Omnibus edition

STAR TRAP
and

AN AMATEUR CORPSE

GW00536374

Simon

Back-In-Print Books Ltd

Published by Back-In-Print Books Ltd 2003
ISBN 1 903552 40 0
Previously published in Great Britain by
Victor Gollancz under ISBN 0 575 02299 X and 0 446 35960 2

Printed and bound on demand by
Lightning Source.

Back-In-Print Books Ltd
P O Box 47057
London SW18 1YW
020 8637 0975

When Simon Brett studied at Oxford he became President of the OUDS, appeared in cabarets and directed the Oxford Theatre Group at the Edinburgh Festival Fringe in 1967. Later he worked as a light entertainment producer for BBC radio and TV before taking up writing full time in 1979. Simon created the Charles Paris and Mrs Pargeter detective series and, to his fans' relief, he is still writing more. He also made a name as the author of the radio and TV series *After Henry*. The radio series *No Commitments*, the best-selling *How to be a Little Sod* and the novel *Shock to the System* filmed starring Michael Caine are other fruits of his imaginative mind. He is married, has three children and lives in a village on the South Downs.

This is a Back-In-Print Book.

• This title was out of print for some time but Back-In-Print Books has brought it back in to print because of demand from Simon Brett fans.
• This re-print was produced on demand using digital printing technology.
• Paper and print quality are higher than most conventionally printed paperback novels.
• Digital printing may cost somewhat more but ensures that book titles need not go out of print as long as there are readers who want them.

What other titles are available from BiP?

Check out our web site at www.backinprint.co.uk for other titles released by Back-In-Print Books Ltd and news about forthcoming titles.

Do you want any other titles?

If you know of a title which is out of print and you think there might be a reasonable demand please contact us.

Back-In-Print Books Ltd
P O Box 47057
London
SW18 1YW
020 8637 0975

e-mail: info@backinprint.co.uk

STAR TRAP

To MY PARENTS, WITH THANKS

FOR ALL THAT EDUCATION

And with special thanks to
Bill and Chris,
who know all about it

PART I

London

CHAPTER ONE

'ACTUALLY,' SAID GERALD Venables, after a sip from his wine glass, 'there's a bit more to it than that.'

'Ah,' said Charles Paris. 'I thought there might be.'

Gerald took a long pause and twiddled the stem of his wine glass. Charles wondered what the catch would be. Gerald was a good friend but was unlikely to be offering him a job from purely altruistic motives. And if it were just a gesture of goodwill, he wouldn't have made it over lunch at Martinez.

'In fact,' the solicitor picked out his words like a philatelist handling stamps, 'there may be something rather odd going on in this show.'

'Odd?'

'Well, as you know, a West End musical is a very large financial undertaking and with any large financial undertaking there are probably as many people who wish it to fall as succeed. And the…people whom I represent are very anxious that this particular show should succeed.'

'You mean you've got money in it?' Charles knew this would make Gerald bridle. Though well known in theatrical circles as a speculator, the solicitor would never admit to his involvement.

'One of the people whom I represent,' came the frosty professional reply, 'has a considerable financial stake in the venture. It is on his behalf that I am approaching you.'

Charles winked. Gerald deflated, smiled and moved the conversation away from money. 'Listen, Charles, the reason that we want you in the show is that we need an investigator on the spot to keep an eye open for anything untoward.'

'I see.'

'And, of course' (remembering that even as cynical an actor as Charles Paris had his professional pride) 'because you would be absolutely ideal for the part.'

Charles inclined his head graciously and looked up for more information.

'You see, Charles, the reason I thought of you was because of that business in Edinburgh that you sorted out...the murder of that boy – what was his name – Marinello?'

'Something like that. I'm flattered, Gerald, but I think to say I sorted it out is a slight exaggeration. I was there...'

'It comes to the same thing. And then there was the Marius Steen business.'

'Again I would hardly say that I...'

'Don't worry what you think. I think you can do the job required and I'm asking you. I mean, it may be that there's nothing to investigate. In that case think of it just as an acting job. After the tour, you'd have a contract for nine months in the West End, you'd be pretty well paid – it's not a bad offer, is it?'

'No.'

'And you haven't got anything else major coming up at the moment, have you?'

As an actor, Charles replied instinctively, 'Well, there are one or two things I'm considering, which may possibly...' Then he decided there was no point in trying to impress Gerald. 'No, nothing major.' Or why not be completely honest? 'Nothing minor either, as it happens. And I had a somewhat uncharitable letter from the Inland Revenue this morning.'

'So you'll take the job?'

'I suppose so.'

'That's terrific.' Gerald punctuated the agreement by refilling their wine glasses. He seemed relieved, which amazed Charles. Surely he never thought the offer might be refused. Or perhaps, from his position of extreme opulence, Gerald was unaware of the general scarcity of acting work at a time when theatres were paring down the size of their permanent companies, when big cast plays were no longer being written or produced and when even the BBC was making cutbacks in its programme hours. Nor was he probably aware of the precarious system of final demands and delaying letters by which Charles conducted his financial affairs.

'What about a sweet?' Gerald airily summoned the waiter with a well-tailored gesture and, as often before, Charles was impressed and amused by his friend's smoothness. He did not envy it, he had long ago decided that certain sorts of success did not interest him, but it was still entertaining to see a successful man at work. Everything about Gerald was right – the beautifully cut charcoal grey pin-striped suit, the residual tan from an August spent with his family in their villa in Corsica, the silver hair cut just long enough to be trendy, the chunky gold ring and identity bracelet, the almost imperceptible aura of expensive after-shave. Charles was always amazed by people who could live like figures in glossy magazines and by people who wanted to. For him the basic challenge of getting from day to day more than occupied his time.

The sweets were sorted out and they both tucked into monster slices of strawberry gâteau. Charles wiped a stray blob of cream from the side of his mouth and asked, 'What's been happening, Gerald?'

'In the show, you mean?'

'Yes. There must be something strange for you to go to these lengths to get me involved.'

'Yes. Two things have happened. They may both have been accidents, and they may be completely unconnected, but it's just possible that someone's trying to sabotage the whole venture.'

'What were the "accidents"?'

'The first came on the second day of rehearsal. There was a guy called Frederick Wooland who was rehearsal pianist for the show. As he was on the way to the Welsh Dragon Club where they're rehearsing, he was shot at.'

'Shot at? You mean someone tried to kill him?'

'No, not really. It was only an air rifle. He just got a pellet in his hand. Not very serious except that he won't be able to play for a couple of weeks and they've had to find a new rehearsal pianist.'

'Usually if you hear of someone being shot at with an air rifle, it's just kids fooling about.'

'Yes, I agree. That may well he what it was in this case. It's a fairly rough area down there.'

'Where is the Welsh Dragon Club?'

'Elephant and Castle.'

'Hmm. Presumably the pianist didn't see who shot at him?'

'No. First thing he knew was a stinging pain in his hand.'

'Were the police told?'

'Oh yes. It was all official. They seemed to think it was kids. No great surprise. It's not the first lime that it's happened round there.'

'In that case, I can't see why you think there's anything odd about it. It doesn't sound as if it bad anything to do with the show at all. Perhaps the only lesson is that managements should be prepared to pay a bit more money to get rehearsal rooms in slightly nicer areas.' He pronounced the last two words in his best Kensington Lady accent.

'Okay. Yes, I admit, on its own, that doesn't sound much. But exactly a week later there was another accident. The day before yesterday.'

'What happened this time?'

'One of the actors fell down some stairs and broke his leg.'

'Where? At the rehearsal rooms?'

'No. At his digs.'

'So why should that have anything to do with the show?'

'It's just the coincidence of the two of them, exactly a week apart, at exactly the same time of day, both people in the show.'

'What time of day was it?'

'Early in the morning both times. Frederick Wooland was shot on his way to rehearsal, say at quarter to ten, and Everard Austick was found in his digs at about half past nine this Tuesday.'

'Did you say Everard Austick?'

'Yes.'

Charles burst out laughing. 'You can't be serious.'

'What do you mean?'

'Well, Everard Austick is the greatest piss-artist in the business. He's a bottle-a-day man. Always drunk out of his mind. If you think that him having a fall in his digs is a sign of foul play, you're way off beam. I'd be much more suspicious if a day went by when he *didn't* fall down something.'

Gerald looked discomfited. 'Oh, I thought the coincidence was too great. I mean, both on the same day.'

'Well…it doesn't sound much to me. Listen, Gerald, I'm very grateful to you for getting me this job and certainly once I get inside the company I will investigate anything that needs investigating, but from what you've said, I'm not going to have much to do. Is that really all you've got?'

'Well, I suppose that's all the actual facts. But it means that the show has got off to an unlucky start and we – they don't want anything to go wrong. There's a lot of money at stake.'

'Whose money?'

Gerald didn't rise to the bait. 'Amulet Productions are putting up most of it and they're working in association with Arthur Balcombe, who is one of my clients. Hence my involvement.'

'I see. All the big boys.'

'Yes. And then of course Christopher Milton has a stake because he's got the rights of the show.'

'Christopher Milton?'

'Yes, he bought it as a vehicle for himself.'

'Really?'

'Didn't you know?'

'Gerald, you didn't tell me anything. You just asked if I would be prepared to take a part in a West End musical for nine months and keep my eyes open for any possible sabotage attempts. You've told me nothing about the show. But I see now, it's this musical based on *She Stoops to Conquer*, isn't it?'

'That's right.'

'I've seen stuff about it in the Press. Now let me think... .' He mused facetiously. 'If it's a musical based on *She Stoops to Conquer* for a West End audience, then what would it be called? Um. How about *Conkers*? With an exclamation mark.'

'No, it was going to be,' said Gerald with complete seriousness, 'but then it was decided that that didn't really give the right impression of the sort of show it is.'

'So what's it called now?'

'Lumpkin!'

'With an exclamation mark?'

'Of course.'

'With Christopher Milton as Tony Lumpkin?'

'Of course. That was another reason for the title. It means a neat billing – "Christopher Milton as *Lumpkin!*" See what I mean?'

'Yes, I do. Tony Lumpkin. Of course. One of the all-time great upstaging parts. Hmm. What's the script like?'

Gerald was reticent. 'It's okay.'

'Anything to do with Goldsmith?'

'No. He hasn't any money in it.'

'I didn't mean Goldsmith the impresario. I meant Oliver Goldsmith who wrote the thing.'

'Oh, I'm sorry. I think the show makes the occasional nod in his direction.'

'But presumably it's not designed for fans of Oliver Goldsmith?'

'No, it's designed for fans of Christopher Milton. He's riding very high at the moment, with the telly show at the top of the ratings.'

'What telly show?'

'Oh, come on, Charles, don't be affected. You must have seen *Straight Up, Guv.*'

'I don't think I have. I'm not a great telly viewer.' He did not possess a television in his Bayswater bed-sitter. He was not enthusiastic about the medium. It was a necessary evil for his career as an actor, because it was well paid, but he had never enjoyed the work (or the product).

'Well, let me enlighten your ignorance. The show gets massive audience figures and it has made Christopher Milton just about the hottest property around. He's very big box office.'

'So it doesn't really matter what show you put him in.'

'Ah, but it does, and *Lumpkin!* is just right. Could make a lot of money. That's why I – the people I represent – are so anxious that nothing should go wrong. Either to the show – or to the star.'

'I see. Who's written it?'

'Well, it's basically a show which the Ipswich Warehouse Company put on last year to celebrate the bicentenary of Goldsmith's death.'

'Oh yes, I remember reading a notice of that in *The Stage*. What was it called then?'

'*Liberty Hall.*'

'That's right.'

'Book by a chap called Kevin McMahon, with music by some bloke whose name I forget. Anyway, Christopher Milton's agent, Dickie Peck – do you know him, by the way?'

'By reputation.'

'Well, he went down and saw the show and reckoned it had potential for his boy, got Christopher Milton himself down to see it, and they bought up the rights. I think they got them pretty cheap. Could be a good investment. I mean, the stage show should run at least a couple of years on Christopher

Milton's name, and then there might be a chance of a film...'
'And the script is more or less as at Ipswich?'
'Hardly. No, there's been quite a lot of surgery. They've scrapped the original music and lyrics – or most of them anyway. And got in Carl Anthony and Micky Gorton to write new ones.'
'You look at me as if I should have heard of them.'
'You certainly should, Charles. They've written a whole string of Top Ten hits. *Heart Doctor...Gimme No More Lies...Disposable Man* – all that lot!'
'Really, Charles, you are square.' Gerald prided himself on his sudden knowledge of the pop scene.
'Some of us age quicker than others, man.'
Gerald ignored the dig. 'The new music is excellent. It fits the style of the period, but it's also very...funky.' He tried too hard to deliver the last word naturally.
Charles laughed. 'It sounds a riot. I hope I don't have to sing anything funky. I wouldn't know where to begin. Incidentally, I should have asked before – what part am I playing?'
'You're playing Sir Charles Marlow. Do you know the play?'
'Yes, I did a production of it once in Cardiff – with Bernard Walton of all people, when he was very new in the business. He played Young Marlow – his first starring rôle. And I'm the father...hmm. Only comes in at the end.'
'That's right.'
'Good.'
'Why good?'
'Last act parts are good. You can spend the whole evening in the pub.'
'It was Everard Austick's part,' said Gerald reprovingly. 'Ah yes, that was probably his downfall. A lifetime of last act parts is the short route to alcoholism.'
'Hmm.' Gerald pondered for a moment. 'I sometimes think I drink too much. Difficult to avoid in my line of work. Occupational hazard.'
'That's what I feel about my line of work too,' Charles agreed. 'Though I must admit at times I worry about the amount I put away.'
'Yes.' There was a reflective pause. Then Gerald said, 'How about a brandy?'
'Love one.'
When it arrived, Charles raised his glass. 'Many thanks, Gerald. This is the most painless audition I've ever undergone.'
'My pleasure.'
'Incidentally, I don't know anything about the time-scale on this show yet. What's this – the second week of rehearsal?'
'That's right. Second of five. Then the show does one week in Leeds...'
'Ah, Leeds...'
'Friends up there?'
'You could say that.'
'Then a week at Bristol, a week at Brighton, a week of final rehearsal and

previews in town and then it should open at the King's Theatre on November 27th.'

'Isn't that a bit near Christmas? I mean, it's a dodgy time for audiences.'

Gerald smiled smugly. 'No problem. Christopher Milton's name will carry us over Christmas. And then…we'll be all right. Ideal family entertainment. Nothing to offend anyone.'

'I see. And when do I start rehearsal?'

'Tomorrow morning, if all goes well.'

'If all goes well? You mean, if I'm not poisoned overnight by the mysterious saboteur.'

'You may laugh, but I've a feeling there's something up.'

'I will keep my eyes skinned, word of honour.' Charles made a Boy Scout salute.

'And if you do find out anything…untoward or criminal, let me know first.'

'Before the police?'

'If possible. We have to watch the publicity angle on this.'

'I see.'

'We don't want the fuzz queering our pitch.'

Charles smiled. It was reassuring to hear Gerald dropping into his thriller slang. The solicitor had always had the sneaking suspicion that crime held more exciting dimensions than the minor infringements of contracts which occupied his working life. His thirst for criminal glamour had to be satisfied by thrillers and, in moments of excitement, his language showed it. Gerald was excited now. He thought they were on to a case.

Charles didn't. He felt certain that the whole idea of saboteurs had been dreamt up by nervy managements suddenly counting up the amount of money that they had invested in one stage show and one star. They were scared and they had to give what frightened them a tangible form. Sabotage was as good an all-purpose threat as any other.

Still, he wasn't complaining. Nine months' work, however boring it might be, was nine months' work. It could sort out the taxman and one or two other pressing problems.

'I'll be very discreet, Gerald, and tell you everything.'

'Good.'

'Now let me buy you a brandy.'

'I wouldn't worry. It's all on Arthur Balcombe. You didn't really think I was taking you out on my own money?'

'No, Gerald, I know you never do anything on your own money. Still, let's have another brandy on Arthur Balcombe and imagine that I've bought it to thank you for the job.'

'Okay. There is one thing, though.'

'Yes.'

'I've offered you the job, you've accepted it, but in a way it isn't mine to offer.'

'Now he tells me.'

'I mean, I don't think there'll be any problem, but it's just that you'll have to go and see Dickie Peck before it's all definite.'

'Oh.'

'Just to check details of your contract.'

'*Just* to check details of my contract.'

'Well, it's also...sort of...to get in know you, to see if you are the kind of person who's likely to get on with Christopher Milton, if you see what I – '

'What you mean by that formula of words is that Christopher Milton has an Approval of Cast clause in his contract and I've got to go and see Dickie Peck to be vetted.'

Gerald tried to find another formula of words, but eventually was forced to admit that that was exactly what he meant.

'I get it. When do I see Peck?'

'You've got an appointment at four o'clock.'

CHAPTER TWO

DICKIE PECK WORKED for Creative Artists Ltd, one of the biggest film and theatre agencies in the country, and he was big. His clients were said to be managed by 'Dickie Peck at Creative Artists' rather than just by 'Creative Artists'. In the agency world this designation often preceded a split from the parent company when an individual member of the staff would set up on his own (usually taking his best clients with him). But Dickie Peck had had his individual billing ever since anyone could remember and showed no signs of leaving the Creative Artists umbrella. There was no point in his making the break; he was a director of the company and worked within it in his own way at his own pace.

It was the pace which was annoying Charles as he sat waiting in the Creative Artists Reception in Bond Street. He had been informed by the over-made-up girl on the switchboard that Mr Peck was not yet back from lunch and as the clock ticked round to half past four, Charles felt all the resentment of someone who has finished lunch at half past three.

He was not alone in Reception. A young actress with carefully highlighted cheek-bones was reading *The Stage* and sighing dramatically from time to time; an actor whose old, hollow eyes betrayed his startlingly golden hair gave a performance of nonchalance by staring at his buckled patent leather shoes. The girl on the switchboard kept up a low monologue of 'A call for you...,' 'I'm sorry, he's tied up at the moment...' and 'Would you mind hanging on?' She deftly snapped plugs in and out like a weaver at her loom.

It was nearly a quarter to five when Dickie Peck came through Reception. The girl on the switchboard stage-whispered, 'Mr Peck, there've been a couple of calls and there's a gentleman waiting to see you.'

He half-turned and Charles got an impression of a cigar with a long column of ash defying gravity at its end. Ignoring his visitor, the agent disappeared into his office. Five minutes later a summons came through on the receptionist's intercom.

The office was high over Bond Street and Dickie Peck's chair backed on to a bow-window. Cupboards and dusty glass-fronted book-cases lined the walls. The paint-work must once have been cream, but had yellowed with age. The dark red carpet smelt of dust. Nothing much on the desk. A current *Spotlight*, Actors L–Z (to check what Charles Paris looked like) and a circular ash-tray in the centre of which was a decorative half golf-ball. The channel around this was full of lengths of cigar ash, long and obscene, like turds.

The ash was long on the cigar that still drooped from the agent's lips. It was an expensive one, but the end was so chewed and worried that it looked like the cheap brown-wrapping-paper sort.

The face which the cigar dwarfed was grey and lined, crowned by a long tongue of hair brushed inadequately over baldness. The head was disproportionately small and accentuated the stocky bulk of body below it. Dickie Peck was dressed in a dark grey suit with thin lapels. A plain blue tie askew across a grubby white shirt. Tie and jacket dusted with cigar ash. It was not the traditional image of the big show business agent; more like a Town Hall clerk.

'Charles Paris, isn't it? Take a chair.' He gestured expansively, but the ash at the end of his cigar miraculously stayed intact.

Charles sat on a low gilt chair whose red plush upholstery was as hard as wood.

'Now, Mr Paris, I gather you've seen a representative of Amulet Productions about this part.'

'Yes.' So Gerald wasn't just acting as solicitor for Arthur Balcombe.

'And he explained what it was about?'

'Yes.'

'Good. As you gather, the part became vacant due to an accident to one of the cast.'

'I know.' Charles didn't volunteer any comment. Gerald had been uncertain whether Dickie Peck shared his suspicions of sabotage or not and had asked Charles to play it carefully. The fewer people knew that there was an investigator in the company, the better.

Dickie Peck gave no sign of suspicion. He took a long draw at his cigar, extending the column of ash to an even more precarious length. He leant back and blew a slow jet of smoke to the ceiling. 'This show, Mr Paris, is a very big one.'

'So I gather.' Charles was getting tired of being told about the size of the operation.

'It's likely to be a very big success.'

'Good,' said Charles, feeling that some sort of comment was required.

'And so it's important that everything about it should be right.'

Again Charles helped out the pause with a 'Yes'.

'Because what we have here is a show with a very big star. Christopher Milton, no less.'

Here a longer pause was left for some comment of amazed approbation. Charles produced a grunt which he hoped was appropriate.

'Yes, Christopher Milton. Let me tell you, Mr Paris, I have been in this business a very long time and I have never before seen someone who had so much star quality written all over him.'

'Ah.' Charles found it difficult to get interested in the idea of stardom. It was not the end of show business in which he was involved.

But Dickie Peck's litany had started and couldn't be stopped. 'Oh yes, I've seen them all sitting in that chair. They've all come to me for advice. Because they know, if they want to get ahead in this business, then they should come and see old Dickie Peck. Oh yes.' For the first time in the interview he looked at the crumbling end of his cigar, but decided it didn't need attention yet. 'I remember once back in 1960, I had four young men from Liverpool in this office. Four ordinary lads, got their own group – would I be interested in representing them? And you know who they were? Only the Beatles.

'They asked my advice and I gave it. I said, Lads, you've got a lot of talent, but the act isn't right. What you've got to do is split up, go your own ways, separate careers, that's what you need if you're really going to make it.' He paused for dramatic emphasis, then delivered his triumph. 'And look at them now – separate careers.'

He leant back with satisfaction, then, instinctively sensing the imminent collapse of his cigar ash, deposited another neat cylinder into the ash-tray.

'There have been others too – Frank Sinatra once when he was over here, wanted a hit of advice on which way I thought his career should go. Glenda Jackson, Tom Jones, oh yes, they've all sat in that chair and asked for a bit of help from old Dickie Peck.'

Charles looked at the chair on which he was sitting with what he hoped was due reverence and didn't believe a word of it.

'But let me tell you, Mr Paris, of all the big stars I've ever seen, Christopher Milton is the biggest. That boy has so much talent, he can do anything. I mean, when you think that he is now only thirty-four, a mere baby, at the beginning of his career, I tell you in the future there's going to be no stopping him. And *Lumpkin!* is the show that's really going to put him in the big time.' Realising that this could be constructed as diminishing his protégé, he covered himself. 'Not of course that he isn't in the big time already. With the television show, a few films, oh yes, he's right at the top. And it's not that we haven't had offers – oh, there have been plenty of scripts come along, plenty of managements with ideas, chance of a big musical on Broadway, Hollywood positively begging, but we said no. We preferred to bide our time, wait for the right show, the one that was absolutely right. Christopher Milton had got the telly, he was doing okay, he could afford to wait. That's an important thing in this business, choosing the right work. Oh yes, you've got to be selective.'

Which is nice if you can afford to be selective, thought Charles. Most actors have to do what comes along or starve.

Dickie Peck's monologue was evidently self-propelled, so Charles gave up providing nods and yesses and grunts of agreement to stimulate it. 'Now, of course, when you're talking about an artist of Christopher Milton's calibre, you want to be sure that all the work he does is done in the right atmosphere, that he works with people who he gets on with, people who are sympathetic to what he's doing.' Charles pricked up his ears. They were finally getting round to the vetting part of the interview. 'Because what happens when you get someone with more talent than most people is that you do tend to get jealousy developing. And that doesn't make for a healthy working atmosphere in a company. Now Christopher Milton is a charming boy, very easy to get along with, but he is a person of considerable genius and he does have strong ideas. Now because of his great sense of theatre his ideas are very often right. And obviously in the context of a show being rehearsed under pressure, too many arguments over the way things are done can only be counterproductive. Do you see what I mean?'

He leant back, nursing another two inches of cigar ash. This time a response was definitely needed.

And it was not an easy one to give. Oh yes, Charles knew what Dickie Peck meant. Through all the verbiage, the message was quite clear – if you want this job, you will have to undertake to do as Christopher Milton says. He's not the director of the show, but his word is law, and if you don't like the sound of that, remember he has an Approval of Casting clause and the world is full of unemployed actors.

Under normal circumstances Charles liked to think he'd tell the agent to stuff his job and walk out. But these weren't normal circumstances. He tried to conciliate his conscience. Gerald had offered him the job, and Gerald was a friend. It wouldn't do to let him down. Anyway, it wasn't really an acting job. He was being infiltrated into the company as an investigator of sabotage. Yes, it was quite legitimate for him to accept the conditions; it would only raise suspicion if he didn't. But as he replied, he knew that his real motive was the tax bill lying on the table in his room in Hereford Road. 'Yes, I fully understand, Mr Peck. I know that Christopher Milton owns the rights of the show and so obviously he will be deeply concerned in all aspects of the production, and I'm sure I will respect his ideas.'

Dickie Peck looked at him suspiciously, but evidently decided to take the reply at face value. 'Good, fine. Well, we have Mr Venables' word as to your suitability for the part...' Then, just as Gerald had done, he gave a token nod to actor's pride. 'And of course I know your work. I have a script of the show here. Did Mr Venables tell you about the tour and the length of contract?'

'Yes.'

'Fine. Well, good luck.'

'Thank you. There is just one thing...'

'Oh yes, of course, money.'

'Yes. Look, I'll give you my agent's number. He deals with all that.'

'Fine. Will I catch him there now? I'd like to get this sorted out today. And it's after half past five now.'

'Maurice'll be there. He works from home anyway.'

'Fine. I'll give him a buzz.'

'Well, thank you very much, Mr Peck. I hope that show's going to be a great success.'

'With Christopher Milton in it it's bound to be. That boy is what stardom's all about. Oh yes, it'll be a big success. And if anyone tries to stop it being a success, there'll be hell to pay. Christopher Milton is going right to the top and no one is going to get in his way.'

He said the last words with a fierce, almost religious, intensity.

Charles pressed twopence into the coin-box when he heard the voice say, 'Maurice Skellern Artistes'.

'Maurice.'

'Who's calling him?'

'Oh, for God's sake, Maurice, don't you ever recognise my voice? It's me – Charles.'

'Ah well, can't be too careful in this business. Don't want to give anything away.'

'You don't give much away by answering to your name. Anyway, never mind that. Did Dickie Peck get through to you?'

'Yes, Charles. Sounds very good, this musical. I think it's about time you got into that sort of show. I mean, haven't I been saying for years that you ought to be doing shows that are more…more important?'

'No. You've been saying for years that I ought to be doing shows that are better paid.'

'Ah, now that's not fair, Charles. Okay, I've always said you should keep out of these fringe capers, this experimental stuff, but I've always been thinking primarily of your career, of your artistic development.'

'That's very generous of you.'

'I do my best.'

'So what am I getting for the current artistic development?'

'Well, Charles, Dickie Peck was offering, on behalf of the management, twenty-five for rehearsal, forty on tour end sixty for the run and I said you wouldn't consider it for under forty for rehearsal, eighty on tour and a hundred for the run and I wouldn't budge from that and that was my final word on the subject.'

'So?'

'You're getting thirty for rehearsal, fifty on tour and eighty for the run.'

'Oh well, could be worse. Christopher Milton's in this show. Got any form on him?' While Maurice Skellern was pretty useless as an agent, he was an invaluable source of theatrical gossip.

'Nothing much, no. He doesn't do a lot of work, really.'

'It's just that everything he does is massively successful.'

'Yes, if you look back on his career it's all award-winning shows. Not a lot, but it's all been chosen just right.'

'That's what having a good agent is about.'

Maurice didn't seem to notice the edge in the remark. 'He's a talented boy, Charles.'

'Where did he start?'

'I'm fairly sure he came out of one of the stage schools, but I don't know which one. Think he may have been a child star in films. Not sure, though.'

'Know anything of his working reputation?'

'A bit temperamental, I've heard. But that's third hand. I mean stories like that go around about every big name in the business.'

'Yes. Is he gay or anything?'

'No, I don't think so. Sure not, actually. He married that girl who was in that film...you know.'

'I'm afraid I don't.'

'Oh, the one who played opposite Nigel Thingummy in that...Oh, you know. Name like Elsa or Virginia or – Charlotte Fable, that's it!'

'I've heard of her. Still together?'

'No, I think they split up eighteen months or so ago.'

'Divorce?'

'Haven't seen anything about it. No, I shouldn't think he'd like the publicity. Rather lets down the image of lovability, and that's what the public expects of him.'

'Hmm. Oh well, thanks.'

'If you really want form, ask Johnny Wilson. He worked with him on the telly show.'

'Oh yes. What's that called?'

'*Straight Up, Guv.* Surely you must have seen it.'

'No, I haven't.'

'Oh, it's a very funny show, Charles. I never miss it. It's on tonight at seven-thirty. These are repeats, actually, second time round, or is it third? Think of the money on a show like that. Probably sells round the world. That's what you need, Charles, a big, long-running television series.'

'As part of my artistic development?'

'Of course.'

That evening Charles watched television. He went round to see Jim Waldeman, a fellow actor who lived in Queen's Gardens with his wife Susie and a fairly new baby. He took a bottle of Bell's to ensure his welcome, but it was unnecessary. As he entered the door, both Jim and Susie's eyes lit up and, with a cry of 'Baby-sitter!', they installed him in an arm-chair in front of the television and went off to the pictures. 'Imagine,' said Susie, 'actually going to see a film. The excitement. We used to go about twice a week, but since *that* came along, we just haven't. At all. Bless you, Charles.'

'What happens if it – '

'Oh, he won't. He's terribly good. But if he does, there's some Phenergan on the dresser. Cheerio.' And the door slammed.

'What's Phenergan?' asked Charles weakly, but he realised they couldn't hear. He also realised that the slam of the door had woken the baby.

He switched on the television, determined that the child would soon be asleep again. It was a colour set (Jim's career was obviously flourishing), but Charles caught the end of an old black and white movie. It was British, some story about a small boy bringing together his estranged parents. The father was an airman and there was a lot of stiff upper lip stuff about one last mission. The boy was a beautiful child, with a perfectly proportioned baby face and blond curls. Charles wondered idly if it was Christopher Milton in his child star days.

It was becoming clear that the baby was not going back to sleep. The keening cry sawed through the noise of the television. Charles looked at his watch. Twenty-five past seven. The crying showed no signs of abating and he didn't want to miss the beginning of the show. He went into the night-lit nursery and mumbled soothingly over the cot. The screams redoubled in volume. In the sitting-room music built to an heroic conclusion. He picked up the baby in its blanket and returned to the television.

The film credits flashed past. The child star was not Christopher Milton. Gareth Somebody, another who had no doubt vanished without trace to become an accountant or an estate agent or a double glazing salesman. After the film came a trailer for a programme on Northern Ireland to be shown the following night.

The baby was not taking kindly to its move. The little mouth strained open like a goldfish and the pebble eyes almost vanished in folds of skin as it screamed. It was a long time since Charles had held a baby and he had forgotten the little tricks he had used when his own daughter Juliet was small. He tried rocking the little bundle and murmuring the Skye Boat Song. It didn't work.

On the television screen the credits rolled. Inevitably, 'CHRISTOPHER MILTON' came first. Then 'in *STRAIGHT UP, GUV* – by WALLY WILSON'. Then 'with' the names of a couple of those comedy supports who are never out of work and the inevitable wild studio applause faded into the show proper. (Why do studio audiences always applaud signature tunes and credits? The fact that they clap when nothing has happened casts serious doubts on the credibility of their subsequent reactions.) The episode started; Charles couldn't hear a word above the baby's howls.

In desperation he dipped a finger in his Scotch and proffered it to the bellowing mouth. The tiny lips closed round it as if determined to remove the skin. But there was silence.

It didn't last. After a few moments the suction was released and the bellowing recommenced. Charles hastily dipped his finger back in the glass and the mouth clamped on again. By repeating the process every two minutes he found he could watch *Straight Up, Guv* in comparative comfort.

It was not bad. The show was built around the adventures of a second-rate con-man Lionel Wilkins (played of course by Christopher Milton), whose attempts to pull off the big coup were always crowned with disaster. Wally

Wilson's script was workmanlike, but uninspired; it was Christopher Milton's performance which raised it above the ordinary. Lionel Wilkins was a genuine comic creation, whose doomed cockiness was strangely engaging. He was the original Wobbly Man; every time you pushed him over, he bounced back up again. As catastrophe followed catastrophe and his face crumpled into crestfallen embarrassment, the audience roared. Each time he picked himself up with some new incongruous scheme and the audience roared again. Even Charles found himself laughing out loud at times. Christopher Milton's face in repose was unremarkable, but in the character it seemed capable of infinite comic variation. It was easy to see why the show had become a cult.

And, like many cult shows, it had a catch-phrase. As the worst reversal hit him, Lionel Wilkins paused in horror, the audience laughed in anticipation, and then, with perfect timing, he said, 'I beg yours?' As Charles heard it, he recognised it, recognised it from shouting schoolboys in the street, giggling secretaries in the tube and half-heard impressionists on the radio. 'I beg yours?' was Christopher Milton; he said it and the entire nation followed him.

When Jim and Susie returned, Charles and the baby were still watching television, and between them they'd got through half the bottle of Bell's.

CHAPTER THREE

THE WELSH DRAGON Club near the Elephant and Castle had been built in more elegant times as a meeting-place for expatriate Welshmen of the upper and middle classes. It then boasted four tennis courts (grass), fielded six rugby teams and held very proper dances on Saturdays. The members tended to wear blazers or tweed, they had strong religious principles and, when drunk, broke into mournful song.

The club was now lost in a forest of concrete blocks. Two of the tennis courts had been sold for development and the others were now pink shale stained with moss. The only rugby discussed in the bar was what was seen on the television and the Saturday dances had been replaced by intermittent bookings for disco-parties (which were rarely profitable because of the number of broken windows). The members had gone down in class and numbers. They tended to lounge around in jeans and patterned pullovers, propped against the moth-eaten baize of the old notice-boards, occasionally throwing a desultory dart or pulling without hope at the arm of the one fruit machine. When they got drunk, they still broke into mournful song.

The club had one paid employee, who doubled the rôles of caretaker and barman. His name was Griff and he spent whole days propped over the bar reading an apparently inexhaustible copy of the *Sun*.

The club activities could not possibly make any profit, but the Welsh Dragon stayed open. All its revenue came from hiring out rehearsal rooms. There were two – one where old cue-racks and brass score-boards against treacle-coloured panels accentuated the absence of the long-sold billiard tables, and the other, grandly called the 'Ballroom', a long expanse of bare boards with a tiny stage at one end and a wall of French windows which in the old days were left open for dances after summer tournaments. Many of the window panes had been broken and covered with asymmetrical offcuts of hardboard.

Charles was directed to the Ballroom, where a flotsam of chairs and upturned benches represented the expensive set of *Lumpkin!* (The designs, by Derbyshire Wilkes, were elaborate and featured considerable use of revolves and flown pieces.) The scene was like any morning in any rehearsal room. Actors and actresses sat on chairs round the edges of the room like the sad wallflowers who had once moped there after missing vital backhand returns in the mixed doubles. Little clusters formed round crosswords or gossip. Bleary bodies shuffled slowly out of the cocoons of their coats. A member of the stage management moved purposefully around the room, following some logic of her own. Hangovers and television were discussed, knitting was unwound.

The director, David Meldrum, was poring over the script at a small table isolated in the middle of the room. He was balding, with rimless glasses and somehow managed the pinched look of a clerk from a Dickens serial. Charles knew him by sight and introduced himself.

'Ah, Charles, hello. I gathered your name was being mentioned for the part. Nice to see you.' He did not seem particularly interested in the addition to his cast. 'Gwyneth will give you a rehearsal schedule.'

At the mention of her name, the stage management girl homed in and handed Charles a cyclostyled sheet of times and scenes. Instinctively he assessed her. Old habits die hard and one of the first moves on joining any company is to examine the available crumpet. He decided that Gwyneth looked too dauntingly efficient for his taste. Not a high cuddlability rating.

As he sat down to study the schedule, Charles reflected that it was rather pathetic for him still to be studying the crumpet. He was nearly forty-nine years old and his emotional track record was not spectacular. There was a nice wife, Frances, in Muswell Hill, with whom he hadn't lived for fourteen years (in spite of occasional reconciliations) and who was now reputed to have a boy friend. Apart from her, it was a history of intense casual affairs, which were either too intense or too casual. Thinking about it depressed him, so he channelled his thoughts in another direction.

It was strange that David Meldrum had accepted his appearance so casually. Indeed, it was strange that the director had had no part in his selection for the role. 'I gathered your name was being mentioned for the part.' As if it had nothing to do with him. Charles racked his brains for any stray comments he had heard about the director and from some source he couldn't identify he remembered the words, 'A good technician, love, but about as much imagination as a bread-board. Ought really to be in local government. Approaches a production like planning a car park.' That made sense. David Meldrum was a director who would see that the show got on the stage. He might not have many ideas of his own, but at least he wouldn't argue with anyone else's. Charles felt certain that Christopher Milton's contract also included an Approval of Director clause.

He looked round for the star, but there was no sign of him. Five to ten. Perhaps he was one of those actors who makes a point of arriving just at the moment of the call.

As the room filled up, there were one or two familiar faces from a long time ago. He saw Michael Peyton, with whom he'd worked on his own production of *She Stoops to Conquer* in Cardiff. They grinned at each other across the room. A couple of other actors smiled vaguely, as unable to remember Charles' name as he was to remember theirs.

There were few actresses. Thinking of the original play, Charles could only remember three female characters – Mrs Hardcastle, Kate Hardcastle and Miss Neville. He identified them easily. The middle-aged lady in a tweed trouser-suit and a scallop of blue-grey hair he recognised as Winifred Tuke. Good workmanlike actress. He remembered once overhearing her saying, 'Been a feature player all my life and very happy at it – I've never wanted to be a star.' She must be playing Mrs Hardcastle. The thin girl with aquiline nose and straight blonde hair must be Miss Neville and the shorter one whose mouth and teeth were attractively too large looked absolutely right for Kate Hardcastle.

Michael Peyton came over to chat and confirmed the identification. The girl playing Kate was called Lizzie Dark, apparently only a year out of Sussex University and generally believed to have a glowing future.

'Nice looking kid, isn't she?' Charles observed.

'Yes. Fairly regular boy friend. Often comes and picks her up after rehearsals.'

'Oh, I wasn't thinking...'

'Of course you were.'

'Well...'

'There's always the tour.'

'Hmm.'

'And the dancers.'

'When do they join us?'

'Next week. They're rehearsing separately.'

'How the hell do dancers fit into *She Stoops to Conquer*?'

'If you think this show bears any relation to the play as we did it in Cardiff, you can't have read the script.'

'True. I've only read my scenes.'

'There's an actor for you. I hope you didn't count your lines.'

'No,' he lied.

David Meldrum stood up and moved to the centre of the set in a rather apologetic way. 'Um, perhaps we ought to start.'

He was interrupted by the entry of a man in a donkey-jacket, who whispered something to him and sat down on a chair adjacent to the table. He had brown curly hair and a boyish face with a snub nose, but his skin belied the impression of youth. It had that *papier-mâché* quality which is the legacy of bad acne.

'Who's he?' Charles hissed.

'Spike. He's the stage manager. Nice bloke. He must be down to see if we're actually going to be able to negotiate Derbyshire Wilkes' amazing set. Of course, there's always the stage staff,' he added irrelevantly.

'What do you mean?'

'Potential crumpet.'

'I'm too old.'

'Come off it. Nothing like a warm little props girl to comfort a chap in his old age.'

'Um, I think we should make a start,' said David Meldrum.

'Where's the star, Michael?'

'Oh, he's never called till ten-thirty. It's in his contract.'

In 1773 Oliver Goldsmith decided that Sir Charles Marlow should not appear in his play until the fifth act, so Charles Paris' rehearsal schedule was not too onerous. That much had survived the translation of *She Stoops to Conquer* into *Liberty Hall* and even the transmogrification of *Liberty Hall* into *Lumpkin!* The result was that, although there was ground to be made up and Charles would have to go through his scenes with the assistant director and be taxied off to Soho for a costume fitting that afternoon, he was not actually called for the morning. And because Griff the barman interpreted such concepts as club membership and licensing hours with a commendable degree of independence, by ten-thirty Charles and Michael Peyton were sitting in the bar over a couple of pints of bitter.

Griff was hunched over the *Sun*, reading between the lines of a photograph. In the corner a gloomy figure in denim battledress confronted the fruit machine, willing it to swallow his money and confirm his failure. Charles decided it might be a good moment to find if Gerald's suspicions about the two accidents were shared by an ordinary member of the company like Michael Peyton. 'Funny way of coming into a show for me, you know, Mike. After an accident. Sort of dead men's shoes situation.'

'Ah well, it's an ill wind.'

'Yes. Poor old Everard.'

'No one can expect to drink that much and stay perpendicular. Against the laws of physics.'

'Yes. I suppose he just fell…'

'Suppose so,' said Michael without interest and certainly without suspicion.

'Hm.' No harm in probing a bit further. 'Funny, though, that accident coming straight after the other one.'

'Other one?'

'The rehearsal pianist.'

'Who? Alec?'

'No, the one before him.'

Michael jutted forward his lower lip in an expression of ignorance. 'Didn't know there was one.'

'Oh, I heard some rumour. Must have got it wrong.' Obviously to the ordinary member of the company there was nothing bizarre going on. There was no general feeling of doom, of a 'bad luck' show. Gerald's imagination had been overstimulated by thoughts of the size of his financial investment. For Charles, it was just an acting job. He raised his glass to his lips and reflected on the differences between unemployed drinking and drinking with a nine-month contract. A warm glow filled him.

'Griff love, can you do me a port.' The new voice belonged to a good-looking young man in a smart blazer and check trousers. 'I've got the most frightful throat coming on and David's just sent me to go through my songs with Alec up in the billiard room.'

'Port, eh?'

'It's the only thing for a throat, Griff.'

'Huh.'

'Mark, have you met Charles Paris?'

'No, Mike, I haven't. Hello, I'm Mark Spelthorne.' He left an infinitesimal pause for Charles to say, 'Yes, of course, I recognise your face from the television,' but Charles didn't, so he continued. 'You're taking over from poor old Everard?'

'That's right.'

'Well, don't drink too much of that, or you'll go the same way.'

'I'll be careful.' It wasn't worth objecting to the young man's patronising tone.

'Do you know, Mike,' said Mark Spelthorne, though he was addressing the world in general rather than anyone in particular, 'my agent is a bloody fool. He had a call yesterday from Yorath Knightley – do you know him?'

'No.'

'BBC. Telly. Drama. Wanted me for a play, super part. Rehearsals the week after this opens. Lovely, just what I need. But my damn fool agent says, oh no, out of the question, they may have some rerehearsal and what have you on *Lumpkin!* Honestly. I said, well, surely, love, we can get a few days off, sort round the contract, organise the filming round the schedule for this show. Oh no, he says, you're under contract. No bloody imagination. I think I must get another agent.'

'Sorry it took so long. Had to open a bottle. Don't get much call for port here. One or two of the ladies has it with lemon, but most of the gents drink beer or spirits.'

'Never mind, Griff. Bless you,' said Mark Spelthorne bountifully. He took a sip of the drink and gargled it gently, then swallowed. 'Better.' He repeated the process. Charles and Mike watched in silence as the glass slowly emptied. 'Ah well, better test out the old singing voice.'

'If you want to hear real singing,' said Griff morosely, 'you want to listen to a Welsh male voice choir.'

'Ah.' Mark was nonplussed, not certain what his reaction should be.

'We used to have a choir here at the Welsh Dragon. Lovely singing. Better than anything I've heard since you lot've been here.'

'That's a matter of opinion.' Mark hesitated, uncertain whether or not that was a good enough exit line. Failing to come up with a better one, he exited to the billiard room.

'Should I know him, Mike? He behaved as if I should.'

'Not unless you're a fan of *The Fighter Pilots*, Charles.'

'What's that?'

'You're obviously not. It's an ITV series. Another cashing in on the nostalgia boom. Mark Spelthorne plays Flying Officer Falconer, whose daring missions and dreary love life fill up most of each episode.'

'Oh. I've never heard of him in the theatre.'

'I don't think he's done much. Presumably he did his forty weeks round the provinces to get the Equity card, but I think that's it. He's one of the media mushrooms who has sprung up overnight as a fully developed television star.'

'Then why is he in this?'

'Publicity, Charles. So that he can be billed on the poster as Mark Spelthorne of *The Fighter Pilots*. That's to mop up the one per cent of the population who haven't come to see Christopher Milton of *Straight Up, Guv*.'

'The television take-over is complete.'

'Yes.'

'He seemed to have a fairly inflated opinion of himself.'

'Ah, he would like to be a big star, Charles.'

'And will he make it?'

'I don't know. Somehow I don't think so. Don't think he's got what it takes.'

'What's he playing?'

'Your son, Young Marlow.'

'That's the best part in the play.'

'Was, Charles, was. Maybe that's what Goldsmith intended, but that was before Christopher Milton got his hands on the script.'

'Yes,' the gloomy man at the fruit machine chipped in suddenly and savagely. 'Before Christopher Milton got his bloody hands on the script.'

There was a moment's pause before Michael Peyton recovered himself sufficiently to make the introduction. 'Charles Paris–Kevin McMahon.'

'Ah yes. You wrote *Liberty Hall*.'

'In a previous existence, I think.' His voice had the rough blur of a hangover and there was a large Scotch on a table beside the fruit machine. Having registered his protest, he seemed to lose interest in the two actors and, with an air of self-mortification, pressed another ten pence into the slot. Or maybe he turned away as a deliberate snub to the man entering the bar. 'Morning, everyone. Hello, Griff. Charles Paris, isn't it?'

'That's right.'

'Delighted you're with us on the show.'

Charles took the offered firm handshake and looked into the clear, honest face. 'My name's Christopher Milton.'

CHAPTER FOUR

THE NEXT FEW weeks were an education for Charles. The sort of theatre he had always concentrated on had not depended on stars. Christopher Milton was a star.

At their initial meeting he was charming. There was only a short break in rehearsal, but he devoted it all to the new member of the company. And he had done his homework. He referred to incidents in Charles' career which he could not have guessed at, but which showed genuine interest or research. He spoke flatteringly about the one successful play Charles had written, *The Ratepayer*. In fact all the right things were said and Charles was impressed. He saw once again the distorting mirror of showbiz rumour at work. Reputations get inflated and diminished by gossip and scandal. One bitchy remark by a jealous actor can give the permanent stigma of being 'difficult' to another. Time and again Charles had encountered supposedly 'lovely' people who were absolute monsters and been charmed by supposed monsters. And he found Christopher Milton charming.

As rehearsals developed and he began to feel part of the company, it was increasingly difficult to take Gerald's fears of sabotage seriously. There was an air of tension about the production, but no more than one would expect from any show at that stage of development. Charles' rôle was not an onerous one, and Griff's ever-open bar was an ideal place to toast Gerald's excessive anxiety which had got him the job.

He had a slight twinge of misgiving as the Tuesday approached. Gerald had made such an issue of the fact that the two accidents had taken place exactly a week apart. If there were a psychopathic wrecker about, determined to ruin the show, then he would strike again on the Tuesday.

Charles went to rehearsal that morning with some trepidation but the day passed and there wasn't so much as a cold among the cast. He decided that he had just landed on his feet in an acting job. Eighty pounds a week and sucks to the taxman.

36

He had not seen much of the show except for the scenes which involved him, but on the Wednesday he decided to stay on after he'd finished. They were rehearsing the Chase Scene at the end.

Now Goldsmith did not write a Chase Scene. In his play Tony Lumpkin meets Hastings and describes how he has just led Mrs Hardcastle and Miss

Neville on a circular wild goose chase until, 'with a circumbendibus, I fairly lodged them in the horse-pond at the bottom of the garden'. But description is not the stuff of West End musicals. Kevin McMahon had written a small chase into *Liberty Hall* and had been persuaded to expand it for *Lumpkin!* The result was a massive production number with song and dance, as Tony Lumpkin actually led the two ladies in their coach through mire and thicket. The dancers, playing a series of misdirecting yokels, buxom country wenches and a full-scale fox hunt which would have amazed Goldsmith, were rehearsing elsewhere on their own, and the special effects of fog, rain and snow were not yet available. Nor was it possible to simulate the moving trees and revolving cottages which were to add visual excitement to the scene. But it was already a complicated sequence and an interesting one to watch.

It also gave Charles his first opportunity to see Christopher Milton in action, building a part. The result was impressive. Tony Lumpkin was emerging as a complete comic character, totally different from Lionel Wilkins. The London whine of the television con-man had been replaced by a rich West Country accent and instead of sentimental incompetence, there was a roguishly knowing confidence. Charles began to feel that Dickie Peck's claims for his client's talent were not so ridiculous.

David Meldrum had by now been nicknamed David Humdrum and it fitted. He ordered people round the acting space like a suburban gardener laying a patio. Everything had to be exactly in place, every move exactly matching the neat plans in his script. But it was not the perfectionism of genius; it was the predictability of a man who had worked out his blocking with pins on a stage model long before rehearsals had started.

Still, it was professional and efficient. The production advanced. And for a complex commercial show it's probably better to have a good journeyman than a genius.

Anyway, David Meldrum was only providing the skeleton; the flesh was the performances. And Christopher Milton was fleshing up nicely. He had a song called *Lead 'em Astray*, for which Micky Gorton had written some most ungoldsmithian lyrics.

> *'Get them going*
> *The wrong way.*
> *There's no knowing*
> *What they'll say.*
> *Hey, hey, hey,*
> *Lead 'em astray.'*

If Gorton's lyrics did have a fault it was a tendency to the non-specific. They had been written not to advance the plot, but to be taken out of the show and recorded by pop stars. However, Carl Anthony's tunes were good and *Lead 'em Astray*, in spite of its anachronism, captured the excitement and mischief of Tony Lumpkin. In Christopher Milton's performance, even with just the rehearsal piano, it was a potential show-stopper.

It was also very funny. His movements were beautiful. They showed the clodhopping clumsiness of the character and yet they were very precise. He darted round the two chairs which represented Mrs Hardcastle's coach and wove his way through the other chairs which were trees. On the chorus of the song he froze for a moment, then jerked forward like a car left in gear, then stopped and flashed a look of sheer devilment at the audience. The timing made the gesture hilarious; even the cast who had seen it many times before laughed spontaneously. He seemed encouraged by the reaction and in the next verse his movements became more grotesque and jerky. He bounced up to the coach and pecked forward like a chicken with a head that suddenly seemed disconnected from his body. There was a splutter from Miss Neville, the unmistakable sound of someone 'corpsing'. Christopher Milton rose to it and varied the steps of his dance into a strange little jig. This struck Miss Neville as even funnier and soon she was gaping, incapable with laughter, while tears flowed down her cheeks.

The laughter spread. Mrs Hardcastle started, then one by one, the watching actors caught it. Charles found himself giggling uncontrollably. It was one of those moments of communal hysteria which cannot be explained, but where everything suddenly gets funnier and funnier.

Only Christopher Milton stayed in control. The pianist was laughing too much to continue playing, but the star sang and danced on to the end of the number. His movements got faster and stranger and funnier until suddenly at the end he dropped flat on his back.

The timing was immaculate. It was the perfect end to the sequence. And it was impossible not to applaud. Charles, who was almost in pain from laughing, joined the others clapping.

As the noise subsided into scattered gasps and deep breaths, a strange stillness came over the room. Christopher Milton was still the focus of attention, but the mood had changed. Everyone watched him as he sat up, but he did not seem to be aware of them. He rose pensively to his feet, and moved slowly forward. 'I think we can do more with that,' he said.

The remark did not seem to be addressed to anyone in particular, but David Meldrum, as director, felt that he should pick it up. 'What do you mean, Christopher?'

'I mean there's not enough happening on stage in that number.'

'Well, of course, we haven't got the dancers yet, and the – '

'Shut up. I'm thinking.' He said it dismissively, as if he were swatting a fly. Then slowly: 'We need more movement from me, bobbing up all over the place. ...Yes, we need doubles.'

'Doubles?'

'Yes, doubles for me. People my height, dressed in the same costume. So that I can disappear behind one tree and appear behind another, come out of trap doors, Really make it into a silent film sequence.'

'But it works very well like this and – '

'I told you to shut up. That's how we're going to do it. The whole thing will have to be replotted.'

'But we haven't got time.'

'We'll make time.'

'Look, it's a tight rehearsal schedule – '

'Sod the rehearsal schedule. We can reblock this tomorrow afternoon.'

'We're meant to be doing the Young Marlow/Kate scenes tomorrow.'

'You can do those on Friday.'

'No,' Mark Spelthorne's voice drawled out. 'I can't do Friday. I'm released for the day. Doing a pilot of a radio series.'

'You're contracted here.'

'Agent cleared the release, Christopher old boy.'

'I don't care what your sodding agent's done. You're contracted here.'

'Listen, it's a pilot of my own show.'

'Your own show. Huh.' The laugh was loaded with scorn. 'A pilot for your own show. I wouldn't bother. Don't do it. It'll save you disappointment when they turn the idea down.'

'What do you mean?'

'I mean that you'll never have a show of your own. You haven't got it in you. Adequate, you are. The word adequate was invented to describe people like you.'

'What the hell do you mean?' Mark had risen sharply, as if he were about to strike his antagonist. Christopher Milton looked at him with contempt.

There was a long pause. Then Mark Spelthorne backed away. He muttered, 'Bloody prima donna' in an unsuccessful tone of defiance, and walked out of the room.

A long silence followed. Everyone except Christopher Milton looked horribly embarrassed. But they all waited for him to speak first.

When he did, it was as if the argument had never happened, as if he had just been thinking. 'We'll reblock this Chase Scene tomorrow afternoon.'

'Yes,' agreed David Meldrum. 'Fine.'

Charles was glad when the rehearsals were over that day. The atmosphere was uncomfortable, although Christopher Milton seemed oblivious of it.

By chance, Charles found himself leaving at the same time as the star. They walked out of the Welsh Dragon Club in silence. Charles felt ill at ease, as though he were about to be asked to take sides, to say what he thought of Mark Spelthorne.

But that was not at all what happened. As they emerged from the Club, Christopher Milton was suddenly surrounded by small boys from the tower blocks opposite. One of them must have seen the star go in earlier in the day and spread the word. They were a rough lot, of various colours and degrees of scruffiness. They all clamoured up to Christopher Milton with scraps of paper for autographs.

As the kids moved in, a stocky figure in a dark suit detached himself from a parked Rolls Corniche and moved forward as if anticipating trouble. A gesture from Christopher Milton stopped him and he moved back to lean against the metallic brown flank of the car.

'All right, all right. Who's first?' The voice was instantly that of Lionel Wilkins.

It was exactly what the audience wanted. They all howled with laughter and clamoured even louder for autographs. 'All right, all right. Give me a pen,' whined Lionel Wilkins. A biro was thrust into his hands. He dropped it with a distinctive Wilkins gesture. The audience howled again.

'All right. You first. What's your name?'

'Mahendra Patel.'

The timing was immaculate. An eyebrow shot up, the mouth dropped open and Lionel Wilkins said, 'I beg yours?'

The catch-phrase produced screams of delight and the little crowd jostled and shouted as their hero signed all the grubby comics, pages torn out of school books, and cigarette packets they thrust at him. He was punctilious about getting every name right and signed nearly thirty, by the time he had supplied sisters and cousins (and a few imaginary sisters and cousins to be sold at school for profit).

Eventually, they were all done. With a few more Lionel Wilkins lines and a demonstration of the Lionel Wilkins walk, Christopher Milton edged towards the back door of the Corniche. The driver opened it smartly and the star was inside. The electric window came down and the cabaret continued. The car started, the kids shouted louder, Christopher Milton waved, called out, 'Cheerio, Charles, see you tomorrow,' and the car drew away.

Charles had felt awkward during the autograph session. He didn't want to sneak off quietly, nor to come too much into the centre of things in case it looked as if he wanted to be asked for his signature too. But now Christopher Milton had drawn attention to him by mentioning his name, he felt the focus of a dozen pairs of questioning eyes.

He made a vague wave in their direction and started to turn, hoping something wouldn't happen.

It did. Two little Indian boys, Mahendra Patel and a younger brother, came towards him. 'May I have your autograph?' asked the elder in perfect Cockney.

'Oh, you don't want it.' He tried to laugh it off, but the lolly wrapper which had been thrust forward was not withdrawn. Blushing furiously, he signed. The other boys stood and stared. With an ineffectual cheery wave, he gave the paper to Mahendra. Then he turned and hurried away. But not fast enough to avoid hearing the little Cockney voice say, 'No, it isn't him.'

He drank rather more than he should have done that evening at his depressing local in Westbourne Grove. He felt emotionally raw, on the edge of depression for the first time since the rehearsals had started. And, as he knew from experience, when he felt in that mood, things got out of proportion.

The afternoon's flare-up had left a nasty taste. It cast doubt on the whole atmosphere of the show. Charles realised the fragility of what he had taken to be such a good company spirit. Maybe he had condemned himself to nine months of unnecessary unpleasantness.

But after the third large Bell's he felt more able to analyse what had happened at the rehearsal. All Christopher Milton had done was to be rude to David Meldrum and Mark Spelthorne in a good cause – he had only been thinking of improving the show. And David Meldrum's passivity positively invited rudeness. So did the affectations of that little tit Mark Spelthorne. In fact, all Christopher Milton had done was to express the opinions held by most of the cast. In fact, he had shown pretty good judgement in his choice of butts.

Having rationalised that, Charles felt better. He went and got another large Bell's.

The next day Christopher Milton was all over the *Sun* newspaper. 'It's Nightshirt Week in the *Sun!*' said the front page and the centre-spread was a large photograph of the star in a long Dickensian nightshirt and drooping nightcap, holding a candle. He wore the familiar Lionel Wilkins expression of appalled surprise.

When it comes to nightwear, Christopher Milton, better known as Lionel Wilkins, says a nightshirt's the answer – so long as it's a long one. 'Otherwise you get very cold round the...round the...um, er...round the middle of the night. It's no fun waking up in December with your nightie round your neck.' 34-year-old Christopher is currently rehearsing a big new musical, *Lumpkin!*, which opens in the West End late November. 'The part I'm playing's a bit different from Lionel Wilkins. Tony Lumpkin's a chap who likes making trouble for everyone – oh yes, he's always getting the girls into trouble – Ooh, that's not what I meant. I beg yours!' With lovable Christopher Milton around, *Lumpkin!* should be a show worth seeing.

Lovable Christopher Milton's behaviour at rehearsals became more erratic. There were more breaks in the flow, more orders to David Meldrum to shut up, more long pauses while he worked out how a comic effect should be achieved. It was intolerable behaviour on the part of a professional actor, and yet Charles could forgive it, because he was gaining an increasing respect for the man's theatrical instinct. Christopher Milton was always right, he knew what would work for an audience. And, given David Humdrum's total lack of this quality, *Lumpkin!* needed some inspiration.

But it wasn't popular with the rest of the cast, because Christopher Milton's comic instinct was only applied to his own part. The rest of the action was hurried through and substantial cuts were suggested. Only occasionally would there be a long discussion about one of the straight scenes, and that was only if the opportunity was seen for another entrance by Tony Lumpkin.

'Um, Christopher...'

'Shut up, David. I'm thinking.'

'Look, we want to get on with this first meeting between Young Marlow and Kate.'

'Yes, I was thinking it might be better if Tony Lumpkin overheard this scene. I could be behind the screen and...'

'Oh, for God's sake,' snapped Mark Spelthorne. 'This is one of the most famous scenes in English drama. It would make nonsense of the plot if Lumpkin overheard it. It wouldn't add anything.'

Christopher Milton did not seem to hear the objection; he was still working the scene out in his own mind. 'I mean, it's not a very interesting scene, no jokes or anything. I think it could be improved with Lumpkin there.'

Mark Spelthorne grew apoplectic. 'That's a load of absolute balls!'

'Um, Christopher,' said David Meldrum tentatively, 'I think we probably will be better off doing the scene as it is.'

'Hmm.' Again he was distant, still mentally planning. There was a long pause. 'I'll have a look at it.' He moved from the centre of the stage, picked up his script and sat quietly in a corner looking at it. The rehearsals continued.

Such confrontations were not conducive to good feeling. Griff's bar became a centre of disaffection and at any time of day there would be a little knot of actors there discussing their latest grievance against the star. Mark Spelthorne was always one of the most vociferous. 'I mean, let's face it, when Goldsmith wrote the play, he intended Young Marlow to be the hero. There's no question about that. Which was why I took the part. Of course, my bloody agent didn't check the script, just assumed that I would be playing the lead. At least one has the comfort that all this mucking about with the show is making a complete nonsense of it. It'll never run. Doubt if we'll actually come in, die quietly on the tour, I shouldn't wonder. And that won't do a great deal for the career of Mr Christopher Milton. Maybe teach him the dangers of over-exposure.'

'I don't know, Mark. He doesn't actually do that much work. He's very selective in what he does. Anyway, you can't talk. You're doing plenty yourself.'

'Oh yes, that's always a danger if one's popular. Have to watch it. I mean, no doubt there'll be another series of *The Fighter Pilots*. And then if this radio takes off...'

'Oh yes, that was the pilot show. How did it go?'

'Bloody marvellous. Really went a bomb. The planners'll be fools to themselves if they turn that one down. So I suppose I'll be stuck with doing a series of that early next year. Not that I mind. I mean, radio doesn't take long and in fact I have quite an affection for it. The main thing is it's comedy, and really comedy's my best thing. The radio might persuade the telly boys how good I am at it. That's the trouble in telly, they do so like to pigeonhole people. After this *Fighter Pilots* thing, they seem to think I'm only good for the handsome young hero type, whereas of course...'

There were plenty of others in the company with complaints about Christopher Milton, but Charles put it down to the ordinary ineffectual bitching of actors. No one seemed sufficiently motivated to want to sabotage the show. As time went on, Gerald's fears seemed more and more insubstantial.

It was on the Tuesday of the fourth week of rehearsals that Charles began to wonder. By then the scale of the production had got larger. The dancers had joined the company, though they kept somewhat aloof in their self-contained, camp little world. None of them had identifiable parts, except for the prettiest girl who had been given the wordless rôle of Bet Bouncer. There had also been a music rehearsal with the full orchestra ('We can't afford more than one with the band, because of the expense'), and the musicians added another element of an alien culture. The rehearsals became more concerned with details. There were constant discussions with Derbyshire Wilkes, the designer, and Spike, the stage manager, about exact sizes of parts of the set. The pieces of tape which marked their outlines were constantly rearranged. Actors were continually being rushed off in taxis for final costume fittings. The whole production was building up to its first appearance in a theatre on the Saturday week. On that day, their last in London before the tour, *Lumpkin!* was going to have a run on an improvised set in the King's Theatre.

The presence of the augmented company did not stop Christopher Milton's continual interruption of rehearsals while he worked out new entrances and business for Tony Lumpkin. His fits of temperament did not worry the dancers or musicians. Both were well used to hanging around at the whim of whoever happened to be in charge. Whether the break was for a broken microphone or a tantrum did not make a lot of difference to them. They just waited impassively until it was time to continue. And the male dancers had a stage-struck camp affection for stardom. They would have felt cheated if Christopher Milton hadn't behaved like a star.

On the Tuesday they were rehearsing the closer (that is, the last new song of the show, not the acres of reprises which followed it). It was called *Never Gonna Marry You* ('gonna' was a favourite word in Micky Gorton's lyrics) and it sewed up the Lumpkin side of the plot by getting him out of marriage to his cousin and into marriage with Bet Bouncer (while, incidentally, leaving the rest of the plot totally unresolved). It was the only moment in the show when Charles had to sing, which was a great relief to him. Just one couplet and he was quite pleased with it. The lines rose above the general level of Micky Gorton's wit.

'Marriage is like a hot bath, I confess –
The longer you're in it, the colder it gets.'

It probably wasn't an original line and it didn't rhyme properly, but it was a line that would get a laugh, and that was quite a bonus to an actor in a supporting rôle. Charles cherished it; it was the only laugh he stood to get in the show.

After he had sung the couplet in rehearsal that Tuesday, there was a long pause. Christopher Milton had the next line, but he let the music continue and was silent. He looked at Charles with the preoccupied expression he always wore when he was working something out. As the accompaniment died down to untidy silence, he spoke. 'You know, that line will probably get a laugh.'

'I hope so,' said Charles cheerily. 'Unless I cock it up.'

'Hmm. I think I ought to sing it.'

'I beg your pardon.'

'I think I ought to have the line rather than you.'

'What?' Charles was stunned by the directness of the approach. He was a fairly easy-going actor and didn't make scenes over minor details as a rule, but the brazenness of this took him off his guard. 'Oh, come on, Christopher, you can't have all the laughs in the show.'

'I think I should have that line.' Christopher Milton's voice had the familiar distant quality of previous encounters with other actors whose parts he had raided.

'But it strikes me, Christopher, that that line would come much more naturally from Old Marlow, the man of the world, than from Tony Lumpkin, who, let's face it, is meant to be fairly uneducated and – '

'I think I should sing it.'

'Look, I'm not claiming that I'd deliver it better than you or anything. 'It's just that – '

'Huh.' The laugh came out with great savagery. 'I should think not. You'd hardly expect great delivery of lines from a tired old piss-artist. I'm sure there are lots of actors who get through their careers with your level of *competence*, but don't you start comparing yourself with me.'

The suddenness of the attack hurt like a blow in the face. Charles tried some acid line about people who felt they should have all the lines and about acting being a team effort, but it misfired. He appealed to David Meldrum for a decision and – surprise, surprise – David thought Christopher Milton probably had got a point.

Charles spent the rest of the day's rehearsal in a state of silent fury. He knew that his face was white and he was hardly capable of speech. He felt sick with anger.

As soon as he was released, he got a taxi back to Bayswater. Too churned up even for the distant conviviality of the pub, he stopped at an off licence on the way and went back to his room with a bottle of Scotch.

The room in Hereford Road was an untidy and depressing mess, with grey painted cupboards and yellow candlewick on the unmade bed. Its atmosphere usually reduced him to a state of instant depression, but on this occasion it had too much anger to compete with and he hardly noticed his surroundings.

He just sat and drank solidly until there was a slight shift in his mood and he could think of something other than his fury.

It was only a line, after all. Not even a particularly good line at that. And the show was hardly one that was very important to him or one that was going to make any difference to what was laughingly called his career. It wasn't like him to get so upset over a detail.

And then he began to realise the power of Christopher Milton's personality. From his own over-reactions Charles understood the intensity of resentment that the man could inspire. Which made him think that perhaps there were people who felt sufficiently strongly to sabotage any show Christopher Milton was in.

Charles decided that he would make a belated start to the business of investigation for which Gerald Venables had engaged him. Since he had no rehearsals the following morning, he would go and see Everard Austick.

CHAPTER FIVE

EVERARD AUSTICK'S ADDRESS was a block of flats in Eton College Road, near Chalk Farm Underground Station. Charles found it in the phone book and went along on the off-chance that its owner would be out of hospital. He could have rung to check, but felt disinclined to explain his enquiries on the telephone. Also there was a chance that the dry agony of his hangover might have receded by the time he got there.

In fact the tube journey didn't help much and, as he stood in the old lift gazing ahead at its lattice-work metal door, he felt in need of a red-hot poker to burn out the rotten bits of his brain. The only coherent thought he could piece together was the eternal, 'Must drink less'.

The block of flats was old, with long gloomy corridors interrupted by the stranded doormats of unwelcoming doorways. Number 108 was indistinguishable from the others, the same blue gloss paint, the same glass peep-hole to warn the inmate of approaching burglars, rapists, etc.

Charles' pressure on the door-bell produced no reaction. Perhaps it wasn't working. He pressed again, his ear to the door, and caught the distant rustle of its ring. Oh well, maybe Everard was still in hospital, or away convalescing. One more try.

This time there was a distant sound of a door opening, a muttered curse and the heavy approach of a plaster-cased foot. The door opened and Everard Austick peered blearily out into the shadows of the corridor. He looked a mess. His grey hair stuck out in a series of Brylcreemed sheaves as he had slept on it. He had only shaved sketchily for a few days and the areas he had missed sprouted long bristles. A dilapidated camel dressing-gown was bunched around his large frame. His right leg was grotesquely inflated by its plaster. He was probably only in his fifties, but he looked an old man.

'Can I help you?' he asked in a public school voice furred with alcohol.

'Yes. I'm sorry to trouble you. My name's Charles Paris.'

Fuddled incomprehension.

'We worked together once for a season in Glasgow.'

'Ah. Ah yes, of course.' But he didn't remember.

'Look, I've taken over the part you were playing in *Lumpkin!*'

'Oh. Do you want to come in?'

'Thank you.' Everard Austick backed away and Charles moved past him into the dim hall. A door gave off on to a large sitting-room and he made towards it. 'Er, not in there if you don't mind.'

Charles had seen the smart decor of the room and looked back quizzically at Everard. 'Fact is, old boy, I don't use all the flat. No point in using it all when I'm away so much...I...er, there's a young couple who also live here. Just on a temporary basis. Helps out with the old rent, what?' The jovial tone could not hide the facts. Everard Austick was so hard up that he had to rent out almost all his flat to keep his head above water.

This impression was confirmed when Charles was led into Everard's bedroom, obviously the smallest in the flat. The air tasted as if it hadn't been changed for a fortnight. A pile of dusty magazines against them showed that the windows hadn't been opened for months, and the bed was rumpled not just by one night's occupation, but by long days and nights of simply lying and staring at the ceiling rose.

A half-empty bottle of vodka on the dressing-table was evidence of the only activity the room had seen for some time. 'Sorry it's a bit of a tip,' said Everard, attempting to play the line with light comedy insouciance. 'Can I offer you a drink? There's only the vodka, I'm afraid. Well, I suppose I could make some coffee, but...' His mind was unable to cope with the incongruity of the idea.

'A little vodka would be fine.' A hair of the dog might possibly loosen the nutcrackers on Charles' head.

He received a clouded tooth mug half-full of vodka. Everard Austick's hand shook as he passed it over and topped up his own tumbler. 'Down the hatch, old boy.' The long swallow he took was not an action of relish, but of dependence. He grimaced, shuddered and looked at Charles. 'Now, what can I do for you, old man? Want a bit of help in your interpretation of the part, eh?' Again the cheerfulness sounded forced.

'No, actually I just wanted to pick your brains about something.' Charles paused. It was difficult. He did not want to reveal his rôle as an investigator into the show. He realised that he had not done enough preparation for the encounter; he should have worked out some specious story to explain his interest, or even made the approach in some other identity. Still, too late now. Better to try the direct question and hope that Everard's bemused condition would prevent him from being suspicious. 'You know when you broke your leg – what happened?'

'I fell down the stairs.'

'Just an accident?'

'Oh, God knows. I'd had quite a skinful the night before, met a few chums, celebrating actually being in work, it had been a long time. And I had a few more in the morning, you know, to pull me round, and I managed to leave late, so I was hurrying, so I suppose I could have just fallen.'

'Or?'

'Well, there was this chap on the stairs, ran down from behind me, I thought he sort of jostled me. I don't know though.'

'And that's what caused you to fall?'

'Could have been. I don't know.'

'Did he stop to help you when you fell?'

'No, he seemed to be in a hurry.'

'Hmm. Did you see what he looked like?'

'No.'

'Not even an impression?'

'Nothing.'

'Did you tell the police?'

'No. Who's going to believe me? I'm not even sure it happened myself. Could just have fallen.'

'Yes.' The interrogation did not seem to be getting anywhere. Everard Austick was so fogged with alcohol that he didn't even trust his own memory. No one was going to get anything else out of him. Charles drained his glass and rose to leave.

'You're off?' Everard seemed to accept the departure with as little surprise as he had the arrival. Nothing seemed strange in his half-real world.

'Actually, there is one thing, old boy.'

'Yes?'

'This damned leg, I find it so difficult to get about, you know, get to the bank and so on, a bit short of cash, for the... er... you know, basic necessities of life.'

The expansive gesture which accompanied the last four words was meant to signify a whole range of food and domestic essentials, but it ended up pointing at the nearly-empty vodka bottle.

Out of guilt or something, Charles gave him a fiver. Then a thought struck him. 'Everard, why didn't you use the lift that morning?'

'Wasn't working.'

'Sure?'

'I pushed the button for it and it didn't come for a long time. I told you I was in a hurry.'

'Yes. Thank you.'

Charles walked slowly along the dim corridor until he came to the lifts. He looked at them closely. Both were the old sort with sliding doors. A notice requested users to close both doors firmly. Otherwise the lifts would not function. So it would be possible to immobilise both by calling them to another floor and leaving them with their doors ajar. It would then be possible to linger in the gloomy corridor until Everard Austick staggered out of his flat, watch him call unsuccessfully for the lift and then help him on his way when he started downstairs. Unlikely, but possible.

'Hello, Gerald, it's Charles. I got your message at the rehearsal rooms and I'm afraid this is the first chance I've had to call.'

'Okay. How's it going?'

'Nothing to report really. Nothing else has happened.'

'No tension in the company?'

'No more than in any show with Christopher Milton in it which starts its pre-London tour in a week.'

'Hmm. Maybe I was being alarmist'

'Maybe. Anyway, thanks for the job.'

'Any time. Keep your eyes skinned.'

'Okay. Though I don't know what for. There's nothing to see.'

'Unless something else happens.'

'Hello, is that Ruth?'

'Yes. Who's speaking?'

'Charles Paris.'

'Good God. I thought the earth had swallowed you up long ago.'

'No. Still large as life and twice as seedy.'

'Well, to what do I owe this pleasure? Tidying out your room and just found a seven-year-old diary?'

'No.'

'Joined Divorcees Anonymous have you, and they gave you my number?'

'Actually I'm still not divorced.'

'Separated though?'

'Oh yes.'

'And you just phoned for the Recipe-of-the-Day, did you? It's stew.'

'No, the fact is, I'm in a show that's about to start a pre-London tour and our first week's in Leeds and, with true actor's instinct, I thought, well, before I fix up any digs, I'll see if I've got any old friends in Leeds...'

'You've got a nerve.'

'Sorry, I shouldn't have asked. I'll – '

'No. It might be quite entertaining to see you after all these years. At least a change from the sort of men who hang around divorcees in Leeds. When do you arrive?'

'Sunday.'

As Charles put the phone down, Ruth's voice still rang, ominously familiar, in his ears and he had the feeling that he had done something stupid.

If all went well on the tour, *Lumpkin!* was to take over the King's Theatre from a show called *Sex of One and Half a Dozen of the Other*, which had long outstayed its welcome. It had been put on in 1971 by Marius Steen and had celebrated a thousand performances just before the impresario's mysterious death in which Charles Paris had become involved. As the Steen empire was slowly dismantled, the show had continued under different managements with increasingly diluted casts until even the coach party trade began to dwindle. It limped through the summer of 1975 on tourists, but had no chance of surviving the pre-Christmas slump. The theatre-going public had been too depressed by rising ticket prices and the fear that the terrorist bombs might return with the dark evenings to make the effort to see a tired old show. *Sex of One…*had made its London killing and was now off to pick up the residuals of national tours, the depredations of provincial theatre companies and finally the indignities perpetrated by amateur dramatic societies. On Saturday, October 25th, the last day of London rehearsals, the *Lumpkin!* cast assembled for a pre-tour run-through in the King's. The idea was to gain familiarity with the place before the ceremonial entry on November 27th.

The call was for nine o'clock, so that everything should be ready when Christopher Milton arrived at his contractual ten-thirty. Time was tight. *Sex of One…* had a three o'clock matinée and their set (most of which had been dismantled and piled up against the naked brick walls at the back of the stage) had to be reassembled by two-thirty. This meant that an eleven o'clock start would just allow a full run, with only half an hour allowed for cock-ups.

The run was not to be with costume or props. Everything had been packed up into skips and was already on its way to Leeds. The set was in lorries on the M1, scheduled to arrive for the get-in at ten-thirty that night when the current show at the Palace Theatre (a second-rate touring revival of *When We Are Married*) finished its run. Spike, the stage manager, was going to see the run-through, then leap on to the five-to-four train to Leeds and maybe grab a little sleep in anticipation of the all-night and all-day job of getting the set erected and dressed. The actors' schedule was more leisurely. After the run, their next call was at seven o'clock on the Sunday evening for a technical rehearsal. At eleven the next morning there was a press conference in the bar of the Palace Theatre, a dress rehearsal at one, and at seven-thirty on Monday, October 27th, *Lumpkin!* was to meet a paying audience for the first time.

The audience in the King's Theatre on the Saturday morning had not paid. They were all in the circle. David Meldrum, with a rare display of personality, had taken over all of the stalls and set up a little table in the middle. A Camping Gaz lamp was ready to illuminate his interleaved script and notes when the lights went down. Two chairs were set there, one for him and one for Gwyneth, ever efficient, never passing comment.

Up in the circle were some of the backers, who joked nervously like race-horse owners, frightened of coughs, lameness and nobbling. Dickie Peck was there, salivating over his cigar until it looked like a rope-end. There was a representative of Amulet Productions, who looked as if he had gone to a fancy-dress ball as a merchant banker. Gerald Venables was too cool to turn up himself and reveal his anxiety, but a junior member of the office was there representing the interests of Arthur Balcombe. Some other seats were occupied by press representatives and a few girl and boy friends who had been smuggled in.

The stage manager had imposed dress rehearsal discipline and the cast were not allowed out front. Nor were they encouraged to make themselves at home in the dressing-rooms, so there was a lot of hanging around in the green room and the wings. Charles decided that once the run started he would adjourn to the nearest pub. Even with a totally trouble-free run, Sir Charles Marlow could not possibly be required on-stage until one o'clock. He knew he should really hang about the green room listening to the gossip and trying to cadge a lift up to Leeds. But he hated cadging and would rather actually spend the travel allowance he had received on a train ticket than try it.

He listened to the beginning of the run-through on the Tannoy. It sounded pretty pedestrian. He left a message as to his whereabouts with one of the stage management and started towards the pub.

But just as he was leaving the green room, he met Mark Spelthorne. 'Good God, Charles, it's pitch dark out there on the stage. There's just some basic preset and no working lights on in the wings. I just tripped over something and went headlong.'

'What did you trip over?' he asked, suddenly alert.

'Don't know. Something just by the back exit from the stage.' Charles moved quietly in the dark behind the black tabs which represented the limits of the *Lumpkin!* set. He had a chilly feeling that he was about to discover something unpleasant.

His foot touched a soft shape. Soft cloth. He knelt down in the dark and put his hands forward reluctantly to feel what it was.

Just at that moment someone became aware of the lack of light backstage and switched on working lights. Charles screwed up his eyes against the sudden brightness, then opened them and looked down.

It was a cushion. A large scatter cushion, part of the set dressing for *Sex of One...*, which had been dropped when the set was cleared. Charles felt sheepish and looked round, embarrassed. He was alone. He shut off the flow of melodramatic thoughts which had been building in his head.

Still, he was there in a watchdog capacity. Better safe than sorry, he argued in self-justification. To reinforce this illusion of purpose he went across to the pile of tall, heavy flats leant haphazardly against the brick wall. They did not look very safe, some nearly vertical, some almost overhanging. He inspected more closely. Oh, it was all right, there was a pair of thick ropes crossed over the flats, restraining them. They were fixed to rings at the top and the loose ends were wound firmly round a large wooden cleat on the wall. No danger there. Charles tried not to feel a fool and went off to the pub.

That morning's run-through had all the animation of a bus queue. Nothing went wrong, but, God, it was dull. Everyone seemed to feel this and there was a great sag as they came to the end of the final reprise. 'Excellent,' said David Meldrum's voice from somewhere near the Camping Gaz glow. 'Two hours, fifty-seven minutes,' as if the stopwatch were the only criterion of theatrical excellence. 'Right, well done, everybody. Now we must clear the theatre as soon as possible. I've got one or two notes on that run, but I'll give them to you before the Tech. run on Sunday. Okay. See you all in Leeds. That run was really super, loves.'

The cast, who didn't agree and didn't think saying 'loves' suited him, dispersed grumbling. There was a communal feeling of apathetic gloom. The *Sex of One...* stage crew came on-stage to start rebuilding their set for a few coachloads of sweet-paper-rustling pensioners. Dickie Peck arrived and started to talk in an undertone to Christopher Milton. The star's driver, who had also appeared from somewhere, stood at a respectful distance. The cast hurried off to tie up the loose ends of their shopping, or sex lives, which had to be done before they left London. Charles made for the exit.

It was at that moment that all the working lights went out again. This was greeted by the usual curses and cheap jokes. Then suddenly there was another sound, an ominous heavy scrape of wood. It merged into a thud and a scream of pain. Voices, suddenly serious, shouted, 'Lights!'

The working lights revealed a silent tableau. The pile of flats had toppled forward from the wall and lay almost flat on the ground. Protruding from under them was the torso of Mark Spelthorne. Christopher Milton, his driver and Dickie Peck were frozen where the flats had just missed them. Other members of the cast and stage crew stood aghast.

Suddenly everyone rushed forward and started heaving at the wood and canvas to lift it off Mark's body.

'It's all right,' came the familiar drawl. 'Don't fret.'

The helpers stood back as Mark extricated himself. He stood up and rubbed his shoulder.

'Are you all right?'

'I think I'll have a bit of a bruise tomorrow, but otherwise, fine.'

'God, you were lucky,' said Spike, who was looking at where the top edges of the flats had come to rest. 'Look.'

The wall had been Mark's salvation. Because the flats had been a little longer than the floor on which they fell, they had been stopped short when they met the wall, which had taken their weight. Scraping and chipping on the brick showed the force with which they had fallen.

'No one else under there, is there?'

Spike crouched and looked into the triangle of darkness under the flats. After what seemed a long time he straightened up. 'No. Look, could some of you lads help me to get these back?'

'Certainly. Let me give a hand.' Mark Spelthorne, having inadvertently been cast in the rôle of hero, continued to play it.

'That could have been a very nasty accident,' said Christopher Milton.

'All in a day's work for Flying Officer Falconer of *The Fighter Pilots*,' said Mark Spelthorne smugly.

'Whoever tied up those flats should get his cards,' Spike grunted with professional disgust.

'Don't know who did it,' mumbled one of the *Sex of One*...crew.

'Ah well. It happened, not much we can do about it now,' said one of the dancers brightly. 'Don't want to cry over spilt milk, do we? Just mop it up and squeeze the rag back into the bottle, eh?'

This seemed to break the atmosphere. They all helped to push the flats against the wall again and went off laughing and chatting.

Except for Charles Paris. He had seen how firmly the restraining ropes had been fixed to the cleat. He knew what had happened had not been an accident.

PART II

Leeds

CHAPTER SIX

ON THE TRAIN up to Leeds that Sunday afternoon Charles cursed his lack of detective instinct. He had been present at what was probably a crime and just when his mind should be flashing up an instant recall of every detail of the scene it was providing only vague memories and woolly impressions. Perhaps it was Oliver Goldsmith's fault. By delaying Sir Charles Marlow's entry until the fifth act, he had ensured that Charles Paris had had at least two pints too many at the Saturday lunch time, so that the ideal computer print-out of facts and details was replaced by a child's picture in Fuzzy Felt.

He couldn't even remember exactly who had been there. Christopher Milton, certainly, and Dickie Peck and the driver. And David Meldrum and Gwyneth were somewhere around, though he couldn't remember whether they were on stage or in the auditorium at the time of the accident. Mark Spelthorne had been there, of course, and Spike and some of the King's Theatre stage staff...And then who else? Two or three male dancers – Charles didn't know their names, but he'd recognise them again – and the two girl dancers. Then one or two of the supporting actors and actresses. Charles screwed up his eyes and tried to see the scene again. Lizzie Dark certainly, she'd been there, and Michael Peyton, and some others. The edges of the picture were cloudy.

'Damn!' he snapped, and opened his eyes to find that the word had attracted the gaze of a large Bradford-bound Pakistani family. Embarrassed, he closed his eyes and tried to concentrate again. A little chill of anxiety about seeing Ruth kept getting in the way.

Well, the identity parade of suspects wasn't very impressive, because it was incomplete. But, assuming a crime had been committed, it must have a motive and that might give a clue to the criminal.

The first question – was Mark Spelthorne the intended victim or was it just chance that caught him? Christopher Milton was not far behind and it was possible that the criminal was after him, but misjudged his timing in the dark. Or it could have been meant for any one of the people on stage. Or just a random blow for whoever happened to he there. The last would tie in with Gerald's original view that someone was trying to wreck the show and didn't mind how. If it was a personal vendetta against Christopher Milton, then why had the perpetrator bothered to make his first attacks on the pianist and Everard Austick? Why not go straight to his quarry? And why not use a more selective method than a tumbling pile of flats? If, on the other hand, Mark Spelthorne was the intended victim...

Oh dear. He knew it wasn't getting him anywhere. Any of the people on stage at the time of the accident could have unwound the rope from the cleat. Equally, any of them could have been the intended victim. And since he couldn't remember exactly who had been there, the possibilities were infinite. Add the difficulty of tying the motivation for that crime in with the other two and the problem was insoluble, or at least insoluble to a forty-eight-year-old actor who had spent too long in the bar at King's Cross and who was having serious misgivings about going to stay with a woman with whom he had had a brief and not wholly glorious affair seven years previously.

He looked out of the window at the matt flatness of the Midlands. He closed his eyes, but sleep and even relaxation kept their distance. A new question formed in his mind – Did the 15.10 train from King's Cross to Leeds have a bar? He set out to investigate.

Ruth was disagreeable. As soon as he saw her again he remembered. Not disagreeable in the sense of being unattractive; her trim body with its sharp little breasts and well-defined calf muscles remained as good as ever; she was disagreeable in the sense that she disagreed with everything one said. Charles never had known whether it was a genuine defence from a reasoned feminist standpoint or sheer bloody-mindedness. But it came back to him as soon as she spoke. Her voice was marinated in cynicism. Charles felt a great swoop of despair, as if all his worst opinions of himself were suddenly ratified, as if the thoughts that infected him in his lowest moods had suddenly been classified as gospel. He saw himself as an Everard Austick, an alcoholic whose failure in his chosen profession was only matched by his failure as a human being.

It wasn't that cynicism struck no chord. He himself tended to attribute the worst motives to everyone and was distrustful of optimists. But like all practitioners of an art, he liked to feel that his version of it was a definitive one. His cynicism could still be unexpectedly erased by the sight of a child or the shock of a sudden kindness or a moment of desire, while Ruth's blanket coverage seemed to debase the currency of cynicism.

It wasn't that she'd had a particularly bad life. True, its emotional path had been a bit rocky. In her twenties she had had a series of affairs which never stood a chance of going the distance (Charles would have put himself in that category) and eventually at the age of thirty married a central heating systems salesman five years her senior. The marriage lasted three years until he went off with a croupier and they got a divorce. The fatalism with which Ruth accepted this reverse suggested that she had never had much faith in the marriage and had been undermining it for some time.

'So you came.' She spoke with that exactness of enunciation which is more revealing than an accent.

'Yes, I said I would.'

'Oh yes.' The disbelief in her tone instantly put the clock beck seven years. 'And how are you, Mr Charles Paris?'

'Fine, fine.'

'Good. And your lady wife?'

'I don't know. Well, when I last saw her. It's a few months back now. I believe she has a boy friend, someone from the school where she teaches.'

'Good for her. Not going to wait forever on your filing system, is she? Can I get you a cup of tea or a drink or something? Or should I show you up to your room in true landlady fashion?' She leant against the kitchen table in a way that could have been meant to be provocative. It was always difficult to know with Ruth. But seeing her, Charles remembered how much he had fancied her. That was really all there ever had been to the relationship. If there were nothing to life except bed, they'd still have been together. He felt a warm trickle of desire in spite of all the gloom which she had generated inside him.

He overcompensated by the heartiness of his reply. 'A cup of tea would be really...grand.' Her flash of suspicion made him wish he had chosen another word. He'd forgotten how sensitive she was to anything that could be construed as criticism of her Yorkshireness.

She made the tea and Charles kept up a relentless flow of banter to stop himself from making a pass at her. 'How are things in Headingley then?'

'They don't change. I've lived here thirty-four years and lost hope that they ever will.'

'Still in the same job?'

'Oh yes. I think Perkis and Levy, Solicitors and Commissioners for Oaths, would cease to function without my secretarial assistance.'

'Enjoy it?'

She spread open her hands in a gesture which showed up the pointlessness of the question.

'And socially?'

'Socially life here is okay if you're a teenybopper going down the discos or an elegant blue-rinse who likes bridge and golf. I'm neither.'

'No.' The little gusts of interest which had been propelling the conversation along died down to silence. Charles was morbidly aware of the outline of Ruth's nipples through the cotton of her patterned blouse.

She broke the silence. 'This show you're doing, is it the one at the Palace?'

'Yes.'

'With Christopher Milton in it?'

'Yes.'

'He's good,' she said with more enthusiasm than usual. What's he like?'

The classic question, as asked by every member of the public about every star. And virtually unanswerable. No reply can possibly satisfy the questioner, who usually has only thought as far as the question. Charles tried. 'Well, he's...' And then realised he could not even answer to his own satisfaction. 'I don't know.'

He was glad of the seven o'clock call at the Palace Theatre, as it temporarily took off the pressure of Ruth's presence.

After David Meldrum's tentative notes on the Saturday run-through (interrupted by less tentative ones from Christopher Milton), Charles sorted out a later call with the stage management and set off to investigate the adjacent pub.

It was small and dingy, one of the few old buildings which had survived the extensive modernization of Leeds city centre. A few regulars sat around in despairing huddles while a younger group played silent, grim darts. Charles ordered a large Bell's, which they didn't have, and got a large Haig. As he turned to find a space on one of the railway waiting-room benches, he recognised a figure in a blue donkey jacket hunched against the bar. 'Hello, Kevin.'

The bleary eyes showed that the writer had been there since opening time. Charles received an indifferent drunken greeting.

'Not a bad theatre, is it?'

'Not a bad theatre? Huh. Are you telling me about the Palace Theatre? That's good. I've been seeing shows at the Palace since I was six. Pantomimes, all sorts. I was brought up here. Meanwood. Went to the grammar school. We were always brought on outings to the Palace, when there was anything cultural on, touring companies, all that. Always came to the Palace. It was my ambition, when I was in my teens, to have something of mine done, performed at the Palace. That and losing my virginity.'

'And now I assume you've managed both.'

'One happened, near as dammit, in the back row of the Cottage Road Cinema.' He let out an abrupt, dirty laugh. Then his face darkened. 'But the other...'

'The other you achieve tomorrow. First night.'

Kevin looked him straight in the eyes for a moment before he spoke. 'Oh yes. Tomorrow. First night. But first night of what? Do you think I'll feel any pride in *that*?'

'Don't worry. It's going to be a good show. It's inevitable that everyone's a bit jumpy just before it starts.' Charles had not decided yet what he really thought of the show, but he thought reassurance was required.

As it turned out, he was wrong. 'That's not what I mean. I mean that what'll go on at that theatre tomorrow will have nothing to do with me.'

'Oh, I know it's changed a bit from the original production, but that's inevitable when – '

'Changed a bit – huh! There's almost nothing in that show that I put there.'

'I'm sure a lot of it's still quite close to the original.'

'Balls. I should never have agreed. If I'd known what a total cock-up they were going to make of it…okay, they wanted to get in somebody else to do the music…all right, maybe Joe Coatley's music wasn't that commercial, but I thought at least they'd leave my text alone. I felt bad about dropping Joe at the time, but now I bloody envy him. I'd give anything to be out of it.'

Deliberately crude, Charles mentioned the money.

'Oh yes, there'll be plenty of money. Run forever, a show like this, or at least until his Lordship gets bored with it. You know, I used to think I'd do anything for money – that was when I hadn't got any – thought I'd write anything, pornography, all sorts. I did, I wrote a real hard-core porn book – filth, all about whips and Alsatians, real muck. I got a hundred pounds for that, but I tell you, I'm more proud of that than I will be when this load of shit's running in the West End and bringing me in my so many per cent a week.' He was in full flow, spurred on by the drink. 'Look, I'm a writer, a writer. If I didn't want to be a writer, I'd be some other bloody thing, an accountant, a clerk in the Town Hall, I don't care what. But that's not what I wanted to be. I wanted to be a writer. And why does someone want to be a writer?'

Charles had his own views on the subject, but didn't volunteer them. Anyway, Kevin's question turned out to be rhetorical. 'I'll tell you why someone wants to be a writer. Because what he writes is his own, it may be rubbish, but it's his own rubbish. No one can take that away from him. He wrote it.' He seemed to realise he was becoming almost incoherently repetitive and paused to collect his thoughts before continuing. He swayed slightly.

'And that is why I don't like my work being destroyed by some jumped-up idiot of an actor, who couldn't even write his own name.'

Charles found himself (not for the first time) taking up a position of boring middle-aged reasonableness. 'Kevin, one has to face it that there are some things which work on the page that don't work in performance.'

'I accept that. Good God, I've worked on plays before. I'm used to doing rewrites and changing things and cutting things down, but in the past it's always been a matter of discussing it, not just some prima donna ballsing up whole scenes so that he gets all the lines.'

Charles smarted at the remembrance of his own suffering from Christopher Milton on a line-hunt, but continued his defence. 'Look, I know he's got an unfortunate manner, but he does have a real genius for the theatre. He knows what's going to work and what – '

'He knows what's going to work for him, yes, but he doesn't give a bugger about the rest of the show. He's already made nonsense of the plot by cutting down the Young Marlow scenes to nothing. The show'll be a great shapeless mess.'

'The audience will love it.'

'Audience, huh. What the hell do they know? The audience that comes to this show will be so force-fed with television they won't notice what it's about. They'll spend all their time waiting for the commercials. They'd come and see him if he was peeling potatoes on stage. They'd come and see anything that they saw on their screen. A jug of water, *as featured on the Nine O'Clock News*, that's what they'd come to see.'

He paused for breath. Charles took the opportunity to buy more drinks, hoping to break the monologue. But when he'd handed Kevin a large whisky, raised his own and said 'Cheers', it was instantly resumed. 'There's a lot of good stuff in that show which has just been dumped. Dumped and replaced by corny rubbish. I know. I'm not saying I'm the greatest writer there ever was, but I know when I've written a good line, and I don't write them so that some idiot can just come along and...' He lost his thread and when he came back his voice was cold with concentration. 'If he takes anything else out of this show, I'll kill the bastard. I've warned him, I've warned him that I can get nasty, and I will. Do you know, last Friday he was even saying he didn't know whether *Liberty Hall* was a good number or not. *Liberty Hall*, I mean that's the best number in the show. It's the only one they kept from the original. They had to, they'd never get a better number than that, would they? Go on, you say what you think of it. Of that song.'

Charles, who hated being button-holed for opinions, murmured something about it being a very good number.

'Too right it is. A bloody good number. I tell you, if he tries to get rid of that song, I will kill him.'

Kevin became more violent and unintelligible as the drink seeped in and Charles was relieved when it was time for him to return to the theatre.

As he travelled back to Headingley in the 33 bus, he thought about Kevin. Most of it he put down to the drink, but it was another example of the violent reactions Christopher Milton inspired. Kevin had plenty of motive for wishing ill to the show, if he was really as disgusted with it as he claimed. And he had said something about having warned Christopher Milton, which could be a reference to the previous crimes. And, Charles suddenly remembered, the writer had been on-stage at the King's Theatre when the flats fell. A new thought came into his mind. Suppose the first two accidents were genuine and the campaign of persecution only began with the falling flats. And suppose the object of the persecution was not the show, but just Christopher Milton. Someone hated the star so much that he wanted to kill him.

Back at the semi in Headingley Ruth had gone to bed, but her door was ajar and the light on. Charles knocked softly and went in.

She looked up without surprise. 'So you've finished.' Her voice could imbue the simplest sentence with criticism.

'Yes.' He sat heavily on the bed.

'Drunk, I suppose.'

'Moderately.'

'You're a wreck, Charles.' She said it hard, without affection. Then she reached forward and touched his hand. The scent of talcum powder rose to his nostrils. He looked at her. And then he kissed her.

She responded, as he knew she would. As he had known when he had first heard he was going to Leeds. From that moment a guilty fascination had led him to this. His unwillingness, his positive knowledge that it was idiotic to restart the affair, was swamped by animal urgency. His right hand scrabbled roughly at her nightdress, pulling it up.

'I know what you want.' Even as her hands reached down hungrily to fight with the clasp of his trousers, she made it sound like an accusation.

CHAPTER SEVEN

IN THE AUDIENCE at *Lumpkin!*'s first public performance on Monday, October 27th 1975 were some people with a special interest in the show. There were the Friends of the Palace Theatre who spent the performance preparing witty things to say at the discussion with the cast which their secretary, Miss Thompson, had arranged to take place on stage after the final curtain. There were Kevin McMahon's parents whom he hadn't been able to dissuade from coming. There was Dickie Peck, just arrived from London to see that everyone was doing exactly what his protégé wanted. And there was Gerald Venables, up in theory in his legal capacity to extort money from a wealthy mill-owner, and in fact to keep an eye on his investment and get a progress report from Charles Paris.

The performance they watched was unusual, in that it started with one central character and ended with another. Charles saw it all from the fly gallery. It was strictly against theatre discipline for him to be up there, but he had asked Spike, who didn't seem to mind. Spike was easy-going about most things. He had that equable technician's temperament that never failed to amaze Charles. The ability to continue hard physical work up to seventy-two hours without ever losing his resource and surly good humour. And all without any sort of public recognition. The extrovert actor part of Charles could not understand that. What made people like Spike tick? Where did they come from?

He looked across at the intent acne-ridden face as the stage manager pulled on a thick rope and delicately eased a huge piece of scenery up between two metal bars with their heavy load of lights. Charles instantly remembered stories of flying disasters, of cumbersome pieces plummeting down on actors below, of faulty counterweighting snatching technicians up from the stage to dash them against the chipping machine of the grid in the roof. But the sight of Spike's strength and control put away such thoughts. The eternal stage manager. As the name implied, he could always manage. There was no point in thinking what Spike might have done before; it was impossible to imagine him in any other world.

As the show progressed, Charles' attention soon moved from speculations about the stage staff to the strange transformation which was taking place on-stage, the transformation of the character of Tony Lumpkin. Christopher Milton's performance started as it had been in rehearsal. The knowing yokel dominated the stage, his voice deeply rustic and his movements capturing the clumsy grace of the farm-boy. Charles settled down to enjoy it.

The change, when it came, was quite abrupt. Audience reaction was a bit slow, but no slower than one would expect from a Monday night house of stuffed shirts from the clothing industry and a few stray television fans, awestruck by the unaccustomed space of a theatre. Charles had been in many shows which had got worse reaction at this tender stage of their lives.

But Christopher Milton was worried. His anxiety was not apparent to the audience, but to Charles, who knew the performance well, the fear showed. There was a hesitancy in delivery, a certain stiffness in dancing that betrayed the inward unrest. It came to a head in the *Liberty Hall* number. This involved a parodic country dance for Tony Lumpkin and the dancers. It was a well-choreographed routine, which started with heavy deliberation and speeded up until Christopher Milton was spinning giddily on a rostrum centre stage, from which he did a final jump to a kneeling position, an inevitable cue for applause.

He'd done it perfectly in rehearsal, but on the first night he mis-timed it. He came out of the spin into the jump and landed untidily on one leg. It was not a serious error and certainly did not hurt him, but it was messy. The audience realised it had gone wrong, lost their own natural timing and did not come in with instantaneous applause.

The pause was tiny, the audience goodwill to clap was there, but the mistake had thrown them. Christopher Milton felt the hiatus and came in quickly with the line, 'Ooh, I done it all wrong.'

This time the reaction was enormous. An instant laugh, the loudest of the evening, which melted naturally into vigorous clapping, as if the audience wanted to make up for missing their first cue.

As a professional Charles could recognise Christopher Milton's immaculate timing of the line, but it was not that which struck him most about it. It was the voice in which it had been delivered. The star had not used his own voice, nor that of Tony Lumpkin. The line had been spoken by Lionel Wilkins of the television series *Straight up, Guv*.

And from that point on, Lionel Wilkins took over. For the next ten minutes or so, Tony Lumpkin fought a desultory rearguard action, but he was defeated before he started. The rustic burr was replaced by a London whine. The brown frock coat was thrown into the wings and the part was played in timeless shirtsleeves. Oliver Goldsmith, who had probably done a few gyrations in his grave over the previous weeks, must by now have been turning fast enough to power the National Grid. One of the central themes of his play, the contrast between Town and Country, had just vanished. The plot lost yet another of its tenuous links with sense.

And the audience loved it. Familiarity gave them the confidence they needed to express their enthusiasm. It may have been a bit difficult to follow the twists and exposition of an old-fashioned story, but to be presented with an instantly recognisable character from their television screens, that made it all simple. Charles watched from the fly gallery in amazement. 'What the hell is he doing?' he murmured to Spike, who was leaning on the rail beside him.

'His own thing,' Spike grunted. 'Never does anything else.'

'What will David Humdrum say?'

Charles knew the answer to his question, but Spike supplied it 'He'll say, "Fine".'

And he did. Charles saw the encounter between star and director in the green room at the interval. 'Christ, this needs a lot more work,' said the star.

'It's going fine, Christopher, just fine,' soothed the director.

'That *Liberty Hall* number will have to come out for a start. I always thought it was a load of crap.'

'I'm sure, with a bit more rehearsal – '

'Shut up! It's coming out.' Christopher Milton went up to his dressing-room.

Charles decided that it was in his interests as the show's secret watchdog to keep his eyes on the movements of Kevin McMahon. If the writer lived up to half of his drunken threats, there was going to be trouble.

The trouble started as soon as the curtain had come down on the final call. Kevin McMahon was in the green room to greet the cast as they came offstage. He went straight up to Christopher Milton and shouted, 'What the hell do you mean by performing my stuff like that? This isn't one of your tatty TV comedies!'

The star seemed to look through him and greeted a man with greasy swept-back hair and a cheap suede zip-up jacket. 'Hello, Wally. What did you think?'

'Good bits, bad bits,' said Wally Wilson in broad Cockney.

'Never mind. Nothing that can't be changed.'

'Too right. Soon be up to the *Straight Up, Guv* standard!'

'Now you bloody listen to me, Mr Christopher Bloody Milton....' Kevin began belligerently.

The response came back like a whip-lash. 'Shut up, I'm talking to a writer.'

The implication was too much for Kevin McMahon. With a cry of fury, he drew his fist back for a blow.

Christopher Milton moved fast. He side-stepped with a dancer's ease. Kevin swung himself off balance and at that moment Dickie Peck, who had moved from the doorway at amazing speed when the fracas started, flicked up Kevin's head with his left forearm and smashed a hard right knuckle into the writer's mouth. The knees gave, the body crumpled and blood welled from a cut lip. 'Don't you ever dare lay a finger on him,' Dickie Peck hissed.

The action had all been so quick that it left behind a shocked silence. The unexpectedness of the fight paled into insignificance compared to the transformation of Dickie Peck, suddenly converted from a middle-aged joke figure to a bruiser. Charles recollected a distant rumour that the agent had started his career as a boxer.

Christopher Milton broke the silence. He continued in an even tone, as if nothing had happened. 'Wally, come up to my dressing-room and have a chat.'

'Love to.' Wall's casualness was more studied.

'Um, er, Mr Milton.' A young man who had been hovering uneasily round the edges of the green room, stepped forward, blushing furiously.

'What?'

'I'm, er, um...my name is Bates and, er, I'm representing Mr Katzmann, who, as you know, is, er, the general manager of the theatre and – '

'What the hell are you burbling about?'

'Well, er, as you know, the; er...the, er...' He ran out of syntax. 'The Friends.'

'Are you coming, Wally?'

'Mr Milton.' Panic made the young man articulate again, and he blurted out his message. 'The Friends of the Palace Theatre are about to hold their discussion of the show on stage and, as Mr Katzmann arranged, you and the other members of the cast will be joining in the discussion.'

'I bloody won't. It's the first I've heard of it. If you think I'm going to piss around talking crap to old ladies, you can forget it.'

'But – '

Dickie Peck cut the young man short with a gesture and again took control. 'Has this been advertised?'

'Yes. Mr Katzmann arranged it months ago.'

'Not through me, he didn't. You'd better do it, Chris.'

'Look, I've just done a bloody performance, I've just been assaulted by a lunatic hack-writer, I'm not going to – '

Dickie Peck raised his hand and the voice petered out. 'You've got to do it, Chris. It's a bloody lumber and – ' with a glance at Mr Bates, who trembled visibly – 'there'll be hell to pay for someone in the morning when I find out who made the cock-up. But if it's been advertised, you can't afford to get the reputation of someone who jacks out of that sort of thing.'

Christopher Milton swore obscenely and loud, but accepted the logic of the argument. He went upstairs to take off his makeup and, as often happened when he left the room, the atmosphere relaxed. People started to drift away. Charles went across to Kevin McMahon, who had dragged himself quietly to a sofa and was dabbing at his lip with a handkerchief. 'I think it's time to take the money and run, Kevin. Put this down to bad experience. Reckon that it's just a grant of money to buy you time to go off and write what you really want to.'

'I really wanted to write *Liberty Hall*.'

'Yes, but there must be other things, more original, more your own that you want to get on with.'

'Oh yes, things where I express the real me, things that the world has been waiting to have written by some genius who only needs time to get on with it.'

Charles ignored the heaviness of the irony. 'Yes, that sort of thing.'

'Don't you patronise me!' Kevin stood up. 'I'm going to kill the bastard,' he said and walked out of the theatre.

'But,' said Mrs Crichton-Smith, whose husband owned a sock factory and played off an eight handicap, 'I remember doing *She Stoops to Conquer* at school and I must say a lot of the original plot seems to have been obscured in this production.'

Christopher Milton flashed her a frank, confiding smile. 'I agree, Mrs Crichton-Smith, but Goldsmith was writing for his time. This is 1975, we can't just do a production as if nothing has changed since the play was written. And, anyway, this is not *She Stoops to Conquer*, this is a new musical. What we're trying to do, and I think our writer, Kevin McMahon, would agree with me here,' he added, as if to impress the image of a big-happy-family, all-working-towards-the-same-end company, 'is to create an original show. I mean, entertainment is variety. Your husband wouldn't think much of you if you produced the same meal for him every night – however good it was.'

His middle-class half-joke produced the right middle-class half-laugh and Charles was once again impressed with Christopher Milton's ability to adapt to any audience and say the right things. It was not an intellectual gift; he probably did not have the intelligence or knowledge to argue the merits of the piece on a literary level; it was just an instinct that never failed.

Miss Thompson, the secretary, next introduced a question from: 'Mr Henry Oxenford, one of our keenest members, who's interested in all things theatrical.' Mr Oxenford, one of the bow-tied types who hang about amateur dramatic societies, content to be precious rather than queer, stood up and put his well-rehearsed enquiry, 'I would like to know whether you, as a performer, be it as Tony Lumpkin or Lionel Wilkins, find the danger that a part tends to take over your private life and you become like that person?'

Christopher Milton laughed boyishly. 'You mean when I'm working on the television series, do I go around trying to con money off everyone I meet?'

'Well, not exactly.'

'Oh, I beg yours.' The Lionel Wilkins line was, as ever, perfectly delivered and got its laugh. Charles watched Christopher Milton's eyes and saw him decide to continue in the Wilkins voice and prolong the misunderstanding. 'Oh, I see what you mean – do I go up to people in the street and say, Look 'ere, I've got this great project. Wouldn't you like to buy shares in the first motel on the moon? Not only do you get the normal dividends, but you also get a free weekend every year once the motel is completed. Now the shares aren't yet officially on the market, but I can let you have some at a price which...' And he was away, re-creating the plot of a recent episode of *Straight Up, Guv*. The Friends of the Palace Theatre loved it.

As he drew to the end of his routine, before Miss Thompson could introduce Mrs Horton who had been waving her arm like a schoolgirl know-all between each question, he glanced at his watch. 'Oh, look at the time. I'm afraid we've gone on much longer than we intended. We've still got a lot of work to do on this show – oh, you may have liked it, but there are a good few things to he altered yet – so we must draw it to a close there.'

The Friends of the Palace Theatre started to leave through the stalls. An autograph cluster gathered round the star. The other members of the cast, who hadn't got much of a look-in on the discussion, trickled back through the curtains. Mark Spelthorne dawdled, seeing if there were any fans of *The Fighter Pilots* on the autograph trail. When it became apparent there weren't, he vanished smartly.

Christopher Milton finished the signings and waved cheerily from the stage until the last Friend had gone out of the doors at the back of the stalls. When he turned his face was instantly twisted with rage. 'Cows! Stupid, bloody cows!' He pushed through the curtains, shouting imperiously, 'Wally! Dickie! Come on, we've got to get this script altered, even if we have to work all bloody night.'

As Charles waited to hear the inevitable news that there would be a rehearsal call at ten the following morning, he began to understand the personality-splitting pressure of a public image.

Gerald Venables was sitting waiting in his car, a Mercedes 280 SL, with the lights doused, by the stage door. He had the collar of his raincoat turned up and was slumped against the window in an attitude cribbed from some B-movie. He was trying so hard to be inconspicuous that Charles saw him instantly. 'Hello.'

'Ssh. Get in.' The passenger door was slipped open. Charles climbed in clumsily. 'So, what gives?' Gerald hissed, his eyes scanning the empty road ahead.

'Just been a bit of a dust-up, boss,' Charles hissed back.

Gerald didn't realise he was being sent up, but ran out of slang. 'What? You mean a fight?'

'Too right, boss.'

'Irons?'

'I beg your pardon.'

'Irons – you know, guns. God, don't you watch any television?'

'Not much.'

'Well, give us the dirt. Who swung a bunch of fives at whom?' The grammatical resolution of the question rather weakened its underworld flavour.

Charles gave a quick account of the scene in the green room and the solicitor nodded knowingly. 'So you reckon this McMahon could be our cookie?'

'Our saboteur, the man devoted to the destruction of the show...?'

'Yes.'

'I don't know. Certainly he hates Christopher Milton. If anything were to happen to the star tonight, I would have no doubt about who to look for. But I don't think Kevin can have been responsible for the other accidents, not the first two, anyway.'

'Why not?'

'Because why should he? When the pianist was shot at, Kevin didn't know what was going to happen to his script, rehearsals had hardly started. I reckon at that stage he must have been full of excitement, you know, his first West End show and all that.'

'But it can't have taken long for him to realise the way things were going.'

'Yes, I suppose he could have built up a sufficient head of resentment by the time Everard Austick met with his accident.'

'Yes, surely, and – '

'There's another snag, Gerald. Kevin's resentment is completely against Christopher Milton. Sniping at these minor figures may be bad for the show, but it doesn't hurt the star much. Christopher Milton doesn't care who his supporting cast are, so long as they don't argue with him or do anything better than he does. If Kevin McMahon did want to get at anyone he'd go straight for the one who was bugging him – and, with the star out of the way, there might be a chance that his musical could survive in another production.'

'Yes. So we've got to look for someone else as the mastermind behind the whole sequence of crimes.'

'If there is a sequence, Gerald, if there are any crimes. So far the only evidence I have of misdoing is what happened at the King's Theatre. I know someone tampered with the rope holding those flats up. All the others could be genuine accidents. In fact, the thing at the King's may have a perfectly legitimate explanation.'

'I don't know, Charles. I still have the feeling that they're all linked and that something funny's going on.'

There was a silence. 'Hmm. Yes, I can feel a sort of foreboding too, but I don't know why.'

As he spoke, light spilled across the road from the stage door. Christopher Milton, Dickie Peck, Wally Wilson and the show's musical director, Pete Masters, came out, escorted by Milton's driver, who smartly moved forward to the parked Corniche and opened the doors. They all got in. 'Let's follow them,' whispered Charles, more to satisfy Gerald's love of the dramatic than anything else.

They let the Rolls disappear at the junction on to the main road, confident that Leeds' central one-way system would make it difficult to lose their quarry, and started up in pursuit.

Gerald's 'Follow that car' routine was as exaggerated as his 'I am waiting unobtrusively' one, involving many sudden swivels of the head and bursts of squealing acceleration alternating with dawdling so slowly that it drew, hoots of annoyance from other road-users. But the inhabitants of the Rolls did not appear to notice them. There were none of the sudden right-angled swerves up side-roads beloved of gangsters in movies. They drove sedately round the one-way system and into Neville Street, where they swung off the main road and came to rest at the entrance of the Dragonara Hotel. Gerald, who hadn't been expecting the stop, overshot, screeched to a halt and reversed to a spying position, flashed at by the righteous headlights of other drivers in the one-way street.

The party disembarking from the Corniche still did not take any notice of their pursuers. The four of them walked straight into the foyer and the driver slid the car away to the hotel car park.

'Well...' said Gerald.

'Well, I guess we've found out where he's staying.'

'Yes. Yes, we have.'

'I could have asked him and saved us the trouble.'

'Yes, but at least this way we can tell if he's lying.'

'What on earth do you mean? Why should he lie about staying in the newest, poshest hotel in Leeds?'

'I don't know.' They both felt very foolish.

'By the way, Gerald, why aren't you staying at the Dragonara? I thought that was your usual style.'

'I didn't know it existed. Polly, my secretary, booked me into the Queen's. More traditional, I think...I'm only here for the one night. I suppose I could try and get transferred, see if there's a room here.'

'What good would that do?'

'Well, then I'd be in the hotel, I could spy, I...'

'What are we spying on? What do we want to find out?'

'I don't know.'

'All we want to do is see that Kevin McMahon doesn't get a chance to have a go at Christopher Milton.'

'Yes.'

'And since he's got Dickie Peck and his driver in the hotel there with him, I think we're superfluous.'

'So what should we do?'

'Go to our several beds,' said Charles, with mingled desire and depression at the thought of his.

'All right. I suppose we'd better. Mind you, we're going to feel pretty silly in the morning if we hear that Christopher Milton's been murdered.'

They needn't have worried. Christopher Milton survived the night unharmed. But Kevin McMahon was found beaten up in the car park by the bus station.

CHAPTER EIGHT

CHARLES DIDN'T HEAR about the new accident until he reached the theatre for rehearsal. A silent breakfast with Ruth had been followed by a silent lift in her Renault 5L to the city centre. She started work at nine, so he had time to kill. They parted in silence and he wandered off in the direction of the Dragonara for no apparent reason.

To occupy his mind with trivialities, he pretended he was trailing the man in front of him. The head he followed was completely bald with enormous ears like the handles of a loving cup. Charles varied his pace, playing a game with himself, committing details to memory, checking the time. At five to nine the man went in the front entrance of the Dragonara and the game was over.

Charles looked round for someone else to use as a dummy and then felt a wave of hopelessness. What was the point of playing at detectives when his performance was so abysmal on occasions that required real detective abilities?

The 'what was the point?' gloom deepened to embrace his emotional life too. Another night of angry sex with Ruth had depressed him. What was the point of it? He had left Frances to get away from the ties and twists of a 'relationship', hoping to find some kind of freedom. And he had accepted the limitations which the emotional free-lance shares with all other free-lances – delays between engagements and sudden terminations of contracts. But it wasn't just that. Casual sex didn't give him enough and anything deeper soon got claustrophobic. If he was going to go through all the hard work of making something work, he might just as well try again with Frances. At least he had got a start there.

But Frances had got a boy friend. So the rumour went, and he had no cause to disbelieve it. And that seemed to change it all. It twisted his emotional outlook. He would not admit to himself that he was prey to so simple an emotion as jealousy, but the fact that Frances was not floating unattached in the background made any other relationship more threatening, as if now he was really looking for something lasting. Which he wasn't...Oh, hell, why couldn't he just think of Ruth as a nice time in Leeds, all to be over and forgotten in a week? But guilt crept in, and though he was conscious of his depression over-dramatising everything, he was unable to get out of the pointless spiral of his thoughts.

He quickly got news of Kevin's accident when he arrived at the theatre. The police were there. They had taken over one of the dressing-rooms, where they were questioning members of the cast. There were constant assurances that no one in the company was suspected, but certain facts had to be established – who Kevin was, where he was staying and so on.

The details of the beating spread quickly. Kevin was in the Infirmary though he was not seriously hurt. Apparently he had spent the evening drinking, moving on to a small club when the pubs closed. He had been kicked out of there at about two, and wandered round for some time – he couldn't remember how long – and then been jumped by someone who punched him in the face, kicked him about the rest of his body, left him unconscious and stole his wallet. The police regarded it as a simple mugging and were looking for someone local.

They did hear about the altercation between Kevin and Dickie Peck and when the agent arrived with his protégé at ten-thirty, he was questioned. But it transpired that the two of them, along with Wally Wilson and Pete Masters, the young musical director, had been up most of the night working on a new number to replace *Liberty Hall*. They had mutually dependent alibis.

That was a blow to Charles' simple reading of the situation. He had leapt to the conclusion that Dickie Peck must have got at Kevin, continuing the scene that had started in the green room. And if there had only been Christopher Milton and Wally Wilson to corroborate Dickie's alibi, he would still have believed it. But if Pete, the M.D., also vouched for him, that changed things. He was not one of the star's immediate entourage and the most unlikely person to submit to intimidation. So maybe it was just an attack by a mugger unknown. But it did seem too much of a coincidence.

And if it was a coincidence, it was a very happy one for Christopher Milton. There was no dissenting voice when he announced that *Liberty Hall* was to be dropped and that the whole day until the evening performance would be spent rehearsing the new number which had been written overnight.

He was very ebullient and cheerful. He made no pretence now that David Meldrum was directing the show and leapt around the stage telling everyone what to do and demonstrating. He showed no fatigue after the long night and was supremely creative. His enthusiasm for the new song was infectious and they all worked hard to give it life.

Pete Masters, the M.D., had written a simple but catchy tune and was very pleased with himself. Wally Wilson had written the lyric and when Christopher Milton first sang it through with the piano, Charles could feel the gyrations of Oliver Goldsmith in his grave accelerate yet again.

When you're out on the fiddle
And you're trying to pull a con
And the cops come in the middle
Of the trick you're trying on,
Then all you've gotta do
Is just give a little pause,
Give a little smile
And come back with 'I Beg Yours?'

Not 'I beg to differ' or 'I beg to remain...'
Not 'I beg your pardon', but an easier refrain,
Not 'I've lost my bottle' and not 'I've lost my drawers' –
The answer's very simple –
All you say is 'I Beg Yours?'

When you're selling some jew'l'ry
And the jew'l'ry don't exist
And the victim of your fool'ry,
(Who you thought was very...drunk)
Turns out to be a cop
And says he'll bring down the laws,
Don't lose your cool,
But come back with 'I Beg Yours?'

Not 'I beg to differ' or...and so on through four more verses of variable scansion and anachronism. Christopher Milton ended the song with a flourish and Charles couldn't help joining in the applause that followed it. He was once again struck by how good Christopher Milton was. The applause was not sycophancy; it was the genuine praise of professionals.

But in spite of the performance, the song was hopelessly wrong for the show. Charles knew it and felt he had to say something. He was just assembling a tactful objection when Mark Spelthorne came in with his own drawling complaint. Typically, it was completely selfish. 'But we can't really have that number there, Christopher. I mean, that would make it three solos for you in a row. Surely, it would be better for the balance of the show if we had an ensemble number at this point.' (What he really meant was, 'I had a lot to do in *Liberty Hall*. Now I've lost a number.')

Christopher Milton did not snap back at Mark. He didn't bother when Dickie Peck was present to do it for him. 'That's nonsense,' barked the agent. 'The audience will have come here to see Christopher Milton and the more of him they see, the happier they'll be.'

'There is such a thing as over-exposure,' Mark Spelthorne observed in a voice that wouldn't remain as cool as he wanted it.

'Something you're never going to have to worry about, sonny,' Dickie flashed back. 'No, it's a great number. Really good. Just done overnight, you know – ' (appealing for admiration from the company. Charles' admiration conformed with Dr Johnson's comment about a dog walking on its hinder legs – 'It is not well done, but you are surprised to find it done at all.') ' – No, I think this is going to be the number of the show. Make a great single too. I don't see actually why it shouldn't be the title of the show. *I Beg Yours?*, I mean it's catchy and it's – '

'All the publicity's already gone out,' David Meldrum interposed, thus at least killing that ridiculous idea. But Charles still thought someone ought to question the suitability of the number for a show which, in spite of major surgery and transplants, was still set in the eighteenth century and was about Tony Lumpkin rather than Lionel Wilkins. It would stick out like go-go dancers in the middle of the Ring Cycle.

He cleared his throat to remonstrate, but fortunately Winifred Tuke anticipated him. 'We can't have this song.'

'Why not?' asked Dickie Peck aggressively, pausing with a match held up to a new cigar.

'Well, honestly, darling, I mean, I know we're not doing *She Stoops...* straight, but this does make nonsense of it.' It was daring and impressive and she should have left it at that. Instead she went on, getting more actressy and vague. 'I mean, the whole thing about this play is that it's Town life versus Country and we're already losing that by playing Tony London, but if we start putting in bits from other shows then – '

'It isn't a bit from another show,' said Christopher Milton softly.

'Not exactly, darling, but this song is absolutely based on that divine character you play in the telly, and I mean it just isn't Tony Lumpkin...is it?'

Her ginny voice faltered as he gazed at her coldly. The tableau was held in silence for a full minute. Then Christopher Milton turned to David Meldrum and said, unfairly, 'Come on, we should be rehearsing if we're to get this number in by tonight.'

'And are we?'

'Yes, we bloody are. For Christ's sake assert your authority.' Which was rich, coming from the person who had done most to undermine it.

I Beg Yours? was in the show on the Tuesday night. It was under-rehearsed and a little untidy, but the audience loved it. Once again, Christopher Milton's instinct seemed to have been vindicated. The reaction to the rest of the show was mixed, but they latched on to that number.

Ruth was out front. Charles had given her a ticket, though after their silent parting in the morning he wasn't certain that she'd come. However, there she was at the stage door after the show. When he saw her, he felt an awful sense of shame. It was not exactly that he was ashamed of her, but he felt wrong with her. He tried to hurry her away, but Michael Peyton called out to him just as they were leaving, 'Hey, everyone's going out for a curry. You want to come?'

Charles started to refuse, but Ruth chipped in and said she hadn't eaten and would love to go.

He hated the meal, because he hated being thought of in conjunction with Ruth. He knew how cruel it was to resent someone's company in that way and the knowledge only made him feel guiltier. Ruth, on the other hand, enjoyed herself. Surprisingly, Christopher Milton and Dickie Peck had joined the party, the star having decided to be one of the boys for a night, and he chatted up Ruth shamelessly. She luxuriated in this and Charles, embarrassed by her naive questions and provincial tastes, was annoyed to find that he felt jealous too. To be jealous about a woman whom he was embarrassed to be with, it all got far too complicated to cope with. He drank heavily and wished Frances were there.

Ruth was drunk too and drove back unsteadily, chattering about Christopher Milton, to the grim inevitability of bed.

There was a small paragraph in the *Yorkshire Post* on the Wednesday morning, which mentioned the mugging of Kevin McMahon. From the management's point of view, it could have been worse. It didn't make a big issue of the incident and, on the bonus side, it was a free advertisement for the show.

The morning's rehearsal schedule was more work on *I Beg Yours?*, which didn't involve Charles, so, hoping to shrug off the depression engendered by the scene with Ruth, he set off for the home of Kevin McMahon's parents. Remembering a mention of Meanwood in their conversation in the pub, he easily found the right McMahons in the phone book and rang them to check that Kevin was out of the Infirmary.

He travelled by bus. The pebble-dash semi had a two-tone doorbell.

Mrs McMahon was small and sixtyish, with fuzzy white hair. She went on about how nice it was for one of Kevin's friends from the play to come along and treated Charles like one of her son's school friends. She also muttered regretfully about this terrible thing happening to Kevin on the night of his great triumph.

'You enjoyed the show on Monday?'

'Oh, we thought it was grand. That Christopher Milton, he's lovely, isn't he? I bet he's one of those who's just the same offstage as he is on. No *side*, if you know what I mean, isn't that right?'

Charles replied appropriately, making a mental note that Kevin was beyond the age for confiding in his parents. The writer was in his childhood bedroom and seemed to have grown younger to match his surroundings. There was a poster of the Leeds United team of 1961. Uneven piles of magazines and carefully dusted Airfix aeroplane models suggested that his mother had kept his room 'just as he liked it' for whenever he decided he needed the comfort of home. But this could hardly have been the return she had hoped for.

Kevin's eyes were nearly closed by puffy blue lids. Face criss-crossed with strips of plaster and open scratches. His right hand was bandaged in gauze and one finger stiffened with the square outline of a splint. No doubt the covers hid comparable injuries on the rest of his body.

'How're you doing?'

'Not too bad, Charles. It's good of you to come.' He was subdued and formally polite, as if his surroundings brought back years of being taught good manners.

'No problem. I wasn't called for rehearsal this morning. They're doing the new – something that doesn't involve me.'

Kevin showed no interest in what was happening to the show. There was a silence.

'Was it very bad?'

'I don't know. I think I was more or less anaesthetised by alcohol at the time it happened.' Charles chuckled encouragingly. 'And when I came round, the hangover was so bad I hardly noticed my injuries. It's only today I'm really beginning to feel it.'

'Sorry.'

'Not too bad. Just very stiff all over. As if every bone in my body has been pulled out of its socket and reassembled by an enthusiastic amateur.'

'Hmm. Do you mind talking about it?'

'No, but there's nothing to say.'

'Why not?'

'I was so honked I can't remember anything. There was one bloke, that's all I know. And no, I didn't get a look at him. The police have asked me all this.'

'You couldn't even say whether he was old or young?'

'No. Why do you ask that?'

Charles decided honesty might elicit the best response. 'I was wondering if it was Dickie Peck who got at you.'

'Dickie Peck? Why?' The question was dully asked; there was no animation.

'Well, you had that fight earlier in the evening…'

'Yes.' He sounded very tired. 'Look, Charles, I was mugged. It's not nice, but it happens. I have no reason to believe it was anyone I know who did it. My only comfort is that it was hardly worth his while. I'd drunk away practically all the money I had, so all he got was a couple of credit cards.'

'Did he say anything to you, or just hit?'

'Just hit.' Kevin winced at the recollection.

'Surely the average mugger starts by asking for the goods and then comes in with the heavy stuff when you refuse.'

'I don't know.' The intonation was meant to end the conversation, but Charles had to continue. 'Kevin, Dickie Peck protects Christopher Milton like a eunuch in a harem. If anyone argues with his blue-eyed boy, he stops them. And I don't think he's too fussy about his methods. He used to be a boxer and, as we saw the other night, he's still pretty tough.'

'I was mugged,' said Kevin doggedly.

'You're not holding out on me? There is nothing to make you think it could have been Dickie?'

'I am not holding out on you. There is nothing to make me think it could have been Dickie,' came the repetition on a monotone.

Charles sighed. 'Okay. Thanks. Well, I expect you'll soon feel better. What'll you do – come down and join us in Bristol?'

'No, I don't think I'll bother.'

'What?'

'I think I'll follow your earlier advice – take the money and run. What was it you said – that I must think of it as a grant to buy time to go off and write what I really want to? That's what I'll do. There's no point in going on banging my head against a brick wall.'

'Or having your head banged against a brick wall.' But Kevin did not rise to the bait. Whoever it was had got at him had achieved the objective of the Christopher Milton/Dickie Peck camp. There would be no more interference in *Lumpkin!* by the writer of *Liberty Hall*.

He managed to get a word with Pete Masters, the musical director, during a break in the morning rehearsal. 'Good number, that *I Beg Yours?*' he offered. Compliment is always conducive to confidence.

Pete, however, showed discrimination. 'It's all right. Rather cobbled together. I don't really think it's that great. Lyric could do with a bit of polishing. The basic tune's okay, but it needs a proper arrangement. I'll do it as soon as I get time.'

'Still, the product of one night. A whole song. Did you find it hard?'

'What, doing it in the time? Not really. Did lots of revue at — university and got used to knocking up stuff quickly.'

'People who hesitate before they say "university" either went to somewhere so unmentionably awful that they're afraid of shocking people or went to Oxbridge and are afraid of being thought toffee-nosed.'

Pete's boyish face broke into a smile. Charles' guess had been right. 'Cambridge, actually.'

'Ah, the Footlights.'

'Exactly. By the way, you're right, people do get a bit shirty if you talk about it. Especially in the music business.'

'Did you read music?'

'Yes.'

'So this is slumming for you.'

Again the tone had been right. Pete laughed. 'You could say that.' As he relaxed, his nondescript working-with-musicians voice gave way to his natural public school accent.

'Tell me, when you wrote that new song, did you actually stay up all night?'

'Oh yes.'

'In the Dragonara?'

'In Christopher Milton's suite, yes.'

'And you all worked on it, him and you and Wally and Dickie Peck?'

'Yes. Well, we talked it through first and then Wally and I went down to the ballroom, which was the only place where there was a piano. I think Christopher Milton and Dickie may have got some sleep while we did that.'

'Or I suppose they could have gone out.'

Pete treated the idea as a joke rather than as grounds for suspicion, which was just as well. 'What, in Leeds? There's nothing to do here during the day-time, leave alone at night.'

Charles chuckled. 'So how long did it take you and Wally actually to write the number?'

I don't know exactly. I suppose we went down to the piano about two-thirty and maybe finished about five.'

So it was possible that Dickie Peck could have left the hotel to get Kevin McMahon. If, of course, he knew where to find him. Which was unlikely. But possible. The case seemed full of things that were possible, but not likely.

Charles wandered aimlessly around Leeds, trying to work it out, just to get one line of logic through all the strange events of the past few weeks. But it seemed as impossible to impose a pattern as it was to work out the geography of Leeds town centre. After half an hour of circling round identical pedestrian shopping precincts, he went into a little restaurant called 'The Kitchen' in Albion Street.

Over the Dish of the Day and a glass of red wine, he got out a notebook and pencil bought for the purpose in a W. H. Smith's he'd passed three times in the last half hour. James Milne, whom he'd met in Edinburgh over the Mariello murder the previous summer, had taught him the advantages of writing things down to clarify thoughts.

Three headings – 'Incident', 'Suspect' and 'Motive'. In the first column – 'Pianist shot at', 'Everard Austick pushed downstairs', 'Flats allowed to fall' and 'Kevin McMahon beaten up'. He filled in a question mark after the first two, thought for a moment, and put one after the third. He started on 'Suspects'. Dickie Peck and Christopher Milton's driver for the second two 'Incidents' and question marks for the first two. 'Motive' offered 'Protection of CM., seeing that he gets his own way', again only for the second two. More question marks.

If only he could get some line which linked the first two victims with the later ones. He'd asked Michael Peyton about any altercations between the star and the pianist or Everard and received the information that, in the first case, the two didn't even meet at rehearsal, and in the second, an atmosphere of great cordiality had been maintained. So, unless there were some unknown link in the past, the motive for the first two attacks couldn't be the same as for the subsequent ones. Oh dear. He had another glass of wine.

In one respect at least the attack on Kevin McMahon had changed the situation. It had been publicly recognised as a crime by the cast, the police, the press. That meant that any subsequent incidents might be related by people other than Charles and Gerald Venables. The criminal, if criminal there were, would have to be more careful in future.

Having come to this conclusion, Charles looked at his watch. Five to two. God. There was a two-thirty matinée on Wednesday and if he hadn't signed in at the theatre by the 'half', there'd be trouble.

In fact, there was trouble, but not the sort he feared. It was gastric trouble, and it only affected one member of the cast, Winifred Tuke.

Very interesting. If the pattern of accidents Charles suspected did exist, and if the motivation he had assumed were correct, then it was natural that Winifred Tuke should be the next victim. Since her clash with Christopher Milton over *I Beg Yours?*, she had made no secret of her feelings and, being a theatrical lady, she made no attempt to make her umbrage subtle. Gastric trouble also fitted. After the dramatic fate of Kevin, the criminal was bound to keep a low profile. Winifred Tuke had to be punished for opposing the will of Christopher Milton, but it couldn't be anything too serious, just an embarrassing indisposition which would put her out of action while the new number was rehearsed and became an established part of the show.

She had started to feel queasy at the end of the matinée, and only just managed to get through the last number. She did not appear for the curtain call. The company manager questioned her in her dressing-room and gathered, not so much from her genteel explanations as from her constant departures to the Ladies, that she was suffering from acute diarrhoea. She was sent back to her digs in a taxi, moaning imprecations against the previous night's curry, and her under-rehearsed understudy took over for the evening performance.

Charles was not convinced about the curry. For a start, he would have expected food poisoning to manifest itself more quickly, and also it seemed strange that Winifred Tuke should be the only one affected by it. The meal had been one of those occasions when everyone ordered something different and had a bit of everything.

But nobody else seemed worried and certainly no one talked of links between the incident and Kevin's mugging. It seemed strange to Charles that in a large company of actors, who are the most superstitious of people, no one had spoken of bad luck or a jinx on the show. Perhaps he was too close to it. If it hadn't been for his unconventional recruitment, he probably wouldn't have found anything odd himself.

But at least this could be investigated. If Winifred Tuke had been slipped something, the chances were it had happened in the theatre. So, in the dead time between the matinée and evening performance, Charles took a look around.

The silence of empty dressing-rooms is almost tangible. He could feel the great pull of sentimentality which has led songwriters to maunder on about the smell of grease-paint, the limpness of unoccupied costumes, the wilting flowers, the yellowing telegrams of congratulation and all that yucky show business rubbish. Distant sounds from the stage, where the indefatigable Spike and his crew were going through yet another flying rehearsal, served only to intensify the silence.

Fortunately, Winifred's hasty exit had left her dressing-room unlocked. Inside it was almost depressingly tidy. A neat plastic sandwich-box of make-up, a box of tissues and a Jean Plaidy paperback were the only signs of occupation. Someone with Winifred's experience of touring didn't bother to settle in for just a week.

What Charles was looking for was not in sight, but it didn't take him long to find it. His clue came from the smell on Winifred Tuke's breath during rehearsals and, more particularly, performances. It was in the bottom of the wardrobe, hidden, in a pathetic attempt at gentility, behind a pair of boots. The middle-aged actress's little helper, a bottle of Gordon's gin.

The investigation was an amateur detective's dream. It was so easy Charles almost felt guilty for the glow of satisfaction it gave him. He opened the bottle and sniffed. Gin all right. He took a cautious sip and immediately felt suspicious. It wasn't the taste, but the consistency, the slight greasiness the drink left on his lips.

He poured a little into a glass and his suspicions were confirmed. Though it didn't show through the dark green of the Gordon's bottle, in the plain glass it was clear that the liquid had separated into two layers. Both were transparent, but the one that floated on top was viscous and left a slight slime round the glass. He dabbed at it and put his finger to his tongue. Yes, he wouldn't forget that almost tasteless taste in a hurry. It was his prep school matron's infallible cure for constipated boys – liquid paraffin.

He was excited by the discovery, but controlled his emotions while he washed up the glass. The slime clung on stubbornly and he had to wipe at it with a tissue.

A doubt struck him. If he had discovered the doctoring of the drink so easily, why hadn't Winifred noticed it? But the concealment of the gin bottle in the wardrobe answered that. If she kept her drinking a secret (or at least thought she did), then probably she would only whip the bottle out for a hasty gulp and pop it straight back to its hiding place. And if she'd been drinking during the show, she would probably put the greasy taste down to make-up on her lips.

Charles felt breathlessly excited. Here at last was evidence. Though every other apparent crime could have been an accident or the work of a vindictive outsider, the bottle was evidence of deliberate misdoing, committed within the company.

He had to keep it. In a case where facts were so thin on the ground he couldn't afford not to. Winifred Tuke was far too genteel to report its disappearance and, considering the bottle's contents, he was doing her a favour by removing it.

His holdall was in the green room, so he set off there, gin bottle in hand. Stealth was unnecessary; nobody would be in for the evening performance for at least an hour. He trod heavily on the stairs, awaking the echoes of the old building. He pushed open the green room door with a flourish and realised that he had forgotten the stage staff.

Spike and some others were slumped on sofas, reading newspapers. Charles made an involuntary movement to hide the bottle.

He needn't have worried. Spike was the only one who stirred. He looked up mildly and said, 'Didn't think that was your usual tipple, Charles.'

Charles made some half-joke about ringing the changes, put the bottle in his holdall and went out to the pub. He gave himself a mental rap over the knuckles for bad security. It didn't really matter, because only Spike had seen him. But it could have been someone else and it was his job as investigator to keep a low profile.

Still, he'd got the bottle. Perhaps a diarrhoea weapon lacked the glamour of a murder weapon, but it certainly warranted a large whisky.

Now all he had to do was find a link between the bottle and his chief suspect. Difficult. Dickie Peck had returned to London that afternoon. Never mind, the investigation would keep until he rejoined the company.

Significantly, with the agent away, in spite of occasional flashes of temper from Christopher Milton, there were no more incidents while *Lumpkin!* was in Leeds.

PART III

Bristol

CHAPTER NINE

CHARLES WAS GLAD to get to Bristol. He hadn't enjoyed the previous few days. Investigations apart, Leeds had ended in scenes of cynical recrimination with Ruth. After a final fierce coupling on the Sunday morning and a silent drive to the station, he had had a long slow journey to King's Cross for her unspoken accusation to fester in his mind. He couldn't just laugh it off. As many times before, he cried out for the ability to say, that was good while it lasted, or that didn't work, oh well, time to move on. But he was bad at the sort of insouciance that should have accompanied his style of sex life. Feelings kept snagging, he kept feeling sorry for people, kept feeling he was using them. And, as always, lacking the self-righteousness necessary for anger, he ended up feeling self-disgust.

A half-day in London hadn't helped his mood. The bed-sitter in Hereford Road had not got less depressing in his absence. With the change in the weather it was as cold as a morgue when he opened the door. Nor did Sunday papers he'd bought offer any cheer. Bombs in London restaurants and the continuing apparent hopelessness of the Herrema siege led to fears of the imminent collapse of society, that terrible plunging feeling that tomorrow everything will stop and animal chaos will reign.

He rang his wife Frances in an attempt to shift the mood. But her phone just rang and rang and he stood, his finger dented by the twopence in the coin-box and his mind drifting, trying to remember what she had said in their last conversation about this new man she was seeing, forming silly fantasies of her with the new man, even of her upstairs in their bed with him, hearing the phone and saying, 'Shall we answer it?' and him saying, 'No'. It was stupid, childish; it was as if he were again a sixteen-year-old, his stomach churning as he asked his first girl out to the pictures. And this was Frances, for God's sake, Frances whom he knew so well, who was so ordinary he had left her. But his feelings swirled around, unanchored. He put the phone down.

Back in his room (the telephone was outside on the landing) he had turned immediately to the obvious solace, a half-full (or, in his current mood, half-empty) bottle of Bell's. He drank with the kamikaze spirit of self-pity, sadly identifying with Everard Austick.

So Bristol, by comparison, was pleasant. He got a lift down on the Monday morning with a couple of the dancers who lived in Notting Hill and, apart from the fact of being in company, the staged sparkle of their camp chatter put him in a good mood. Then there was where he was staying. Julian Paddon, an actor friend from way back, was a member of the resident company at the Old Vic and had issued an immediate invitation when he heard *Lumpkin!* was coming to Bristol. His wife Helen was charming and had the enormous advantage after Ruth that Charles didn't fancy her at all (and even if he had, she was eight months pregnant and thus satisfactorily *hors de combat*).

Julian, whose nesting instinct, always strong, had been intensified by regular employment and the prospect of an addition to his family, had rented a flat in a Victorian house in Clifton and Charles was made to feel genuinely welcome.

Lumpkin! too responded to the new town. The day's break after the heavy rehearsal schedule in Leeds meant that everyone came to it with renewed vigour. The makeshift musical arrangement for *I Beg Yours?* had been improved and expanded by Leon Schultz, an American arranger flown over at enormous expense by an edgy management. The song was greatly enhanced and on the first night in Bristol it stopped the show. Once again Christopher Milton's theatrical instinct had been vindicated. The management was so pleased with the song that they asked Schultz to do new arrangements for all other numbers in the show. It would mean a lot more rehearsal, but in the new mood of confidence no one complained.

Away from the gloom of Leeds, Charles found it difficult to believe in thoughts of sabotage. The long sequence of crimes he had rationalised became unreal, another part of the general confusion over the show and Ruth which Leeds had meant for him. When he unpacked at Julian's flat, he had to look closely at the Gordon's gin bottle to convince himself that anything criminal had ever happened.

Part of his relaxation was due to Dickie Peck's absence. His suspicions had now homed in firmly and until the agent rejoined the company, he did not fear further incidents. What he should do when another occurred was something he tried not to think about.

Anyway, rehearsals kept him busy. Desmond Porton from Amulet Productions was to come and see the show on the Thursday and give the final all-clear for the scheduled first night at the King's Theatre on Thursday, November 27th. That gave a sense of urgency and a healthy edge of determination to everyone in the show.

The first two nights made Charles begin to think he was, for possibly the first time in his life, about to be connected with a success. Apart from reflections on the irony of a fate which withheld major triumph from shows he had cared about in favour of the commercial banality of *Lumpkin!*, it was a pleasant feeling.

* * * * *

He was sitting in the pub during the Tuesday performance (having dutifully checked in for the 'half' and let the stage manager know where he'd be) when the girl approached him. Her pale blue eyes had the unfocused stare of contact lenses, but there was nothing vague about her manner. 'Are you in *Lumpkin!*?' she asked, the directness of the question emphasised by an American accent.

'Fame at last,' he replied with irony. 'Yes, I am.'

'Good, I thought I recognised you. I saw the show last night.'

'Ah.' Charles left the pause for comment on his performance which no actor can resist.

But the girl didn't pick up the cue. 'My name's Suzanne Horst,' she said. 'I'm a free-lance journalist.'

He emitted another 'Ah', again succumbing to an actor's instinctive reaction that the girl wanted to write something about him.

She soon put him right on that. 'I'm trying to make contact with Christopher Milton.'

Of course. He blushed for having suspected anything else, and let out another multi-purpose 'Ah'.

'Would you introduce me to him?'

'Well...' This was rather difficult. The past month with Christopher Milton had revealed to Charles how carefully the star's contact with the press and media was regulated by his agent. To introduce an unexpected journalist could be a serious breach of professional etiquette. 'I think probably the best thing you could do would be to make contact with his agent. It's Dickie Peck of Creative Artists.'

'I don't want to mess about with agents. Anyway, I'm here in Bristol. What's the point of contacting a guy in London about someone who's only a hundred yards away at this moment?'

There wasn't a great deal of logic about it, but that was the way stars worked, Charles explained.

She was not put down. 'Yes, I know that's the correct way to go about things, but I don't want to go the correct way. I want to go the way that'll get me the interviews I'm after.'

'Well, I don't know what to suggest.' Charles felt churlish, but thought he was probably doing the right thing. 'What are these interviews you are after?'

'One's for radio. Only got Radio Brighton interested at the moment, but I'm sure I'll be able to get it on one of the networks. That's only secondary, anyway. The main thing I want him for is an article I'm doing on the nature of stardom. Want to know what makes him tick, you know.'

'Who's that for?'

'Don't know who I'll offer it to yet. *Cosmopolitan*, maybe.'

'It hasn't been commissioned?'

'No, but I'll sell it all right.' Whatever Miss Horst lacked, it was not confidence.

In fact she didn't lack much. Certainly not looks. Her shoulder-length hair was that streaky yellow which might be the natural result of sun on brown hair or the unnatural result of hairdressers on any colour. Her belted Burberry formalised but did not disguise her lithe figure, and though her overpowering confidence might be a slight deterrent, the general effect was distinctly tangible. 'Can I get you a drink?'

'Thank you. A vodka and tonic, please.' The barman eyed Charles knowingly as he supplied the drink. Suzanne didn't seem to notice. 'Are you sure you can't introduce me?'

'Honestly, it is difficult. You know, people like Christopher Milton have to guard their privacy very carefully. I'm afraid they tend to be a bit resistant to journalists.'

'But, look, I'm not going to do a big exposé or anything. It'll be an appreciative piece. I mean, I'm a fan.'

'I don't think that's really the point. It's rather difficult to get near him.'

'But you see him at rehearsal, don't you?'

'Well, yes, but – '

'Then you could ask him if he'd be prepared to do an interview with me.'

Her persistence didn't make it easy. Charles cringed with embarrassment at the thought of putting the girl's request to Christopher Milton. It was difficult to explain to someone outside the closely defined relationship that exists between actors in a working context. 'Look, I'm sorry, I really don't think I can.'

'Why not? You do know him, don't you?'

'Yes, I do, but – '

'Well then,' she said, as if that concluded the syllogism.

'Yes.' Under normal circumstances he would have given a categorical 'No', but under normal circumstances the people who made this kind of request didn't look like Suzanne Horst. He said something about seeing if he had a chance to raise the matter at rehearsal (which he had no intention of doing) and asked the girl how much journalism she had done.

'Oh, quite a lot in the States. I got a degree in it, but the scene over there isn't very interesting, so I decided to check it out over here.'

'What, you've given yourself a sort of time limit to see if you can make it?'

'Oh, I'll make it.'

Charles was beginning to find this self-conviction a little wearying, so he brought in a damper. 'Yes, unfortunately it's a bad time to get started in that sort of area at the moment. Journalism's getting more and more of a closed shop. It's like acting, getting increasingly difficult to make the initial break into the business.'

'Don't worry,' said Suzanne, as though explaining to a child, 'People with talent always get through.'

He couldn't think of anything to say after that.

But Suzanne suddenly got an idea. 'Hey, you could actually be quite useful on this stardom article.'

'In what way?'

'Well, you could give me a bit of background on Christopher Milton. After all, you're working with him.'

Charles was hesitant, but overruled. She had whipped out a new shorthand notebook and a freshly-sharpened pencil and was poised in the attitude of someone who had taken a degree in journalism. The question came out formal and rehearsed. 'Tell me, as an actor, what do you think it is that makes some people stars?'

'And some dreary old hacks like me? Hmm. Well now – ' dropping into an American accent – 'what is a star? What is it that picks out one from the myriad throng of the moderately talented and gives him that magic name? What is it that sets one talent glowing in the limelight, that scatters the moondust of stardom on that one chosen head? Is it of the earth or is it made in heaven? Perhaps in that Great Casting Agency in the Sky, there sits the one Eternal Agent who – '

'Look, are you taking the rise out of me?'

He lapsed back into his normal voice. 'No, sorry. I was just getting my bearings. Stardom? I don't know really. In the sort of theatre I normally do it's rarely an issue.'

'But I suppose, if I had to give an opinion...Well, talent certainly, that must be there. Not necessarily a great deal of it, nor anything very versatile. In fact, there should be no versatility. The star must always be recognisable – if he puts on voices, he must put them on almost badly, so that everyone knows it's him. That's talent. Okay. What else? Dedication certainly, the conviction that what he does is more important than anything else in the world.'

'Isn't that likely to lead to selfishness?' Suzanne interposed with studied professionalism.

'Inevitably. Bound to. Hence, presumably, all the stories that one hears of stars hating competition and being temperamental and slamming dressing-room doors and that sort of thing.'

He realised that it could get a little awkward if Suzanne asked him to relate his last observation to the star of *Lumpkin!*, and hurried on before she had the chance. 'I think there's also something about the way the entertainment industry works, certainly for actors. Being an actor is, potentially, the most passive function on earth. Most actors are completely dependent on directors, because it's directors who control the jobs. Some manage to assert themselves by deep commitment to their work, or by directing or writing and devising shows. Some do it by political affiliations...starting street theatres, workshop communes, even – in cases of extreme lunacy – joining the Workers' Revolutionary Party. Some do it by forming their own companies, that kind of thing. But what I'm getting at is, that, given this lack of autonomy, when an actor becomes very much in demand, as a star might be, he wants to dictate his own terms. It's years of frustration at living on someone else's terms. It's also a self-preservation thing – once someone's got to the top, he tries to do everything to ensure that he stays there, and that may involve being careful about the people he works with, seeing that none of them are too good. I mean, often when you see a show with one big star name above the title and the rest of the cast nonentities, it's not just because the star's fee has exhausted the budget, it's also so that he shows up in such mediocre company. The Whale among Sprats syndrome.

'Then there's management, which is very important. Choosing work, not doing anything that's beneath the star's dignity, or anything in which he's not going to shine. Can't take a risk, everything that is done has to be right, even at the expense of turning work down. For that reason you often find that a real star won't do anyone a favour, won't step in if someone's ill. It's not just bloody-mindedness, it's self-preservation. When someone's at the top, there are any number of people sniping, ready to read the signs of a decline, so it never does to be too available.'

'Do you think a star has *magic*?' asked Suzanne, with awe-struck italics.

'I don't know. I – '

'Oh, Mr Paris, there you are.' Gwyneth of the stage management stood before him, her customary calm ruffled by anxiety. 'You should have been back in the theatre half an hour ago.'

On the Wednesday morning they were rehearsing the first act finale, *Ooh, What a Turn-up*, which had been rearranged by Leon Schultz. Pete Masters, the M.D., was not in the best of moods. Having seen his own arrangements thrown out of the window, he found it galling to have to teach the new ones to the impassive band. The musicians had long since lost any spark of interest that they may have had for the show and sat mentally sorting out their VAT returns, eyes occasionally straying to their watches to see if the rehearsal would spread over into another session at M.U. rates. Christopher Milton was onstage directing, while David Meldrum sat at the back of the stalls reading *The Stage*.

The rehearsal had reached an impasse. Leon Schultz's new arrangement introduced a short violin figure which bridged from the verse into the chorus and there was no dancing to cover it. The cast tried freezing for the relevant three seconds, but that lost the pace of the number. A couple of the dancers improvised a little jig, which looked alien and messy. There was a long pause while Christopher Milton stood centre stage, the ominous faraway expression in his eyes.

Suddenly he was galvanised into action. 'Where's the sodding choreographer?'

'She wasn't called for this rehearsal,' said the musical director smugly, 'following assurances that the new arrangements would not involve any major changes in the choreography.'

Christopher Milton seemed not to hear the dig. It was as if his mind could only focus slowly. 'Then what can we do?' He enunciated the words very clearly and without emotion.

'No idea.' Pete Masters shrugged. 'Unless we cut the meaningless little bit of schmaltz altogether.' His tone was calculated to provoke, but produced no reaction. Emboldened, he pressed on:

'Or go back to the original arrangements, which were quite as good and a darned sight less fussy.'

'What, your arrangements?' Christopher Milton asked slowly.

'Yes.'

'Your sodding arrangements.' The build to anger was slow, but now it had started it built to a frightening intensity. 'Your little tuppenny-ha'penny amateur tea-shop quartet arrangements. This is the bloody professional theatre, sonny, not some half-baked student revue. Your arrangements! This isn't Penge Amateur Operatic Society, you know.'

Pete Masters' face had gone very red, but he fought to keep his voice calm and give a dignified reply. 'There's no need for you to speak to me like that. You may prefer the new arrangements to mine, but there's no need to be offensive about it.'

'Oh, I'm sorry, was I being offensive?' The last word was pronounced with savage mimicry that exactly echoed Pete's public school tone. 'How foolish of me. I had forgotten that I was speaking to someone who has a degree in music and therefore knows everything about the subject. What a silly-billy I am.'

The impersonation was funny and, though Charles cringed in the wings and the musicians continued to stare impassively, it did produce an unidentified laugh from somewhere up in the flies where the stage crew were invisibly watching the proceedings. It gave Christopher Milton a stimulus and he continued to vent his lacerating irony on Pete.

Eventually the M.D. struck back. Still he tried to sound in control, but his wavering voice let him down. 'Listen, if you're going to speak to me like that, I'm going.'

'Go. See if anyone cares. Just don't think you can treat me like that. You've got to get it straight, boy, what matters in this show. You don't. You go, there are a hundred second-rate musicians can take over tomorrow. I go, there just isn't a show. Get your priorities right, boy.'

Pete Masters mouthed, but couldn't produce any words. He did the only possible thing in the circumstances and walked off stage. The musicians looked at their watches with satisfaction. A row like this made it almost certain that they'd go into another session. The atmosphere in the theatre was heavy with embarrassment.

It blew over. Of course it blew over. That sort of row can't go on for long. The pressures of keeping the show going don't allow it. Pete and Christopher Milton were working together again within a quarter of an hour, with neither apologising or commenting on the scene. All the same, Charles Paris was relieved that Dickie Peck had not been present to witness the latest challenge to his protégé.

* * * * *

It wasn't just the clash at rehearsals that morning, but something changed the company mood on the Wednesday afternoon. Perhaps it was a small and silent house at the matinée. Perhaps it was Desmond Porton's impending visit and the fear of having the show assessed. Or perhaps it was The Cold.

Actors, whose working tools are their voices, are naturally terrified of colds, sore throats, 'flus and other infections which threaten their precious vocal cords. They all have their own favourite remedies and preventative methods when germs are in the air, or, in some cases, even when they aren't. Large doses of Vitamin C are swallowed, dissolved or crunched. (So are most other vitamins of the alphabet, with a kind of pagan awe.) Strange elixirs of lemon and honey (with bizarre variations involving onions) are poured down tender throats. Aspirin, codeine, paracetamol, Anadin, Veganin and others are swilled down, discussed and compared as connoisseurs speak of malt whiskies. Names of doctors who can 'do wonders for throats' (as well as others who deal with backs and nervous twinges) are exchanged like rare stamps. It is all taken very seriously.

When a show involves singing, the panic and precautions are doubled. Vocal sprays are brought into play. Little tins and envelopes of pills are ostentatiously produced and their various merits extolled. Some favour Nigroids, small pills which 'blow your head off, dear, but really do wonders for my cords'; others will not stir without 'The Fisherman's Friend' – 'quite strong, darling, but they really relax the throat'; there are Friar's Balsam, Vocalzones, Sanderson's Throat Specific and a whole gallery of other patent medicines available, all of which have their staunch adherents.

The Cold started with one of the dancers, who had difficulty in preventing his sneeze during the matinée. Then Mark Spelthorne, quick to seize any opportunity for self-dramatisation, thought he might have one of his throats coming on. During the evening performance many of the cast were walking round backstage massaging their throats, talking in whispers ('conserving the voice, dear – may have a touch of 'flu coming on') and generally putting on expressions of private suffering which they had learnt when rehearsing Chekhov. It helped to make the atmosphere around *Lumpkin!* suddenly spiky.

Charles just made it to the pub as time was being called after a sedate Bristol house had given its qualified support to the evening performance. He was the only one of the company who went. Most went straight home to nurse themselves in anticipation of The Cold.

He managed to get in an order for a pint of bitter (performing always made him thirsty) and was letting the first mouthful wash down when the girl came up to him. The American voice twanged. 'Did you ask him?'

'Who? What?' He pretended innocence, but knew full well what she meant.

'Christopher Milton. You were going to ask him about the interview.'

'Oh yes, of course. I hadn't forgotten. Trouble is, today was very busy, what with the two shows. And we were rehearsing some new arrangements this morning.' It sounded pretty feeble.

But she didn't seem to notice. 'Never mind. You'll do it sometime.' Surprisingly benign. He'd expected her to tear him apart for his omission. 'Some time,' she repeated and he realised that she was drunk.

'Can I get you a drink?'

'Haven't they closed?'

'Nooo. Never. Barman. What is it, Suzanne?'

'Vodka tonic.'

'One of those, please.'

She took the drink and gulped it down like water. She stood close to him and swayed so that they almost touched. 'How'd the show go?'

'Not world-shattering.'

''Smy birthday today.'

'Ah.'

'Had a few drinks to celebrate. Alone in a foreign country.'

'Ah.'

She leant against him. 'Give me a birthday kiss. Back in the States I never go without a birthday kiss.'

He kissed her dryly on the lips as if she were a child, but he felt uncomfortably aware of how unchildlike she was. Her breasts exercised a magnetic attraction as she swayed towards him. He drained his beer. 'Well, better be off. They'll be turfing us out shortly.'

'You going to see me home?' she asked kookily. Miss Suzanne Horst with a few drinks inside her was a very different proposition from the hyper-efficient lady who was about to set British journalism afire.

'Is it far?'

'Not far. Staying at a hotel.'

'Ah.' Charles found he said a lot of 'Ahs' in conversation with Suzanne. Because he couldn't think of anything else to say.

They hadn't got far from the pub when she stopped and rolled round into his arms. 'Kiss me properly,' she mumbled. Light filtered across the road from the lamp over the stage door.

He held her warm and cosy in his arms. He didn't kiss her. Thoughts moved slowly, but with great clarity through his mind. The girl was drunk. He was nearly fifty. He should keep away from women; it always hurt one way or the other. The silent resentment of Ruth was too recent a memory. And before that there had been Anna in Edinburgh. And others. A wave of tiredness swept over him at the eternal predictability of lust.

He felt a shock of depression, as if the pavement in front of him had suddenly fallen away. What was the point of anything? Women could alleviate the awareness of the approach of death, but they could not delay it. He was cold, cold as though someone was walking over his grave. The intensity and speed of the emotion frightened him. Age, it must be age, time trickling away. He thought of Frances and wanted her comforting touch.

The girl in his arms was still, half dozing. He took her elbow and detached her from him. 'Come on. I'll get you back to your hotel.' Gently.

At that moment he heard the clunk of the stage door closing and looked across to see Pete Masters emerge with a brief-case under his arm. The M.D. didn't see him, but started to cross the road, going away from him.

The Mini must have been parked near by, but Charles wasn't aware of it until it flashed past. He turned sharply, seemed dumb for a moment, then found his voice, too late, to shout, 'Look out!'

Pete Masters half-turned as the wing of the Mini caught him. He was spun round on his feet and flung sprawling against a parked car. From there he slid down to lie still in the road. The Mini turned right at the end of the street and disappeared.

CHAPTER TEN

AND DICKIE PECK had not been in Bristol at the time of the accident. Charles tried to reason round it, but the fact was incontrovertible. According to Christopher Milton, the agent was not expected to come and see *Lumpkin!* again until Brighton. In case that information wasn't reliable, Charles went to the extreme of phoning Creative Artists to check it. He used a disguised voice and pretended to be a policeman investigating the accident to Pete Masters. It was a risky expedient, one that had turned sour on him before, but he couldn't think of another. As soon as he put the phone down, he realised that if Dickie Peck had anything to hide, he was now going to be a hundred times more careful. And he could well have been lying about his movements anyway.

All the same, Charles had already started to remove the agent from the front rank of his suspicions. Though he might be involved, might be directing operations, Dickie Peck wasn't the one to do the heavy stuff. The more Charles thought about it, the more incongruous it became – a successful agent, with a lot of artists on his books, going round running people over and slipping them liquid paraffin? No. What was needed was a logical reappraisal of the situation.

He sat in Julian Paddon's sitting-room on a bright autumn day and once again wrote down James Mime's headings, 'Incident', 'Suspect' and 'Motive'. He only filled in the middle column. Three names – Dickie Peck, Christopher Milton and Christopher Milton's driver.

Then, as if imposing logic by committing conjecture to paper, he wrote another heading, 'Reasons for Innocence'. Against Dickie Peck's name he filled in, 'Not on scene of last incident (i.e. in London) – position to keep up – discovery would ruin career'. Against Christopher Milton – 'Last point above to nth degree – v. concerned with public image – could not afford the risk of personal action'. Against the driver he put a neat dash, then changed his mind and wrote, 'The only question is who he's taking orders from – D.P. or C.M. – or is he acting off his own bat?'

Written down it looked convincing. Charles felt a satisfaction akin to completing *The Times* crossword. He couldn't imagine why he hadn't thought of the driver before. Very distinctly he remembered the first time he had seen the man, advancing threateningly towards the crowd of boys who mobbed Christopher Milton outside the Welsh Dragon Club. He remembered how the driver had been halted by a gesture and how he had hovered protectively until the star wanted to leave. Like a bodyguard. It was quite logical that Christopher Milton should have a bodyguard. People in the public eye are instant targets for freaks and lunatics. And in a way everything untoward that had happened on the show could be put down to an exaggerated interpretation of a bodyguard's rôle. Whether the man interpreted it that way for himself or at someone else's suggestion was a detail which could wait until there was some actual evidence of guilt.

In Charles' new mood of logical confidence he felt sure that proof would not be difficult to find now that he had a definite quarry. He took his sheet of paper with the winning formula on it and burnt it carefully in the grate of the fireplace, pulverising the black ash until it could yield nothing to forensic science. Even as he did so, a sneaking suspicion that he concentrated too much on the irrelevancies of detection started to bore a tiny hole in his shell of confidence.

'Charles, what the hell's going on?'

'What do you mean, Gerald?'

'Well, there's a little piece in the *Evening Standard* about this M.D. being run over.'

'Ah.'

'It also mentions Kevin being mugged in Leeds. No comment, just a juxtaposition of the two facts. It's worse than if they actually said it's a bad luck show.'

'Oh, come on. If someone's run over, it doesn't necessarily mean there's anything odd. Accidents do happen.'

'But don't you think this is another in the series?'

'As a matter of fact I do, but nobody else does. There's no talk about it in the company, beyond the sort of relish actors always have for dramatic situations.'

'Have the Press made much of it down there?'

'Not a lot. Small report, just the facts. M.D. of *Lumpkin!* – hit and run driver in stolen car – details of injuries, that's all.'

'What were his injuries?'

'Mainly bruising. I think he may also have broken his patella.'

'His what?'

'Kneecap to you.'

'And he's out of the show?'

'Certainly for a bit. Leon Schultz has taken over as M.D..'

'Has he?' Gerald sounded gratified. 'Ah, well, it's an ill wind. Good. I always said they should have got a big name from the start rather than that boy. It'll bump the budget up a bit.'

The welfare of the show seemed to be Gerald's only concern. So long as his investment was protected, nothing else mattered. Charles felt bitter, particularly as his friend continued, 'But look, do keep a watchful eye on Christopher Milton. If he gets clobbered, the show really is a non-starter.'

'And if anyone else gets clobbered, it doesn't matter?'

'Well, yes, it does, of course, because it's very bad publicity for the show, but it's Christopher Milton who's the important one. And they must be aiming for him eventually, otherwise there's no point in all this, is there?'

'That's not the way I see it. I don't think I should worry about Christopher Milton; I should be protecting everyone else in the show.'

'What do you mean?'

'Nothing. I can't explain it now. Suffice to say that my view of the case has changed since we last spoke.'

'Oh. But do you know who's doing it all?'

'Yes. I think I do.'

'Well, get him arrested and stop him.'

'I haven't got any evidence yet.'

'Then get some.'

'I will.'

Charles felt furiously angry when he put the phone down. The whole thing was getting out of proportion. The protection of Christopher Milton must continue, whoever got hurt on the way. It was hearing such blinkered lack of consideration from Gerald that made him so cross. The world, even his friends, would forgive anything done in the name of Christopher Milton. Gerald had asked for evidence and an arrest and he'd get them, though they might not be what he expected. Charles felt a wave of anger against the whole star set-up, the charming public persona that needed the support of thuggery to survive. Whether or not Christopher Milton was directly involved in the crimes, the rottenness and meanness of what had been going on should be exposed to the public. From now on Charles wasn't working for Gerald Venables representing Arthur Balcombe. He was working for himself.

After the Thursday show, he dressed carefully for his midnight jaunt. As an actor, he knew how much the right costume could help in a difficult role, and the role in which he had cast himself was a very difficult one.

He wore a pair of his own black trousers and a black sweater borrowed from Julian (in what he hoped was a casual manner). He had bought a pair of plimsolls in Woolworth's and, since Woolworth's don't sell ready-dirtied plimsolls for house-breakers, he had shabbied them up with earth from Julian's garden. Other investments were a balaclava helmet and a pencil torch. He knew the preparations were over-elaborate, but they took his mind off what he had to do.

With the balaclava on, he looked like a very young photograph of himself as Second Sentry in *Coriolanus* ('Leaden production' – *Richmond and Twickenham Times*). Without it, he looked a cross between himself as Lightborn in a modern dress *Edward II* ('Flamboyantly sinister' – *Birmingham Evening Mail*) and as Jimmy Porter in *Look Back in Anger* ('Ill-considered' – *Luton Evening Post*). He crept down the stairs to the front door and realised he was using the walk he'd perfected for *Rookery Nook* ('Uneven' – *Jewish Telegraph*).

Unfortunately he met Julian coming in. 'Where are you going dressed like that, Charles? You look as if you're about to commit a burglary.'

That didn't help.

Residents of the Holiday Inn in Bristol park their cars in the adjacent multi-storey car park. It was a simple matter to walk in. He found Christopher Milton's distinctive Rolls on the first level without any problem.

And his luck held. The Corniche was unlocked. He slipped in by the passenger door and closed it quickly to douse the interior light. He reached to get the torch out of his pocket, but his hand was shaking too much. He closed his eyes and practised rib-reserve breathing, trying to keep the thought of what he was doing at bay. But a schoolboy fear of being found out remained. He wished he could remember some of the relaxation exercises various experimental directors had tried to put him through. None came.

Still, the deep breathing helped. He opened his eyes and, very slowly, like a man under water, he got out the torch and switched it on.

The glove pocket opened easily. A tin of boiled sweets came first into the light. He prised it open and found nothing but the sugary debris that should have been there. Next a large stiff envelope. He felt inside. The shiny surface of photographs. He pulled one out and shone the torch on it. Christopher Milton grinned cheerily at him. Fan photographs. The sight of the familiar face brought on another pang of guilt. At the same moment he noticed that his thumb had left a perfect print on the photograph. The light caught it on the shiny surface. That was one that the police wouldn't need powder to spot. He wiped at it roughly, but seemed only to add more prints. He shoved the photograph back into the envelope and replaced it.

Sweat prickled on his hands and he thought he'd done enough. His grandiose schemes for following the raid on the car with a search of the driver's hotel bedroom were evaporating fast.

Finish the glove pocket and go. He ran his fingers along the angle at the back and felt some small bead-like objects under his finger-nails. He picked one out, held it between thumb and forefinger and turned the light on it.

And at that moment his whole attitude to what he was doing changed. What he held was a small-waisted piece of lead. The shape was unmistakable. It was an airgun pellet. Just the sort of airgun pellet which had hit *Lumpkin!*'s first rehearsal pianist in the hand on the second day of rehearsal. It was evidence.

He grabbed three or four more of the slugs and put them in his pocket. His panic had changed to surging confidence. He reached forward for one more sweep into the glove pocket and his hand closed round the firm outline of a small bottle. Hardly daring to hope, he drew it out and flashed the torch on it. LIQUID PARAFFIN (Liquid Paraffin BP). The bottle was half-empty. He could not believe his good fortune.

There was a noise of a door banging. He turned. Someone was coming from the direction of the hotel. A guest going to another car. He'd wait for them to drive off and then beat a hasty retreat. He shrank down into the leather seat and slipped the balaclava helmet over his head. He pulled it round to cover his face.

The silence was unnaturally long. No slam of a car door, no choking of an engine. He began to think that the visitor must have gone out down the ramp and slowly eased himself up to look.

At that moment there was a click of the door opening and he felt light through the latticed wool of the balaclava. He was face to face with Christopher Milton's driver, who was leaning forward to get into the car.

The man's eyes bulged as he saw the intruder and in shock he jerked his head back sharply. There was a loud crack which shook the car and he slid gracefully from view.

Charles, his mind full of ugly pugilistic visions, edged slowly across to the driver's seat and looked down over the edge.

The driver lay neatly on the ground with his eyes closed. He was out cold. Charles got out of the car, shut the door to put the light out and turned his torch on the body on the ground.

There was no blood. Regular breathing. Strong heart-beat. Strong pulse. Probably just concussion. He loosened the man's tie and put a cushion from the back of the car under his head.

Then, with the precious pellets and bottle in his pocket, Charles crept down the stairs out of the garage. As he emerged into the street, he removed the balaclava.

There was a phone-box opposite. It seemed a natural conclusion to the dream-like flow of luck which had characterised the previous half-hour. Charles dialled and asked for the ambulance service in his own voice before thinking to disguise it. When he was connected, he had a moment's agonising decision choosing a voice. Northern Irish seemed the most natural for this sort of thing, but it might be unduly alarmist in a bomb-conscious Britain. The voice that came to hand was American-Italian. Sounding like something out of *The Godfather*, he said, 'Could you send an ambulance to the big car park beside the Holiday Inn.' He was tempted to say, 'There's a stiff there', but made do with, 'There's somebody injured'.

'What's happened to them?' asked the voice and it was only by putting the phone down that Charles could prevent himself from saying, 'Someone made him an offer he couldn't refuse'.

He hung about until he saw the ambulance safely arrived, and then went briskly back to Julian's place, using the walk he'd developed when playing a gangster in *Guys and Dolls* ('This guy didn't like it and nor did the doll he was with' – *Bolton Evening News*).

CHAPTER ELEVEN

CHARLES WOKE IN an excellent mood. The events of the previous night were very clear to him. It was as if he had found the instant cure-all he had always dreamed must exist somewhere. All his problems had been resolved at once. He now had evidence of the wrong-doing of the driver and just to make his job easier, the driver himself was temporarily removed from the scene. There was still the minor question of what he should do about it – confront the villain and threaten police proceedings, go direct to the police or send them an anonymous deposition advising investigation – but that would keep. The warm completed-*Times*-crossword sensation had developed into an even better feeling, as if his solution to the puzzle had won a prize.

Helen Paddon cooked him an enormous breakfast, which he consumed with that relish which only a fulfilled mind can give. She was pleased to have something to do. The last heavy weeks of pregnancy were dragging interminably.

He finished breakfast about nine and took the unusual expedient of ringing Gerald at home. After pleasantries and must-see-you-soons from Kate Venables, the solicitor came on the line. 'What gives?' he asked in his B-film gangster style.

'It's sorted out.'

'Really?'

'Uhuh.' Charles found himself slipping into the same idiom.

'You know who's been doing it all?'

'I know and I've got evidence.'

'Who?' The curiosity was immediate and childlike.

'Never mind.' Charles was deliberately circumspect and infuriating. 'Suffice to say that I'll see nothing else happens to threaten the show, at least from the point of view of crime or sabotage. If it fails on artistic grounds, I'm afraid I can't be held responsible.'

'Is that all you're going to tell me?'

'Yes.'

'Damn your eyes.' Charles chuckled. 'But you're sure that Christopher Milton is in no danger?'

'I don't think he ever has been in any danger from anyone but himself.' On that cryptic note he put the phone down, knowing exactly the expression he had left on Gerald's face.

* * * * *

There was a ten-thirty call for the entire company to hear what Desmond Porton of Amulet Productions had thought of *Lumpkin!* and what changes he had ordered before the show could come into London. Charles ambled through the streets of Bristol towards the theatre, his mood matched by the bright November sun. The people of the city bustled about their business and he felt a universal benevolence towards them. His route went past the Holiday Inn and he could hardly repress a smile at the memory of what had happened the night before. It was strange. He felt no guilt, no fear that the driver might have been seriously hurt. That would have spoiled the rounded perfection of the crime's solution.

The people of Bristol looked much healthier than those of Leeds. His mind propounded some vague theory about the freedom of living near the sea as against the claustrophobia of a land-locked city, but it was let down when the sun went in. Anyway, the people didn't look that different. In fact, there was a man on the opposite side of the street who looked exactly like the bald man with big ears whom he'd idly followed in Leeds. He kicked himself for once again trying to impose theories on everything. Why could he never just accept the continuous variety of life without trying to force events into generalisations?

There was a lot of tension at the theatre. The entire company sat in the stalls, exchanging irrelevant chatter or coughing with self-pity to show that they'd got The Cold. There were three chairs on the stage and, as Charles slumped into a stalls seat, they were filled by the company manager, David Meldrum and Christopher Milton.

David Meldrum stood up first as if he were the director and clapped his hands to draw attention. The chatter and coughing faded untidily. 'Well, as you all know, we had a distinguished visitor in our audience last night, Desmond Porton of Amulet, who, you don't need reminding, are putting up a lot of the money for this show. So for that reason, if no other, we should listen with interest to his comments and maybe make certain changes accordingly.'

'Otherwise the show will never make it to London,' added the company manager cynically.

'Yes.' David Meldrum paused, having lost his thread. 'Um, well, first let me give you the good news. He liked a lot of the show a lot and he said there is no question of the London opening being delayed. So it's all systems go for November 27th, folks!' The slang bonhomie of the last sentence did not suit the prissy voice in which it was said.

'And now the bad news...' For this line he dropped into a cod German accent which suited him even less. 'We were up quite a lot of the night with Desmond Porton going through the script and there are quite a lot of changes that we're going to have to make. Now you probably all realise that over the past few weeks the show has been getting longer and longer. Our actual playing time is now three hours and eight minutes. Add two intervals at fifteen minutes each and that's well over three and a half.'

A derisive clap greeted this earnestly presented calculation. David

Meldrum appeared not to hear it and went on. 'So that means cuts, quite a lot of cuts. We can reduce the intervals to one, which would give us a bit of time, and the King's Theatre management won't mind that because it saves on bar staff. But we've still got half an hour to come out of the show. Now some of it we can lose by just shortening a few of the numbers, cutting a verse and chorus here and there. We can probably pick up ten minutes that way. But otherwise we're going to have to lose whole numbers and take considerable cuts in some of the dialogue scenes.

'Now I'm sorry. I know you've all put a lot of work into this show and I know whatever cuts we make are going to mean big disappointments for individuals among you. But Amulet Productions are footing most of the wage bill and so, as I say, we have to listen carefully to their views. And after all, we have a common aim. All of us here, and Amulet, we all just want the show to be a success, don't we?'

The conclusion of the speech was delivered like Henry V's 'Cry God for Harry, England and St George!' but was not greeted with the shouts of enthusiasm which follow Shakespeare's line in every production. There was an apathetic silence punctuated by small coughs until one of the dancers drawled, 'All right, tell us what's left, dear.'

David Meldrum reached round for his script, opened it and was about to speak when Christopher Milton rose and said, 'There was another point that Desmond made, and that was that a lot of the show lacked animation. Not enough action, not enough laughs. So as well as these cuts, there will be a certain amount of rewriting of the script, which Wally Wilson will be doing. It's all too sedate at the moment, like some bloody eighteenth-century play.'

'But it is a bloody eighteenth-century play.' Charles kept the thought to himself and nobody else murmured. They were all resigned – indeed, when they thought about it, amazed that the major reshaping of the show hadn't come earlier. They sat in silence and waited to hear the worst.

David Meldrum went through the cuts slowly and deliberately. They were predictable. Oliver Goldsmith, whose revolutions in his grave must by this time have been violent enough to put him into orbit, was left with almost nothing of his original play. The trouble with most musicals based on other works is that the songs are not used to advance the action. A musical number is merely a break in the continuity and, when it's over, you're four minutes further into the show and only two lines further into the plot. Carl Anthony and Micky Gorton's songs, written with an eye to the Top Ten and continuing profitable appearances on LPs, were particularly susceptible to this criticism. But because the songs were the set-pieces and the items on which most rehearsal time and money had been spent, they had to survive at the expense of the text. Charles, who remembered Goldsmith's play well from his own Cardiff production, saw the plot vanishing twist by twist, as one of the most beautiful and simple comic mechanisms in English literature was dismantled and reassembled without many of its working parts.

But the cuts were selective. It was clear that Christopher Milton had been up through the night with David Meldrum and Desmond Porton, watching each projected excision with a careful eye. Tony Lumpkin's part came through the massacre almost unscathed. One rather dull number was cut completely and a verse and chorus came out of another. And that was it. While all the other characters had their parts decimated.

The one who suffered most was the one who Goldsmith, in his innocence, had intended to be the hero, Young Marlow. Cut after cut shredded Mark Spelthorne's part, until he had about half the lines he had started the day with.

For some time he took it pretty well, but when the proposal to cut his second act love duet with Lizzie Dark was put forward, his reserve broke. 'But that's nonsense,' he croaked. (He was suffering from The Cold and was determined that no one should miss the fact.)

'Sorry?' asked David Meldrum mildly, but the word was swamped by a sharp 'What?' from Christopher Milton.

'Well, putting on one side for a moment the fact that the play no longer has a plot, if you cut the love duet, there is absolutely no romantic content from beginning to end.'

'Yes, there is. There's my song to Betty Bouncer.'

'But that song has nothing to do with the plot. Betty Bouncer doesn't even appear in the original play.'

'Sod the original play! We aren't doing the original play.'

'You can say that again. We're doing a shapeless hotch-potch whose only *raison d'être* is as a massive trip for your over-inflated ego.'

'Oh, I see. You think I'm doing all this work just to give myself cheap thrills.'

'I can't see any other reason for you to bugger up a plot that's survived intact for two hundred years. Let's face it, it doesn't matter to you what the show is. We might as well be performing a musical of the telephone directory for all you care. Just so long as you've got all the lines and all the jokes and all the songs. Good God, you just don't know what theatre's about.'

'I don't?' Christopher Milton's voice was ominously quiet. 'Then please tell me, since I am so ill-informed on the matter, what the theatre is about.'

'It's about team-work, ensemble acting, people working together to produce a good show – '

'Bullshit! It's about getting audiences and keeping in work. You go off and do your shows, your "ensemble theatre" and you'll get nobody coming to see them. People want to see stars, not bloody ensembles. I'm the reason that they'll come and see this show and don't you kid yourself otherwise. Let me tell you, none of you would be in line for a long run in the West End if this show hadn't got my name above the title. So don't you start whining about your precious lines, Mark Spelthorne. Just think yourself lucky you've got a job. You're not going to find them so easy to come by now they've dropped that bloody awful *Fighter Pilots*.'

That got Mark on the raw. 'How the hell did you know that?'

'I have contacts, sonny. As a matter of fact, the Head of London Weekend Television was down this week trying to get me to do a series for them. He told me.'

'It's not definite yet,' said Mark defensively. 'They're still considering it. The producer told me.'

'It's definite. The producer just hasn't got the guts to tell you the truth. No, your brief taste of telly stardom is over and let me tell you, no one's too anxious to pick up the failed star of a failed series that didn't make the ratings. So if I were you, I'd keep very quiet in this show, take what you're given and start writing round the reps.'

The public savagery of the attack gave Mark no alternative but to leave the theatre, which he did. What made the denunciation so cruel was that it was true. Mark Spelthorne had risen to public notice in advance of his talents on the strength of one series and without it he wasn't much of a prospect.

As usual the star continued addressing his audience as if nothing had happened. 'Now the next scene we come to is the Chase, the *Lead 'em Astray* sequence. I don't think we need cuts in this one. In fact I don't think we've begun to develop that scene yet. I discussed this with Desmond Porton and he agrees that we can add a whole lot more business and make it a really funny slapstick sequence. We're going to do it in a sort of silent film style, with a lot more special effects. And I think we can pep up the choreography a bit in that scene. Really get the girls jumping about.'

'You try jumping about in eighteenth-century costume,' complained an anonymous female dancer's voice.

Christopher Milton did not object to the interruption; he continued as if it were part of his own train of thought. 'Yes, we've got to change the girl's costumes there. Get more of an up-to-date feel. Like go-go dancers. Really get the audience going.'

'Why not have them topless?' drawled one of the dancing queens.

'Yes, we could – no.' His objection was, needless to say, not on grounds of anachronism. 'We've got to think of the family audience. I think this Chase Scene can be terrific. Wally Wilson's working on it now and we can make it into something really exciting. Going to mean a lot more work, but it will be worth while. Oh, that reminds me, we're going to need flying equipment for it...'

'What?' asked David Meldrum weakly.

'Flying equipment for the Chase Scene. I'm going to be flown in on a Kirby wire. Have we got the stuff?'

'No, I don't think so. We'd have to get it from London.'

'Well, get it. Who organises that?'

'I suppose the stage manager.'

'Is he about?'

'Yes, I think he's backstage somewhere.'

'Then get him to organise that straight away. I want to start rehearsing with it as soon as possible.' As if under hypnosis, the man whose title was 'director' wandered offstage to find Spike.

'Now, in that sequence, we're also going to be making a lot more use of the trap-doors and doubles for me...Okay. It's going to make that bit longer, but I think it'll give the show a great lift towards the end...'

Charles' part was so small that, short of cutting it completely (and in the current climate, that did not seem impossible), the management could not do it much harm. As it was he lost four lines and left the theatre for the pub feeling that it could have been a lot worse. Just as he went through the stage door, he met Spike coming in. 'Oh, they were looking for you. Something about a Kirby wire.'

Spike's *papier-mâché* face crumpled into a sardonic grin. 'They found me. Yes, so now his Lordship wants to fly as well as everything else. It'll be walking on the water next.'

Charles chuckled. 'I wonder if he's always been like this.'

'What do you mean?'

'Always ordering everyone about. I mean, he couldn't have done it when he started in the business, could he?'

'With him anything's possible.'

'Where did he start? Any idea?'

'Came out of stage school, didn't he? Suppose he went straight into rep.'

'You've met lots of people in the business, Spike. Ever come across anyone who knew him before he became the big star?'

There was a pause. 'I don't know. I'm trying to think.' Spike wrinkled his face; when the acne scars were in shadow, he looked almost babylike. 'There was an actor I once met who I think had been with him a long time back. Now what was his name...? Seddon...Madden, something like that. Paddon, that's right.'

'Not Julian Paddon?'

'Yes, I think that was the name. Why, do you know him?'

'I'm only staying with him here in Bristol.'

Mark Spelthorne was sitting in the corner of the pub. It was only eleven-thirty and there weren't many people about. Charles felt he couldn't ignore him. 'Can I get you a drink?'

'Brandy, please. Medicinal. For the cold.' He looked frail. His nose was comically red, the lines of his face were deeply etched and for the first time Charles realised that the hair was dyed. Mark Spelthorne was older than the parts he played. As Christopher Milton had said, overcoming the current setback in his career wouldn't be easy.

Charles ordered the brandy and a pint of bitter for himself. That meant he was in a good mood. He drank Scotch when he was drinking to change his mood or delay a bad one and beer when he wanted to enjoy the one he was in.

'Cheers.' They drank. Charles felt he could not ignore what had happened.

'Sorry about all that this morning. Must've been pretty nasty for you.'

'Not the most pleasant few minutes of my life.'

'That I believe. Still, he says things like that in the heat of the moment. He doesn't mean them.'

'Oh, he means them.'

Though he agreed, Charles didn't think he should say so. He made do with a grunt.

'Yes, he means them, Charles, and what's more, he's right.'

'What do you mean?'

'They aren't going to do any more *Fighter Pilots*.'

'Well, so what? Something else will come up.'

'You reckon? No, he's right about that too. They launched that series to see if it caught on. If it had, I'd have been made, got star billing from now on. But now it's failed, nobody'll touch me.'

'Oh, come on. You'll keep in work.'

'Work, yes. Supports, but not star billing. My career's ruined.' Charles tried to remember if he'd ever thought like that. So far as he could recollect, his aim in the theatre had always been for variety rather than stardom. Still, it obviously mattered to Mark. He tried another optimistic tack. 'But there'll be other chances. I mean, you made this pilot for your own radio show...'

'Yes. They don't want it. It's been heard and they don't want to make a series.'

'Ah, ah well.' Charles searched through his store of comforts for such situations and could only come up with cliché 'Never mind, one door closes, another one opens.' It was patently untrue. In his own experience life's doors worked like linked traffic lights – one closed and all the others closed just before you got to them. Mark treated the platitude to the contemptuous grunt it deserved. 'My God, he's such a sod. I feel so angry, just so angry.'

'Yes,' Charles said, inadequately soothing.

'And the world loves him. *Lovable* Christopher Milton. Every time he's mentioned in the press, there it is, lovable Christopher Milton. Doesn't it make you puke? If only his precious public could see him as he was this morning, could see all the meanness that goes to make up his lovability. My God, do people have to be that unpleasant to appear lovable?'

'He works hard at his public image. It's all very calculated.'

'Yes, calculated and untrue. He has no integrity, his whole life is a masquerade.' Mark Spelthorne spoke from a position of extreme righteousness, as if his own life had never been sullied by a shadow of affection. 'You know, I think I'd give anything to expose him, show him to the public for what he really is – a mean-minded, egotistical, insensitive bastard.'

'But talented.'

'Oh yes. Talented.' Even in the violence of his anger Mark could not deny the facts.

Charles thought a lot about what Mark had said. Because possibly he held in his hands the power to expose the star. If the series of accidents which had happened to *Lumpkin!* and been perpetrated by his driver could ever be traced back to Christopher Milton, that would be exactly the sort of scandal to bring the star down in the public estimation.

And yet Charles did not believe that Christopher Milton was directly involved. True, all the crimes turned out to the star's advantage, but Charles was convinced that the driver had either been acting off his own bat or on the orders of Dickie Peck. Either way, the motive had been a protective instinct, to keep the star from the harsh realities of life (like people disagreeing with him). Somehow Christopher Milton himself, in spite of all his verbal viciousness, retained a certain naiveté. He assumed that everything should go his way and was not surprised to find obstacles removed from his path, but his was more the confidence of a divine mission than the gangster's confidence in his ability to rub out anyone who threatened him. The star might have his suspicions as to how he was being protected, but he was too sensible to ask any questions about such matters. And far too sensible to take direct action. For a person so fiercely conscious of his public image it would be insane and, when it came to his career, Christopher Milton seemed to have his head very firmly screwed on.

The Friday performance was scrappy. The cuts had been only partly assimilated and the show was full of sudden pauses, glazed expressions and untidy musical passages where some of the band remembered the cut and some didn't. With that perversity which makes it impossible for actors ever to know what will or won't work onstage, the audience loved it...

Charles was taking his make-up off at speed – even with the cuts, it was still a close call to the pub – when there was a discreet knock on his door. Assuming that someone must have got the wrong dressing-room, he opened it and was amazed to be confronted by his daughter Juliet and her husband Miles. What amazed him more was that Juliet, who had a trim figure and was not in the ordinary way prone to smocks, was obviously pregnant.

'Good heavens. Come. Sit down,' he added hastily, over-conscious of Juliet's condition. It confused him. He knew that everything about having children is a continual process of growing apart and could remember, when Frances first brought the tiny baby home, the shock of its separateness, but seeing his daughter pregnant seemed to double the already considerable gulf between them.

'Enjoyed the show very much,' Juliet volunteered.

'Oh good,' Charles replied, feeling that he should have kissed her on her arrival, but that he'd been too surprised and now he had missed the opportunity (and that the whole history of his relationship with his daughter had been missed opportunities to show affection and draw close to her). 'I didn't know you were coming. You should have let me know. I could have organised tickets,' he concluded feebly, as if free seats could compensate for a life-time of non-communication.

'I didn't know I was coming till today. Miles had to come to a dinner in Bristol and then I was talking to Mummy yesterday and she said you were in this show and I thought I'd come and see it.'

That gave him a frisson too. He had not told Frances about *Lumpkin!* How had she found out? At least that meant she was still interested in his activities. He couldn't work out whether the thought elated or depressed him.

'I didn't see the show, of course,' Miles stated in the plonking, consciously-mature manner he had. 'I had to attend this dinner of my professional body.'

Charles nodded. He could never begin to relate to his son-in-law. Miles Taylerson did very well in insurance, which was a conversation-stopper for Charles before they started. Miles was only about twenty-five, but had obviously sprung middle-aged from his mother's womb (though, when Charles reflected on Miles' mother, it was unlikely that she had a womb – she must have devised some other more hygienic and socially acceptable method of producing children). Miles and Juliet lived in a neat circumscribed executive estate in Pangbourne and did everything right. They bought every possession (including the right opinions) that the young executive should have and their lives were organised with a degree of foresight that made the average Soviet Five-Year-Plan look impetuous.

When Miles spoke, Charles took him in properly for the first time. He was dressed exactly as a young executive should be for a dinner of his professional body. Dinner jacket, but not the old double-breasted or now-dated rolled-lapel style. It was cut like an ordinary suit, in very dark blue rather than black, with a discreet braiding of silk ribbon. Conventional enough not to offend any senior members of the professional body, but sufficiently modern to imply that here was a potential pace-setter for that professional body. The bow tie was velvet, large enough to maintain the image of restrained panache, but not so large as to invite disturbing comparisons with anything flamboyant or artistic. The shirt was discreetly frilled, like the paper decoration on a leg of lamb. In fact, as he thought of the image, Charles realised that that was exactly what Miles looked like – a well-dressed joint of meat.

Recalling a conversation that Miles and he had had two years previously on the subject of breeding intentions, he could not resist a dig. 'When's the baby due?' he asked ingenuously.

'Mid-April.' Juliet supplied the information.

'You've changed your plans, Miles. I thought you were going to wait a couple more years until you were more established financially.'

'Well, yes...' Miles launched into his prepared arguments. 'When we discussed it, I was thinking that we would need Juliet's income to keep going comfortably, but of course, I've had one or two rises since then and a recent promotion, so the mortgage isn't taking such a big bite as it was, and I think the general recession picture may be clearing a little with the Government's anti-inflation package really beginning to work and so we decided that we could advance our plans a little.'

He paused for breath and Juliet said, 'Actually it was a mistake.' Charles could have hugged her. He spoke quickly to stop himself laughing. 'I'm sorry I can't offer you anything to drink...I don't keep anything here.' With a last act entrance and an adjacent pub, there didn't seem any need.

'Don't worry, I'm not drinking much, because of the baby.'

'And I had up to my limit at the dinner. Don't want to get nabbed on the M4.' The image came of Miles sitting at the dinner of his professional body, measuring out his drinks drop by drop (and no doubt working out their alcoholic content with his pocket calculator).

'You say you heard from your mother yesterday,' said Charles, with what attempted (and failed) to be the insouciance of a practitioner of modem marriage, unmoved by considerations of fidelity and jealousy.

'Yes.'

'How was she?'

'Fine.'

'How's the new boy friend?' He brought in the question with the subtlety of a sledge-hammer.

'Oh, what do you...?' Juliet was flustered. 'Oh, Alec. Well, I don't know that you'd quite call him a boy friend. I mean, he just teaches at the same school as Mummy and, you know, they see each other. But Alec's very busy, doesn't have much time. He's a scout-master and tends to be off camping or climbing or doing arduous training most weekends.'

Good God. A scout-master. Frances must have changed if she'd found a scout-master to console her. Perhaps she'd deliberately looked for someone as different as possible from her husband.

Juliet tactfully redirected the conversation, a skill no doubt refined by many Pangbourne coffee mornings. 'It must be marvellous working in a show with Christopher Milton.'

'In what way marvellous?'

'Well, he must be such fun. I mean, he comes across as so...nice. Is he just the same off stage?'

'Not exactly.' Charles could also be tactful.

But apparently Christopher Milton united the Taylersons in admiration. Miles thought the television show was 'damn funny' and he was also glad, 'that you're getting into this sort of theatre, Pop. I mean, it must be quite a fillip, career wise.'

'What do you mean?'

'Well, being in proper commercial theatre, you know, West End, chance of a good long run, that sort of thing. I mean, it's almost like having a regular job.'

'Miles, I have done quite a few shows in the West End before, and if I have spent a lot of my life going round the reps, it's at least partly because I have found more variety of work there, more interest.'

'But the West End must be the top.'

'Not necessarily. If you want to be a star, I suppose it might be, but if you want to be an actor, it certainly isn't.'

'Oh, come on, surely everyone in acting wants to be a star.'

'No, actors are different. Some want to open supermarkets, some just want to act.'

'But they must want to be stars. I mean, it's the only way up. Just as everyone in a company wants to be managing director.'

'That principle is certainly not true in acting, and I doubt if it's true in the average company.'

'Of course it is. Oh, people cover up and pretend they haven't got ambitions just because they see them dashed or realise they haven't got a chance, but that's what everyone wants. And it must be the same in the theatre, except that the West End stars are the managing directors.'

'If that's the case, where do I come on the promotion scale?'

'I suppose you'd be at a sort of...lower clerical grade.' And then, realising that that might be construed as criticism, Miles added, 'I mean, doing the job frightfully well and all that, but sort of not recognised as executive material.'

They were fortunate in meeting the managing director on the stairs. Christopher Milton was leaving alone and, suddenly in one of his charming moods, he greeted Charles profusely. Miles and Juliet were introduced and the star made a great fuss of them, asking about the baby, even pretending to be interested when Miles talked about insurance. They left, delighted with him, and Charles reflected wryly that if he'd wanted to organise a treat, he couldn't have come up with anything better.

Christopher Milton's mood of affability remained after they'd gone. 'Fancy a drink?'

'Too late. The pubs have closed.'

'No, I meant back at the hotel.'

'Yes. Thank you very much.' Charles accepted slowly, but his mind was racing. The offer was so unexpected. If Christopher Milton were behind the accidents which had been happening over the past weeks and if he knew that Charles had been inspecting his car the night before, then it could be a trap. Or it could be an innocent whim. Acceptance was the only way of finding out which. And Charles certainly felt like a drink.

'Good. I've got a cab waiting at the stage door.'

'I thought you usually had your car.'

'Yes. Unfortunately my driver had an accident last night.'

The intonation did not sound pointed and Charles tried to speak equally casually. 'Anything serious?'

'Got a bang on the head. Don't know how it happened. He'll be in hospital under observation the next couple of days, but then he should be okay.'

'Do you drive yourself?'

'I do, but I don't like to have that to think about when I'm on my way to the theatre. I do quite a big mental build-up for the show.' Again the reply did not appear to have hidden layers of meaning. No suspicion that Charles was mildly investigating the accident to Pete Masters.

In his suite at the hotel Christopher Milton found out Charles' predilections and rang for a bottle of Bell's. It arrived on a tray with a bowl of cocktail biscuits. The star himself drank Perrier water. '...but you just tuck into that'

Charles did as he was told and after a long welcome swallow he offered the biscuits to his host.

'I don't know. Are they cheese?'

Charles tried one. 'Yes.'

'Then I won't, thanks.'

There was a long pause. Charles, who had the feeling he was there for a purpose, did not like to initiate a topic of conversation. Christopher Milton broke the silence. 'Well, how do you think it's going?'

'The show? Oh, not too bad. A lot of work still to be done.' Clichés seemed safer than detailed opinions.

'Yes. This is the ugliest part.' Christopher Milton paced the room to use up some of his nervous energy. 'This is where the real work has to happen.' He stopped suddenly. 'What do you think of the cuts?'

'Cuts were needed.'

'That tells me nothing. We both know cuts were needed. I'm asking what you thought of the cuts that were made.'

'Well, it depends. If you're thinking of how much sense we're now making of Goldsmith's play – '

'We're not. We're thinking of the audience. That's what theatre's about – the people who watch the stuff, not the people who write it.'

'I agree with you up to a point, but – '

'What you're trying to say is that the cuts could have been spread more evenly, that I myself got off pretty lightly. Is that it?'

'To an extent, yes.' Asked a direct question, Charles felt bound to give his real opinion.

'I thought you'd think that. I bet they all think that, that it's me just indulging my oversized ego.' Charles didn't confirm or deny. 'Go on. That's what they think. That's what you think, isn't it?'

The sudden realisation came that all the star wanted that evening was someone to whom he could justify himself. The fact that it was Charles Paris was irrelevant. Christopher Milton was aware of the bad feeling in the cast and he wanted to explain his actions to someone, to make him feel better. Obviously he had more sensitivity to atmosphere than Charles had given him credit for. 'All right,' Charles owned up, 'I did think other cuts would have been fairer.'

Christopher Milton seemed relieved that he'd now got a point of view against which to deliver his prepared arguments. 'Yes, and I bet every member of the cast is sitting in his digs tonight saying what a bastard I am. Well, let me tell you, all I think is whether or not this show is going to be a success, and I'm going to do my damnedest to see that it is. That's my responsibility.

'You see, *Lumpkin!* just wouldn't be on if I weren't in it. *She Stoops to Conquer*'s been around for years. No commercial management's likely to revive it unless they suddenly get an all-star cast lined up. I suppose the National or the RSC might do a definitive version for the A-level trade, but basically there's no particular reason to do it now. But I said I was interested in the project and the whole band-wagon started.

'Now we come to the point that I know you're thinking – that we're buggering up a fine old English play. No, don't deny it, you're a kind of intellectual, you're the sort who likes literature for its own sake. What I'm trying to tell you, to tell everyone, is to forget what the play was. We're doing a show for an audience in 1975. And that, in your terms, is probably a debased audience, an audience force-fed on television. Their ideal night out at the theatre would probably be to see 'live' some soap opera which they see twice a week in the privacy of their sitting-rooms. Okay, that's the situation. I'm not saying it's a good situation, it's just the way things are, and that's the audience I'm aiming for.

'Because of television, I'm one of the people they want to see. And they want to see a lot of me. They don't give a bugger about the twists and turns of Goldsmith's quaint old plot They want to see Lionel Wilkins of *Straight Up, Guv*, simply because he's something familiar. I've only realised this since we started playing the show in front of audiences. That's why I stopped playing Lumpkin rustic – oh, yes, I saw the expression of disapproval on your face when I did that. But I am right. Give the audience what they want.'

'All right, I agree they want to see you, but surely they'd be even more impressed if they saw your range of abilities, if they saw that you could play a very funny rustic as well as Lionel Wilkins.'

'No, there you're wrong. They want what they recognise. Popular entertainment has got to be familiar. This is a mistake that a lot of young comedians make. They think the audience wants to hear new jokes. Not true, the average audience wants to hear jokes it recognises. No, in this show they see sufficient variety in me, they see me sing and dance – most of them probably didn't know I could do that – but they never lose sight of Lionel Wilkins, and it's him they came for. And it's my business to give them Lionel Wilkins.

'So, when I said to Mark Spelthorne this morning that I felt responsible for the entire company, I meant it. It's up to me to hold this company together and if that looks like just ego-tripping, well, I'm sorry.'

Charles couldn't think of anything to say. He had been surprised to hear such a cogently reasoned justification and, although he could not agree with all the arguments, he could respect it as a point of view. Christopher Milton himself obviously believed passionately in what he said. He broke from the unnatural stillness he had maintained throughout his exposition and started his restless pacing again. He stopped by a sofa and began rearranging the cushions. 'And it's the same reason, my duty to the audience, which makes me so concerned about my public image. I just can't afford to do anything that lowers me in their estimation.

'Oh, don't look so innocent, as if you don't know why I've moved on to this subject. People think I'm blind, but I see all the little looks, the raised eyebrows, the remarks about me putting on the charm. Listen, my talent, wherever it came from, is all I've got. It's a commodity and, like any other commodity, it has to be attractively packaged. I have to be what the public wants me to be.'

'Even if at times that means not being yourself?'

'Even if that means most of the time not being myself. That's the way of life I've chosen.'

'It must put you under incredible strain.'

'It does, but it's what I've elected to do and so I must do it.' This messianic conviction seemed almost laughable when related to the triviality of *Lumpkin!*, but it was clear that this was what made Christopher Milton tick. And though the strength of his conviction might easily overrule conventional morality, he was never going to commit any crime whose discovery might alienate the precious audience whom he saw, almost obsessively, as the arbiters of his every action.

Charles left the Holiday Inn, slightly unsteady from the whisky, but with the beginnings of an understanding of Christopher Milton.

CHAPTER TWELVE

THE LIGHTS WERE still on in Julian's flat when Charles got back there, though it was two o'clock in the morning. Julian himself was in the front room, marooned wretchedly on an island of bottles, glasses and ash-trays. 'Oh, Charles, thank God you've come back. I need someone to talk to. It's started.'
'Started?'
'The baby.'
'Oh yes.' He nearly added 'I'd completely forgotten', but decided that might show an unwelcome sense of priorities.
'Waters broke, or whatever it is they do, about nine. I took her down to the hospital, they said nothing'd happen overnight, suggested I came back to get some sleep. Sleep, huh!'
'She'll be okay.'
'Yes, I'm sure she will, but that doesn't make the time till I know she is any easier. It's like quoting the statistics of normal childbirths, it doesn't make you any more convinced that yours is going to be one.'
'No. Well, you have a drink and keep your mind off it'
'Drink, huh, I've had plenty of drinks.' Julian was playing the scene for all it was worth. Charles had the feeling that he often got with actor friends in real emotional situations, that they rose to the inherent drama and, though their feelings at such moments were absolutely genuine, their acting training was not wasted. 'Oh God,' Julian went on, 'the waiting. It's much worse than a first night.'
'For a small Paddon it is a first night'
'Yes. Oh God!'
'Talk about something else. Take your mind off it.'
'All right. What shall we talk about?'
'The Irish situation? Whether *Beowulf* is the work of one or more writers? The Football League? Spinoza's *Ethics*? Is pay restraint compatible with democracy? Is democracy compatible with individual freedom? Is individual freedom compatible with fashion? Is fashion compatible with the Irish situation? Do stop me if you hear anything that sounds interesting.'
'Nothing yet. Keep talking.'
'You sod.'
'All right. Let you off. Tell me what you've been doing all day. I'm sure the wacky world of a pre-London tour must be more interesting than a day of

rehearsal in a resident company.'

'Yes, I suppose today has been quite eventful. Desmond Porton of Amulet came down last night to pass sentence.'

'And are you still going in?'

'Oh yes, but today has been spent disembowelling the show.'

'Ah, that's familiar. A different show every night. Oh, the thrills of the open road.'

'You sound very bourgeois as you say that.'

'Well, I am. Respectable. Look at me – regular company, in the same job for at least six months. Married...'

'Prospective father...'

'Oh God!'

'I'm sorry. I'm meant to be taking your mind off that. I wonder what that makes you in the hierarchy.'

'What?'

'Being in a resident company. I suppose it's not quite a managing director but it's better than a lower clerical grade. A sort of rising young executive. Middle management, that's probably the level.'

'What are you talking about?'

'Nothing. I'm sorry. I'm a bit pissed.'

'Well, get stuck into that whisky bottle and get very pissed.'

'Okay.'

'Who have you been drinking with until this time of night?'

'With no less than Christopher Milton. The Star. Tonight I was given the honour of being the repository of his guilty secrets.'

'Not all of them, I bet.'

'Why, what do you – oh, of course, you knew him.' Spike's words of earlier in the day suddenly came back. 'You knew him before he was big.'

'Yes, I had the dubious pleasure of being with him in the first company he went to as an adult actor. He'd done quite a lot as a child, but this was his first job as a member of a company. Cheltenham, it was.'

'How long ago was this?'

'I don't know. Fifteen years – no, twenty. I remember, I celebrated my twenty-first birthday there.'

'Christopher Milton must have been pretty young.'

'Eighteen, I suppose.'

'No, fourteen. He's only thirty-four now.'

'My dear Charles, you must never allow yourself to be a victim of the publicity men.'

'What do you mean?'

'Christopher Milton is thirty-eight, at least.'

'But it says in the programme – '

'Charles, Charles, you've been in the business too long to be so naive. As you know, in this game everyone gets to play parts at the wrong age. People who play juveniles in the West End have almost always spent ten years grafting round the provinces and are about forty. But it doesn't have quite the right ring, does it? So when Christopher Milton suddenly became very big, he suddenly shed four years.'

'I see. It figures. Do you remember him from that time?'

'Difficult to forget.'

'What – the star bit?'

'Oh yes, give him his due, he never made any secret of what he wanted to be. He spent a good few years rehearsing for the big time.'

'Was he good?'

'Very good. But no better than any number of other young actors. Indeed there was another in the company at the time who was at least as good. He'd come from the same drama school, also done the child star bit – what was his name? Garry Warden, that was it. And who's heard of that name now? I don't know what happens to the products of the stage schools. They almost always vanish without trace...'

'Perhaps most of them haven't got Christopher Milton's single-mindedness.'

'Single-mindedness is a charitable word for it. God, he was terrible. Put everyone's backs up. Used to do charming things like ringing up other actors in the middle of the night to give them notes. And as you know it's very difficult to have that sort of person in a small company.'

'Did he drive everyone mad?'

'Funny you should say that.' Julian held his glass up to the light and looked through it pensively. 'No, he drove himself mad.'

'What do you mean?'

'He had a breakdown, complete crack-up. Couldn't live with an ego that size, maybe.'

'What form did the breakdown take?'

'Oh, the full bit None of this quiet sobbing in corners or sudden keeling over in the pub. It was the shouting and screaming that everyone was trying to murder him sort. He barricaded himself in the dressing-room with a carving knife. I tell you, it was the most exciting thing to happen in Cheltenham since the Ladies' College Open Night.'

'Did he go for anyone with the knife?' Charles was beginning to feel a little uncomfortable.

'Went for everyone. One of the stage staff got a nasty gash on the forearm. It took three policemen to calm him down. Well no, not calm him down, hold him down. He was screaming blue murder, accusing us all of the most amazing things. Yes, it was a pretty ugly scene.'

'And did he come back to the company when he'd recovered?'

'No, he was taken off in a traditional little white van and that's the last time I saw him. Then suddenly four or five years ago I started reading all this publicity about the great new British star and there he was.'

'And you've no idea what happened to him after Cheltenham?'

'Not a clue. I suppose he went to some loony bin and got cured or whatever they do to people with homicidal tendencies.'

'Yes. Strange, I've never heard about that incident before.'

'Well, he's not going to go around advertising it. Lovable Lionel Wilkins, the well-known loony.'

'No, but it's the sort of story that gets around in the business.'

'Probably he's deliberately tried to keep it quiet. I suppose there aren't many people who would know about it. The Cheltenham company was pretty small – what was it the director used to call us? "A small integrated band." A cheap integrated band, anyway. God, when I think of the money they used to give us, it's a wonder we didn't all die of malnutrition.'

'You don't still see any of them?'

'No, not for years. I should think a lot of them have died from natural causes – and one or two drunk themselves to death.'

'Can you remember who was in that company?'

'Yes. Let me think – ' At that moment the telephone rang. Julian leapt on it as if it were trying to escape. 'Hello. Yes, I am. What? When? But you said nothing would happen till the morning. Well, I know, but – what is it? Good Lord. Well, I...um...I mean...Good Lord. But I wanted to be there. Can I come down? Look, it's only five minutes. No, I'll be there straight away. Good God, having effectively stopped me being there, you can bloody well keep them up for five minutes for me to see them!' He slammed the receiver down and did a jaunty little walk over to the fireplace. He turned dramatically to Charles and threw away the line, 'A boy. Just a little boy. Damian Walter Alexander Robertson Paddon.'

'Congratulations. That's marvellous.'

'Yes, it is rather good, isn't it? I must dash. The cow on the phone wanted me to wait till the morning. God, I should take her something.' He started frantically scanning the room. 'I don't know what – grapes or...where would I get grapes at three in the morning? Oh, I'd better just – '

'Julian, I'm sorry, but who was in that company?'

'What?'

'In Cheltenham.'

'Oh look, Charles, I've got to rush. I – '

'Please.'

'Well, I can't remember all of them.' He spoke as he was leaving the room. Charles followed him through the hall and out of the front door to the car. 'There was Miriam Packer, and Freddie Wort...and Terry Hatton and...oh, what's the name of that terrible piss-artist?'

Charles knew the answer as he spoke. 'Everard Austick?'

'Yes.'

'And was there a pianist called Frederick Wooland?'

'Good Lord, yes. I'd never have remembered his name. How did you know? Look, I've got to dash.'

Julian's car roared off, leaving the road empty. And Charles feeling emptier.

It was with a feeling of nausea, but not surprise, that he heard next day that Mark Spelthorne had been found hanged in his digs.

PART IV

Brighton

CHAPTER THIRTEEN

IT SEEMED STRANGE to continue working with Christopher Milton after that. Or perhaps the strangeness lay in how easy it was, how much of the time it was possible to forget the grotesque suspicions which had now hardened in Charles' mind. And they were busy. *Lumpkin!* was scheduled to open at the King's Theatre on November 27th and the problems of re-rehearsing great chunks of the show were now exacerbated by extra rehearsals for Mark Spelthorne's understudy. (The management were dithering in London as to whether they should leave the part in the understudy's hands or bring someone else with a bit more name value. The boy who'd taken over wasn't bad...and he was cheaper than his predecessor...but was his name big enough...? Or with Christopher Milton above the title, did one perhaps not need any name value in the supports...? And after the cuts Young Marlow wasn't much of a part anyway...The usual impersonal management decisions continued to be made a long way from the people they concerned.)

There was not much fuss over the death. Police were round asking about Mark's state of mind before the incident and there were rumours that some representatives of the company might have to attend the inquest, but the assumption of suicide was general. The coincidence of the failure of the radio pilot, the demise of the *Fighter Pilots* and troubles over *Lumpkin!* were thought to be sufficient motive. To a character like Mark Spelthorne, whose life was driven by ambitions of stardom, this sequence of blows, with the implication that he was never going to make it in the way he visualised, could be enough to push him over the edge.

Even Charles found the explanation fairly convincing and tried to make himself find it very convincing. But other thoughts gatecrashed his mind.

An unwelcome logical sequence was forming there. What he had heard from Julian provided the thread which pulled all the wayward strands of the case together into a neat little bundle. Christopher Milton's history of mental illness was just the sort of thing that he would fight to keep from his adoring public. The mass audiences for popular entertainment are not the most liberal and broad-minded section of the population and they would not sympathise with anything 'odd'.

Everard Austick and the pianist Frederick Wooland had passed unnoticed through Dickie Peck's Approval of Cast net and Christopher Milton must have recoiled in shock when he saw them at rehearsals. They were links with the one episode in his past he was determined to keep quiet and so far as he was concerned, they had to be removed. Not killed or even badly injured but kept out of *Lumpkin!* Hence the airgun pellet and the shove which sent poor, pissed Everard downstairs. Charles kicked himself for being so blinkered about the evidence he had found in the Corniche. He had been looking for something to incriminate the driver and had found what he wanted, without considering that its location could be equally damning to the car's owner.

Because now he had no doubt of Christopher Milton's personal involvement. Apart from anything else, at the time of Mark's death, Dickie Peck was in London and the driver was in hospital. And everything became quite logical if the star was considered as potentially unbalanced. In his morbid self-obsession he saw everyone who challenged him as a serious threat to his personality and as such someone who should be removed or punished. It wasn't a case of Dickie Peck or the driver being overprotective; it was a paranoid man protecting himself. And it meant that Charles was dealing with a madman.

Only a madman would believe that he could continue to behave like that without ultimate discovery and disgrace. Only someone totally locked in his own world, someone who had lost touch with everyday reality. Christopher Milton's unshakable belief in his talent was matched by a belief in his immunity from discovery.

And he had been skilful. All of the crimes had the appearance of accidents or unrelated acts of violence. Charles felt certain that no one else in the company saw any pattern in them. And because *Lumpkin!* was on the move, it was unlikely that the different police forces involved would be aware of a sequence of crimes.

But now, with the death of Mark Spelthorne, the whole situation became more serious. Beating up people who get in your way is one thing; killing them puts you in a different league.

And Charles was still left with the dilemma of what he should do about it. Gerald's original instructions to him to protect the show and its star from sabotage now seemed grotesquely irrelevant. The situation had got beyond that. But he still did not have enough evidence to go to the police with a tale which must strain their credulity. The airgun pellets and the liquid paraffin were unsubstantiated evidence; he could have planted them, and anyway his own behaviour in snooping around the Holiday Inn car park could be liable to misinterpretation. He didn't have any proof that Christopher Milton was at the scene of most of the incidents.

He considered the possibility of talking directly to his suspect, but he couldn't imagine what he would say. A quiet word in the ear may stop a schoolboy from smoking behind the cycle sheds, but in a case of murder it's seriously inadequate. And if he was dealing with a potentially homicidal maniac, it was asking for trouble to draw attention to such suspicions. But the alternative was sitting and waiting for someone else to get hurt or even killed.

He wanted to discuss it with someone, but Gerald Venables, who was the only suitable confidant, was too involved in the situation and might panic.

So he would have to work it out on his own. He thought through the known facts and wished there were more of them. He made vague resolutions to find out as much as he could about Christopher Milton's past and current activities. One useful idea did come into his head. He recollected that the first two crimes had been committed between nine and ten in the morning and suddenly tied this up with the unusual 'no calls before ten-thirty' clause in the star's contract. It would be interesting to find out what he did in the mornings. Was it just that he liked a lie-in? That did not tally with the voracious appetite for work he demonstrated the rest of the day. He was prepared to stay up all night getting a new number together and yet the day never began until half past ten. That was worth investigating.

But it was one stray positive thought in a scrambled mind. Everything else circled round uselessly, tangling with emotions and producing nothing.

The Queen's Theatre, Brighton, was one of the great old touring theatres of Britain. It had been built for more spacious times, in the 1870s, before the cinema had cheapened illusion by comparisons with the real thing. When the Queen's was put up, people went to the theatre for spectacle and they got it. Entertainments were built round special effects – shipwrecks, fires and falling buildings, magic, ghosts and live animals. And the theatres were designed to cope.

The original stage machinery had been built for the Rise and Sink method of set changing, whereby the stage was made up of separate narrow sections, which could be raised and lowered with different sets on them by an elaborate system of pulleys and counterweights. There was a cellar below the stage as deep as the proscenium was high and above the audience's sight lines there was equivalent space in the flying gallery. The complex of girders and hawsers in the cellar was a feat of engineering comparable to one of the great Victorian railway bridges.

When the stage was designed, it had been equipped with the full complement of trap doors which were written into many plays of the period. Downstage were the corner traps, small openings used for the appearance or disappearance of one actor. Often these would be used as Star Traps, so called because the aperture was covered with a circle made up of triangular wooden segments like cake slices, hinged with leather on the outside, which would open like a star to deliver the actor on to the stage and then fall back into place.

Then there was the Grave Trap centre stage, which was always used for the

Gravediggers' scene in *Hamlet*. And originally the theatre had had the most elaborate trap of all, the Corsican Trap, or Ghost Glide. This had been developed for the 1852 play *The Corsican Brothers* and enabled a ghost to rise from the grave as he moved across the stage.

Charles found it fascinating. He had always been intrigued by the mechanics of theatre and just being in the old building gave him that pleasantly painful feeling of hopeless nostalgia which always comes from the knowledge that, however much one exercises the imagination, however much one researches, it is never possible to know what earlier times were really like. He picked the brains of Len, the stage doorman, about the theatre's history and tried to spend as much time as he could alone there, sensing the building's past, hearing echoes of old triumphs, tantrums and love affairs.

But it was not easy to indulge this sentimentality. For one thing, the theatre had undergone many changes. The divided stage had been replaced in the forties and now most of the old equipment was boarded over. Only the Star Trap on the fore-stage was still kept working for the annual pantomime appearances of the Demon King (complete no doubt with miscued puff of smoke).

Then again the frantic re-rehearsal schedule for *Lumpkin!* was not conducive to luxuriating in nostalgia. But, most of all, the looming problem of what should be done about his knowledge of Christopher Milton's criminal activities kept Charles' mind naggingly full.

As in the other towns of the tour, the local press greeted the arrival of *Lumpkin!* in Brighton with a big spread about the show's star. There was a photograph of Christopher Milton in one of his lovable poses and the column was headed 'BACK TO SCHOOLDAYS FOR LIONEL WILKINS'. Intrigued, Charles read on.

> *Lovers of television's Straight Up, Guv are in for a surprise this week at the Queen's Theatre when they see the show's lovable star Christopher Milton in a different role as an eighteenth-century rogue by the name of Tony Lumpkin.*
>
> *'Actually, he's not that different from Lionel,' confides boyish 34-year-old Christopher. 'They're both con-men. I think, if anything, Tony Lumpkin is slightly more successful than Lionel. Well, let's face it – that wouldn't be difficult.'*
>
> *Offstage, Christopher Milton is nothing like his bungling television counterpart. He is a hard-working performer with a great belief in the live theatre. 'Television is strange,' he muses. 'It's in one way the most intimate of the media, because everything you do on it is very small, you know, just for the camera, and because the viewers are just sitting in their living-rooms to watch. And yet in a strange way, for the performer, it's a distant feeling playing to a camera, even when there's a studio audience. It doesn't bear comparison with the contact you can get with a live theatre audience. That's electrifying, intoxicating, magic.'*

For Christopher, being in Brighton is almost like coming home. 'I spent seven years of my life here at Ellen da Costa's Stage School. I came when I was a very young ten-year-old and left when I went into full-time professional theatre. In many ways, Ellen taught me all I know. I think she's retired now, but I certainly hope to see her while I'm in Brighton. I hope she'll come and see the show – and no doubt rap me over the knuckles for sloppy enunciation! She used to be very hot on enunciation. I can't think that she'd approve of Lionel Wilkins' style of speech...'

The article went on to complete the plug for *Lumpkin!* with information about Carl Anthony and Micky Gorton. It made no mention of Mark Spelthorne's death. But then the whole thing read like an Identikit PR interview which had been prepared long in advance.

Still, the information about the stage school was interesting. If the key to Christopher Milton's behaviour lay deep in his past, then it might be worth paying a visit to Miss Ellen da Costa.

The rehearsals were hard. They started with a ten-thirty call on the Monday morning and it was like working on a new show. Wally Wilson's typewriter had been busy and few scenes had escaped 'improvement'. The charming cadences of Goldsmith's lines had now completely vanished and were replaced by the staccato banality of television comedy. There was more work for everyone. At enormous cost, the band had special rehearsals with Leon Schultz. The choreographer kept snaffling dancers away to learn new routines in the theatre bar. Actors were rarely seen without scripts in their hands as they tried to flush the old lines out with the new. Wherever there was a piano it was surrounded by a knot of actors struggling to pick up altered songs. The atmosphere was one of intense pressure.

But surprisingly it was cheerful. The company seemed more united than ever. And this was almost solely due to Christopher Milton. His enthusiasm was infectious and he inspired everyone to greater and greater efforts, he made them think that they were working on the greatest show that had ever happened and that every change was only going to make it that much greater. Charles could not help admiring the Pied Piper strength of the man's personality. The company was carried along on the wave of his vitality. Even the previous doubters, like Winifred Tuke, made no more comments on the evisceration of Oliver Goldsmith. The triumph of the Christopher Milton was total.

He was everywhere. David Meldrum no longer even made a pretence of directing. He acted as a glorified messenger boy for the star, organising rehearsal schedules as instructed and fixing the details of the increasingly elaborate technical side of the show.

Christopher Milton shared Charles' fascination for the mechanics of theatre and seemed to feel the magic of the old building. But he didn't just want to stand and dream while a sense of history seeped into him; he wanted to recapture that history and recreate the splendours of Victorian illusion. The Star Trap was quickly enlisted into the Chase sequence to fire Tony Lumpkin on to the stage from the bowels of the earth. (It was hoped to accompany this entrance with a flash from an electrically-fired maroon, but with the IRA bombers again in action, managements were nervous of sudden bangs in their theatres.) Moments later, Tony Lumpkin descended from the flies on a Kirby wire, then shot behind a tree only to reappear within seconds (thanks to the judicious use of a double) rising from the Grave Trap flanked by two eighteenth-century go-go dancers. The sequence was a far cry from *She Stoops to Conquer*, but it was moving towards the Chaplinesque quality the star wanted. Of course as the business got more and more detailed, so it expanded and yet more of the original plot had to be cut to accommodate it. At the current rate of progress, by the time the show got to London it would have no more substance than a half-hour episode of *Straight Up, Guv*. 'This week lovable con-man Lionel Wilkins fools some supporting actors into believing that a private house is a pub – with hilarious consequences.'

But *Lumpkin!* was beginning to work. Taking Christopher Milton's advice and forgetting Goldsmith, Charles began to see what was emerging, and it was something with enormous potential. In his own strange way, Christopher Milton was a considerable artist. His instinct for the theatrical and particularly the comic was unerring. Charles began to see the situation as a Faustian one in which the star was achieving earthly success at the cost of his immortal soul. The dark side of madness and crime was a necessary complement to the genius of the public image.

After a very hard day's rehearsal on the Tuesday Charles was leaving the theatre to grab a quick bite before the evening performance when he met Suzanne Horst 'Ah,' she said accusingly, 'there you are. Have you asked him yet?'

'What?' His mind was completely blank. He could only remember Suzanne drunk in his arms at the time of Pete Masters' accident.

'About the interview. You said you'd ask him.'

'Oh, did I?' He tried to sound ingenuous and squirm out of it. 'Yes, and you didn't do it in Bristol, which means I've lost some time. So look, I want to do the radio interview this week. It's for Radio Brighton and I've promised them I'll do it while he's down here.' The last sentence was not an appeal for help from a position of weakness; it was a reproof to Charles for failing to discharge a duty. Suzanne was a sharply efficient young lady once again; the warmth of their last encounter was only a product of the drink. Either she had forgotten it or was determined that it should be forgotten. 'So look, when am I going to be able to do it?'

'Well, I don't know,' he prevaricated. 'We're rehearsing very hard at the moment and – '

'Have you asked him yet?'

Faced with the point-blank question, Charles could only admit he hadn't.

Suzanne Horst gave a contemptuous grunt. 'Do you realise, you've wasted a lot of my time. I thought you were asking him.'

'I'm sorry,' he mumbled inadequately, trying to remember how he'd got into the position of agreeing to help her. 'Does that write off the magazine article as well?'

'No, it only slows that down too.' Her mind did not accommodate the idea of failure. 'But I've been doing quite a lot of background research on it.'

'Oh.'

'Yes, I went to see the old lady who ran his stage school, that sort of thing.' A firm reminder to Charles that that was his next priority. He started to make leaving noises, but did not escape without the final rap over the knuckles. 'I'm very disappointed in you, Charles. I was relying on you. Now I'll have to try my own more direct methods.'

Maybe it was the meeting with Suzanne that decided Charles to present himself at the Ellen da Costa Stage School in the guise of a journalist, or maybe it was just the obvious rôle to take when seeking information. Some inner warning mechanism told him not to go as Charles Paris.

There were some good old-clothes shops near the station in Brighton and he had kitted himself out well. The suit was cheaply cut, but looked newish, and the tie was a touch of psychedelic bravado, too young for its wearer and too old to be fashionable. His hair was greyed and Brylcreemed back like raked grass. A pair of pebble glasses changed the shape of his face and made seeing almost impossible. He stained two fingers of his right hand yellow and bought a packet of cigarettes. He didn't shave and rubbed a little Leichner No. 16 on to darken his jowl. Then an unfamiliar after-shave to cover the grease-paint smell.

He studied the effect in the mirror and thought he looked sufficiently anonymous. The face that looked back at him was like a child's Potato Man, random features stuck on to a vegetable. He adopted a slightly hunched stance, as if shrinking from the cold. It looked all right.

'Now just a name and a voice. He fabricated Frederick Austick from the names of the first two victims of the accidents, then decided it was too obvious and amended it to Alfred Bostock. Despite temptations to go fancy or double-barrelled, he stuck at that. He tried a few words in his *Moby Dick* voice ('Allegorically inconsistent' – *Coventry Evening Telegraph*), but was more satisfied with the one he'd used as Bernard in *Everything in the Garden* ('Authentic suburban twang' *Surrey Comet*).

He didn't really know who he was disguising himself from – the rest of the *Lumpkin!* company were rehearsing on the Wednesday morning – but as usual he felt more able to cope with a difficult task in character.

The Ellen da Costa Stage School had closed some years before, but its principal still lived in the building (and still kept her hand in by giving elocution lessons to the young people of Brighton who had impediments or social aspirations). The school was a tall Victorian private house off one of the sea-front squares. Its owner's reduced circumstances were indicated by the cluster of tenants' doorbells attached with varying degrees of permanency to the old front door frame. Charles pressed the one whose plastic window showed a copperplate 'Ellen da Costa' cut from a visiting card.

She answered promptly, a long gaunt lady in black, whose flowing dress and shawl combined with a tangle of hanging beads to make her look like a bentwood hat stand. Her hair was swept back in flamenco dancer style, as if to justify her Spanish surname, but the white line at the roots gave the lie to its sleek blackness. The skin of her face was drawn tight over her cheekbones, as if, like the hair, its tension was maintained by the system of asymmetrical combs at the back of the head. She was made up with skill, but a skill which belonged to an earlier age and survives now only in opera.

But she had style and must once have been a beautiful woman. Though probably seventy, she behaved with the assurance of a woman who has no doubt of her sexual magnetism. There was no coquetry, but a grace and dignity, heightened by her theatrical manner.

'Good morning,' she enunciated with the attention to each vowel and consonant which she had instilled into generations of young hopefuls.

'Hello, I'm Alfred Bostock.' He slipped easily into his *Everything in the Garden* twang. 'I'm a journalist. I'm researching an article on Christopher Milton and I'm here because I've heard that you had so much to do with shaping his early career.'

She laughed a clear, tinkling laugh, only shown to be staged by the over-dramatic intake of breath which followed it. 'Ah, dear Christopher. Everyone wants to know about him.'

'Other members of the Press, you mean?'

'Yes, dear boy. There was the cub from the local rag, then a charming American girl, and now you.'

'Yes, I hope you don't mind going over the ground again.'

'Mind? But, *mon cher*, I am always delighted to speak about my little ones. And when it is *the* one, the one of all others who had the *je ne sais quoi*, the unknowable something that is stardom, why should I refuse? We who serve genius must do our duty. Do come in.'

Charles, who was beginning to find her language a bit excessive, followed her up a couple of staircases to a dark sitting-room. It needn't have been as dark as it was, but much of the window was obscured by an Art Deco glass fire-screen with a colourful design of a butterfly. The splashes of pale green, blue and red which the sun cast over the floor and furniture gave an ecclesiastical flavour to the room and this was intensified by the rows of photographs in ornate metal frames on the walls. They looked like images of saints and youthful miracle-workers, with their slicked hair and unearthly smiles. They were presumably the 'little ones', the pupils who had taken their theatrical orders under Miss da Costa's guidance and gone on to work in the field.

Two untimely candles added to the stuffy atmosphere of Italian

Catholicism which the room generated. Every surface was crowded with souvenirs, more tiny framed photographs, dolls, masks, gloves, programmes, massed untidily like offerings before a shrine.

The votaress sank dramatically into a small velvet chair and lay back so that the candle-light played gently over her fine profile. It reminded Charles of *Spotlight* photographs of ten years before, when every actor and actress was captured in a fuzzy light which picked out their bones in a murk of deepening shadows. (Nowadays actors tend to be photographed as if they've just come off a building site or are about to start life sentences for rape.) 'Well,' she said, 'you want to ask me about Christopher.'

She didn't ask for any credentials, which was a relief, because Charles hadn't thought through the details of what Alfred Bostock was meant to be researching.

'Yes, I'm after a bit of background, you know, what was he like as a child?' Charles mentally practised his Alfred Bostock voice by repeating 'Ford Cortina', 'double glazing' and 'ceiling tiles' to himself.

'Christopher came to me when he was ten.' Ellen da Costa settled down to her recitation from *Lives of the Saints*. 'Just a scrap of a boy, but with that same appealing charm and, of course, the talent. Even then, when he was unformed, the talent was there. Quite exceptional. His parents had died, in a car crash, I think, and it was an aunt who brought him to me. Very self-possessed he was.'

'When was this that he first came to you?'

Ellen da Costa gave him a look for talking in prayers, but she answered his question, revealing that she had not been in on the shedding of four years considered necessary to the star's career.

She then continued at some length describing the evolution of the embryo talent under the ideal laboratory conditions of her school. Charles was beginning to feel sated with superlatives when she offered to illustrate her lecture with a collection of press cuttings pasted into large blue ledgers.

They weren't very revealing. One or two good notices for the young Christopher Milton, but nothing which suggested a performer set to take the world by storm. Charles mentioned this to Ellen da Costa in suitably reverential tones.

'Ah well, the press has never been notorious for its recognition of true quality, particularly in the theatre. I once knew an actor...' the pause was deliberately left long to summon up images of years of wild passion. '...a very great actor, who was nearly crucified by the critics. It was a martyrdom, a true martyrdom, very *triste*. Pardon my speaking so of your chosen occupation – ' for a moment Charles couldn't think what she was talking about – 'but in my experience the press has never, in this country anyway, had the *delicatesse* to understand the workings of genius.'

Charles did not attempt to defend his assumed calling, but murmured something suitable. 'Also,' she continued, her finely modulated voice drawing out the final 'o' almost to breaking point, 'perhaps Christopher was not fully realised at first. The potential was there, massive potential. Of course, with my experience I could see that, I was *sympathique* to it, but it was slow to blossom. At first there were others who appeared more talented than he, certainly who attracted more public notice, more press reaction, more work.'

'They worked while they were here?'

She at once became guarded, as if this were a patch of coals over which she had been hauled before. 'Most stage schools also act as agencies for child performers and a lot of our pupils do a great deal of work, subject of course to the legal restrictions of only working forty days in the year and with adequate breaks. All the children are chaperoned and – '

But Charles was not writing a muck-raking article on the exploitation of child actors, so he tactfully cut her short, and asked if she would show him some of the early photographs of Christopher Milton.

She obliged readily. 'Here are some from 1952.' They looked very dated. Styles of period stage costume change quite as much as current fashion and the starched ruffs and heavy Elizabethan garments the children wore had the same distant unreal quality as Victorian pornography. 'This is from a production of *Much Ado* my students did. Christopher was playing Claudio.'

Charles took the photograph she proffered. Christopher Milton's face was instantly recognisable, even under a jewelled and feathered hat. All twenty-three years had done was to cut the creases deeper into his skin.

But it was the other two children who intrigued Charles. They were beautiful. Their grace in the heavy costumes made them look like figures from an Elizabethan painting and showed up Christopher Milton as very twentieth century, almost gauche in doublet and hose. The girl had a perfect heart-shaped face and long-lashed eyes whose grave stare, even from the old photograph, was strongly sensual. She appeared to be looking at the boy, who returned her gaze with the same kind of intensity. He had the epicene grace which some adolescent boys capture before they coarsen into adults. The face was almost baby-like in its frame of long blond curls. The eyes were deep-set and powerful.

'Claudio,' Charles repeated after a long pause. 'That's not the best part in the play. Presumably this young man played Benedict?'

'Yes.'

'Was he good?'

'Yes, he was very good. He did a lot of film work in his teens. Gareth Warden, do you remember the name?'

'It rings a bell.' Yes, Julian Paddon had mentioned it and, now he saw the photograph, Charles realised that Gareth Warden had been in the film he'd caught the tail-end of on Jim Waldeman's television. That seemed so long ago it was like a memory from a previous incarnation. 'And the girl?'

'Prudence Carr. She was a clever little actress, so clever.'

'And she played Beatrice?'

'Yes.'

'Any idea what happened to her? Or to Gareth Warden, come to that?'

'I don't know, Mr Bostock. The theatre brings its share of heartbreaks to everyone who is involved in it.' She gave a long sigh, which was a good demonstration of the breath control so vital for elocution and which was also meant to imply a lifetime of theatrical heartbreaks. 'Neither of them did much so far as I know. Dear Garry had the misfortune of early success. It's so difficult for them to make the transition from playing child parts to adult ones. As you see, he was a beautiful boy. Perhaps he lost his looks as he got older. Perhaps he decided the theatre was not the career he wanted. *Je no sais pas*. He hasn't kept in touch at all.'

'And the girl?'

'The same story. I haven't seen her since she left my care. Maybe she didn't go into the theatre.'

'She should have done. With looks like that. And if she could act as well as you say.'

'Ah, she was magic. But things change. Fate takes a hand. Maybe she settled down and got married. How many promising careers have been cut short by matrimony. And how many only started by the failure of matrimony,' she added mysteriously with a suffering gaze out of the window to some distant memory. 'But *c'est la vie*. Some rise and some fall. Of those three, all the same age, all so talented, one was chosen, one who was more talented, one who had the real magic of stardom, and that was dear Christopher. He triumphed and left his rivals standing.'

With recent knowledge of Christopher Milton's methods of leaving his rivals standing, Charles wondered if there was some story from the past which might show a parallel. 'Presumably, Miss da Costa, with three students who were so talented in the same area, there must have been moments of jealousy between them?' he probed.

'Ah, the young are always jealous. They are so afraid, they feel that if they are not the absolute best in the world, then they are the absolute worst. Only with time can they understand that most are destined to be fairly good or fairly bad, that the world is made up of mediocrity and that only a chosen few, like dear Christopher, will be the best.'

Charles tried to move her from generalisations to the specific. 'You mean they were jealous of each other?'

'But of course. They would not be normal if they weren't.'

'And was that jealousy ever expressed in violence?'

'Violence?' Her eyes widened and again she stiffened as if he were trying to find scandal. 'Of course not I kept a respectable school, Mr Bostock. Nowadays, if one can believe the newspapers, violence in the classroom is commonplace. I did not allow it in my school.'

'No, of course not. That's not what I meant.' Charles covered his retreat clumsily, realising that he wasn't going to get any answers to that question. But then it struck him that a bit of well-placed journalistic boorishness might be productive. 'Of course, Miss da Costa, another thing we keep reading about in the newspapers is sex in the classroom.'

'Sex.' She gave the word Lady Bracknell delivery.

'Yes, I mean, a group of young adolescents together, it's inevitable that they're going to form relationships. I was wondering, I mean, say these three youngsters, was there also some kind of emotional attachment between them?' He was glad he had come in disguise. Charles Paris could sever have managed this crudeness of approach.

The question touched a nerve which had apparently been exposed before. 'Mr Bostock, I don't think there is any need to go over this ground again. The investigation by the local education authority in 1963 revealed that I was quite blameless in that matter.'

Intriguing though it was, Miss da Costa's dark secret had no relevance to his current enquiries, so Charles tried to retrieve some of the ground he had lost. 'I'm sorry, I think you misunderstand me. I'm not talking about 1963. As you know, I'm interested only in Christopher Milton. What I meant by my question was, was there maybe some early schoolboy romance we could mention? You know, the women readers go for all that stuff. "My first romance." It was a perfectly innocent enquiry.'

It worked. 'Oh, I see.' She sat back. 'I'm sorry, but I have had cause in my life to be somewhat wary of the press. When one has figured in the private life of the great...' Again she left the hint of her wildly romantic past dangling to be snapped up by anyone interested. Charles wasn't, so she continued after a pause. 'Well, of course, when you are speaking of young people, of beautiful young people, yes, *l'amour* cannot be far away. Oh, I'm sure at one time or another, all three of them were in love with each other. All such sensitive creatures. Yes, I have seen the two boys wildly, madly in love. I have seen them both look at Prudence in a way... in a way one can recognise if one has seen it directed at oneself. Then one understands. Ah, I sometimes wonder if one has loved at all if one has not heard a lover's voice reciting Swinburne soft in one's ear. Don't you?'

He thought that Charles Paris, and Alfred Bostock's answers to that question might well be identical, so he tried to get the conversation back on the subject and avoid the Ellen da Costa Anthology of Love Poetry. 'Hmm,' he offered, in a way that he hoped dismissed Swinburne. 'I was wondering, do you know if either of the affairs with Prudence continued after they left the school?'

'Mr Bostock, I do not like your word "affair"; it implies impropriety at my school.'

'I'm sorry. You're misunderstanding me again. I just meant, you know, the...friendships.'

'That, Mr Bostock, I'm afraid I don't know. For the first year after they left, I heard a little of them – well, that was inevitable. I act as agent for all my pupils for their first year out of school.'

'You mean you put them under exclusive contract?'

'I prefer to think that I protect them from some of the sharks and exploiters in the agency business. But after the year, I heard nothing of Garry or Prudence. Of course, I heard a great deal about Christopher. Everywhere these days, one hears about Christopher. Did you see this in the local paper?' She opened one of the blue ledgers and pointed to the cutting from the previous day's edition. It was already neatly glued in. Charles found the promptness of its filing sad. It opened a little window on to the great emptiness of the old lady's life. He told her that he had seen the article and rose to leave.

Now she seemed anxious to detain him. 'Did you notice, he said in the interview that he'd try to come and see me while the show's down here?'

'Yes. Well, I believe that the company are doing a great deal of rehearsal at the moment.'

'Oh yes, I fully understand.' She reclined elegantly in her chair, the High Priestess of the Cult, prepared to wait forever for her Mystic Experience.

CHAPTER FOURTEEN

CHARLES RANG JULIAN Paddon from a phone-booth on the front. 'Hello, how's the family?'

'Sensationally well. Damian has inherited my own innate sense of the theatre. I went to see them yesterday and he shat all over the nurse who was changing him. What timing. I think he'll grow up to be a critic.'

'And Helen?'

'Fine. Uncomfortable, which is I believe a feature of the condition, but extremely cheerful. Normal cervix, I understand, will be resumed as soon as possible. No hint of purple depression or whatever it is. Can't wait to get home.'

'When will that be?'

'Monday, I hope.'

'Listen, Julian, I wanted to pick your brains again. You remember we were talking last week about the old Cheltenham company you were in with Christopher Milton.'

'Oh yes.'

'You did say that an actor called Gareth Warden was also in the company?'

'Yes.'

'Seen anything of him since?'

'No. Why do you ask?'

'Oh, it's just something I'm trying to work out You've no idea what happened to him?'

'Vanished off the face of the earth so far as I know.' Julian's words gave substance to a thought which had been forming in Charles' mind. Christopher Milton tended to make people who challenged him 'vanish off the face of the earth'. Was the key to the current set of crimes in a crime which had been committed long before?

'Hmm. I see. Another thing – you don't remember by any chance what Christopher Milton's sex-life was like at the time?'

'Good God. What do you want – times, dates, with whom, number of orgasms achieved? It was twenty years ago, Charles. It's hard enough to remember what my own sex life was like.'

'I mean just in general terms.'

'Blimey. Well, let me think – I don't remember him being gay, though I could be wrong. I don't remember him taking up with anyone in the company – mind you, there wasn't much spare there, they tended to get snapped up pretty quickly. I don't even recall a sort of regular popsie coming down for weekends. Oh, it's a long time ago. I honestly don't know, Charles. I mean, keeping a track of actors' love-lives is like doing a National Census of rabbits. Sorry, I just can't remember.'

'Oh well, never mind. And you can't ever recall hearing him speak of a girl called Prudence Carr?'

'Nope.'

'Does the name mean anything to you?'

'Nope.'

'Oh. Well, I – ooh, one last thing – when he had his breakdown, was it caused by anything personal, you know, a girl who'd chucked him or...'

'I don't think so, Charles. I think it was solely due to the fact that the world did not at that time share his inflated opinion of himself. As I remember him, sex was a long way down his list of priorities. In fact everything was a long way down his list of priorities – except for his career and becoming a star.'

The strain of the extra rehearsals and the difficulties of remembering a continuously changing text began to show on the Wednesday evening performance. Perhaps the matinée was the last straw which made the cast suddenly realise how tired they were. Whatever the reason, the mood of united endeavour was replaced in a moment by an atmosphere of bad temper and imminent disintegration.

It was small things that went wrong. Lines were missed and lighting cues were slow. As the show progressed, the contagion spread and by the end everyone felt they were doing everything wrong. There weren't any major errors of the sort that an audience is likely to notice, but they worried the cast and undermined the communal confidence.

The Chase Scene was all over the place. Entrances were missed and special effects failed to function. The Star Trap didn't work. Because of other stage management crises, the crew forgot about it completely and Christopher Milton rushed down to the cellar to find the locking bar which held the wooden platform firmly in position and no sign of the four members of the crew who were meant to man the ropes and eject him on to the stage. As a result he had to rush back up on stage mouthing obscenities at everyone and make a very tame entrance from the wings. The comic timing of the scene's slapstick was ruined.

Even Charles didn't escape the epidemic of cack-handedness. He actually fell over in his first scene. To give him his due, it wasn't his fault. Because of the general panic of the stage management, including some local help who'd only been brought in that day, the rostrum on to which he had to move at a given point had not been anchored to the ground and was free-moving on its wheels. So, as soon as he put his foot on it, it sped away, forcing an ungainly splits movement which deposited him flat on his face. It got a good laugh from the audience, but, since it took place in the course of Tony Lumpkin's romantic song to Bet Bouncer, it was perhaps not the sort of laugh the show wanted.

The only person who came through the performance unscathed was Lizzie Dark. In fact, she was at her very best. She had an advantage. She was only eighteen months out of Sussex University and still had a lot of friends there who had come *en masse* to see her. They were wildly partisan and applauded her every action. The general mediocrity of the performance made her seem even better and the reaction grew increasingly fulsome. It was only a small group in the audience, but they were noisy. At the curtain call, they screamed and shouted 'Bravos!' and 'Encores!' at her. It was an elaborate private joke, recapturing no doubt the heady atmosphere of a campus first night, and it was out of place in a professional theatre. But Lizzie seemed to be carried along by it, to be instantly transported back to amateur night. She played to her gallery shamelessly.

Christopher Milton exploded as soon as the curtain was down. Surprisingly he didn't turn on Lizzie or any other of the cast who had miscued him or let him down. He let the stage management have it. Of all the errors of the show, it was his ignominious return to the stage from the Star Trap which really rankled. He bawled them all out. Four-letter words flew around as he lambasted their incompetence, called them amateurs, provided a few choice images of things he wouldn't trust them with and some equally vivid ones of fates that would be too good for them. This display of temper was the most violent Charles had witnessed from the star and it made him uncomfortable. The great hiss of anger came like steam from a pressure cooker and before long the pressure cooker was going to explode and scald everyone in sight. Charles couldn't keep his knowledge to himself and do nothing much longer.

The inefficiency which had characterised the performance continued. While the star was unleashing his diatribe onstage, a group of schoolkids had somehow eluded Len the stage doorman's vigilance and invaded the dressing-rooms. They had only been driven by enthusiasm and were in fact fans of Christopher Milton, but he was in no mood for one of his sudden switches to charm. He added a few lacerating sentences against Len and said he'd remain on stage until the fans had been cleared. The rest of the cast shuffled sheepishly off to get changed.

Charles started to follow them. He was in a bad mood; the limping performance and the ensuing row had ruled out any possibility of getting to the pub before closing time. But just as he was at the pass door he noticed Christopher Milton going off into the wings and down the stairs to the cellar. Presumably just to have another look at The offending Star Trap. What made it interesting was that Lizzie Dark followed him.

There was another way down to the cellar backstage. Charles moved silently, though there was no one about The cellar was lit by a couple of isolated working lights, but the vertical and horizontal girders of the old stage machinery made forests of shadow through which he could creep to a good spying position. Somewhere over the other side Spike or one of the stage crew was hammering nails into a broken flat, but he paid no attention to the intruders.

As Charles anticipated, Christopher Milton was looking balefully at the Star Trap mechanism. Four wooden beams boxed in the small platform on which the person to be ejected stood. The platform was in the up position, almost flush with the stage underneath the hinged Star top. The locking bar, a solid piece of two by four, was firmly in position, blocking any movement The star slapped it petulantly. He seemed aware of Lizzie Dark's presence, but, though he spoke out loud, he did not speak to her.

'Sodding thing. Why we're stuck with this sort of old-fashioned crap I don't know. Four people to operate it. You'd think with a system of counterweights, you could make it self-operating. Get this bloody locking bar out and leave it pre-set, so that it's ready when I am and not when the bloody stage crew are.'

'But,' Lizzie hazarded tentatively, 'if you took out the locking bar and had it down for too long someone onstage might step on and fall through.'

'Yes, so we're back relying on incompetents.' His anger had drained away, leaving him tired and listless.

'Christopher...'

'Yes.'

'I wanted to apologise for tonight.'

'Eh?'

'That load of lunatics in the audience. My so-called friends. I'm afraid they did rather misbehave. It can't have made it any easier for you to concentrate.'

'Oh, never mind. There are good nights and bad nights.' His voice was philosophical and very tired. The violent outburst Charles had expected didn't come. That was what made being with Christopher Milton so exhausting. There was never any indication of which way he was going to jump.

'Well, I'm sorry. I shouldn't have played up to them. It was a bit unprofessional.'

'Never mind.' He put his arm round the girl's waist affectionately. 'We all have to learn.'

This avuncular, kindly Christopher Milton was a new one on Charles and he found it unaccountably sinister. The arm stayed round her waist as Lizzie asked, 'How do you think it's going, Christopher?'

'It's going all right. It'll be very good – if we all survive to see the first night.'

'Am I doing all right?'

'Yes, you're good. Could be better in bits.'

No actress could have resisted asking which bits.

'That song in the second half, the romantic one. There's a lot more to be got out of that.'

'Yes, I'm sure there is, but the trouble is, David never actually gives any direction and I'm not experienced enough to know what to do myself...It's difficult.'

'I'll take you through it when I've got a moment.'

'Would you?'

'Sure. When? What's the rehearsal schedule tomorrow?'

'The afternoon's free. We're all meant to be in need of a rest.'

'And how.' The deep weariness in the two words reminded Charles of the intense physical pressure that the star had been under for the past months. 'But okay. Let's go through it tomorrow afternoon.'

'No, I don't want to take up your time. I...'

'Here. At three o'clock.'

'Well, if you really...'

'I really.'

'Thank you. I'm sorry, I just feel so amateur in this company. I mean, it's jolly nice getting good jobs, but I've only done a year round the reps and I've got so much ground to make up.'

'Don't worry. You'll make it. You've got talent.'

'Do you really mean it?'

'I do. You'll be a big star. Probably bigger than me.'

'Come off it.'

'I'm serious. It's a long time since I've seen an actress who had your kind of potential. There was a girl I was with at drama school, but no one since then.'

'What was her name?'

'Prudence.'

'And what happened to her?'

'Ah.' There was a long pause, during which Charles felt that water, defying the laws of gravity, was being poured up his back. 'What does happen to talented girls who work with me?'

Christopher Milton moved suddenly. The hand on Lizzie Dark's waist was brought up sharply to her neck where his other hand joined it. Charles started forward from his hide to save her.

They didn't see him, which was just as well. Because far from being strangled, as he feared, Lizzie Dark was being passionately kissed. Charles melted back into the shadows. The hammering in the distance continued, but otherwise the cellar was silent as he crept out, feeling like a schoolboy surprised with a dirty book.

The next morning Alfred Bostock took over the case again. For the next part of the investigation it would not do to be recognised and, after the previous night's unsatisfactory spying, Charles wanted the comfort of disguise.

He'd hung around the stage door until Christopher Milton and Lizzie Dark left the building. They had come out separately and set off in opposite directions. Charles trailed Christopher Milton to the Villiers, his sea-front hotel. (It was so near the theatre that there was no point in having a car, even for a star.) That made him think that Lizzie at least was safe for the night. What had gone on in the cellar after he'd left fed his imagination. It was a good half-hour before they emerged, so most things were possible.

But the urgency of the case was inescapable. The star's violent outburst, the strangeness of his behaviour with Lizzie, and a vague but unpleasant idea of what had happened to Gareth Warden and Prudence Carr made Charles realise that he could dither no longer. And the most obvious thing to do was to find out what Christopher Milton did during that missing hour in the morning.

Charles was very organised. He got up at five o'clock after a disbelieving look at the alarm clock and started making up as Alfred Bostock.

At six-thirty he rang the Villiers. A night porter answered. Charles said he was ringing on behalf of Dickie Peck, Mr Milton's agent, and was Mr Milton up, he knew he sometimes got up very early. No, Mr Milton was not up. Yes, he was in the hotel, but he was sleeping. Yes, he was certain that Mr Milton had not gone out, because he'd been on all night. Yes, he thought it would be advisable if the representative of Mr Peck rang back later. Mr Milton normally ordered breakfast in his suite at eight o'clock. And, incidentally, the Villiers Hotel looked forward to Mr Peck's arrival later in the day.

At eight o'clock the representative of Mr Peck – who incidentally used the accent Charles Paris had used as Voltore in *Volpone* ('Lamentably under-rehearsed' – *Plays and Players*) – rang again and asked to be put through to Mr Milton. He was connected, but as soon as Christopher Milton spoke, there occurred one of those unfortunate cut-offs which are a feature of the British telecommunications system. Charles Paris, in a phone-booth on the sea-front opposite the Villiers Hotel, knew that his quarry was inside and was determined to follow him wherever he went. He had checked the entrances and exits and, unless Christopher Milton left through the kitchens (which would be more conspicuous than the main door in terms of witnesses), he would have to come out on to the front. Now it was just a question of waiting.

Charles sat in a shelter with a miserable-looking couple of old men who were realising their life-time's ambition of retiring to the south coast. They depressed him. It was cold. He saw himself with the deadly X-ray eye of a third person. A middle-aged actor play-acting on the front at Brighton. Someone who'd never managed to create a real relationship with anyone, a man whose wife was forced to take solace with a scout-master, a man whose daughter spoke the language of another planet, a man who would sink into death without even disturbing the surface of life, unnoticed, unmourned. How would he be remembered? As an actor, not for long. Maybe the occasional unfortunate accident might stick in people's minds: 'There was an actor I knew – what was his name? – Charles Paris, that's right, and he...' Or would he just live on as a sort of Everard Austick, an archetypal heavy drinker in the mythology of the theatre? 'There was an incredible piss-artist in a company I was once in, bloke called Charles Paris, and he used to drink...' No, he wasn't even an exceptional drinker, not the sort of wild alcoholic around whom Rabelaisian stories gathered. He drank too much, but not interestingly too much.

Perhaps it was the sea-front in winter that made him so introspective, but he found big questions looming in his mind, big unanswerable cliché questions, all the *whys?* and *why bothers?* and *what does it matters?* Life was very empty.

There was a man walking along the street towards the Villiers Hotel. Charles stiffened. Here at last was something, something real and tangible.

The man he saw was bald, with big ears. When he had seen them in Leeds, Charles had thought the ears looked like handles of a loving cup. The man had hardly registered in Bristol, Charles had just thought he looked like the one in Leeds, but now seeing him for the third time there was no question. It was the same man.

And each time the man had appeared near Christopher Milton's hotel early in the morning. Charles felt he was near to solving the mystery of who did the star's dirty work.

He crossed the road and followed the bald man into the Villiers Hotel. He hadn't really planned his next move, but it was made easy for him. There was temporarily no one in Reception. The bald man rang for a lift. Charles stood by his side, assessing him. A bit old for a heavy, but he was well-built and had the bear-like shape of a wrestler. His mouth was a tight line and the eyes looked mean.

The lift came. The bald man got in and asked for the fourth floor. Charles, who hadn't acted in fifties detective films for nothing, also got in and asked for the fifth. There wasn't one. 'Oh, so sorry,' he said, feeling that this wasn't a very auspicious start. 'I mean the fourth – third.'

The bald man did not seem to notice his companion's gaucheness and Charles was decanted on the third floor. It was a matter of moments to find the stairs and scurry up to the fourth. He hid behind the fire-door and watched the bald man walk along the corridor to room 41, knock and enter.

Charles followed, treading noiselessly in the soft pile of the expensive carpet. He stopped by room 41 and put his ear to the door. He could hear two voices, one of them recognisably Christopher Milton's, but they were too far away for him to distinguish the words.

Anyway, he was in a rather exposed position for listening. A Hoover stood unattended in the corridor and muffled singing also indicated the presence of cleaners. He'd have to move quickly.

The cleaners had left a key with its heavy metal label in the door of room 42. He opened the door and sidled in.

He had expected an immediate confrontation with a suspicious cleaner but miraculously the suite was empty. He moved to the wall which was shared with room 41 and put his ear to it. They were still talking, but, though the speech was clearer, it was again impossible to hear individual words. The effect was of badly tuned radio.

Remembering another movie, Charles fetched a tooth-glass from the bathroom. Pressed against the wall it improved the sound quality, but still not enough to make it intelligible. People who paid for their privacy at the Villiers Hotel did not waste their money.

He was almost despairing when he thought of the balcony. A sea view was another of the perks for those who were prepared to pay the astronomical rates charged for a fourth-floor suite at the Villiers.

He slid the galvanised steel door back. The cold slap of air made him realise how grotesquely over-heated the hotel was.

The balcony of room 42 adjoined that of 41. Only a bar separated them. By sliding along the wall of the building, Charles could get very close to Christopher Milton's window and still remain out of sight from the room. The window was slightly open in reaction to the central heating. Charles could hear what was being said inside quite clearly.

He stood high above the sea-shore on a cold November morning in Brighton and listened.

Christopher Milton's voice came first, strangled with passion. '...and I can't stand the way they are always looking at me, always assessing me. I hate them all.'

'What do you mean, you hate them?' The other voice was toneless, without any emotion.

'I mean I want something to happen to them.'

'What?'

'I want them out of my way. The others went out of my way.'

'Yes.' The dry voice gave nothing. 'What do you want to happen to them?'

'I want them to die. I want them all to die.' He could hardly get the words out.

'Who are you talking about?'

'All of them.'

'Not all. We can't just kill them all, can we? Who do you really want dead?'

'Charles Paris.' The name was hissed out. 'I want Charles Paris dead.'

CHAPTER FIFTEEN

AT THAT MOMENT someone came into the room behind Charles and let out an incomprehensible shriek. It was one of the cleaners, a slender Filipino girl in a blue nylon overall. She looked at him with widening black eyes. He had to think quickly. 'Room 32?' he offered. And then, to cover himself in case she knew the occupant of Room 32, 'Toilet? Toilet?' Unaccountably the words came out in a comedy sketch Spanish accent.

'Toilet,' the girl echoed, as if it were a word she had heard before, but did not understand.

'Si, si,' Charles continued insanely, 'dondo este el toilet?'

'Toilet,' the girl repeated, now uncertain whether she had actually heard the word before.

'Si, toiletto.' He thought adding the final 'o' might help, but it didn't appear to. The girl looked blank. Charles pointed to his fly as a visual aid to the word 'toilet'.

This time the girl understood. Or rather she misunderstood. Throwing her hands in the air, she cried 'Rape!' and rushed out into the corridor.

Charles followed at equal speed. He too wanted to get away in a hurry. Unfortunately the Filipino girl took his movement for pursuit and redoubled her screams. They rushed along the corridor in convoy, because she had chosen to run in the direction of the lifts. Doors opened behind them and bewildered faces stared. Charles decided he couldn't wait for the lift and took to the stairs. He managed to get out of the building without being stopped.

He sat in the shelter opposite the Villiers Hotel and tried to control the breath which was rasping in his throat. It wasn't only the physical effects of the chase that made him feel so shaky. It was also the unpleasant feeling which comes to people who have just heard a contract being taken out on their lives. He gasped and trembled and, although a diluted sun was now washing the sea-front, the morning seemed colder.

The two old men were still sitting in the shelter, overtly ignoring him, but with sly side-glances. They didn't depress him now. They were part of a humanity he did not want to leave. Dr Johnson's adage about the proximity of death concentrating the mind wonderfully was proving true. The depression he had felt so recently seemed a wicked affront to life, to all the things he still wanted to do. And yet within fifty yards of him a lunatic was giving a paid killer instructions to murder him.

It was ridiculous. He had that feeling he could recall from prep school of getting into a fight and suddenly realising that it was becoming more vicious than he'd expected and suddenly wanting to be out of it. Like a recurrent nightmare in which, after a long chase, he always capitulated and apologised and pretended it had all been a joke. But this was not a joke.

The question of what to do about the whole case had now taken on more than a dilettante interest. It had become an issue of red-hot urgency. But the answer didn't come any more readily.

Though the sequence of Christopher Milton's (or his hit-man's) crimes and their motives were now clear as daylight, Charles still had no real evidence. Just the gin bottle, the airgun pellets and the liquid paraffin, but none of those could be pinned on the criminals and none related to the most serious crimes.

He still needed positive proof of wrong-doing, Or, since he was apparently the next person to be done wrong to, positive proof of the intention to do wrong might be preferable. He decided to follow the bald man in the hope of catching him red-handed. (The details of how he would himself catch red-handed someone whose criminal mission was to eliminate him he left for the time being. They would supply themselves when the occasion arose.)

He counted his advantages and there weren't many. First, he knew they were after him, so he was on his guard. Secondly, he was in disguise and so could spy on them without automatic discovery. Not much, but better than nothing.

At about five past ten the bald man came out of the hotel. He walked without suspicion, no furtive glances to left and right. Charles had the advantage of hunting the hunter.

The bald man was an ideal candidate for tailing. He walked straight ahead at a brisk pace, not stopping to look in shop windows or dawdling aimlessly. All Charles had to do was to adjust his own pace to match and follow along about fifty yards behind. Brighton was full of shoppers and the pursuit was not conspicuous.

It soon became clear that the man was going to the railway station. He walked briskly and easily up the hill, fitter than his appearance suggested. Charles thought uncomfortably of the strength he had seen in middle-aged wrestlers on the television. If it came to direct physical confrontation, he didn't reckon much for his chances.

The man didn't stop to buy a ticket. He must have a return, because he showed something at the barrier. He went on to Platform 4, for trains to London. At first Charles was going to buy a single, but that showed a depressing lack of faith in the outcome of his mission, so he got a return.

He also bought a *Times* for burying his face in. Tabloid newspapers, he decided, must be unpopular with the criminal fraternity; they hide less.

The train came soon, which implied that the bald man knew the times and was hurrying for this specific one. Charles began an irrelevant conjecture about the idea of the commuting assassin, always catching the same train. 'Had a good day at work, dear?' 'Oh, not too bad. Had a bit of trouble with one chap. Had to use two bullets. Still, always the same on a Friday, isn't it?' But the situation was too tense for that sort of fantasy.

The assassin got into an open-plan carriage, which was ideal. Charles went into the same one by another door and positioned himself in a seat from which he could see the man's leg and so would not miss any movement. He opened *The Times*, but his eyes slipped over the words without engaging or taking them in. He turned to the crossword on the principle that mental games might take his mind off the icy trickling in his stomach.

'I know that death has ten – several doors / For men to take their exits – Webster (8).' The fact that he recognised the quotation from *The Duchess of Malfi* and could fill in the word 'thousand' gave him small comfort.

He felt ill, on the verge of violent diarrhoea. He could still see the man's leg round the edges of the seats. It didn't move, but it mesmerised him. He tried to imagine the mind that owned the leg and the thoughts that were going through it. Was the man coolly comparing methods of killing, trying to come up with another crime that could look like an accident? Had his paymaster given him a deadline by which to get Charles Paris? The word 'deadline' was not a happy choice.

Come to that, if his quarry was supposed to be in Brighton, why was he going to London anyway? Charles' fevered mind provided all kinds of unpleasant reasons. There was some particularly vicious piece of killing equipment that had to be bought in London. Or the job was going to be subcontracted and the bald man was on his way to brief another hit-man with the details. Even less attractive solutions also presented themselves.

The pressure on his bowels was becoming unbearable. He'd have to go along to the toilet at the end of the carriage.

That meant going past the bald man. Still, it might be useful to get a closer look. Charles walked past. The man did not look up.

His reading matter was unlikely for a hired killer. *The Listener* was open on his lap and a *New Scientist* lay on the seat beside him. Obviously a new class of person was turning to crime. Presumably in times of rising unemployment, with a glut of graduates and a large number of middle-aged redundancies, the criminal social pattern was changing.

Charles felt a bit better after he had used the lavatory, but the face that stared at him from the stained mirror as he washed his hands was not a happy one.

The Alfred Bostock disguise made him look seedier than ever. The pebble glasses perched incongruously on the end of his nose (the only position in which they enabled him to see anything). The make-up on his jowl looked streaked and dirty. The bright tie mocked him. What was he doing? He was forty-eight, too old for this sort of masquerade. What was he going to do when he got to London? He couldn't spend the rest of his life following the bald-headed man. The confidence that he would know what to do when the, occasion arose was beginning to dissipate.

The journey to Victoria took just over an hour and during that time the assassin sat quietly reading *The Listener*. Charles supposed that one would have to relax and behave normally in that line of work or go mad. 'His own *Times* lay unread on his knee and no subsequent crossword clues were filled in.

At Victoria the man got out and gave in his ticket at the barrier. Charles tried a little detective logic. If the man had a return ticket and yet was carrying no luggage except his newspapers, it was possible that he had started from London that morning, gone down to Brighton just to get his instructions and was now returning to base. This deduction was immediately followed by the question, 'So what?'

The bald man walked purposefully to the Underground with Charles in tow. He bought a 15p ticket from the machine and Charles did likewise. The man went on to the platform for the Victoria Line northbound. Charles followed.

They travelled in the same compartment to Oxford Circus. The bald man was now deep into his *New Scientist*, apparently unsuspicious.

He climbed out of the Underground station and walked along Upper Regent Street into Portland Place. He walked on the left, the British Council side rather than the Broadcasting House one. His pace was still even. Nothing in his behaviour betrayed any suspicion. And equally nothing in his behaviour would make any passer-by think of him as anything but a professional businessman on his way to work.

He turned left at New Cavendish Street, then right up Wimpole Street and left on to Devonshire Street. After two hours of tailing, Charles was becoming mesmerised and he almost overshot the man when he stopped.

Though they were only feet apart, the bald man still did not notice his pursuer. He walked in through the yellow-painted front door of a white Georgian house.

Charles, in a panic over nearly bumping into his quarry, walked on a little so as not to make his behaviour too obvious, then turned back and walked slowly past the house. It was expensive. Net curtains prevented snooping inside. A worn brass plate on the door – 'D. M. Martin'. No initials after the name, no indication of professional qualifications.

Charles paused, undecided. It was an expensive area of London. Contract killing must be a lucrative business, if the man lived there. All around were expensive private doctors and architects. He looked up and down the road. A policeman about fifty yards away was watching him curiously.

That decided him. The Law was there to back him up if need be, and the thing had to be done. He couldn't stand the strain of being under sentence of death any longer. It was time to take the bull by the horns.

The door gave easily when he turned the handle and he found himself in a carpeted hall. The smartly suited girl behind the desk looked up at him, surprised. 'Can I help you?'

It was all too ridiculous. He had seen films about organised crime where the whole operation was run like big business with secretaries and receptionists, but he never expected to see it with his own eyes.

He was no longer afraid. Somehow here in the centre of London he felt safe. There was a policeman just outside. He could manage. 'Did a bald man just come in here?' he asked brusquely.

'Mr Martin just arrived, but – '

'Where is he?'

'He's in his room, but do you have an appointment?'

'No. I just want to see him.'

The girl treated him warily, as if he might be important.

'Look, if you like to take a seat in the waiting-room, I'll speak to Mr Martin and see what we can do. He's got someone coming to see him at twelve, but I'll – '

'Waiting-room!' It was farcical. Charles started to laugh in a tight, hysterical way. 'No, I'm not going to sit in any waiting-room. I haven't come along with a list of names of people I want killed. I – '

The noise he was making must have been audible from the next room, because the door opened and Charles found himself face to face with the assassin. 'What's going on, Miss Pelham?'

'I'm not sure. This gentleman – '

'I've come to tell you I know all about what you've been doing, Mr Martin. There's a policeman outside and I have proof of what's been going on, so I think you'd better come clean.' Somehow the denunciation lacked the punch it should have had. The bald-headed man looked at him gravely. 'I'm sorry. I've no idea what you're talking about.'

'Oh really. Well, I'm talking about Christopher Milton and the instructions he gave you.'

The name had an instantaneous effect. Mr Martin's face clouded and he said coldly, 'You'd better come in. Ask the twelve o'clock appointment to wait if necessary, Miss Pelham.'

When they were inside, he closed the door, but Charles had now gone too far to feel fear. He was going to expose the whole shabby business, whatever it cost him.

'Now what is all this?'

'I know all about what you and Christopher Milton have been doing.'

'I see.' The bald man looked very displeased. 'And I suppose you intend to make it all public?'

'I certainly do.'

'And I suppose you have come here to name a price for keeping your mouth shut?'

'Huh?' That was typical, the feeling that money can solve anything. 'No, I intend to let everyone know what's been going on. You won't buy me off.'

'I see. You realise what this could do to Christopher Milton?'

'Nothing that he doesn't fully deserve. He may think he's a god, but he's not above the law. He is a public danger and should be put away.'

'It's that sort of small-minded thinking that delays progress. If you –

'Small-minded thinking! I don't regard disapproving of murder as small-minded. What, do you subscribe to the theory that the artist is above the law, the artist must be cosseted, the artist – ?'

'What the hell are you talking about? Who are you?'

'Charles Paris.' This was no time for pretence.

The name certainly registered with Mr Martin.

'Yes, I'm Charles Paris. I'm in the company with Christopher Milton. You know all about me.'

'Oh yes. I know about you. So it was you all the time. And now, blackmail.'

It was Charles' turn to be flabbergasted. 'What are you talking about?'

'Christopher Milton mentioned that a lot of sabotage had been going on in the show, that someone was trying to get at him. It was you. And now you want to expose what he does with me.'

The voice was sad, almost pitying. It checked the impetus of Charles' attack. "What do you mean? It's Christopher Milton who's been responsible for the sabotage and you're the one who's done the dirty work for him. And this morning he gave you orders to kill me. Don't try to pretend otherwise, Mr Martin.'

The bald man gazed at him in blank amazement. 'What?'

'I know. I saw you in Leeds, and in Bristol, and in Brighton. I know you did it. All those early morning meetings when he gave you instructions. You are Christopher Milton's hit-man.'

'Mr Paris,' the words came out tonelessly, as if through heavy sedation, 'I am not Christopher Milton's hit-man. I am his psychotherapist.'

Charles felt the ground slowly crumbling away beneath his feet. 'What?'

'As you may or may not know, Christopher Milton has been prone in the past to a form of mental illness. He has had three or four major breakdowns, and has been undergoing treatment by me for about seven years. His is a particularly stressful career and at the moment the only way he can support the pressures it places on him is by having an hour of psychotherapy every day of his life.'

'And that's why he always has his call at ten-thirty?'

'Exactly. The hour between nine and ten is our session.'

'I see. And so you travel round wherever he goes?'

'He doesn't leave London much. Under normal circumstances he comes to me. This tour is exceptional.'

'And what happens to your other patients or subjects or whatever they're called?'

'It was only the week in Leeds when I had to he away. I commuted to Bristol and Brighton. Mr Milton is a wealthy man.'

'I see.' Money could buy anything. Even a portable psychiatrist. 'Needless to say, the fact that Mr Milton is undergoing treatment is a closely-guarded secret. He believes that if it got out it would ruin his career. I've argued with him on this point, because I feel this need for secrecy doubles the pressure on him. But at the moment he doesn't see it that way and is desperately afraid of anyone knowing. I only tell you because of the outrageousness of your accusations, which suggest that you have completely – and I may say – dangerously misinterpreted the situation.'

'I see.' Charles let the information sink in. It made sense. It explained many things. Not only the late morning calls, but also the obsessive privacy which surrounded the star. Even little things like Christopher Milton's non-drinking and unwillingness to eat cheese would be explained if he were on some form of tranquillisers as part of his treatment.

'I take it, Mr Paris, from what you said, that you overheard part of our session this morning and leapt to a grotesquely wrong conclusion?'

'Yes. I may as well put my cards on the table. I was brought into the show by the management to investigate this sabotage business.'

'If that's the case then I apologise for suggesting that you were responsible for the trouble. It seems that both of us have been victims of delusions. But, Mr Paris, why did your investigations lead you to eavesdrop on our session this morning?'

'The fact is, Mr Martin, that my investigations so far have led me to the unfortunate conclusion that Christopher Milton is himself responsible, either directly or indirectly, for all of these incidents.'

The psychotherapist did not reject the suggestion out of hand. 'I can understand what you mean – that all of the...accidents have in fact benefited him, that they disposed of people he wanted out of the way.'

'Exactly.'

'Yes. The same thought had crossed my mind.' He spoke the words sadly.

'You know his mental condition better than anyone. What do you think?'

'I don't know.' He sighed. 'I don't think so.'

'Having heard the violence of what he said about me this morning.'

'Yes, but that is a feature of the analysis situation. You mustn't take it literally. The idea of analysis is – in part – that he should purge his emotions. He says the most extreme things, but I don't think they should be taken as expressions of actual intent.'

'You don't sound sure.'

'No.'

'I mean, at the time of his first breakdown he attacked people with a knife.'

'I see you've done your homework, Mr Paris. Yes, there is violence in him. He's obsessed by his career and he is slightly paranoid about it. He does turn against anyone who seems to threaten him in even the tiniest way. I mean, I gather that the crime which provoked this morning's outburst was your falling over and getting a laugh during one of his songs.'

'An accident.'

'Oh yes, I'm sure, but he's not very logical about that sort of thing.'

'But he has expressed antagonism to most of the other people who've been hurt.'

'Yes, I'm afraid so. And a strange bewildered relief after they've disappeared from the scene. I suppose it is just possible that he could have done the crimes. You say you have evidence?'

'Some. Nothing absolutely conclusive, but it seems to point towards him.'

'Hmm. I hope you're wrong. It would be tragic if it were true.'

'Tragic because it would ruin his career?'

'No, tragic because it would mean the ruin of a human being.'

'But you do think it's possible?'

'Mr Paris, I think it's extremely unlikely. Behaviour of that sort would be totally inconsistent with what I know of him from the past and with all that I have ever encountered in other cases. But I suppose, if you force me to say yea or nay, it is just possible.'

Charles Paris looked at his watch. It was a quarter to one. In two and a quarter hours Christopher Milton had a meeting arranged on the stage of Queen's Theatre, Brighton, with the girl who had stolen the show from him the night before.

CHAPTER SIXTEEN

THERE IS no stillness like the stillness of an empty theatre. As Charles stepped on to the stage, he could almost touch the silence. And the fact that the building wasn't completely empty seemed to intensify the loneliness. Somewhere behind the circle people were busy in the general manager's office. In a distant workshop someone was using an electric drill. Traffic noise was filtered and reduced by the ventilation system. But onstage there was a deep pool of silence.

Len the stage doorman had not been in his little room, though he had left his radio on and was presumably somewhere around in the silent building. But he didn't see Charles enter.

It was ten to three. The stage had been preset for the evening performance after the morning's rehearsal. One light in the prompt corner alleviated the gloom. Charles stood behind a flat down right in a position from which he could see the entire stage. He looked up to the fly gallery. If sabotage were planned, the easiest way would be to drop a piece of scenery or a bar loaded with lights from above. But the shadows closed over and it was impossible to distinguish anything in the gloom.

The old theatre had an almost human identity. The darkness was heavy with history, strange scenes both on- and offstage that those walls had witnessed. Charles would not have been surprised to see a ghost walk, a flamboyant Victorian actor stride across the stage and boom out lines of mannered blank verse. He had in his bed-sitter a souvenir photograph of Sir Herbert Tree as Macbeth from a 1911 *Playgoer and Society Illustrated*, which showed the great actor posed in dramatic chain mail, long wig and moustache beneath a winged helmet, fierce wide eyes burning. If that apparition had walked onstage at that moment, it would have seemed completely natural and right.

There was a footfall from the far corner near the pass door. Charles peered into the shadows, trying to prise them apart and see who was approaching. Agonisingly slowly the gloom revealed Lizzie Dark. She came to the centre of the stage, looked around and then sat on a rostrum, one leg over the other swinging nervously. She looked flushed and expectant, but a little frightened.

She hummed one of the tunes from the show, in fact the song with which Christopher Milton had promised to help her. It was five past three, but there was no sign of her mentor.

As Charles watched, she stiffened and looked off into the shadows of the opposite wings. She must have heard something. He strained his ears and heard a slight creak. Wood or rope taking strain maybe.

Lizzie apparently dismissed it as one of the unexplained sounds of the old building and looked round front again. Then she rose from her seat and started to move gently round the stage in the steps of the dance which accompanied the song she was humming. It was not a flamboyant performance, just a slow reminder of the steps, the physical counterpart to repeating lines in one's head.

Charles heard another creak and slight knocking of two pieces of wood from the far wings, but Lizzie was too absorbed in her memorising to notice. The creaks continued, almost in rhythm, as if something were being unwound. Lizzie Dark danced on.

Charles looked anxiously across into the wings, but he could see nothing. His eye was caught by a slight movement of a curtain up above, but it was not repeated. Just a breeze.

The noise, if noise there was, had come from the wings. He peered across at the large flat opposite him and wished for X-ray eyes to see behind it. There was another, more definite movement from above.

He took in what was happening very slowly. He saw the massive scaffolding bar with its load of lights clear the curtains and come into view. It hung suspended for a moment as if taking aim at the oblivious dancing girl and then started its descent.

With realisation, Charles shouted, 'Lizzie!'

She froze and turned towards him, exactly beneath the descending bar.

'Lizzie! The lights!'

Like a slow-motion film she looked up at the massive threatening shape. Charles leapt forward to grab her. But as he ran across the stage, his feet were suddenly jerked away from him. His last thought was of the inadvisability of taking laughs from Christopher Milton, as the Star Trap gave way and plummeted him down to the cellar.

CHAPTER SEVENTEEN

THE FIRST THING he was conscious of was pain, pain as if his body had been put in a bag of stones and shaken up with them. And, rising above all the others, a high, screaming pain of red-hot needles in his right ankle. He lay like an abandoned sack at the bottom of the Star Trap shaft. It was even darker in the cellar. He didn't know whether or not he had passed out, but time, like everything else, seemed disjointed. He remembered crying out to Lizzie, then crying out as he fell and then he remembered being there swimming in pain. There was an interval between, but whether of seconds or hours he didn't know.

He was aware of some sort of commotion, but he couldn't say exactly where. Onstage maybe, or in the auditorium. A door to the cellar opened and light flooded in.

Len was the first to arrive. The old doorman came towards him nervously, as if afraid of what he would see. 'It's all right. I'm alive,' Charles said helpfully, hoping he was speaking the truth.

'Who is it? Mr Paris?'

'That's right. Is Lizzie all right?'

'Lizzie?'

'Lizzie Dark. Onstage. There was a bar of lights that – '

'It missed her. She's all right.'

'Thank God.'

'Can you move?'

'I wouldn't like to make the experiment.'

Other people came down to the cellar. Lizzie. She looked pale and on the verge of hysterics. Some of the staff from the general manager's office who had heard the commotion arrived. So did Dickie Peck. Spike and a couple of his stage crew came from the workshop. Charles lay there in a daze of pain. He knew that he had been the victim of another of Christopher Milton's insane jealousies, but there seemed nothing to say and talking was too much effort.

They carried him upstairs. Spike and another of his men took an arm each. As the shock of the various pains subsided, it was the ankle that hurt most. It was agony when it dragged on the ground, so they lifted him up to sit on their joined hands. It still hurt like hell.

Since the dressing-rooms were up more stairs they took him into Len's little room by the stage door. There was a dilapidated sofa on which he was laid. The general manager's staff went back to phone for an ambulance. Len went off to make some tea, which was his remedy for most conditions. Dickie Peck and Lizzie Dark vanished somewhere along the way. Spike stayed and felt Charles' bones expertly. 'Used to do a bit of first aid.' His diagnosis was hopeful for everything except the ankle. Charles wouldn't let him get near enough to manipulate it, but Spike insisted on removing his shoe. Charles nearly passed out with pain.

'Spike,' he said, when he was sufficiently recovered to speak again. 'That Star Trap, it must have been tampered with.'

'Yes.'

'The locking bar was right out of position.'

'Yes, and someone had scored through the leather hinges with a razor blade. It was a booby-trap, meant for anyone who stepped on it.'

'I think it was meant specifically for one person.'

'What do you mean?'

'Never mind. You'll all know soon enough.'

'Hm.'

'Well, this sabotage to the show can't go on, can it?'

'You think it's a connected sequence of sabotage?'

'Sure of it. And after today I think a police investigation can be started. It's sad.'

'Sad?'

'Sad because we're dealing with a madman.'

'Ah.'

There was no point in hiding the facts now. It would all come out soon. 'Christopher Milton. A good example of the penalties of *stardom!*'

'So it was him all along. I wondered.' There was suppressed excitement in Spike's voice as if at the confirmation of a long-held suspicion.

'Yes.'

A pause ensued and in the silence they both became aware of Len's radio, which was still on. '...so all I can say in answer to that question is – I beg yours?'

It was Christopher Milton's voice. An American female voice came back, 'Well, on that note, thank you very much, Christopher Milton.'

A hearty male voice took it up. 'Well, there it was – an exclusive for us here in the studio on Radio Brighton – for the past half hour you've been listening to Christopher Milton live. And just a reminder that *Lumpkin!* is at the Queen's Theatre until tomorrow and it opens in the West End at the King's Theatre on November 27th. And incidentally the interviewer with Christopher Milton was Suzanne Horse.'

'Horst,' said Suzanne's voice insistently.

Spike went to turn off the radio. Too quickly. He turned back defensively to Charles. The light caught him from behind and only the shape of his face showed. The blurring marks of acne were erased and the outline of his features appeared as they must have done when he was a boy.

Charles recognised him instantly and like the tumblers of a combination lock all the details of the case fell into place and the door swung open. 'Gareth Warden,' he said softly.

'What?'

'Gareth, if Christopher Milton has just been in the studio at Radio Brighton, he couldn't have been here tampering with the Star Trap.'

'He could have done it earlier and left it as a booby-trap.'

'And released the bar of lights to fall on Lizzie Dark?'

There was a silence. Spike, or Gareth Warden, seemed to be summoning up arguments to answer this irrefutable logic. The ambulance arrived before he had mustered any.

Len fussed around as Charles was loaded on to a stretcher and taken to the ambulance. The doors were about to close when Charles heard Spike's voice say, 'I think I'll come with him.'

The realisation of the true identity of the criminal he had been seeking seeped slowly into Charles' mind. Strangely he didn't feel afraid to have the man beside him in the ambulance.

They travelled in silence for some minutes. Then Charles asked softly, Why did you do it all?'

Spike's voice had lost its hard professional edge and now showed more signs of Ellen da Costa's painstaking elocution lessons. 'To show him up. To let people see what he was really like.'

'What do you mean?'

'I mean I just realised his ambitions. All he ever wanted to do was to get his own way and destroy anyone who challenged him. He was always totally selfish. And yet the public loved him. Look at the Press, everywhere – it always says '*lovable*' Christopher Milton. I just wanted to show the public what a shit their idol really was. All I did was to put into action what he was thinking. It was wish-fulfilment for him. Everyone who got in his way just vanished. That's what he wanted.'

'But he never actually hurt anyone.'

'But he wanted to, don't you see? He was never lovable, just evil.'

'And you hoped to bring public disgrace on him?'

'Yes.'

'But how? You must have realised that sooner or later you were going to make a mistake, commit some crime at a time when he had an alibi. Like this afternoon, for instance. He'd never have been convicted.'

'He didn't need to be convicted. The disgrace of the allegation would have been enough. Reports of the investigation would have brought up all the rows at rehearsals and showed the kind of person he really was.'

'But what made you think that there would be an investigation? The management have done everything to keep the whole affair quiet.'

'Au, but they put you in the cast.'

'You knew I was there to investigate?'

'I was suspicious early on and when I saw you with Winifred Tuke's gin bottle, I was certain. That's why I fed you so much information, why I planted the clues for you in his car, why I told you to ask Julian Paddon about him.'

'I see.' Charles' detective achievements were suddenly less remarkable. Why did you hate him so much?'

'I've known him a long times He's always been like this.'

'No, there's more to it than that. Has it anything to do with Prudence Carr?'

Spike/Gareth flinched at the name. 'What do you know about her?'

'Just that you were all three at stage school together, that she was very beautiful and talented, that nothing has been heard of her for some time, that you and he were both maybe in love with her.'

'I was in love with her. He was never in love with anyone but himself. His marriage broke up, didn't it?'

'But he wasn't married to Prudence,' Charles probed gently.

'No, he wasn't. He didn't marry her.'

'What do you mean?'

'He just took up with her, he unsettled her. He...I don't know...changed her.'

'In what way?'

'He destroyed her confidence. He crushed her with his ego. She could have been...so good, such a big star, and he just undermined her. She never stood a chance of making it after she met him.'

'A lot of people don't make it in the theatre for a lot of reasons.'

'No, it was him. He destroyed her. Because he knew she was better and more talented than he was. She stood in his way.' His words were repeated in the monotone of obsession.

'And where is she now?'

'I've no idea. But wherever she is, she's nothing – nothing to what she could have been.'

'And you loved her?'

'Yes.'

'Did she love you?'

'Yes, at first. Then he came along...I wanted to marry her. She refused. Said she loved him. That's impossible. There is nothing about him to love.'

'And what happened to you? Why did you give up acting? I know you started at Cheltenham.'

'My, you have done your homework. Why did I give up acting? I gave it up because nobody wanted to employ me. I'd had a good run as a child star, but it's difficult to make the break from child to juvenile. And I lost my looks, which didn't help. I developed this acne, my hair turned darker. Nobody thought I was pretty any more. I had three years of nothing. And then I thought, stuff it, I'll go into the stage management side.'

'But didn't Christopher Milton recognise you when you started on this show?'

'I don't know. I doubt it. He's totally unaware of other people.' There was another pause. The ambulance moved slowly through the Friday afternoon traffic. Charles began again. 'But, Spike, why? I can see that you hated him, I can see that you wanted revenge, but why do it this way?'

'I had to show him up in public for what he was,' Spike repeated doggedly.

'But the things you had to do to achieve that…I mean, beating up Kevin McMahon, running Pete Masters over…It's all so cruel, so mean.'

'Exactly,' said Spike as if this proved his point. 'Christopher Milton is cruel and mean. That's what I had to show the public. I have seen inside his mind. That's what he would have wanted to happen to people.'

'But he didn't do it, Spike. You did it.'

'He wanted to.' The line came back insistently.

'But, Spike, people got hurt. Mark Spelthorne got killed. That's murder, Spike.'

'It was suicide. I had nothing to do with that.'

'Do you mean it?'

'Christopher Milton drove him to suicide.'

'And you didn't help him on his way?'

'No.' The answer came back so casually that Charles believed it.

'But, Spike, I still can't understand why you did it.'

'Perhaps you can't, but then you didn't grow up with him, you didn't see him use people, destroy people, always. You didn't see the smile of satisfaction on his face when someone was removed from his path. You didn't feel him all the time undermining your confidence. You didn't see him grinning with triumph every time he came out on top. He is a monster and the public should know it. Someone like that shouldn't be allowed to win all the time.'

'What do you think made him like that?'

'Ambition for stardom, He wants to be the best. Oh, I know what it's like. I was big in my teens. I was hailed as the great white hope of English theatre. I was going to get to the top. I understand the kind of pressure that puts you under. And I know that you've got to get out of it and love people, not treat them like dirt.'

'Hmm.' Charles was about to comment on how Spike had treated people but he went on on another tack. 'Do you think he's happy?'

'Happy? So long as he's on top, yes.'

So Charles told him what he had discovered that morning, how Christopher Milton could not face life without an hour of psychoanalysis a day, how he lived in fear of discovery of his weakness, how his life was split between public acclamation and private misery. 'How can he be happy when he doesn't even know who he is? His changes of mood are so violent because he has no real identity. That's why he clings to his fictional self. Lionel Wilkins is more real to him than Christopher Milton and it is only when he is in that character, hearing the adulation of an audience, that he feels alive. You hate him, you can despise his behaviour, but don't ever think he's happy. His desperate concern for his career is only because he lives through it. Take it away and you kill him.'

There was another long silence. Then Spike grunted, 'He's a bastard.' His mind couldn't cope with an idea that challenged his long-held obsession.

The ambulance swung round into the gates of the hospital. Charles felt weak. The pain in his ankle was burning fiercely again. 'The question now is,' he said with effort, 'what are we going to do about it.'

'I suppose you'll report me to the police.' Spike's voice was dull. 'That's presumably what the management put you into the company to do – find the wrong-doer and see him brought to justice.'

'On the contrary, they brought me in to the company to find the wrong-doer and to hush up the whole affair.'

'Ah.'

'And I don't see why I shouldn't do just that. That is, if you've been persuaded of the pointlessness of your vendetta. You cannot do worse to him than he does to himself. You cannot destroy the real Christopher Milton, because it doesn't exist.'

'So in fact you're letting me off?'

'Yes, but, by God, if anything else happens in this show, you'll have the entire police force descending on you from a great height.'

'And if I actually strike at the *star* himself?'

'I don't think you will.'

'Well, thanks.' The ambulance came to a stop and the men got out to open the back door. 'So you reckon he's a real wreck?'

'Yes. If that gives you any cause for satisfaction.'

'Oh, it does, it does.'

'What will you do – leave the show?'

'I'll have to, won't I?'

Charles was pulled out and placed on a trolley. Spike still didn't seem able to leave. He wanted to taste the last drop of news of his rival's degradation. 'So it's driven him mad. That happens. There's a danger of that with anyone who's ever been even vaguely in contact with stardom. They lose all touch with reality.'

'Yes,' said Charles, but, locked in his own world, Gareth Warden seemed unaware of the irony.

PART V

First Night

CHAPTER EIGHTEEN

THE FIRST NIGHT of *Lumpkin!* at the King's Theatre on Thursday, November 27th 1975 was a major social and theatrical event. Everyone was there.

Included in everyone, though less famous and glamorous than many of the rest of everyone, were Charles Paris and his wife Frances. She had somehow heard about his accident and come down to visit him in the Brighton hospital. His injuries were not too bad. Apart from extensive bruising, the only real damage was a broken ankle. In fact, the rather gloomy young doctor who dealt with him described it as a Pott's fracture and said that with a fall like that, he was lucky not to have crushed a few vertebrae, fractured his calcaneum and broken his sternum. He was out within a week, complete with a cartoon plaster on his foot and a pair of authentic-looking tubular crutches. There was no chance of his appearing in the show and there was talk of compensation from the company. The wheel had come full circle; his identification with Everard Austick was now complete.

It was difficult to say where he stood with Frances. She had accepted his invitation to the first night and there had been no mention of Alec, the scoutmaster. And yet she seemed distant. Perhaps just making her point that she was no longer around whenever he needed picking up out of depression. It wasn't a tangible change, but it made him feel that if really he did want her back, he'd have to work for her.

It was like going out with someone for the first time, not knowing which way the evening would turn out.

In the crowded foyer they met William Bartlemas and Kevin O'Rourke, a pair of indefatigable first-nighters resplendent in the Victorian evening dress they always affected for such occasions. Why, Charles...' exclaimed Bartlemas.

'Charles Paris...' echoed O'Rourke.

'What *have* you been doing to yourself...?'

'You have been in the wars...'

'What was it – some tart stamp on your foot...?'

'I don't think you've met my wife, Frances.'

'Wife? Dear, oh dear. Never knew you were married...'

'Lovely to meet you though, Frances...'

'Lovely, Frances darling. Such a pretty name…'

'But Charles, I thought you were *in* this show…'

'But obviously the leg put you out. You know what it was, O'Rourke, someone wished him luck. You know, the old theatrical saying – break a leg…'

'Break a leg! Oh, that's too divine…'

'Going to be a marvellous show tonight, isn't it, Charles…?'

'Well, of course you'd *know*, wouldn't you? I mean, you've been working with him. Such a clever boy, isn't he, Christopher...?'

'Clever? More than clever. That boy is an A1, thumping great star. If the national press don't all agree about that in the morning, I'm a Swedish *au pair* girl…'

'Oh, but they will. He is such a big star. I think he's really brought stardom back into the business. We've had all those dreary little actors with Northern accents who spend all their time saying how they're just like ordinary people…'

'But stars shouldn't be like ordinary people. Stars should be larger than life…'

'And Christopher Milton is…so big. We were reading an interview with him in one of the Sundays…'

'By some American girl, Suzanne somebody...very good it was…'

'Oh, super. And you've been working with him, Charles. That must have been wonderful…'

'Yes, but wonderful.

It was very strange seeing a show he had been with for so long from out front, but perhaps less strange with *Lumpkin!* than it would have been with anything else. It had changed so much since he last saw it that it was like seeing a new show. The cast must have been working every hour there was since Brighton. And they did well. The first-night sparkle was there and they were all giving of their best.

The show had gained in consistency of style. Wally Wilson had also been working away like mad and, for all the part he played in the final product, Oliver Goldsmith might as well have taken his name off the credits. Charles reflected that in the whole case there had only been one murder – that of *She Stoops to Conquer*.

The changes had involved more cuts and now Tony Lumpkin's part totally overshadowed all the others. In less skilled hands than those of Christopher Milton it would have overbalanced the show, but the star was at his brilliant best. He leapt about the stage, singing and dancing whole new numbers with amazing precision and that perfect timing which had so struck Charles at the early rehearsals in the Welsh Dragon Club. The show would be a personal triumph. It was bound to be if it succeeded at all, because no other member of the cast got a look in.

At the interval there was a buzz of satisfaction in the audience. Charles, who was feeling tired and achey after his bruises, couldn't face the rush for the bar and sat quietly with Frances. Greatly daring, like a schoolboy on his first date, he put his hand on hers and squeezed it. She returned the pressure, which made him feel ridiculously cheerful. Their hands interlocked and he felt the familiar kitchen-knife scar on her thumb.

He looked at the busy stalls. He could see Kevin McMahon in the middle of a congratulatory throng, smiling with satisfaction. Gwyneth, David Meldrum's assistant, was coming up the aisle towards him. They were like creatures from a previous existence.

Gwyneth stopped by his seat to ask how he was. He told her, but she hung around, for the first time in their acquaintance seeming to want a conversation. He asked a few idle questions about the company and production details. Running out of things to say, he asked, 'Who's the new stage manager?'

'New one? Why, it's still Spike.'

'Still Spike?'

'Yes, of course. He's in charge in the fly gallery tonight.'

A familiar cold trickle of anticipation crept into Charles as the lights dimmed for the second act.

It continued to go well. The audience, enlivened by their gins and tonics, seemed more relaxed and receptive. The show was building up to the climax of the Chase Scene. The profusion of comic business meant that no one was aware of the butchery that the plot had undergone. The audience exploded with laughter time and again. Only Charles Paris was silent.

The Chase Scene arrived and the audience roared. Charles held his breath when it came to the Star Trap moment, but the machinery of the King's Theatre delivered its burden safely on stage at the correct time and gained an enormous laugh.

But the respite for Charles was only temporary. He knew what was happening behind the scenes. While doubles onstage continued their interweaving and dancing, the real Tony Lumpkin climbed to the gallery where he would have the Kirby wire attached to the corset he was already wearing. The audience laughed away at the action onstage while Charles fought with the nausea of horror.

Bang on cue, Christopher Milton appeared. He descended slowly from the heavens and his appearance gathered the round of applause that always attends spectacular stage effects.

The pace of his descent suddenly accelerated. The applause died as if it had been switched off. No longer was the star coming down at a controlled speed; he was free-falling. The real panic in his eyes and the jerking of his arms and legs communicated his fear to the audience. For about twenty feet he fell and then sharply the wire was taken up again and he came to rest bobbing about five feet above the stage.

There was a long pause while Charles could feel the agony of the corset cutting under the star's arms. Then Christopher Milton pulled a Lionel Wilkins face and said, 'I beg yours?' The house erupted into laughter and applause.

And that was how the rest of the show went. Everything that should have got laughs did, every song was applauded to the echo and Christopher Milton could do no wrong. At the end there were twelve curtain calls and the audience was still shouting for more when the curtain came down for the last time.

Afterwards Charles, who was the least showbiz-conscious person in his profession, felt he had to go round backstage. There was an enormous mêlée of people outside the stage door.

He met one of the stage management struggling out against the crowd (no doubt sent by thirsty actors to stock up with drinks before the pubs closed). She recognised him. 'How are you? Wasn't it marvellous tonight?'

'Great. Barbara, where's Spike?'

'Well, that's strange. I don't know. He was in the gallery and then there was that cock-up in the Chase Scene. Did you notice it?'

'I think the whole audience noticed it.'

'Oh no. Apparently most of them thought it was deliberate. Anyway, Spike went off straight after that. It was very strange, he said something about some things you can't beat and that he was leaving and wouldn't be coming back. And he went. Amazing, isn't it? He always was a funny bloke.'

'Yes,' said Charles. 'He was.'

At that moment the stage door crowd surged forward and Charles and Frances found themselves swept into the theatre. Standing in the green room (he had been mobbed before he could even get to his dressing-room) was Christopher Milton. He was smiling, radiant, happy, as the world milled around him and everyone said how marvellous he was.

He saw Charles and reached out a hand to wave across the throng. 'Hello. Are you better? What did you think of it?'

'Bloody fantastic,' said Charles. And he meant it.

AN
AMATEUR CORPSE

DEDICATED TO SOPHIE

CHAPTER ONE

THE CAST PARTY for the Breckton Backstagers' production of *The Seagull* was held, like all their cast parties, in the rehearsal room. Drinks were served in the bar (known to the members as the Back Room) and were paid for by a collection made during the run by the Assistant Stage Manager. The choice, displayed on the bar, was cheap Spanish red in two-litre bottles or cheap Spanish white in two-litre bottles.

Charles Paris was the first to arrive in the Back Room after the curtain fell on the Saturday night. His friend Hugo Mecken had stopped off in the Gents on the way from the theatre. The cast were still creaming off their make-up and slipping out of costumes and most of their hangers-on were hanging on in the dressing rooms, spraying out wild congratulations and faint praise. Hugo, Charles noticed without surprise, had not gone backstage to congratulate his wife Charlotte on her performance as Nina.

Charles was conscious of his interloper status. So, judging from his sour expression, was the thin man in a cravat who stood behind the bar. Charles tried, 'A glass of red, please.'

'Are you a member?'

It was a perfect example of what Charles remembered being taught about in Latin school – a question expecting the answer no. It got it.

'Then I'm afraid I can't give you a drink.'

'My name is Charles Paris. I was invited down here this evening to see the show because I'm leading the Critics' Circle discussion on Tuesday.'

'Ah. Well, in that case, a member will be able to get. you a drink.'

'But I can't get one for myself?'

'Not unless you are a member.'

Charles was beginning to get angry. 'And how much would it cost me to become a bloody member?'

'Two pounds a year Social Membership or five pounds Acting Membership. Though for that, of course, you have to pass an audition,

With difficulty Charles didn't say what he thought of the idea of himself, as a professional actor, having to audition for a tin-pot suburban amateur dramatic society. He channelled his annoyance into slamming two pounds down on the counter. 'Right, there you are. I'm a Social Member. Now give me a drink.'

'I'm afraid your application has to be endorsed by a member.'

Hugo appeared slap on cue from the Gents. 'Right, here's my endorsing member – Hugo Mecken. I'm Charles Paris, there's my two pounds, now give me a drink.'

'What's the trouble, Charles?' asked Hugo.

'I'm joining the bloody society, so that I have a license to breathe in this place."

'Oh, you don't need to – '

'I've joined. Red wine, please.'

'And for me too, Reggie.'

Sour Reggie paused for a second, searching for another rule that was being contravened. Failing to find one, he ungraciously half-filled two wine-glasses.

They drank. Charles contemplated Hugo. Olive-coloured skin. his head a bald dome fringed with black hair, dark eyes darting about uneasily. The lips, heavy with indulgence in the good things of life, turned down, registering that the Backstagers' Spanish plonk wasn't among them.

Charles was conscious of the 'silence. He often had difficulty in thinking of what to say to Hugo. It had always been the same, even when they first met at Oxford back in 1947. They had been friends, but conversation had never flowed easily.

And when they had remet a couple of months previously it had been exactly the same. A great warmth, affection for each other, but not a lot to say. A good working-relationship, socially no overt strain. Just a slight tension within Charles from a sense of Hugo's dependence on him. Hugo was almost too hospitable, inviting Charles down to Breckton all the time, pressing a spare house key on him, telling him to use the place as his own.

But the re-established contact had been a godsend at least from the financial point of view. Hugo seemed likely to put a lot of work his way after what had been a very lean year, even by the modest standards of Charles Paris's theatrical career.

Hugo Mecken was the Creative' Director of Mills Brown Mazzini, a small but thriving advertising agency in Paddington, and he had introduced Charles to the lucrative world of commercial voice-over work. It was a strange world to Charles, one that he was still trying to come to terms with, to fit into his picture of what being an actor meant.

The pause had gone on too long for comfort. Charlotte's very good.' Charles volunteered.

'Should be. Professionally trained.' The shortness of Hugo's response confirmed his suspicion that all was not well with the marriage.

'I feel like 'getting obscenely pissed,' Hugo continued suddenly, and drained his glass.

It was a familiar cry. The word 'pissed' was of the seventies but the intention was one which Charles had often heard from Hugo thirty years before at Oxford. Sometimes it had been a danger signal. A sudden lurch of mood, a lot to drink and then bizarre midnight exploits, wild destruction of college windows or other fierce extravagances until the passion subsided into somnolence and, later, self-abasing recrimination.

While Hugo outstared sour Reggie into refilling their glasses Charles reviewed his friend's marital history. First wife, Alice, married straight out of Oxford. Rather swish do in Worcester College Chapel at which Charles had been present. Two children soon after, all set on conventional course.

Then, over twenty years later, news from a mutual friend, Gerald Venables, that Hugo had contacted him in his professional capacity as a solicitor and wanted a divorce. He had upped and left Alice with two teenagers, and moved in with sonic twenty-two-year-old actress with whom he'd done a commercial.

A couple of years later, a scribbled note on Snoopy paper (strong contrast to the heavy die-stamped invitation to Worcester Chapel) asked Charles to a post-registry office piss-up in an expensive Soho trattoria.

Through hazes of alcohol, Charles could recall that riotous meal. Hugo and Charlotte dressed in identical oyster-grey velvet suits, a lot of advertising people, a lot of showbiz. A truly glittering occasion. Charlotte so young, so unbelievably beautiful, her complexion glowing and red hair sparkling in the coloured lights of the restaurant. And' Hugo boisterous as a schoolboy, his bald dome gleaming, his face alive with the knowledge that every man in the room envied him.

Then it had all seemed possible. That one could start again. It even convinced Charles how right he had been to leave his own wife Frances. Somewhere, round some corner, there was a perfect young girl waiting for him, someone who could make it all happen again.

Mostly it had been the drink thinking for him. But there had been more than that. Hugo, in a good mood, was a fierce romantic and he could infect others with his enthusiasm. He could make everyone believe that the world was perfectible, that it was only a matter of time before paradise was re-established on earth.

Charles remembered acting in a play which Hugo had written at Oxford, a play full of soaring, impossible romanticism. But that had been a long time ago, when Hugo had been going to he the world's greatest playwright, when he had been in love with Alice, when he'd 'been on a permanent high.

As he returned with the drinks, Hugo was patently not on a high. He looked ill at ease, vulnerable, potentially petulant.

The rehearsal room was beginning to fill up now, as the stars of the Backstagers emerged in their party finery. Charles was relieved to see they all got the same vinegary reception from Reggie at the bar. (Maybe he had made the mistake of trying the wine.)

Hugo seemed to know many of the people who came in. Though not involved in the acting side, he was a regular of the Back Room, using it as his local, often dropping in for a drink on his way home from work. He dished out some abrupt nods and deterrent smiles to acquaintances, but seemed anxious to stay with Charles. It was reminiscent of parties in their first terms at Oxford, staying together shy against the wall until they had had enough to drink to risk a social foray.

A young man in jeans and a denim shirt came over to them. His face still glowed with the scrubbing it had taken to remove the make-up and there were streaks of greasepaint behind his ears. Charles recognized him from the stage, where less than half an hour before he had gone out to shoot himself in the character of Konstantin. In his own character, he didn't look suicidal. Cocky would be a better word. A handsome young face, pulled out of true by lines of arrogance around the mouth.

'Hugo! How'd you like it?' He must have been nearly thirty years younger, but the tone was patronizing.

'Fine.' Hugo was unexpansive.

'Little lady did well.'

Hugo flicked a one-frame smile across his face.

Konstantin looked speculatively at Charles. Then, deciding that Hugo was not going to introduce them, he reached out a man-of-the-world hand. 'I'm Clive Steele.'

'Charles Paris.'

'Thought you must be. Charlie said the old man was bringing you.' Charles felt Hugo stiffen. Difficult to tell whether it was at his wife's nickname or his own designation. The boy continued with a self-deprecating smile. 'Well, how did it seem to you, Charles? How did the stumbling efforts of the amateurs seem to you as a professional theatre man?'

The boy was not really asking his opinion; he was fishing for compliments. Charles didn't know whether to give a vague reassurance as he would to any professional actor after a performance or to do exactly as he had been asked and give professional criticism. It was something he was going to have to sort out before the Critics' Circle on the Tuesday.

He made some trimming remark about the show with an ambiguous comment on Clive's performance. It was a waste of ambiguity; Clive took it as a straight compliment.

The conversation eddied. Clive, unprompted, but assuming its unfailing interest, provided his life story. He was becoming an accountant. The next week he had to go to Melton Mowbray on an audit. All bloody week. He had done a lot of productions with the Breckton Backstagers, mostly leads.

Charles couldn't resist it. 'Yes, amateur dramatic societies are always hard-up for young men.

But Clive was well armoured with self-opinion. 'Certainly for ones who can act and are anything like decent-looking.'

Charles didn't bother any more. The conversation was nearly dead, now he had withdrawn. But the boy kept talking. Like Hugo, Clive didn't seem to want to leave this particular corner. They both seemed to be waiting for something. Charles. wondered if it was Charlotte.

A new couple came over and gave the conversation the kiss of life. This time Hugo remembered his social graces. 'This is Charles Paris. Charles, Denis and Mary Hobbs.'

'Oh dear,' Mary giggled, 'you're the one who's going to pass judgment on our performance. Now I do hope you'll treat us just like professionals.'

It took him a minute or two to place her. She looked so different in the turquoise trouser suit, orange silk blouse and rainbow lamé slippers. And the blonded hair and too-young make-up. But when he added a rust-coloured pre-Revolutionary Russian dress and a high-piled black wig... 'Of course. Madame Arkadina. I'm so sorry. I just didn't recognize you.'

Yes, he was full of admiration for her make-up. On her performance he hoped he wouldn't be drawn. That kind of criticism could well wait till the Tuesday. In spite of himself, he found he was forming phrases of his real critical opinion. Such a pity that amateurs are always tempted by classic plays. Just because they're classics, it doesn't mean they're easy to do. In fact, often just the reverse. Arkadina is one of the great roles of the theatre and not to be handed out at random to anyone who happened to have' recited nicely at the Women's Institute Concert. Amateurs should stick to what's within their range – Agatha Christies, frothy West End comedies, nothing that involves too much subtlety of characterization. Leave Chekhov to the professionals.

Good God, there were only two people in that cast tonight who got within a mile of what it was about – Charlotte as Nina and the guy who played Trigorin. The rest should take up something else to fill their evenings – like stamp-collecting.

Even as he framed the thoughts, he knew he was overreacting. It was the irrational but instinctive response of anyone who made his living by acting. The very existence of amateur dramatic societies seemed to cast doubt on the seriousness of his profession.

Mary Hobbs was in full theatrical spate. 'Oh God, there was a terrible moment in the first act, when we were meant to be watching Konstantin's play and I had 'this line about there being a smell of sulphur, and I think one of the stage managers had brought some fish and chips into the wings, because suddenly we all got this amazing whiff of vinegar across the stage, and I caught Geoff's eye and I'm afraid I just went. Total, absolute corpse. I turned upstage. I don't know if anyone noticed in the audience...'

Charles had noticed. Any experienced actor would have been aware of the tell-tale snort and sudden movement. And how typical of the Backstagers that they should have: all the theatrical slang. A 'corpse' was a breakdown into laughter on stage.

Mary Hobbs appealed to her husband. 'Did you notice it, Den?'

'Blimey, no. Couldn't take my eyes off your missus, Hugo, I didn't see much else, eh?'

He erupted with laughter. Not particularly amused laughter, just the sort that some 'hearty people use around their speech like quotation marks.

The reactions to his remark were interesting. Hugo grimaced in an irritated way, as if he didn't want to be reminded of Charlotte's existence. Mary Hobbs flashed a look of reproof which quelled her husband. He looked like a schoolboy who had spoken out of turn., gauche as if he shouldn't have said anything in his rough voice while his wife was present to elocute for the two of them.

Mary's admonition was over in a second and she resumed her theatrical reminiscence. 'Of course, Geoffrey didn't break up. He is marvellous. Didn't you think he was marvellous, Charles? Geoffrey Winter, our Trigorin. He's so clever. We really all think he ought to go on the stage professionally. He's so much better than most professional actors you see on the telly-box.'

Charles didn't know whether this was meant to be deliberately rude, but let it pass. Mary Hobbs didn't seem to need reaction to impel her dialogue. She sighed dramatically, 'Oh, It's all over. *Quelle tristesse.*'

'Till the next one.' Denis supplied her cue promptly, as if to make up for his earlier faux pas.

'Till the next one. *Winter's Tale.* Dear old Shakespeare. Start rehearsing next week.'

There was a moment of silence and Hugo seemed to wake up to some sort of social duty. But his question showed he had not been listening to the conversation. 'Now the show's over, Denis, will you be able to get some weekends down at the cottage?'

Denis gave his punctuation of laughter. 'Yes, not before time. I must say we've been living Chekhov this last couple of months. And what with all the Sunday afternoon rehearsals, we only got away one weekend since August.'

'Still we are going away this weekend.' Again the edge of reproof in his wife's voice.

Denis compensated quickly. 'Oh yes. It's just one of the penalties of marrying talent, eh?' Another unmotivated eruption. Mary smiled and he reckoned he could risk a little joke. 'She's spent so much time here recently I kept saying why didn't she move in? After all, we're only next door.' This too was apparently very funny.

Mary graciously allowed him this little indulgence and then felt it was time to draw attention to her magnanimity. 'Still, this weekend I'm going to make it all up to you, aren't I?' She took her husband's hand and patted it with a coquettishness which Charles found unattractive in a woman in her fifties. 'First thing in the morning, when all the rest of the naughty Backstagers are sleeping off their hangovers; we'll be in the new Rover sweeping off down to the cottage for a little delayed weekend. All tomorrow, and all Monday – well, till nine or so when we'll drive back. Just the two of us. A second honeymoon – or is it a third?'

'Three hundredth,' said Denis, which was the cue for another explosion of merriment.

Charles escaped to get more drinks. Soon the wine would cease to taste of anything and his bad temper would begin to dissipate.

While he queued at sour Reggie's bar, he looked around at the kindling party. There was music now, music rather younger than the average age of those present. But the pounding beat was infectious.

As the room filled, he was increasingly aware of the common complaint of amateur dramatic societies – that there are always more women than men. And some of them were rather nice. He felt a little glow of excitement. No one knew him down in Breckton. It was like being given a whole new copybook to blot.

Some couples were dancing already. Charlotte Mecken was out there, with her arms around Clive Steele. They were moving together sensuously to the slow pounding of the music. But what they were doing was paradoxically not sexy. It had the air of a performance, as if they were still on stage, as if their closeness was for the benefit of the audience, not because it expressed any real mutual attraction.

The same could be said of the Trigorin, Geoffrey Winter. He was dancing with a pretty young girl, whose paint-spattered jeans suggested she was one of the stage staff. They were not dancing close, but in a jerky slow motion pantomime. Geoffrey moved well, his body flicking in time to the music, like a puppet out of control. But again it was a performance of a body out of control, not genuine abandon. Each movement was carefully timed; it was well-done, but calculated.

Charles had noticed the same quality in the man's stage performance. It had been enormously skillful and shown more technique than the rest of the cast put together, but it had been mannered and ultimately artificial, a performance from the head rather than the heart.

The man was good-looking in an angular way. Very thin, with grey hair and pale eyes. He wore a black shirt, black cord jeans and desert boots. There was something commanding about him, attractive in not just the physical sense of the word.

As Charles watched he saw the man change partners and start a new dance with another little totty. 'Enjoying himself, isn't he?"

He turned to the owner of the voice which had spoken beside him. A young woman of about thirty. Short mousy hair, wide green eyes. Attractive. She was following Charles's gaze towards the dancing Trigorin. 'My husband.'

She said it wryly. Not bitterly or critically, but just as if it were a fact that ought to be established.

'Ah. I'm Charles Paris.'

'Thought, you must be.' Charles felt the' inevitable actor's excitement that she was going to say she recognized him from the television. But no. 'You're the only person down here I didn't recognize. And I knew you'd be in tonight because you're doing the crit on Tuesday, so, by a process of elimination...'

'I'm Vee Winter, by the way. Though I act here under my maiden name, Vee le Carpentier. I always think if people see in programmes that the leads are played by people with the same surname, they get to think the Backstagers are awfully cliquey.' Before Charles had time to take in this statement, she went on, 'Have you met Geoffrey?'

'No, just seen him on stage. He's very talented.' Charles didn't volunteer whether he thought the talent was being appropriately used.

'Yes, he's talented.' She changed the subject abruptly.

'Since you're coming down to do this thing on Tuesday, why not have a meal with us beforehand?'

'That's very kind,' said Charles, wondering if he ought to check whether Hugo and Charlotte were expecting him.

Vee took it as assent. 'About half-past seven. The Critics' Circle isn't till eight-thirty. I'll give you our phone number in case you have problems.'

'Fine.' Charles made a note of the number. Then he added, because he was beginning to understand suburban timetables, 'Seven-thirty then. After the children are asleep.'

'We don't have any children,' said Vee Winter.

Sour Reggie dispensed Charles's order for drinks as if the country were threatened by imminent drought. Vee helped carry the glasses back to the group.

She seemed to know them all. She made some insincere compliment to Mary Hobbs about her Arkadina.

'Oh, that's sweet of you to say so, darling. Actually. The voice dropped with the subtlety of a double declutch on a worn gear-box. '.1 still think you would have made a better Nina, but, you know, Shad gets these ideas....

The circle had enlarged in Charles's absence to include an elderly man with a white goatee beard. And Hugo's mood had shifted into something more expansive. 'Charles, I don't think you've met Robert Chubb. Bob, this is Charles Paris. Bob's the founder of the whole set-up. Started the Backstagers back in....ooh...'

'Nineteen hundred and mind-your-own-business,' supplied Robert Chubb jovially. 'First productions in the Church Hall, mind you. Come some way since then. Started the fund for this complex in 1960...and ten years later it was all finished.' He gestured to the rehearsal room and theatre.

It was an impressive achievement. Charles bit back his cynical views on the subject of amateur theatre and said so.

Robert Chubb seemed to have been waiting for this cue to launch into the next instalment of his monologue. 'Well, I thought, I and a few like-minded cronies, that there should be some decent theatre in Breckton. I mean, it's so easy for people in the suburbs to completely lose sight of culture.

'So we damned well worked to set up something good – not just your average amateur dramatic society, performing your Agatha Christies and your frothy West End comedies, but a society with high professional standards, which kept in touch with what was happening in the theatre at large. And that's how the Backstagers started.'

Charles felt he was being addressed like a television interviewer who had actually asked for this potted history. And his interviewee continued. 'And now it's grown like this. Enormous membership,. great waiting list of people from all over South London keen to join in the fun. Lots of Press coverage – particularly for our World Premières Festival.

'It just keeps getting bigger. Now we run our own fort-nightly newsletter to keep people informed of what we're up to – called *Backchat*, don't know if you've seen it?'

'No.'

'Then of course this bar's called the Back Room.'

'I see, everything's Back-something-or-other?'

'Yes, Rather nice, isn't it?'

Charles's mind began seething with new permutations of Back-, most of them obscene. It was perhaps as well that Hugo spoke before he launched into any of them. 'We must get Charles down here to do a production, eh, Bob?'

It was Charles's turn to be self-deprecating. 'Oh, come on, Hugo, I'm a professional actor. Much as I'd like to do it, I'm likely to be off touring or something at a moment's notice.'

'Nonsense. This voice-over campaign's really going to take off. You'll be stuck in London with more work than you can cope with.'

'When that happens – ' Charles joked, 'and I won't believe it until it does – I'll be prepared to do a production for the Backstagers.' That seemed to get him safely off the hook.

But a new voice joined the circle and qualified his remark. 'If,' of course, you do a successful One-Act Productions Audition and your choice of play is 'approved by the Directorial Selection Sub-Committee.' Charles was not surprised to find that the voice came from sour Reggie, the walking rule-book.

'Oh, Charles has had rather a lot of experience as a director.' It was Hugo coming to his rescue. Charles didn't' want rescuing. He thought doing a production for the Breckton Backstagers was a consummation devoutly to be avoided. The atmosphere was getting claustrophobic.

But Hugo's defence was quite impassioned. Again Charles was conscious of the other man's need for him. He was being paraded for the benefit of Hugo's local crowd. In a strange way, it seemed to tie in with Charlotte's behaviour, as if Hugo's ignoring his wife was justified by the fact that he had a genuine professional actor to show off.

Charles was being used and he didn't like it, but Hugo continued with his sales campaign. 'Charles is, a bit of a playwright too. You should get him to write something for the World Premières Festival.'

Charles made some suitably modest response, but Robert Chubb seized on the cue. 'Oh really, if you've got something that hasn't been performed tucked away in a cupboard, do let us see it. We're getting the next Festival sorted out at the moment and one of our expected scripts has just fallen through, so we'd be very interested.'

Charles was tempted. There was in fact an unperformed play sitting in a drawer in his room in Hereford Road. He'd written it after his one successful play, *The Ratepayer*. A light comedy, called *How's Your Father?* It would be quite gratifying to have it done under any circumstances.

But the patronizing tone in which Robert Chubb continued changed his mind. 'It could do you a lot of good,

Charles. Lots of plays we've premiered here have gone on to do awfully well. It's a real chance for an unknown playwright. I don't know if you know George Walsh's *Doomwomb?*'

Charles shook his head. Robert Chubb smiled indulgently at his ignorance. 'That started here.'

'Really?' Suddenly he wanted to scream, wanted to do something appalling, be very rude to someone, break something, get the hell away from all these pretentious idiots.

Rescue came from an unexpected source. He felt an arm round his waist and a female body pressed close to his. 'Dance with me.'

It was Vee Winter.

CHAPTER TWO

SHE WAS A strange woman. She clung to him tightly and he could feel the nervous excitement coursing through her body. In other circumstances, he would have interpreted this as a sexual message and responded in kind, but that somehow didn't seem appropriate. The excitement had nothing to do with him. He was being used for some purpose of her own. Certainly she was working to give the appearance of a sexual encounter, but it was for the benefit of the rest of the room, not for her partner.

Charles wondered at first if it was a ploy to make her husband jealous. Geoffrey was across the room, dancing with circumscribed abandon in front of yet another little dolly and Vee was very aware of his presence. But her behaviour did not seem designed to antagonize him; instead Charles received an inexplicable impression of complicity between husband and wife, as if their performances were co-ordinated parts of an overall plan and would later be laughed over when they were alone together.

This annoyed him. Again he was being used as a counter in a game he didn't understand. The heavy beat of a rock number changed to a soupy ballad and Vee snuggled closer, pressing the contours of her body tightly against his. He realized with surprise that he didn't find this arousing. Vee Winter was an attractive woman, but he didn't fancy her. this gave him a perverse sense of righteousness, as if confirming that his randiness was not absolutely indiscriminate.

He commented rather coldly on her forwardness. 'is this to give food for scandal to the gossip columnist of *Backbite*?'

'Backbite?'

'Your fortnightly magazine.

'That's called *Backchat*.' She corrected him without humour. 'Anyway, it doesn't have a gossip columnist.'

Charles unwisely chose to continue in facetious vein. 'So there's no one to chronicle the backslidings of the Backstagers bopping to Burt Bacharach and their bacchanalian orgies?'

'No.' Vee's reply was absolutely straight. Charles wouldn't have minded if she had said it as a put-down (his attempt at humour had been pretty feeble), but for her not to notice even that the attempt had been made, that he found galling.

'Do you act much here?'

She laughed with incredulity at his question, rather as if someone had

asked the Queen if she had any jewelery. 'Oh I have done a few things, yes.'
'But not *The Seagull*?'
'No.' She stiffened slightly. 'I really' felt I needed a rest. Also I've played
so many leads in the past year, I didn't want it to look as if Geoff and I were
monopolizing the entire society. Ought to give some of the newer members a
chance. And then Shad, who directed, had this strange notion that Nina ought
to have red hair. He's a rather quirky director, if you know what I mean.'
Through the excuses, Charles knew exactly what she meant.

He took the end of a record as an opportunity to end their clinch. He looked
over at the group round Hugo and couldn't face it yet. He needed just to get out
of the place for a moment. The sweet wine was making him feel sick. Pausing
only to pick up someone's full glass off a table, he left the rehearsal room.
The change was as welcome as he had anticipated. In spite of the summery
days of that fall, October was nearing its end and the evenings were chilly.
The slap of cold air was refreshing. He leaned against the inside of the porch
and breathed deeply.
Then he heard the voices. Charlotte Mecken and Clive Steele. Arguing in
fierce whispers. First Charlotte's voice, the veneer of drama school thinned
by emotion to reveal its Northern Irish origin. 'I'm sorry, Clive, you've got it
completely wrong. I never knew you were thinking that.'
'Whit was I meant to think, after all those rehearsals, when you suddenly
got all emotional and confided in me when I drove you home?'
'I'm sorry. I shouldn't have broken down. I just…it was all too much…'
'Well, I made the perfectly natural assumption that – '
'It may have seemed perfectly natural to you, but – '
'It bloody well did. Look, if it's your husband you're worried about, forget
it. It's bloody obscene you being married to him anyway. Reminds me of all
those jokes about young girls on their wedding nights feeling old age
creeping all over them – '
'Clive. stop it. You've got the wrong end of the stick. So completely the
wrong end. It's all much more complicated than you can begin to imagine.
Look, I'm sorry if you've been hurt, but I can assure you – '
'Oh, stuff that! All right, you've made your point. I see what's been
happening now. There is a word for women who lead men on you know.'
'Clive, if I'd had any idea of what was going through you mind – '
'Oh shut up. I'm going.'
'Be careful.'
'Don't worry, I will. I'm not like Konstantin – I'm not going to go off and
shoot myself because some tart's let me down. If I were to do anything, I can
assure you it would be something a lot more practical. Goodbye!'
Charles heard a few brisk footsteps across the gravel, a car door open and
slam, then a powerful sports car engine starting and tires screeching off down
the road.

He assumed Charlotte was still there. He gave her two minutes, then, not being an actor for nothing, did his impression of someone coming noisily out of the rehearsal room.

He was aware of her perfume before he saw her. It was very expensive, very distinctive. Whatever Hugo's relationship with his wife, he didn't stint her expenses. Her clothes were also of the best. She was a trendy fashion plate amidst the pervading dowdiness of the Backstagers.

She was leaning against the bonnet of a Volvo in the car park and didn't look as if she had moved for some time. Her face was infinitely miserable.

'Hello, Charlotte. What's up?'

'I don't know. Last night blues,' she lied. 'You should understand about that.'

'Yes. What I usually do is get wildly pissed. Then I don't notice. And the next morning I feel so bad physically that I forget about any emotional upset.'

'Hmm. I'm rather off alcohol at the moment.'

Silence. She looked sensational in the bluish light shed from the rehearsal room. The pain of her expression increased rather than diminished her beauty. The face framed in red hair looked pale and peaky in the thin light. Very young, very vulnerable, a child being brave.

Charles found being with her a relief. She seemed more like a real person than the lot in the rehearsal room. He felt protective towards her. And that made him feel better. He didn't like the boorish bloody-mindedness which the massed Backstagers kindled in him.

'You know, your Nina was very good.'

'Thank you. What are you going to say – I ought to take it up professionally?'

'That's what you were trained for.'

'Yes. A bit pathetic, isn't it really – fully trained actress mucking about with amateur' dramatics.'

'Oh, I don't know. I'm sure, if you pass your Juvenile Lead Audition and are approved by the Big Parts Selection Sub-Committee, you'll get some very juicy roles here.'

Charlotte laughed. 'You seem to have caught on to the atmosphere of the place very quickly. God, what a load of creeps they all seem when you think of them objectively. All with their oversize egos and silly stage names – all those abbreviations and hyphens and extra middle names – it makes me sick when I think about it. I make a point of using their proper names just to annoy them.'

'Do you think you'll do more here?'

'Maybe. I don't know. What's the alternative? I can't see Hugo being keen on my having a real acting career. Anyway, I've lost all the few contacts I ever had in the theatre. Just a housewife with dreams, I suppose.'

'I'm sure you could make it in the real theatre.'

' "You should go on the stage," says Arkadina. 'Yes, that is my one dream,' replies Nina. 'But it'll never come true." '

'Could do.'

But Charlotte's temporary serenity was broken by some memory. 'No, it'll never – oh, everything's such a mess. God knows what's in store for me anyway.'

'Anything you can talk about?'

She hesitated for a moment, on the verge of sharing her burden. But decided against it. 'No. Thanks for the offer, but I'm rather against shoulders to cry on at the moment. It's my own mess and I must sort it out somehow.' She moved resolutely away from the Volvo.

'Are you coming back in, Charlotte?'

'No, I can't face that lot right now. I'm just going to…don't know…have a bit of a walk, try to clear my head or…I don't know, Charles. Tell Hugo I'll be back later. You're staying with us tonight, aren't you?'

'If that's okay.'

'Sure. I'll see you in the morning.' She walked off into the night, pulling her long Aran cardigan round her against the cold.

Hugo had been hard at the Spanish red when Charles got back into the. rehearsal room. But the mood that was settling in was one of catatonic gloom rather than manic violence.

They both continued to drink, resolutely and more or less silently. The party was livening up, with more and more couples clinched on the dance-floor. There were still plenty of spare women, but Charles had lost interest. The intensity of Vee Winter and Charlotte's troubled words had changed his mood. He and Hugo drank as they might have done thirty years earlier at an Oxford party where all the women had been bagged before they arrived.

It was about three when they left. Charles murmured something about Charlotte making her own way home, but Hugo didn't react. He drove them back to his house with the punctilious concentration of the very drunk.

As the Alfa-Romeo saloon crunched to a halt on the gravel in front of the house, he said determinedly. 'Come in and have a nightcap.'

Charles didn't want to. He was tired and drunk and he had a potentially difficult day ahead of him. Also he had a premonition that Hugo wanted to confide in him. Ignobly, he didn't feel up to it.

But Hugo took his silence for assent and they went into the sitting room. Charles stood with his back to the empty fireplace, trying to think of a good line to get him quickly up to bed, while Hugo went over to the drinks cupboard. 'What's it to be?'

He opened the door to reveal a neat parade of whisky bottles. There were up to a dozen brands. Hugo always rationalized the size of the display on the grounds that everyone has a favourite Scotch, but it was really just the potential alcoholic's insurance policy.

Charles missed the opportunity to refuse and weakly chose a Glenmorangie malt. Hugo poured a generous two inches into a tumbler and helped himself to a Johnnie Walker Black Label.

Then they just stood facing each other and drank. Hugo kept the Johnnie Walker bottle dangling in his free hand. The silence became oppressive.

Charles downed his drink in a few long swallows and opened his mouth for thank you and goodnight.

Hugo spoke first. 'Charles,' he said in a voice of uneven pitch, 'I think I'm cracking up,'

'What do you mean?' "

'Cracking up, going round the bend, *losing control*.' The last two words came out in a fascinated whisper.

'Oh come on, you're pissed.'

'That's part of it. I drink too much and I just don't notice it. It doesn't make me drunk, it doesn't calm me down, I just feel the same thing – I'm...losing control.'

'Control of what? What do you think you are going to do?'

'I don't know. Something terrible. I'm going to say something awful, hit somebody or. ...All the constraints I've built up over the years, they're just breaking down...' He mouthed incoherently.

'Oh come on. You've just had too much to drink. It's nothing.'

'Don't tell me it's nothing!' Hugo suddenly screamed. As he did so, he hurled the whisky bottle at the stone mantelpiece to the right of Charles. It shattered. Glass fell into the fireplace and spirit dripped down on to it.

Charles thought the outburst contained more than a dash of histrionics. If his friend wasn't going to believe him, then Hugo was damned well going to give a demonstration of his lack of control. 'Like that, you mean?' asked Charles. 'Out of control like that?'

Hugo looked at him defiantly, then sheepishly, then with a hint of a smile, seeing that his bluff had been called. He sank exhausted into a chair. 'No, not like that. That was just for effect. I mean worse than that. 1 get to a flashpoint and I feel I'm going to lash out – I don't know, to kill someone.'

Charles looked straight at him and Hugo looked away, again slightly sheepish, admitting that the homicidal threat was also for effect.

'Who are you going to kill?' Charles teased. 'Charlotte?' Hugo was instantly serious. 'No, not Charlotte. I wouldn't touch Charlotte. Whatever she did, I wouldn't touch her.'

'Then who?'

Hugo looked at Charles vaguely, distantly, as if piecing together something that had only just occurred to him. Then he said slowly, as if he didn't believe it, 'Friends of Charlotte'.

Charles took a risk and laughed. Hugo looked at him suspiciously for a moment and then laughed too. Soon after they went to bed.

Charles didn't think too much about what Hugo had said. Obviously his friend was under pressure and all wasn't well with his marriage, but most of the trouble was the drink. Anyway, Charles had domestic problems of his own to worry about. His last thought, before he dropped into the alcohol-anaesthetized sleep which was becoming too much of a habit, was the next day he had to see his wife for the first time in five months. At the christening of their twin grandsons. Grandsons, for God's sake.

CHAPTER THREE

THE CHRISTENING WENT okay, he supposed. Difficult to say, really. It was a long time since he had been tu one with, which to compare it. The twins were healthy five-month-old boys and they were successfully received into the Church of England in Pangbourne in Berkshire, which was where Charles's daughter Juliet and her husband Miles (who was apparently carving a successful career for himself in insurance) lived. The boys were named Damian and Julian, which would not have been their grandfather's choice. So everything went as it should have done. But it was not an easy day for Charles. Being with Frances and behaving as if they were still conventional man and wife had been strange. In some ways seductively appealing. His mind was still full of the bourgeois morality of Breckton and he found himself wondering whether it could have worked, he and Frances as a couple, growing old together, building a family, having Juliet and the kids over for Sunday lunch and so on. But deep down he knew that he'd followed the only course open to him when he'd left Frances in 1961. He still loved her, still often would rather spend time with her than anyone else, but he never wanted to get back into the claustrophobia of always being there, always being answerable.

In a way, his leaving her had been as romantic as Hugo's leaving of Alice. But, unlike Hugo, Charles hadn't thought it was all possible, that a new woman could make it all all right again. He had left so as to keep some illusions. He didn't want just to sink into a middle age of disappointed bickering. Nor did he want to feel guilty if he had affairs with other women.

Of course, it hadn't worked. Guilt had remained in some form in all his affairs and much of the time he had been just lonely. But his single state gave him a kind of perverse integrity.

The situation had been complicated when it transpired that Frances had developed some sort of boyfriend. Charles never knew how serious the relationship was. The only thing he did know was that, illogically, it made him jealous.

And so, even more illogically, did seeing Frances so wrapped up in the twins. He felt excluded, as he had when she had been pregnant with Juliet.

That was the trouble. Whenever he saw Frances, unwelcome emotional confusion crowded into his mind. When he didn't see her, he could exist quite happily from moment to moment, without thinking all the time that feelings had to be defined and formalized.

At the christening he hardly saw her. It was a public occasion, there were other people there, he had no real chance to ask her the sort of questions he wanted to. Or felt he ought to.

He went through it all in the train on the way back to London. He must ring Frances – soon. They must meet and talk, really talk.

The day had increased the unease which the atmosphere between Hugo and Charlotte had fomented in him.

He tried to think if there was anything comforting that had emerged. Only the fact that his son-in-law Miles, Mr. Prudent, king of the insurance world, with a policy for every hazard, had not insured against twins.

The Monday recording session was for a series of radio commercials, which was much less hairy than the voice-to-picture session which had preceded it. All Charles had to do was to read some copy in the same voice that he had used in the television commercials.

Not very hard work. And well spread out. Even this simple job was to be done in two sessions: half of the commercials were to be recorded the following Tuesday morning.

The whole voice-over business still puzzled him. Giving a couple of dozen readings of a banal endorsement for some product which no self-respecting housewife should be without didn't fit into his definition of acting.

Still, the money was good, potentially very good. And it was different. And so long as one didn't take it too seriously, it was better than sitting at home waiting for the telephone to ring.

It had started out of the blue some two months before with a bewildered call from his agent, Maurice Skellern. Someone from Mills Brown Mazzini had been enquiring about Charles Paris's availability for voice-over work. That had led to a series of in-house voice tests in a tatty studio at the advertising agency.

Presumably (though no one ever actually told him so) these had been successful because within a week he had been summoned to a session of voice-to-picture tests. These had been more elaborate, in a swish professional dubbing theatre, and attended by an enormous gallery of advertising people, all of whom, it seemed, had the right to give him notes on his performance.

Again (though nobody actually said so) he must have been successful, because soon after he was summoned to put his voice to three television commercials, which were apparently on test transmission in the Tyne-Tees area.

It was Hugo Mecken he had to thank for this new development in his acting career. It seemed that Hugo had secured the account for a new bedtime drink which was being launched by a huge Dutch-owned drugs company. The drink was to be called Bland and the campaign had been agreed on some months before. It was to be led by a cartoon character called Mr. Bland who wore a top-hat and tails. In the launching series of animated television commercials he was to visit a tribe of little fuzzy red creatures called the Wideawakes. When presented with cups of Bland on a silver salver by Mr. Bland, they gradually turned pale blue and fell asleep. Over their snoring, Mr. Bland intoned the words, 'Bland soothes away the day.'

The voice of Mr. Bland, which, if the campaign took off as it was hoped, would be a very lucrative assignment, had gone to Christopher Milton, a well-known stage and television actor (who, apart from his current success in the musical *Lumpkin!* at the King's Theatre, was said by Hugo recently to have signed a contract for £25,000 to do an in-vision commercial for instant coffee).

All this had been agreed with the Brand Manager for Bland, the animation voice-track was recorded and the animation work was started. From which point all should have gone well until the launching of the product.

But during the interval between the agreement of the campaign and the completion of the three test commercials the Brand Manager for Bland had been appointed European Marketing Manager for the huge Dutch-owned drugs company. His successor on Bland, a Mr. Farrow, saw the commercials and, as a matter of principle, didn't like them. Because of the proximity of the launch date and because of the enormous cost of the animation, he couldn't afford to make radical changes in the campaign. So he homed in on the voice.

It was totally wrong. he cried. Far too patronizing, too light, it didn't treat the product seriously enough, suggested that the whole sales campaign was a bit of a joke. Hugo and his associates held back their view that little fuzzy red figures called Wideawakes were not going to look very serious however funereal the voice that addressed them and said yes, of course he was right and they had rather suspected this might be a problem from the start and they'd go straight off and find another voice.

By coincidence, on the very evening of the meeting at which this decision had been made, Charles Paris was appearing in a television play. It was one of the few jobs he had had in a very lean year and he was playing an avuncular Victorian solicitor. His voice was somewhat deeper than usual because he had had a cold at the time of the recording.

Whether it was this odd voice quality or the fact that he had worn tailcoat and top-hat that made him seem to Hugo to be the ideal Mr. Bland, Charles never knew. Secretly he thought it was partly that Hugo knew that he would be easy to work with and that the Creative Director desperately needed to come up with something new. It was evident that Hugo, in a business that thrives on ideas, was beginning to run out of them.

He could feel the pressure from the inventive minds of younger copywriters and the task of finding the new voice for Mr. Bland was a competitive issue in the agency. There were other members of the staff with other candidates and the results of the voice-to-picture tests could well cause some realignment in the creative hierarchy of Mills Brown Mazzini.

So when the new Bland Brand Manager, Mr. Farrow, chose Charles Paris from the test, Hugo was over the moon. It was then that he had started the showing off and parading of his new discovery which had so annoyed Charles at the Backstagers' party.

(For Charles the success was not without irony, because it involved getting one up on Christopher Milton, whose path he had crossed during the accident-haunted rehearsals for the musical *Lumpkin!*)

Charles was now familiar with the small commercial recording studio where he was to work. Through the glossy foyer with its low glass desks and low oatmeal couches, downstairs to the tiny Studio Two.

God knows what the building had been before conversion. A private house maybe, with the studio as a larder. The conversion had consisted mainly of sticking cork tiles on every available surface. In spite of the expensive recording hardware, the whole operation looked unfinished and temporary, as if all the cork could be stripped off and the studio equipment dismantled in half an hour so that the real owner would never know what his premises had been used for during his absence.

Hugo and Farrow were already sitting in the control cubicle. Hugo looked tired and nervous.

They started recording. The copy was so similar to the television version that any notes on performance given in those sessions were still applicable, but Farrow was determined to give them all again. Like all Brand Managers (indeed it is an essential qualification for the job), he was without artistic judgement.

Charles had now done enough of these sessions to know how to behave. Just take it, do as you're told even if it's wrong, don't comment, don't suggest, above all don't try to put any of yourself into it. The agency and, indirectly, the client had hired his voice as a piece of machinery, and it was their right to use it as they thought fit, even if the owner of the machinery knew it wasn't being used in the best way. At worst, there was the comfort that the session was only booked for an hour and he was being paid for it. Thirty-five quid basic, with possible repeats.

So, with his voice lowered an octave to recapture the coldy quality of his Victorian solicitor, Charles gave every possible reading of the lines. He hit each word in turn to satisfy Farrow. BLAND soothes away the day. Bland SOOTHES away the day. Bland soothes AWAY the day. Bland...It did seem a rather pointless exercise for a grown man.

Within half an hour all possible inflections of the lines had been recorded and Charles went from the studio into the control cubicle Farrow was still not happy. After some deliberation, he pronounced, 'I think it may not be the actor's fault this time.' Charles found that charming. 'No, I think it's the copy that's wrong.'

Hugo's voice was extremely reasonable as he replied. 'But you have already passed the copy as suitable for the television commercials, and I thought the idea was to keep the two the same.'

'If so, the idea was wrong,' said Farrow accusingly.

'Well, it was your bloody idea,' Hugo suddenly snapped.

Farrow looked at him in amazement, as if he must have misheard. In times when there was so much competition for big accounts, no member of an agency would dare to disagree with a client. After a pause, he continued as though Hugo had not spoken. 'I'm afraid you advised us wrongly on that. The radio campaign must be entirely rethought. I can see it's easy for you to use the same copy but I'm not the sort of man to take short cuts. I care about this product arid I'm looking for a campaign that's going to be both effective from the sales point of view and also artistically satisfying.'

This was too much for Hugo. 'Christ, now I've heard it all. Artistically satisfying – what the hell do you know what's artistically satisfying? I've listened to enough crap from you and all the other jumped-up little commercial travellers who try to tell me how to do my job. Stick to what you're good at – peddling pap to the masses – and leave me to get on with what I'm good at – making advertising.'

There was a long pause. Mr. Farrow collected together his papers and put them in his briefcase. Had he left the room in silence, it could have been a dignified exit. But he let it down by trying an exit line. 'More powerful men than you, Mr. Mecken, have tried to beat me and failed.'

This delivered in his nasal London whine was suddenly unaccountably funny, and Charles and Hugo both erupted with laughter almost before the door had closed behind the aggrieved Brand Manager.

Hugo's laughter was a short, nervous burst and when it had passed, he looked ghastly, drained of colour. 'Oh shit I shouldn't have done it. I'll have to go after him and apologize. I wasn't thinking – or I was thinking about other things. I just snapped.'

He rose to leave: Suddenly Charles was worried about him, he couldn't forget their drunken conversation on the Saturday night. The outburst against Farrow had sounded like an overdue expression of home truths, but now he wondered if it had been a more fundamental breakdown of control.

Hugo stood dazed for a moment and then started for the door. 'I've booked a table at the Trattoria for twelve-thirty. See you there. I'll get along as soon as I can.'

CHAPTER FOUR

CHARLES WALKED ROUND Soho until it was time to go to the restaurant for another expense account meal. He gave Hugo's name and was shown to a table where there were already two young men.

One he recognized as Ian Compton, a bright copy-writer of about twenty-four who was under Hugo at Mills Brown Mazzini. He was wearing a double-breasted gangster-striped suit over a pale blue T-shirt. Around his neck hung a selection of leather thongs, one for a biro, one for a packet of Gauloise, one for a Cricket lighter and others whose function was not immediately apparent. His lapels bristled with badges, gollies, teddy bears, a spilling tomato ketchup bottle and similar trendy kitsch.

The other was more soberly dressed in a dark jacket and open-necked brown shirt. 'Diccon, this is Charles Paris. I told you about him.' Ian's tone implied that what he had told hadn't been wholly enthusiastic. 'This is Diccon Hudson.'

'Hello.' The name rang a bell. Charles had heard Diccon spoken of as one of the few who made a very good living exclusively from voice-over work.

Diccon looked at him appraisingly. Not rudely, just with great interest, sizing him up professionally. 'So you're the guy who got the Mr. Bland campaign.'

''Fraid so,' said Charles inanely.

'Oh, don't apologize. You win some, you lose some.' So Diccon had been one of his rivals for the job. Intuition told him that he was facing Ian Compton's candidate.

'Who's your agent?' asked Diccon suddenly.

'Maurice Skellern.'

'Never heard of him.' Was there a hint of relief in the voice? 'You want a specialist voice-over agent if you're going to get anywhere in this business.'

'Where's the old man?' asked Ian, as Charles ordered a Scotch.

'Hugo? Oh, he's...he'll be along shortly.' Charles felt it prudent to keep quiet about the scene with Farrow.

It was Diccon's turn for a sudden question. 'Do you know Charlotte?'

'Hugo's wife? Yes.'

'How is she?' The inquiry was poised midway between solicitude and insolence.

'Fine.' Not the moment to share her anxieties of the Saturday night. 'You know her well?'

'Used to. Before she got married. Drama school together. Used to go around with her.' There was a shading of sexual bravado in his tone. 'Quite cut up when she went into the geriatric ward, I was.'

Charles ignored the implied rudeness. 'But now you've managed to forgive Hugo?'

Diccon looked at him very straight. 'Well, he's work, isn't he, love?'

At that moment the subject of their conversation arrived. He was deathly pale. It was impossible to guess at the outcome of his interview with Mr. Farrow. He was in need of a drink. 'Got a lot of catching up to do. Marcello, vodka and Campari for me, please. And the same again for the others.'

Hugo started drinking as if he were trying to catch up on a whole lifetime. He became very jovial, swapping flip dialogue, scandal and crude anecdotes with the two young men in a way that was jarringly out of character. Charles didn't like the sight of Hugo being one of the boys. And he didn't like the way the two young men were responding to it either. Hugo didn't seem to notice the covert smiles that passed between Ian and Diccon, or the hint of mockery in their tones as they spoke to him. It was not just at home that Hugo had problems.

As the drink got through, he became increasingly like a salesman in a dirty joke. At one point he leaned nudgingly across to Diccon. 'What do you say to that bit over there? Chick by the wine rack, eh? Lovely pair of tits.'

'Not bad.' Diccon gave a superior smile. He knew Hugo was making a fool of himself and was enjoying every minute of it.

'That's what women should be like,' Hugo went on in drunken man-of-the-world style. 'Nice firm' little tits. Don't let 'em have children. Never have children. Not worth the effort. Little buggers don't give a damn about you and look what they do to their mothers – make 'em bloody sag, ruin their figures, stop 'em being sexy. That's what women should be about – they're meant just to give you a bloody good time in bed, that's all.'

They had reached the coffee stage. Charles looked round desperately for a waiter to come and bring a bill. He couldn't bear to see Hugo destroying himself much longer.

Diccon Hudson leaned across the table and said to Hugo in a very sincere voice, 'So I take it you and Charlotte won't be starting a family?'

'No chance. I've been through all that and it doesn't work.'

So you've managed to persuade her to go on the Pill. Funny, she always used to be against the idea.'

Diccon's ambiguous indiscretion had been quite deliberate, but Hugo didn't rise to it. 'Huh,' he snorted, 'there are other ways, you know. We didn't have any Pills in our young days, but we managed, didn't we Charles? Eh, we managed.'

Charles had had enough of this barrack-room talk. He rose, 'I've got to be going now actually, Hugo.'

'No, don't go.' The appeal was naked, almost terrified. Charles sat down.

* * * * *

They left the Trattoria an interminable half-hour later, just after three. Diccon Hudson (who had drunk Perrier water through the meal) said he had to go off to his next recording session.

'They keep you busy,' Charles observed and was rewarded by a complacent smile.

'Got an evening session tonight, have you, Diccon?' asked Ian in his usual insolent style.

Diccon coloured. 'No,' he said and left without another word.

After Ian Compton had also gone, Charles turned to his friend. 'Well, Hugo, thanks for the lunch. Look, I'll no doubt see you tomorrow down in Breckton for this Critics' – '

'Don't go, Charles. Let's have another drink. 'S a little club in Dean .Street where I'm a member. C'mon, little quick one.'

The club was a strip joint with gold chairs and a lot of hanging red velvet. A party of Japanese executives and a few morose single men watched a couple of girls playing with each other.

Hugo didn't seem to notice them. He ordered a bottle of Scotch. The boisterous, vulgar stage of drunkenness was now behind him; he settled down to silent, cold-blooded consumption.

Charles drank sparingly. He had the feeling that Hugo was going to need help before the day was out.

He tried asking what was the matter; he offered help.

'I don't want help, Charles, I don't want talk. I just want you to sit and bloody drink with me, that's all.'

So they sat and bloody drank. Clients came and went. The girls were replaced by others who went through the same motions.

Eventually, Hugo seemed to relax. His eyelids flickered and his head started to nod. Charles looked at his watch and put his hand on his friend's arm. 'Come on, it's nearly six. Let's go.'

Hugo was surprisingly docile. He paid the bill (an amount which took Charles's breath away) without noticing. Out in the street he looked around blearily. ''S find a cab, Charles. Get the six-forty-two from Waterloo.'

They were lucky to find one and got to the station in good time. Charles went off to buy a ticket and returned to find Hugo on the platform with a copy of the *Evening Standard* tucked under his arm. Charles made to move a little further down the platform. 'No, Charles, here. Right opposite the barrier at Breckton.'

Sure enough, twenty minutes later they got out of the train opposite the ticket collector. Hugo showed his season ticket with an unconscious reflex movement, turned right out of the station and started to walk along a footpath by the railway line. After a few steps he stopped.

'Come on, Hugo, let's get back to your place. See Charlotte.'

'Charlotte.' There was a deep misery in his echo.

'Yes, Come on.'

'No,' Hugo dithered like a recalcitrant two-year-old. 'No, let's go up to the Backstagers and have a drink.'

'Haven't we had enough drinks?' Charles spoke very gently.

'No, we bloody haven't! Don't you try to tell me when I've had enough!' Hugo bunched his fist and took a wild swing. Charles was able to block it harmlessly, but he felt the enormous strength of frustration in the blow.

Hugo went limp. 'I'm sorry, Charles. I'm sorry. Silly. Come on, come to the Backstagers – just for a quick one. Often go there for a quick one on the way home.'

'All right. A very quick one.'

In the Back Room bar (manned that evening by Robert Chubb) Hugo recommenced his silent, systematic drinking. Charles, himself no mean performer with a bottle, was amazed at his friend's capacity. What made it unnerving was the fact that after the outburst by the station, it no longer seemed to have any effect. Hugo spoke with great care, but without slurring. And still the alcohol poured in, as if fuelling some inner fire, which must soon burst out into a terrible conflagration.

There were a good few Backstagers about. Apparently, this was one of their rare lulls between productions. The Critics' Circle for *The Seagull* the next day and then, on Wednesday, rehearsals for *The Winter's Tale* would start. Charles visualized Shakespeare getting the same perfunctory treatment as Chekhov.

Hugo introduced him liberally to everyone in sight and then left him to fend for himself. Geoffrey Winter was lounging against the bar with a middle-aged balding man dressed in a navy and white striped T-shirt, white trousers, plimsolls and a silly little blue cap with a gold anchor on it.

This refugee from *H.M.S. Pinafore* turned out to be Shad Scott-Smith, director of *The Seagull*. 'Now, Charles,' he emoted when they were introduced, 'promise me one thing – that when you do the Critics' Circle you will really criticize. Treat us just as you would a professional company. Be cruel if you like, but please, please, do be constructive. There's an awful tendency for these meetings to end up just as a sort of mutual admiration society, which really doesn't help anyone.'

'I'll do my best to avoid that.'

'Oh, super. I'm just here actually buying the odd drink of thanks for members of my hardworking cast – libations to my little gods, you could say. Oh, the whole gang did work so hard. I tell you, I'm still a washed-out rag at the end of it all. Still, I at least get a bit of a break now. Do you know, Geoff's going straight on to play Leontes in *The Winter's Tale*. Honestly, I don't know where he get the energy. How do you do it, Geoff?'

Geoffrey Winter shrugged. Charles thought that was a pretty good answer to a totally fatuous question. He warmed to the man.

Shad went on. 'Oh, something happens, I know. The old adrenaline flows.

Leave it to Doctor Footlights, he'll sort you out.'

He breathed between gushes and changed the subject. 'By the way, Geoff, do you know if Charlotte's going to be in this evening? I do want to buy my darling Nina a drink.'

'I've no idea what she's up to. Ask Hugo.'

Charlotte's husband was hunched over a large Scotch at the bar. Shad swanned over. 'Any idea what the little woman's up to this evening?'

'Little woman?' Charles heard a dangerous undertone in Hugo's echo.

'Darling Charlotte,' Shad explained.

'Darling Charlotte...' Hugo began, unnecessarily loud.

'Darling Charlotte may be in hell for all I know. Don't ask me about Charlotte the harlot. She's a bloody whore!'

After the shocked silence which followed this pronouncement, Shad decided that he'd ring Charlotte from home. As he minced away, other Backstagers joined the exodus with desultory farewells. Charles felt guilty, responsible.

'Geoffrey, has Hugo driven them away? He's drunk out of his mind.'

'No, it's not that. This place is used to dramatic outbursts. The mass evacuation is due to the telly. *I, Claudius* tonight. Nine o'clock. Becoming a great cult show. I haven't seen any, been rehearsing. But I'm told it's just the thing for bourgeois commuters' wish-fulfilment. Lots of rapes and murders.'

'Living vicariously.'

'Yes, well, we don't get all that at home. At least, not many of us.'

Charles laughed. 'Actually, I'd better get Hugo home. I hate to think how much alcohol he's got inside him.' He moved over to the bar. 'Hugo, time to go, don't you think?'

Once again this suggestion touched some trigger of violence. Hugo shouted, 'Just keep your bloody mouth shut!' and dashed his glass of Scotch in Charles' face.

Charles was furious. Unaware of the shocked gaze of the remaining Backstagers, he turned on Hugo. 'You're drunk and disgusting!'

'Get lost!'

'You ought to go home. You've had enough.'

'I'll go home when I bloody choose to. And that won't be before closing time.' Hugo banged his glass down on the bar and then, as if to deny the force of his outburst, asked politely, 'May I have another Scotch, please?'

As Robert Chubb obliged with the drink, Charles stormed out. In the lobby he found Geoffrey Winter had followed him. Geoffrey offered a blue and white handkerchief to mop up his jacket. 'Thanks. Is there a phone?'

'There. Just behind the door.'

Charles got through to Charlotte. 'Look, I've just left Hugo. He's in the Backstagers' bar. Says he won't be leaving till it closes. He's extremely drunk.'

'Won't be the first time,' she said dryly. 'Thanks for the warning.'

Geoffrey Winter was still waiting outside. 'I'd offer you a lift, but we don't run a car. Still, I can show you a quick way down to the station. There's a footpath.'

'Thank you.'

'They walked past a large house next door to the Backstagers. It was neo-Tudor with diamond window panes. No light on. Outside the porch, horrible out of period, a pair of grotesque stone lions stood on guard.

Charles drew in his breath sharply with distaste. Geoffrey followed his glance and chuckled. 'The Hobbses. Mr. and Mrs Arkadina. Advertising their money. Ostentatious buggers. But, nonetheless, a good source of free drinks.'

Charles laughed, though inwardly he was still seething from the encounter with Hugo.

'By the way,' said Geoffrey, 'I gather we see you tomorrow.'

'Yes, Vee invited me down for a meal. If that's still okay.'

'Fine. Love to see you. I'll show you the way when we get to the main road.'

They walked across a common where a huge pile of wood and rubbish announced the approach of Bonfire Night.

'Good God, November already,' observed Geoffrey. 'Guy Fawkes to be burnt again on Friday. How time flies as you get older.'

'You think you've got problems,' Charles mourned. 'It's my fiftieth birthday this week.'

They talked a little on the way to the main road, but most of the time there was silence except for the soft pad of their rubber soles on the pathway. Charles didn't notice the lack of conversation. His mind was still full of hurt after the clash with Hugo.

He didn't really notice saying goodbye to Geoffrey. Or the train journey back to Waterloo. He was still seething, almost sick with rage.

CHAPTER FIVE

CHARLES SPENT AN unsatisfactory Tuesday mooching round his bedsitter in Hereford Road, Bayswater. It was a depressing room and the fact that he stayed there to do anything but sleep meant he was depressed.

He was still fuming over the scene with Hugo. No longer fuming at the fact that Hugo had hit him, but now angry with himself for having flared up. Hugo was in a really bad state, possibly on the verge of a major breakdown, and, as a friend, Charles should have stood by him, tried to help, not rushed off in a huff after a drunken squabble.

As usual, his dissatisfaction with himself spilled over into other area of his life. Frances. He must sort out what his relationship with Frances was. They must meet. He must ring her.

Early in the afternoon he went down to the pay-phone on the landing, but before he dialled her number, he realized she wouldn't be there. She was a teacher. Tuesday in term-time she'd be at school. He'd ring her about six, before he went down to Breckton.

To shift his mood, he started looking through his old scripts. How's Your Father? He read the first few pages. It really wasn't bad. Light, but fun. A performance by the Backstagers would be better than nothing. Rather sheepishly, he decided to take it with him.

He left without ringing Frances.

Vee Winter opened the door. She had on a P.V.C. apron with a design of an old London omnibus. She looked at him challengingly again, part provocative, part exhibitionist.

'Sorry I'm a bit early, Vee. The train didn't take as long as I expected.'

'No, they put on some fast ones during the rush-hour. But don't worry, supper's nearly ready. Geoff's just got in. He's up in the study. Go and join him. He's got some booze up there.'

The house was a small Edwardian semi, but it had been rearranged and decorated with taste and skill. Or rather, someone had started rearranging and decorating it with taste and skill. As he climbed the stairs, Charles noticed that the wall had been stripped and rendered, but not yet repapered. In the same way, someone had begun to sand the paint off the banister. Most of the wood was bare, but obstinate streaks of white paint clung in crevices. The house gave the impression that someone had started to renovate it with enormous vigour and then run out of enthusiasm. Or money.

The soprano wailing of the Liebestod from Wagner's Tristan und Isolde drew him to Geoffrey Winter's study. Here the conversion had very definitely been completed. Presumable the room had been intended originally as a bedroom, but it was now lined with long pine shelves which extended at opposite ends of the room to make a desk and a surface for an impressive selection of hi-fi. The shelves were covered with a cunning disarray of hooks, models, old bottles and earthenware pots. The predominant colour was a pale, pale mustard, which toned in well with the pine. On the wall facing the garden French windows gave out on to a small balcony.

Geoffrey Winter was fiddling with his hi-fi. The Wagner disc was being played on an expensive-looking grey metal turntable. Leads ran from the tuner to a small Japanese cassette radio.

'Sorry, Charles, just getting this on to cassette. So much handier. It's nearly finished.'

'This room's really good, Geoffrey.'

'I like it. One of the advantages of not having children – you have space.'

'And more money.'

Geoffrey grimaced. 'Hmm. Depends on the size of your mortgage. And your other bills. And how work's going.'

'What do you do?'

'I'm an architect.' Which explained the skill of the decor.

'Work for yourself?'

'Yes. Well, that is to say, I work for whoever will pay for my services. So at the moment, yes, I seem to work just for myself. No one's building anything. Can I get you a drink?'

'Thank you.'

'It's sherry or sherry, I'm afraid.' And, Charles noticed, not a particularly good sherry. Cypress domestic. Tut, tut, getting spoiled by the ostentatious array of Hugo's drinks cupboard. It would take a distressingly short time to pick up all the little snobberies of materialism.

While Geoffrey poured the drinks, Charles moved over to the shelves to inspect a theatrical model he had noticed when he came in. It was a stage set of uneven levels and effectively placed columns. Plastic figures were grouped on the rostra.

Geoffrey answered the unspoken question as he handed Charles his sherry. 'Set for The Caucasian Chalk Circle. I'm directing it for the Backstagers in the new year.'

'You're a meticulous planner.'

'I think as a director you have to be. In anything to dowith the theatre, in fact. You have to have planned every detail.'

'Yes, 1 could tell that from your Trigorin.'

'I'm not sure whether that's meant to be a compliment or not, Charles.'

'Nor am I.'

Geoffrey laughed.

'No, Geoffrey, what I mean is, you had more stagecraft than the rest of the company put together, but occasionally one or two tricks – like that very slow delivery on key lines, separating the words, giving each equal emphasis – well, I was conscious of the artifice.'

Geoffrey smiled, perhaps with slight restraint. 'Don't waste it, Charles. Keep it for the Critics' Circle. Professional criticism.'

The record had ended. The stylus worried against the centre groove. Geoffrey seemed suddenly aware of it and, with a look at Charles. he switched off the cassette player. He replaced the disc in its sleeve and marshalled it into a rack.

The conversation clipped. Charles found himself asking about the previous night's television. Dear, oh dear. Slip-pine into commuter habits. 'Did you get back in time for your ration of rape and murder in 1, Claudius last night?'

'No. I was back in time but I left Vee to watch it on her own. I did some work on Leontes. Trying to learn the bloody lines.'

'Shakespearean verse at its most tortured. How do you learn them? Have you any magic method?'

'"Fraid not. It's just read through, read through. Time and again.'

'It's the only way.'

At that moment Vee called from downstairs to say the meal was ready.

There was quite a crowd in the Back Room before the Critics' Circle. And for once they had a topic of conversation other than the theatrical doings of the Breckton Backstagers.

Denis and Mary Hobbs had been burgled. They had come home from their weekend cottage at about midnight the previous night and found the house full of police. A burglar had smashed one of the diamond panes in a downstairs front window, reached through and opened it, gone upstairs and emptied the contents of Mary's jewel box.

That's what's so horrible about it,' she was saying into her fourth consolatory double gin, ' – the idea of someone in your house, going through your things. It's ghastly.'

'Were they vandals too? Did they dirty your bedclothes and scrawl obscenities on your walls?' asked sour Reggie hopefully.

'No, at least we were spared that. Remarkable tidy burglars, closed all the cupboards and doors after them. No fingerprints either, so the CID. boys tell us. But   After her proprietory reference to the police force, she warmed to her role as tragic queen. '...that only seems to make it worse. It was so cold-blooded. And the idea of other people invading our privacy – ooh, it makes me feel cold all over.'

'Did they get much?' asked Reggie, with morbid interest.

'Oh yes, there was quite a lot of good stuff in my jewellery box. Not everyday things – I dare say a lot of them I don't wear more than twice a year. But I'd got them out of the bank for this Masonic do of Denis's last Monday and it didn't seem worth putting them back, because next week there's this dinner-dance thing at the Hilton – did I tell you about that?'

The snide expressions on the faces of the surrounding Backstagers suggested that Mary missed no opportunity to give them details of her posh social life. Anyway, the question seemed to be rhetorical. The role was shifting from tragic queen to wonderful person.

'Oh, I don't care about the stuff as jewellery. I'm not materialistic. But they're presents' Den's given me over the years, birthday, Christmases and so on. That's the trouble-the insurance will cover the value in money terms, but it can never replace what those things mean to me.

'It serves us bloody right,' said her husband. 'We've talked enough times about having a burglar alarm put in. But you put it off. You think it'll never happen to you.'

'Do the police reckon there's a chance of getting the culprits?'

'I don't know. Never commit themselves, the buggers, do they? But I think it's unlikely. They seem to reckon the best chance . was missed when Bob first saw the light.'

'What light?'

'Oh, didn't you hear?' You tell them, Bob.'

Robert Chubb took his cue and graciously moved to centre stage. 'I was the one who discovered the ghastly crime. Proper little Sherlock Holmes. Perhaps I should take it up professionally.

'I'd been sorting through some stuff in the office last night after I handed the bar over to Reggie and I was walking home past Denis and Mary's at about ten-fifteen, when I saw this light.'

Years of amateur dramatics would not allow him to miss the pregnant pause. 'The light was just by the broken win(low. It shone on the jagged glass. I thought immediately of burglars and went back to the office to phone the police. Incidentally – ' he added in self-justification, in case Denis's last remark might be construed by anyone as a criticism, 'the boys in blue told me I was absolutely right not to try to tackle the criminal. Said they get as much trouble from members of the public who fancy themselves as heroes as they do from the actual crooks.

'Anyway, my intervention does not seem to have been completely useless. They reckon the burglar must have seen me and that's what frightened him off. He appears to have scampered away in some disarray.'

'Yes,' Mary Hobbs chipped in, temperamentally unsuited to listening to anyone for that length of time. 'He left his torch behind in the window sill. The police are hoping to be able to trace him through that.'

Robert Chubb, piqued at losing his punch-line, changed the subject. Like a child who dictates the rules of the game because it's his ball, he brought them back to his dramatic society. 'Oh, Charles, about the World Premières Festival, did you bring along that play of yours? The committee would really like to have a look at it. Need a good new play, you know.'

Embarrassed at the fact that he actually had got it with him, Charles handed over the script with some apology about it being very light.

'Oh, the lighter the better. I'm sure it has the professional touch. And, talking of that, I do hope that in your criticism this evening you will apply professional standards to *The Seagull*. We always do and hope others will. So please don't pull your punches.'

'All right. I won't.'

As soon as Charles started speaking to the rows of earnest Backstagers in the rehearsal room, it was clear that they did not like being judged by professional standards.

He began with a few general observations on Chekhov and the difficulties that his plays presented. He referred to the years of work which had gone into the Moscow Arts Theatre's productions. He then went into detail on Chekhovian humour and stressed the inadvisability of playing Russian servants as mugging Mummerset yokels.

He moved on from this to the rest of the cast. He gave a general commendation and then made detailed criticism. He praised Charlotte's controlled innocence as Nina and the technical skill of Geoffrey's Trigorian. He faulted Clive Steele's Konstantin for lack of discipline and regretted that the part of Madame Arkadina was beyond the range of all but a handful of the world's actresses. But, rather against his better judgement and to sugar the pill, he congratulated Mary Hobbs on a brave attempt.

He thought he had been fair. Out of deference to their amateur status and because he had no desire to cause unpleasantness, he had toned down the criticism he would have given a professional cast. He thought his remarks might have been overindulgent, but otherwise unexceptionable.

The shocked silence which followed his conclusion indicated that the Backstagers did not share his opinion. Reggie, who seemed to get lumbered with (or perhaps sought after) all official functions, was chairing the meeting. He rose to his feet. 'Well, some fairly controversial views there from Mr. Parrish. I don't think everyone's going to agree with all that.' A murmur of agreement came back from the audience. 'Still, thank you. Any questions?'

There was an 'after you' silence and then Shad Scott-Smith rose to his feet. He spoke with a heavy irony which obviously appealed to the mood of the gathering. 'Well, first of all, I'd like to thank Mr. Parrish for his comments and what I'd like to offer is not so much a question as a humble defence.'

'As perpetrator of the terrible crime of *The Seagull*.

This sally drew an appreciative titter. 'I feel I should apologize, both to the cast, whom I misled so disastrously, and to the good folk of Breckton, who so unwisely bought all the tickets for all four performances and who made the terrible mistake of enjoying the production very much.'

This got an outright laugh of self-congratulation. 'And I would also like to apologize to the local newspaper critics who, out of sheet malice and stupidity, gave such good reviews to my production of The Cherry Orchard last year, since they didn't know they were dealing with someone who had no appreciation of Chekhov. And while I'm at it, I'd better tick off the adjudicators of the Inter-Regional Drama Festival who were foolish enough to award my production of The Bear a Special Commendation.'

He sat down to a riot of applause. Charles saw he was going to have an uphill fight. 'All right, I'm sorry. I had no intention of offending anyone. I am here as a professional actor and director and I'm giving you my opinions as I would to the members of a professional company. Everyone keeps saying that these Critics' Circles are not just meant to be a mutual admiration society.'

'No, they're certainly not,' said Robert Chubb with unctuous charm. 'I set them up as a forum for informed discussion, for the give-and-take of intelligent ideas. I'm sure we can all take criticism and that's what we are all here for.'

Charles thought maybe at last he had got a supporter. But Robert Chubb soon dispelled the idea as he went on. 'The only comment I would have is that it does seem to me rather a pity that the only member of the cast for whom you managed unstinting praise was one of our newest members and that you were somewhat dismissive of some of our most experienced actors and actresses. Particularly of a lady to whom we all owe many splendid performances, not least her Lady Macbeth last year.'

This spirited defence of Mary Hobbs produced another warm burst of applause. Charles was tempted to ask what relevance a performance in a production of Macbeth he couldn't possibly have seen should have to a production of *The Seagull* he had seen, but there didn't seem any point.

He had misjudged the nature of the meeting entirely. All that had been required of him had been a pat on the back for all concerned, not forgetting the charming young man who tore his ticket and the good ladies who made the coffee for the interval. All he could do now was to insure that that meeting ended as soon as possible and get the hell out of the place. And never come back.

Mentally he cursed Hugo for ever letting him in for it, or at least for not briefing him as to what to expect.

He then realized with a slight shock that Hugo wasn't there. Nor was Charlotte. Nor Clive Steele. It seemed strange.

As he thought about it, he started again to feel guilty about the way he had left Hugo the night before. He hated to let things like that fester. Stupid misunderstandings should be cleared up as soon as possible. He was too old to lose friends over trivialities. Once he'd stopped the Backstagers baying for his blood, he'd go round and see Hugo and apologize.

But there was still more Critics' Circling to be weathered. It was hard work. There was no common ground for discussion. The Backstagers were only capable of talking about the Backstagers. When Charles made a comparison with a West End production of The Three Sisters, someone would say, 'Well, of course, when Walter directed it down here   When he praised the comic timing of Michael Hordern, someone would say, 'Oh, but Philip's a wonderful actor too. If you'd seen him in The Rivals. . .' It was like talking to a roomful of politicians. Every question was greeted, not by an answer, but by an aggrieved assertion of something totally different.

It did end. Eventually. Reggie gave an insipid vote of thanks with some vague remarks about 'having been given lots of food for thought...interesting, and even surprising, to hear the views of someone from the outside.'

Charles prepared his getaway. He thanked Geoffrey and Vee for the meal and made for the exit, hoping that he was seeing the last of the Breckton Backstagers.

As he reached the door, he overheard a lacquered voice commenting, 'Don't know who he thinks he is anyway. I've never seen him on the television or anything.'

Charles Paris knew who they were talking about.

Hugo opened the front door. His eyes were dull and registered no surprise at the visit. He was still wearing the clothes he had had on the day before and their scruffy appearance suggested he hadn't been to bed in the interim. The smell of whisky which blasted from him suggested that he hadn't stopped drinking either.

'I came round to apologize for going off like that last night.'

'Apologize,' Hugo echoed stupidly. He didn't seem to know what Charles was talking about.

'Yes. Can I come in?'

'Sure. Have a drink.' Hugo led the way, stumbling, into the sitting room. It was a mess. Empty whisky bottles of various brands bore witness to a long session. He must have been working through the collection. Incongruously, the scene was cosily lit by an open fire, heaped with glowing smokeless fuel.

'Was cold,' Hugo mumbled by way of explanation. He swayed towards the fire and removed the still burning gas poker. 'Shouldn't have left that in.' He unscrewed the lead with excessive concentration. 'Whisky?'

'Thank you.'

Hugo slopped out half a tumbler of Glenlivet and handed it over. 'Cheers.' He slumped into an armchair with his own glass.

Charles took a long sip. It was welcome after the idiocies of the Critics' Circle. 'Where's Charlotte?'

'Huh. Charlotte.' Hugo spoke without violence but with great bitterness. 'Charlotte's finished.'

'What do you mean?'

'Charlotte – finished. The great love affair, Charlotte and Hugo – over.'

'You mean she's left you?'

'Not here.' Hugo was almost incoherent.

'She wasn't here when you got back last night?'

'Not here.'

'Where do you think she's gone?'

'I don't know. To see lover boy.'

'Is there a lover boy?'

'I suppose so. That's the usual story. Pretty young girl. Middle-aged husband. Don't you read the Sunday papers?' Hugo spoke in a low, hopeless mumble.

'Have you been in to work today?' Hugo shook his head. 'Just drinking?' A small nod.

They sat and drank. Charles tried to think of anything he could say that might be helpful. There was nothing. He could only stay, be there.

After a long, long silence, he started to feel cold. The fire was nearly dead. Charles got up briskly. 'Where's the coal, Hugo? I'll go and get some more.

'You'll never find it. Let me. Come on, I'll show you.' Hugo led the way unsteadily into the kitchen. He picked up a torch and fumbled it on.

They went out of the back door. There was a shed just opposite. 'In there,' said Hugo.

Charles opened the door. Hugo shone the torch.

In its beam they saw Charlotte. She was splayed unceremoniously over the coal. A scarf was knotted unnaturally round her neck. She was very dead.

CHAPTER SIX

CHARLES RANG THE police and stayed beside Hugo in the sitting room until they arrived. Hugo was catatonic with shock. Only once did he speak, murmuring softly to himself, 'What did I do to her? She was young. What did I do to her?'

When the police arrived, Charles steeled himself to go out once again to the coal shed. The beams of their torches were stronger and made the colour of Charlotte's cheeks even less natural, like a detail from an over-exposed photograph.

The richness of her perfume, which still hung in the air, was sickly and inappropriate. The staring eyes and untidy spread of limbs were not horrifying; the felling they gave Charles was more one of embarrassment, as if a young girl had been sick at a party. And his impression of callowness was reinforced by the Indian print scarf over the bruised neck, like a teenager's attempt to hide love-bites.

The bruises were chocolate brown. On one of them the skin had been broken -and a bootlace of dried blood traced its way crazily up towards Charlotte's mouth.

Hugo remained dull and silent and Charles himself was dazed as they were driven to the police station. They were separated when they arrived and parted without a word. Each was taken into a separate interview room to make a statement.

Charles had to wait for about half an hour before his questioning began. A uniformed constable brought him a cup of tea and apologized for the delay. Everyone was very pleasant, but pleasant with that slight restraint that staff have in hospitals, as if something unpleasant is happening nearby but no one is going to mention it.

Eventually two policemen came in. One was in uniform and carried a sheaf of paper. The other was fair-haired. early thirties, dressed in a brown blazer and blue trousers. He spoke with the vestiges of a South London twang. 'So sorry to have kept you waiting. Detective-Sergeant Harvey. Mr. Paris, isn't it?'

Charles nodded.

'Fine. I must just get a few personal details and then, if I may, I'll ask a few questions about.., what happened. Then Constable Renton will write it down as a statement, which you sign – if you're happy with it. Okay?'

Charles nodded again.

'It's late, and I'm afraid this could take some time. Say if you'd like more tea. Or a sandwich or something.'

'No, I'm fine, thanks.'

So it started. First, simple information, name, address and so on. Then details of how he came to know Mr. and Mrs Mecken. And then a resume of the last two days.

As he spoke, Charles could feel it going wrong. He told the truth, he told it without bias, and yet he could feel the false picture that his words were building up. Everything he said seemed to incriminate Hugo. The more he tried to defend him, the worse it sounded.

Detective-Sergeant Harvey was a good poker-faced questioner. He didn't force the pace, he didn't put words into Charles's mouth, he just asked for information slowly and unemotionally. And to damning effect.

'After your lunch on Monday you say that you and Mr. Mecken went on to a drinking club?'

'Yes, a sort of strip joint in Dean Street.'

'And what did you drink there?'

'Hugo ordered a bottle of whisky.'

'So, by the time you left there, you had both had a considerable amount to drink?'

'I didn't drink a great deal in the club.' Immediately Charles kicked himself for prompting the next question.

'But Mr. Mecken did?'

'I suppose he had quite a bit by some people's standards, but you know how it is with advertising people – they can just drink and drink.' The attempt at humour didn't help. It made it sound more and more of a whitewash.

'Yes. But you then both returned to Breckton and continued drinking at the theatre club. Surely that made it rather a lot of alcohol, even for an advertising man.'

'Well, yes, I agree, we wouldn't normally have drunk that much, but you see Hugo was a bit upset and...' Realizing that once again he had said exactly the wrong thing, Charles left the words hanging in the air.

'Upset,' Detective-Sergeant Harvey repeated without excitement. 'Have you any idea why he should have been upset?'

Charles hedged. 'Oh, I dare say it was something at work. He was involved in a big campaign to launch a new bedtime drink – that's what I was working on with him–and I think there may have been some disagreements over that. You know, these advertising people do take it all so seriously.'

'Yes. Of course.' The slow response seemed only to highlight the hollowness of Charles's words. 'You have no reason to believe that Mr. Mecken was having any domestic troubles?'

'Domestic troubles?' Charles repeated idiotically.

'Worries about his marriage.'

'Oh. Oh, I shouldn't think so. I mean, I don't know. I don't think anyone can begin to understand anything about another person's marriage. But I mean Charlotte is a – I mean, was a beautiful girl and...' He trailed off guiltily.

'Hmm. Mr. Paris, would you describe Mr. Mecken as a violent man?'

'No, certainly not. And if you're trying to suggest that – '

'I am not trying to suggest anything, Mr. Paris. I am just trying to get as full a background to the death of Mrs Mecken as I can,' Detective-Sergeant Harvey replied evenly.

'Yes, of course, I'm sorry.' Blustering wasn't going to help Hugo's cause. As his interrogation continued, Charles kept thinking of his friend, in another interview room, being asked other questions. Where were Hugo's answers leading?

'You say Mr. Mecken is not a habitually violent man. Is he perhaps the sort who might become violent when he's had a few drinks? I mean, for instance, did he show any violence towards you during your long drinking session on Monday?'

Charles hesitated. Certainly he wasn't going to go back to Hugo's bizarre outburst while an undergraduate and his instinct was to deny that anything had happened on the Monday. But Hugo's second swing at him had been witnessed by a bar full of Backstagers. He couldn't somehow see that self-dramatizing lot keeping quiet about it. He'd do better to edit the truth than to tell a lie. 'Well, he did take a sort of playful swing at me at one point when I' suggested he ought to be getting home, but that's all.'

'A playful swing.' Detective-Sergeant Harvey gave the three words equal emphasis.

The questioning ended soon after and the information was turned into a written statement. Detective-Sergeant Harvey courteously went through a selection of the questions again and Constable Renton laboriously wrote down the answers in longhand on ruled paper.

Inevitably it was a slow process and Charles found his mind wandering. He didn't like the way it was heading.

Previously he had been numb with shock, but now the fact of Charlotte's death was getting through to him. The feeling of guilt which his initially casual reaction had prompted gave way to a cold sensation of nausea.

'With it came a realization of the implications for Hugo. As Charles went through the details for his statement, he saw with horror which way the circumstantial evidence pointed.

There were so many witnesses too. So many people who had heard Hugo's denunciation of his wife and his violent burst of aggression towards Charles. Unless Hugo could prove a very solid alibi for the time at which his wife had been murdered, things didn't look too good for him.

At this point it struck Charles that he was assuming Hugo was innocent and he paused to question the logic of this. On reflection, it didn't stand up very well. In fact the only arguments he could come up with against Hugo's guilt were Hugo's own denial that he would ever hurt Charlotte and Charles's own conviction that someone he knew so well would be incapable of a crime of such savagery.

And those weren't arguments. They were sheer emotion, romantic indulgence.

The thought of romanticism only made it worse. It suggested a very plausible motive for Hugo to kill his wife. Hugo was a romantic, unwilling to accept the unpleasant facts of life. He had built up his own life into a romantic ideal, with his writing talent supporting the professional side and his love-affair with Charlotte the domestic.

When it became clear to such a man that the twin pillars of his life were both illusions, anything could happen.

He finished the statement and was asked to read it through, signing each page. At one point he hesitated.

'Anything wrong?' asked Detective-Sergeant Harvey.

'Well, I... it seems so bald, so...' He couldn't think of anything that didn't sound like protesting too much. 'No.' He signed on.

He was amazed, to discover it was nearly five o'clock. Dully he accepted the offer of the lift home in a squad car. He gave his' Hereford Road address.

He didn't notice the drabness of the bedsitter as he entered. He homed in on the bottle of Bells straight away and sank half a tumblerful. Then he lay down on the bed and lost consciousness.

When he. woke, it was still dark. Or rather, he realized after looking at his watch, dark again. Quarter past six. He's slept round the clock.'

He was still dressed. He left the house and walked along Hereford Road to Westbourne Grove. There was a newspaper seller on the corner. He bought and Evening Standard.

It didn't take long to find the news. Hugo Mecken had been arrested, charged with the murder of his wife, Charlotte.

And Charles Paris felt is was his fault.

CHAPTER SEVEN

IN SPITE OF logic, the feeling of treachery remained. Charles Paris had deserted his friend in a crisis. Charles Paris had incriminated his friend by his statement.

He had to do something. At least find out all the circumstances, at least check that no mistakes had been made.

He hurried back to the house in Hereford Road, went to the pay-phone on the landing and dialled Gerald Venables's office number.

Gerald was a successful show business solicitor whom Charles had known since Oxford. Armed with a boyish enthusiasm for the whole business of detection, he had collaborated with Charles on one or two investigations, starting with the strange death of Marius Steen. In the current circumstances, it was an immediate instinct to ring Gerald.

An efficient, husky voice answered the phone.

'Is that Polly?'

'Yes.'

'It's Charles Paris. Could I speak to Gerald, please?'

'I'm sorry, he's not here.'

'Oh, sod it. Is he on his way home?'

'No, he's out with a client, I'm afraid. He was called down to Breckton mid-morning and he's been there all day.'

'Oh my God, of course. He's Hugo Mecken's solicitor, isn't he?'

'Yes. That's who he's with. I gather you've heard the news.'

'Yes.' It wasn't worth going into details of how he had been the first to hear it. 'Stupid of me. I'd forgotten. Gerald sorted out Hugo's divorce, didn't he?'

'Yes. And he was a bit shocked when he discovered what it was about this time.'

'That I can believe. Look, Polly, have you any idea when he'll be back? I mean, is he reckoning to go back to the office?'

'No. He rang about half an hour ago to say he'd go straight to Dulwich from Breckton. And asked me to ring Mrs Venables and say he'd be late.'

'Why didn't he ring her himself?' Charles asked irrelevantly.

'I think it sounds more businesslike if I do.' Polly replied with a hint of humour.

Yes, that was Gerald all over. 'Polly, when he says "very late", what do you reckon that means?'

'I honestly don't know. He said I was to say ten-thirty at the earliest to Mrs Venables.'

'Okay. Thanks, Polly. He didn't say anything else about...you know, the case...or Hugo... or anything.'

'No. Well, there isn't really much to say, is there?'

'I suppose not.'

Charles spent an unsatisfactory evening and drank too much. He thought of ringing Frances, but put it off again. Round eight he realized he hadn't eaten for over twenty-four hours.

He didn't feel hungry, but he thought he ought to have something.

Going out to a restaurant was too much effort. He was too jumpy to sit down and relax over a proper meal. He looked round the room. There was an opened packet of cornflakes on the table. No milk. He tried a handful. They were soft, cardboard.

He rooted through the grey-painted cupboard, shoving aside scripts, half-finished plays, empty bottles, socks and crisp packets. All he came up with was a tin of sardines without a key and a tin of curried beans.

The menu was dictated by his antiquated tin-opener, which wouldn't grip on the sardine tin., He slopped the beans into a saucepan still furred with boiled milk from the previous week and put it on the gas-ring which was hidden discreetly behind a plastic curtain.

The curried beans didn't improve anything. He took a long swill from the Bell's bottle as a mouthwash. Except he didn't spit it out.

Then he addressed his mind to thought. Serious thought. He had been in criminal situations before and he had even, by a mixture of luck and serendipity, solved crimes before. But this one mattered. He had to concentrate, sort it out. He was motivated by his affection for Hugo and his abiding sense of guilt.

His first assumption remained Hugo's innocence. No logic for this, just a conviction.

If only he could see Hugo face to face, talk to him, ask him. Then he would know, he felt sure.

But how do you get to see a man who has just been arrested for murder? Gerald would know. All action seemed to hinge on speaking to Gerald.

Half past nine. The evening was passing, but slowly. Perhaps another generous Bell's would speed up the process.

He looked at the floor through the slopping spirit in his glass. The image was refracted and distorted. Like his thought processes.

The obvious solution was that Hugo had killed his wife. In a wild reaction to the collapse of his dreams he had taken the terrible kamikaze course of the disillusioned romantic. 'Yet each man kills the thing he loves...,' as Oscar Wilde wrote in his despair.

The only way to escape the obvious, solution was to provide a feasible alternative. Either to prove Hugo was doing something else at the time that Charlotte was killed. Or to prove that someone else did it.

Charles's brief experience of the Backstagers told him that emotions ran high in the group. Charlotte had antagonized the established stars by her success as Nina. Vee Winter, for one,., felt herself usurped by the newcomer.

But that kind of jealousy wasn't sufficient motive for murder. A sexual impulse was more likely. A woman as beautiful as Charlotte was bound to cause reverberations wherever she went and no doubt her appearance among the Backstagers had let to the snapping-off of a few middle-aged husbands' heads by middle-aged wives who saw eyes lingering with too much interest. Indeed, Charles had seen evidence of this with the Hobbses.

But that was still not something for which a sane person would kill.

It must be a closer attachment. Clive Steele. Charles thought back over the conversation he had heard in the car park. The young man's passions had been demonstrably immature, but they had been strong. He was supposed to be away working in Melton Mowbray for the whole week, but it might be worth investigating his movements.

Or then again, why should the murderer have anything to do with the Backstagers? Charlotte did have other contacts. Not many but a few. Diccon Hudson, for instance. He had made some sour reference to having gone around with her before her marriage. Probably nothing there, but anything was worth looking into to save Hugo.

After all, Diccon could have been the mysterious lover of whom Hugo had spoken. Charles didn't know whether to believe in this personage or not. It could just be a creation of Hugo's fevered imagination. But if such a person did exist, the possible permutations of violent emotions were considerably increased.

Equally, if he did exist, Hugo's motive for killing his wife was that much stronger. But Charles put the thought from his mind. He had to start by assuming Hugo's innocence.

He was full of nervous excitement. He wanted to do something, get started, begin his task of atonement.

He looked at his watch. Twenty-five to eleven. Thank God, he could try Gerald again. The need to do something was now almost unbearable.

Kate, Gerald's wife, sounded disgruntled. No, he wasn't home yet. Yes, Charles could try again in half an hour if it was important, but not much later because she was going to bed.

Charles stood by the phone, seething with energy. There must be something else he could do. He could start piecing together Hugo's movements from the time he left the Back Room on Monday night. Someone must have seen him leave, someone might even have walked him home. Details like that could be vital.

The only Backstager's number he had was Geoffrey and Vee's. Geoffrey answered.

'Have you heard about Hugo?'

'Yes, Charles. Horrible, isn't it?'

'Horrible. Look, I'm trying to find out what he did when he left the bar on Monday night.'

'Amateur sleuth work.'

'I don't know. Maybe. Thing is, you'd know – who are the real barflies up at that place? Who was guaranteed to have been there at closing time and seen him go?'

'Well, Bob Chubb's the obvious one. He was on the bar, wasn't he?'

'Do you have his number?'

'Yes, sure. I'll get it. I – what's that love?' Vee's voice was asking something in the background. 'Just twiddle the aerial round to the right. Sorry, Charles, our television's on the blink. Extremely unwilling to get a decent picture on BBC2. Comes of buying cheap junk. Ah, here it is.' He gave Charles Robert Chubb's number. 'I only hope it bears fruit. It seems incredible, doesn't it? The idea that Hugo... I keep thinking that it'll all turn out to be a mistake and all be cleared up somehow.'

'It depends what you mean by cleared up. Charlotte will still be dead.'

'Yes.'

Robert Chubb answered the phone. His voice was bland and elocuted. When it heard who was calling, it took on a colder note. And when it heard what Charles wanted to know, it became positively snappish.

'As I have already told the police, Mr. Mecken left the bar at about ten-thirty. On his own. I don't really know why I should waste my time repeating this to you. I know everyone likes to see themselves as a private eye, but I really do suggest, Mr. Parrish, that you should leave criminal investigation to the professionals.'

'And I really do suggest, Mr. Chubb, that you should do the same with the theatre.' Charles slammed the phone down.

He was beginning to run out of small change. He rested his penultimate 10p on the slot and dialled the Gerald's number again,

The solicitor answered, sounding formal, even pettish. 'Oh, hello, Charles,
• Kate said you'd rung. Look, could you ring me later on tomorrow? I'm dog-tired. I've just got in and I'm sure whatever you've got to say will keep.'

'Gerald, it's about Hugo.'

'Oh. Oh yes, of course, you were with him when he found the body – or claimed to find it.'

'Yes. How's it going?'

'What do you mean – how's it going?'

'With Hugo.'

'Charles, I'm sorry.' Gerald sounded exasperated and professional. 'I know you are a friend and we are talking about a mutual friend, but I'm afraid, as a solicitor, I can't discuss my clients' affairs.'

'You can tell me where he is, can't you? Is he in prison – or where?'

'He'll be spending tonight in the cells at Breckton Police Station.'

'And then what?'

Gerald sighed with annoyance. 'Tomorrow morning he'll appear at Breckton Magistrates' Court where he'll be remanded in custody. Which means Brixton. Then he'll be remanded again every week until the trial.'

'Hmm. When can I get to see him?'

'See him – what do you mean?'

'You know, see him. I want to ask him some questions.'

'Well, I don't know. I suppose it may be possible for him to have visitors when he's in Brixton. I'm not sure how soon – '

'No, I want to see him tomorrow.'

'That's impossible.'

'Will you be seeing him?'

'Yes, of course. As his solicitor, I'll be in court and see him before he's taken off to Brixton.'

'Well, can't I come along with you and be passed off as one of your outfit?'

'One of my outfit?' Gerald italicized the last word with distaste.

'Yes, surely you have colleagues in your office, articled clerks and what have you. Pretend I'm one of them.'

'Charles, do you realize what you're saying? You are asking me to indulge in serious professional misconduct. Have you been drinking?'

'Yes., of course I have. But that's not the point. I am completely serious.'

'Charles, I am also serious. This is an extremely serious matter. We are talking about a case of murder.'

'What about the death of Willy Mariello? Wasn't that a case of murder? You were keen enough to help me on that. Indeed, whenever I meet you, you get all schoolboyish and ask me when I'm going to get involved in another case and beg that I'll let you know and work together with you on it."

'Yes, but that's different.'

'No, it isn't. The only difference is that this case happens to be one in which you are already involved professionally. So far as I'm concerned, this is a case of murder which might well need investigation and, according to your frequently expressed desire, I am asking you if you will help me on it.'

Gerald was silent for a moment. When he spoke again, it was with less certitude. 'But, Charles, this is a fairly open-and-shut case. I mean, I know I shouldn't say this about a client, but it seems to me that there's little doubt Hugo did it. It all fits in too neatly. And anyway the police wouldn't have arrested and charged him so quickly if it hadn't been pretty definite.'

'Okay, I agree. It is most likely that Hugo murdered Charlotte. But I feel that so long as there's even the vaguest alternative possibility, we should investigate it. Well, I should, anyway. Just for my peace of mind.'

What do you mean by an alternative possibility?'

'Say an alibi. Suppose Hugo saw someone, talked to someone during that missing twenty-four hours...

'But if he did, surely he would have told the police.'

'Yes, probably. Look, I haven't worked it all out yet, but I feel guilty about it and – '

Gerald was continuing his own train of thought. 'Anyway, we are only talking of a fairly short period for which he'd need an alibi. The preliminary medical report came in while I was down at the Breckton Police Station. They'll get the full post-mortem results in a couple of days. It seems that when you discovered Charlotte's body she'd already been dead for twenty-four hours.'

'Good God. So she was killed on the Monday night.'

'Yes. The police theory is that Hugo arrived back from the theatre club smashed out of his mind, had an argument with his wife – possibly over sexual matters – and then...well, strangled her and hid the body. It fits. He'd had a hell of a lot to drink.'

'I see. And I suppose the theory is that he continued drinking through the Tuesday to get over the shock.'

'Something like that, yes.'

'Hmm. This makes it even more imperative that I see Hugo.'

'Charles, I have a professional reputation to – '

'Oh, stuff that, Gerald. For God's sake. You're always complaining to me how bloody boring your work is, how sick you get of fiddling about with theatrical contracts all day, how you wish you could get involved in something really exciting like a murder. Well, here's one right in your in-tray'

'Yes, and it's just because it's there that I have to treat it with professional propriety.'

'Gerald, stop being so bloody pompous. I've got to see Hugo. Look, there's hardly any risk involved. Okay, so you've got a new Mr. Paris on your staff. No one knows you down in Breckton. No one's going to check.'

'Well...' wavering.

Press home advantage. 'Come on, Gerald. Live a little. Take a risk. Being a solicitor is the business of seeing how far laws can bend – why not test this one out?'

'I'm not sure.'

'Look, you're nearly fifty, Gerald. I don't believe you've ever taken a risk in you life. Even the shows you put money into are all box office certainties. Just try this. Come on, I'll be the one who gets clobbered if anything goes wrong. But nothing will, anyway. Go on, what do you say?'

'Well...Look, if I do agree, and if you do find out there's anything to be investigated, you will keep me in the picture, won't you?'

'Of course.'

There was a long pause. The pay-tone on the phone beeped insistently.

Charles crammed in his last 10p. By the time the line was clear, Gerald had reached his decision.

'Okay, buster. We give it a whirl, huh?'

It was going to be all right. When Gerald started talking like a fifties thriller, he was getting interested in a case.

'But one thing, Charles...'

'Yes.'

'People' who work in my office tend to look extremely smart and well-groomed. So will you see to it, that you are wearing a suit, that you've shaved and that you've brushed your hair? I don't want you rolling up in your usual guise of an out-of-work gamekeeper who's just spent a long night with Lady Chatterley.'

'Don't worry, Gerald. I'll look as smooth as you do.'

CHAPTER EIGHT

GERALD WAS GRUDGING. 'Well, I suppose it'll do.'

'What do you mean – do?' Charles was aggrieved. He had spent the journey down to Breckton in vivid fantasies of Charles Paris, the legal whiz-kid. As an actor, he could never escape being dictated to by his costumes.

'Never mind. I suppose there are scruffy solicitors,' Gerald conceded.

'Scruffy? I'll have you know, in 1965, this suit was considered daringly trendy.'

'Yes, maybe, but one or two things have changed since 1965. In fact, most things have.'

'Except the British legal system, which hasn't changed since 1865.'

Gerald ignored the gibe. He looked preoccupied. 'Charles, I've been thinking about this business. As a solicitor, I will be taking a risk which is really unjustifiable. In the sense – '

'It's decided. I've got to see Hugo.'

'You'll have to give your name when we enter the court. If there ever is any follow-up – '

'Let's assume there isn't. Come on, Gerald, where's your spirit of adventure?'

'Currently hiding behind my fear of being struck off for professional misconduct.'

They entered the Magistrates' Court building. Mr. Venables and his colleague from the office, Mr. Paris, checked in and were directed to the relevant court. They sidled on to a solicitors' bench on which the profession was represented by every level of sartorial elegance.

'That suit on the end's a darned sight older than mine,' Charles hissed. 'Looks like it escaped from a Chicago gangster movie.'

Gerald switched hips off with a look. Charles scanned the courtroom. It all seemed a bit lethargic, like a rehearsal where some of the principal actors were missing and their lines were being read in. The court was as empty as a summer matinee. And as in a theatre, where the audience is scattered in little groups, he was more conscious of the comings and goings in his immediate vicinity than of the main action taking place between the magistrates' dais and the dock. Solicitors shuffled in and out, reading long sheets of paper to themselves in states of bored abstraction.

One disturbing feature of the proceedings, for which his ignorance of the British legal system had not prepared him, was the large number of policemen around. That in itself was not worrying, but it soon became apparent that for each case the arresting officer had to be present. He wasn't sure who the arresting officer would be in Hugo's case, but if it were one of the policemen he had met on the Tuesday night, Charles's imposture could have serious consequences. He decided not to mention this new anxiety to Gerald. It would only upset him.

It was after twelve, and after some dreary cases of drunkeness, thefts and a taking and driving away, that Hugo was called. He came up into the dock accompanied by a policeman whom, thank God, Charles had never seen before. The prisoner was not handcuffed; in spite of the seriousness of the charge, he was not regarded as a public danger.

Charles turned round with some trepidation and discovered to his relief that there were no familiar faces among the policemen who had just entered the court.

He transferred his attention to his friend. Hugo looked lifeless. There was a greyish sheen to his face and bald dome; his eyes were dead like pumice-stone. Charles recognized that extinguished expression. He'd seen it in Oxford tutorials, in recording studios, at the various ports of call during their Monday drinking session. Hugo had retreated into his mind, closing the door behind him. Nobody could share what he found there, no friend, no wife.,

This time the deadness seemed total, as if Hugo had withdrawn completely from the body. His movements when brought to the dock had been those of an automaton. Presumably he must still be suffering from a brain-crushing hangover – it would take a week or so to get over the sort of bender he had been on – but that wasn't sufficient to explain the absolute impassivity of his expression. It was as if he had opted out of life completely.

The proceedings were short. The charge was read by the magistrate, the police said that they were not yet ready to proceed and the accused was remanded in custody for a week.

Suddenly Hugo was being led off down to the cells again. Gerald shook Charles by the shoulder. 'Come on. We go down now.

The jailer was in a lenient mood and gave the two solicitors permission to go into the accused's cell rather than leaving them to conduct their interview through the covered slot in the metal door.

The door was unlocked with caution, but as it swung open, it was apparent that no one need fear violence from the inmate.

Hugo sat on the bed, looking straight at the wall ahead of him. He did not stir as the genuine and false solicitors were ushered in or as the door clanged shut and was locked behind them.

'How are you feeling?' asked Gerald with professional joviality.

'All right,' came the toneless reply.

'Headache better?'

'Yes, thank you.'

Charles took the moment for his revelation. Perhaps it would be the necessary shock to shake Hugo out of his lethargy. 'Look, it's me – Charles.'

'Hello.' The response was again without animation. Without even surprise.

Unwilling to lose his coup, Charles continued, 'I came in under cover of Gerald's outfit.'

The solicitor winced predictably at the final word. To gain another predictable wince and maybe to shift Hugo's mood by humour, Charles added, 'There's no substitute for knowing a bent lawyer.'

Gerald's reaction was as expected; Hugo still gave none. Charles changed tack. 'Look, Hugo, I know this is one hell of a situation and I feel partly responsible for it, because I'm sure if I hadn't said certain things in my statement, you wouldn't be here and – '

Hugo cut him off, which at least demonstrated that he was taking in what was being said. But the voice in which he spoke remained lifeless. 'Charles, if it hadn't been you it would have been someone else. You only told them the truth and that was all they needed.'

'Yes, but – '

So there's no need for you to feel guilty about me or feel you have to make quixotic gestures and come down here to save me from a terrible miscarriage of justice. I don't blame you. I'm the only person to blame, if blame is the right word.'

'What, you mean you think you killed her?'

'That's what I told the police.'

'You've confessed?'

'Yes.'

Charles looked at the solicitor. Gerald shrugged. 'I didn't tell you because you didn't ask. You swept me along with some wild scheme of your own and –'

'But, Hugo, is it true?'

'Oh, Charles.' The voice was infinitely weary. 'I've spent some days going through this, both on my own and with the police. And...yes, I think I did it.'

'But you can't remember?'

'Not the exact details. I know I staggered back from the Backstagers when the bar closed and I was full of hatred for Charlotte and drunk out of my mind. The next thing I remember with any clarity is waking up on the sitting room floor on Tuesday morning with the feeling that I'd done something terrible.'

'But everyone feels like that when they've had a skinful.' Hugo ignored him. 'It's no secret that Charlotte and I hadn't been getting on too well, that...the magic had gone out of our marriage   For the first time, there was slight intonation, a hint of bitterness as he spoke the cliché. 'And it's no secret that I'd started drinking too much and that when I drank, we fought. So I imagine it's quite possible that, if I met her, smashed out of my mind, on Monday night, I laid hands on her and...' In spite of the detachment with which he was speaking, he was unable to finish the sentence.

'But you can't remember doing it?'

'I can't remember anything when I'm that smashed.'

'Then why did you confess to killing her?'

'Why not? It fits the facts remarkable well. The motivation was there, the opportunity. I think my guilt is a reasonable deduction.'

'Did the police put pressure on you to – '

No, Charles. For Christ's sake-' He mastered this momentary lapse of control. 'I reached the conclusion on my own, Charles. I was under no pressure.' Realizing the irony of his last remark, he laughed a little laugh that was almost a sob.

'So you are prepared to confess to a murder you can't even remember just because the facts fit?'

Gerald came in at this juncture with the legal viewpoint.

'I think this may be one of the most fruitful areas for the defence, actually. If you really can't remember, of course we won't be able to get you off the murder charge and that's mandatory life, but the judge might well make some recommendation and you could be out in eight years.'

'You're talking as though his guilt were proven, Gerald.'

'Yes, Charles. To my mind – '

'For Christ's sake, both of you shut up! What does it matter? What's the difference?'

Charles came in, hard. 'The difference is, that if you are found guilty of murder, you'll be put away for life. And if you are not found guilty...' He petered out.

'Exactly.' It was only then that Charles realized the depths of Hugo's despair. His friend was bankrupt of any kind of hope. It made little difference whether he spent the rest of his life in prison or at large. Except if he were free, drink might help him shorten his sentence.

Gerald got to his feet in an official sort of way. 'You see, Charles, I didn't really think there was much point in your coming down here. I'm afraid it's an open-and-shut case. All we can do is to ensure that it's as well presented as possible. Actually Hugo, I wanted to discuss the matter of instructing counsel. I felt – '

'Stop, Gerald, stop!' Charles also stood up. 'We can't just leave it like this. I mean, as long as there's even a doubt...'

'I'm afraid a signed confession doesn't leave much room for doubt. Now come on, Charles, I've taken a foolish risk in bringing you down here; I think we should move as soon as possible and – '

'No, just a minute. Hugo, please, just look at me and tell me that you did it, tell me that you strangled Charlotte, and I'll believe you.'

Hugo looked at Charles. The eyes were still dull, but somewhere deep down there was a tiny spark of interest. 'Charles, I can't say that definitely, because I can't remember. But I think there's a strong chance that I killed Charlotte.'

'And you're prepared to leave it like that?'

Hugo shrugged. 'What's the alternative? I don't see that it's going to be possible to prove that I didn't.'

'Then we'll just have to prove that someone else did.' The remark came out with more crusading fervour than Charles had intended.

It affected Hugo. A new shrewdness came into his eyes. 'Hmm. Well, if you think that's possible, then you have my blessing to investigate until you're blue in the face.'

The new animation showed how little Hugo had even considered the possibility of his innocence. Whether from his own remorse or because of the prompting of C.I.D. men anxious to sew up the case, he had not begun to think of any alternative solution.

But the shift of mood did not last. Hugo dropped back into dull despair. 'Yes, if it'll amuse you, Charles, investigate everything. I'd like to feel I could be of use to someone, if only as something to investigate. And if you can t clear my besmirched name' – the italics were heavy with sarcasm – 'then take up another hobby. Amateur dramatics, maybe?'

Gerald got purposeful again. 'Charles, I think Hugo and I – '

'Just a minute. Hugo, I've got to ask you a couple of things.'

'Okay.' The voice had reverted to tonelessness.

'You said the other evening that Charlotte was having an affair. Do you know who her lover was?'

'Oh God, here we go again. I've been through all this with the police and – '

'Look, Charles, I don't think – ' Gerald butted in instinctively to defend his client.

'No, it's all right, Gerald. I can go through it once again. No, Charles, I don't know who Charlotte's lover was. No, I'm not even certain that she was having an affair. It just seemed a reasonable assumption – like so much else.'

'What led you to that assumption?'

'She was a young, attractive woman. She was trapped in a marriage that was getting nowhere. She was bored, lonely. I spent more and more time out getting pissed. If she didn't start something up, then she had less initiative than I gave her credit for.'

"But you had no proof?'

'What sort of proof do you want? No. I never caught her in flagrante delicto, no, I never saw her with a man, but if coming in at all hours, if going out on unexplained errands during the day, if saying she didn't have to stay with me, she could go elsewhere…if that kind of thing's proof, then I had it.'

'But you never asked her directly?'

'No. Towards the end we didn't talk too much. Only to make domestic arrangements or to shout at each other. Oh, I'm sure she had a man somewhere.'

'When did you start to think this?'

'I don't know. Two, three months back.'

'Round the time she started rehearsing *The Seagull*.'

'Possible. And, in answer to your next question, no, I have no idea whether she was having an affair with any of the Backstagers. I just felt she was having an affair with someone.' Hugo's voice was slurred with fatigue. Charles could feel Gerald's protective restlessness and knew he hadn't got much longer for his questioning.

'Hugo, I'll leave you now. Just one last thing. I want to find out more about Charlotte. Did she have any friends' I could talk to, to ask about her?'

Hugo replied flatly, 'No, no friends in Breckton. No close friends. That's what she always complained about. That's why she joined the Backstagers, to meet people. No, no friends, except lover boy.'

'Didn't she keep in touch with people she'd known before you married?'

'One or two. Not many. Diccon Hudson she used to see sometimes. And there was a girl she'd been at drama school with, used to come round sometimes. Not recently. I didn't like her much. Too actressy, hippy...young maybe is what I mean.'

'What's her name?'

'Sally Radford.'

'Thank you. I will go now, Hugo. I'm sorry to have to put you through it all again. But if there's a chance of finding something out, it'll be worth it.'

Hugo spoke with his eyes closed. His voice was infinitely tired. 'I wouldn't bother Charles. I killed her.'

CHAPTER NINE

CHARLES SAT OVER a pint in the bay-window of a coach lamp and horse brasses pub and looked out at the main shopping street of Breckton.

It was dominated by a long parade of shops with flats overhead, built in the thirties by some neat planning mind which had decreed that this would be enough, that there was room here for a baker, a butcher, a grocer, a greengrocer, a fishmonger, an ironmonger and one of everything else that the area might need. It would all be neat, all contained, all readily accessible.

Maybe it had had five years of this neat, ordered appearance. But soon shops had changed hands or identities and the uniformity of the original white-lettered names had been broken down by new signs and fascias. Now the line above the shop-windows was an uneven chain of oblongs in neon and garish lettering. And the frontages of the flats had been variously painted or pitted with the acne of pebbledash.

The original parade had quickly proved inadequate to the demands of the growing dormitory suburb. New rows of shops had sprung up to flank it, each date-stamped by design, and each with its uniformity broken in the same way.

As the final insult to symmetry, opposite the old parade an enormous supermarket had been built in giant Lego bricks.

The street was crowded with shoppers. Almost all women with children. Outside the pub Charles saw two young mothers, each with a child swinging on the end of one arm and another swaddled in a baby buggy, stop and chat. And he began to feel the isolation of Charlotte in this great suburban incubator.

The whole place was designed for young couples with growing families and all the daytime social life revolved around children.

What could a girl like Charlotte have done all day in a place like this? Little more than a girl when she married, she had presumably come from some sort of lively flat life in London. The shock of her lonely incarceration in the suburbs must have been profound.

What had she done all day? At first there had been thoughts of her continuing her acting career, but, as time went on, the terrible slump of unemployment which all young actors go through while they are building up their contacts must have extended hopelessly to the point where she lost those few contacts she had. Hugo, while probably not actively discouraging her career, had come from nearly twenty years of marriage to a woman who had done nothing but minister to him and, however vehement his protests that his second marriage was going to be totally different from his first, was too selfish to give real encouragement to something that could take his new wife away from home. So Charlotte's horizons were limited before the marriage had gone sour.

What had gone wrong with the marriage? Charles felt he knew. Something comparable had happened to him. With a mental blush he remembered himself equally dewy-eyed two years before, equally certain that a young girl called Anna could put the clock back for him, that he could fall in love like an adolescent in a romantic novel. In his case, the disillusionment had been rapid and total, but he could still feel the pain of it.

With Hugo the realization must have been slower, but even more devastating. As the relationship progressed, he must have understood gradually that he had not married a goddess. only a girl. She wasn't a symbol of anything, just a real person, with all the attendant inadequacies and insecurities. Even her beauty was transient. In the short years of their marriage, he must have seen her begin to age, seen, the crinkles spread beneath her eyes and know that nothing had changed, that he was the same person, growing older yoked to a different woman. And a woman in many ways less suitable than the wife he had left for her.

No doubt the sexual side of the marriage had also palled. Charles knew too well the anxieties men of his age were prey to. Perhaps Hugo had left Alice when their sex-life had started to fail, making the common male mistake of blaming the woman. He had married Charlotte as the new cure-all and then, slowly, slowly found that all the old anxieties had crept back and left him no better off than before.

Once the marriage had started to go wrong, deterioration would have been rapid. Hugo had always had the ability to shrink back into himself. No doubt when love's young dream began to crack, he didn't talk to Charlotte about it. He probably ceased to talk to her at all, morbidly digging himself into his own disappointment. He took to drinking more, arriving home later, leaving her longer and longer on her own. Again the question – what did she find to do all day?

Charles decided that was the first thing for him to find out. And he knew where to start. Still in his pocket was the spare key which Hugo had pressed on him so hospitably. He set off towards the Meckens' house.

The road of executive residences was almost deserted. Distantly an old lady walked a dog. The houses looked asleep, their net curtains closed like eyelids.

Charles felt chilly as he crunched across the small arc of gravel in front of Hugo's house. There was a strong temptation to look round, to see if he was observed, but he resisted it. There was no need to be surreptitious; he was not doing anything wrong.

Inside everything was tidy. Very different from the Tuesday night. The police had been through every room, checking, searching. And they had replaced everything neatly. Too neatly. The house looked like a museum.

He didn't know what he was looking for, but it was something to do with Charlotte. Something that would explain her, maybe even answer the nagging question of how she spent her time. He had thought he understood her in the Backstagers' car park on Saturday night, but it was only since her death that he was beginning to feel the complexity of her character and circumstances.

Like the Winters, Hugo and Charlotte had had the luxury of space in a house designed for a family. Their double bed was in the large front bedroom which had a bathroom en suite. But when Charles had come to stay with them for the first time, some three months before, Hugo had slept in one of the small back bedrooms and used the main bathroom. Husband and wife lived in a state of domestic apartheid.

The bed in the mis-titled master bedroom was strangely pathetic. It was large with a white fur cover, a defiant sexual status symbol. It had been bought for a new, hopeful marriage, a marriage that was going to work. But now the pillows were only piled on one side and one of the bedside tables was empty.

He looked through the books on the other side. Nothing unexpected in Charlotte's literary taste. A few thrillers, a Gerald Durrell, a copy of *The Seagull*. All predictable enough.

On the shelf below was something more interesting. A copy of a Family Health Encyclopaedia. It was not a new book, printed in the fifties, probably something Hugo had brought from his previous married home. Not a great work of medical literature, but useful for spot diagnosis of childish ailments.

But why was Charlotte reading it? Was she ill? And why was she reading it in a slightly surreptitious way, half-hiding the book. Surely, if she thought she were really ill, she'd have gone to a doctor. Or at least consulted some more detailed medical work. Unless it had been the only work of reference to hand. Unless she had a panic about something she didn't dare to discuss...

Good Lord, had Charlotte been worried that she was pregnant? Suddenly, the thought seemed attractively plausible. A lot of what she had said in the Backstagers' car park would be explained if that were the case. That business about being off alcohol. It could be checked through the police post-mortem. Mental note to ask Gerald.

If she were pregnant, a whole new volume of possible motives for killing her was opened. He felt a catch of excitement.

He tried the drawer next. That didn't seem to offer anything unexpected. A couple of rings, a broken string of beads, no doubt awaiting mending, a polythene bag of cotton wool balls, a nail-file, an empty key-ring, a jar of nail polish and...what was that at the back? He pulled it out. A small book covered in red leather.

It was a Roman Catholic missal. Inside the cover was written, 'To Charlotte. On the occasion of her first communion, with love from Uncle Declan and Auntie Wyn.'

Yes of course, the Northern Irish background. Good little Catholic girl. Which might raise problems if she had got herself pregnant. And moral issues over contraception. Difficult to know how strong the Catholic influence would have remained. She had married Hugo in spite of his divorce. But Charles had gathered from his friend's unworthy ramblings in the Trattoria that she had let Hugo take the responsibility for birth control in the relationship. Which might mean that Charlotte would be in danger of getting pregnant if she started sleeping with someone else. Which would make sense.

He opened the fitted wardrobe on Charlotte's side of the room. The sight of her fashionable clothes gave him a sharp pang. She had worn them so well, been so beautiful. And now they hung lifeless, misshapen by the bony shoulders of the clothes hangers..

Charles ruffled through the dresses and looked with care among the litter of shoes in the bottom of the wardrobe. He still didn't know what he was looking for, but he didn't feel the time was wasted. Somehow, among her things, he felt closer to Charlotte, closer to understanding what had been going through her mind in the days before her death.

Her clothes smelt strongly of her scent, as if she were still alive. He wouldn't have been surprised to see her walk in through the door.

The wardrobe revealed nothing unexpected. Nor did the rows of drawers which flanked it. He was about to start looking round the bathroom when he stopped. There had been nothing unexpected among her clothes, but equally there had not been something that might have been expected there either.

Charlotte Mecken had been strangled with a scarf. Hugo had identified it as her own scarf and yet there were no others among her clothes. There were any number of dresses, skirts and shirts for her to choose from, any number of pullovers and pairs of shoes. But only one scarf.

When he came to think of it, Charles realized he had never seen Charlotte wearing a scarf. And what was more, even his sketchy knowledge of current fashion told him that scarves were not 'in'. Certainly not those crude Indian prints like the one he had seen knotted around Charlotte's neck. No, those had had a vogue in the late sixties, they now looked rather dated. Charlotte, with her sharp fashion sense, would not have been...He smiled wryly as his mind formed the phrase 'been seen dead in one.'

What it meant was that Charlotte was most unlikely to have been wearing the scarf with which she was killed. Which made the accepted picture of the murder, of Hugo reaching out to her in a drunken fury and throttling her, unlikely. Whoever killed Charlotte must have gone to get the scarf with which to do it.

The bathroom did not offer much space for secrets. The pale green bath, basin, bidet and lavatory were modern and functional. Fluffy yellow towels hung from the heated rail. Only the mirror-fronted cabinet gave any opportunity for concealment.

The contents were predictable. Make-up, various creams, nail scissors, a tin of throat sweets, shampoo, an unopened box of Tampax, cough medicine, a roll of sticking plaster.

The decor of the bathroom was recent. The walls were olive green and the floor was covered with the same mustardy carpet as the bedroom. It was all very neat, very attractive, like a picture out of Homes and Gardens.

The only blemishes were two small screw-holes above the cabinet. It must have been set too high initially and been moved down to the right level for Charlotte. Maybe it had been moved when Hugo exiled himself to the other bedroom and bathroom.

Now it had been moved down, the cabinet's bottom edges rested on the top row of white tiles which surrounded the wash-basin. As a result it was tilted slightly and there was a narrow triangle of space between it and the wall.

Charles knew there would be something in there. He didn't know why. It was part of the understanding he was beginning to feel for Charlotte. She had been so young, so young, almost childlike in some respects. It was in character for her to have a hiding place for her Secret things, like a girl at boarding school making one 'little corner of total privacy that the teachers would never know about. It was a way of maintaining her identity in a challenging situation.

Charles pressed his face to the wall and squinted along the gap. Then, very calmly, he fished in with a pen and slid out a brown envelope. It was not sealed. As he raised it to shake out the contents, the front door-bell rang.

He shoved the envelope in his pocket and swallowed his first impulse to run and hide. After all, he wasn't doing anything wrong. Hugo had given him the key Without prompting. He wasn't even trespassing on his friend's property.

He tried to calm himself with such thoughts as he walked sedately downstairs, but he still felt as guilty as a schoolboy caught with an apple in his hand in an orchard.

This mood was intensified when the opened front door revealed a uniformed policeman.

'Good afternoon, sir,' said the policeman in a tone that indicated that he was prepared to start quite reasonably, but was ready to get tough when the need arose.

'Good afternoon,' Charles echoed foolishly.

'Might I ask what you're doing here, sir?'

'Yes, certainly.' Charles affected man-of-the-world affability, to which the policeman seemed immune. 'My name's Charles Paris. I'm a friend of Hugo Mecken. I've stayed here a few times. He gave me a key, actually.' Charles reached into his pocket as if to demonstrate until he realized the fatuity of the gesture. 'Said I could drop in any time.'

'I see, sir.' The policeman's tone remained reasonable, but it had a strong undercurrent of disbelief. 'Rather an unusual time to drop in, sir. Or haven't you heard what's been happening here?'

'Oh yes, I know all about it.' Charles replied eagerly and, as he said it, recognized his stupidity. If he'd claimed ignorance of the whole affair, he could just have walked away.

'I see, sir. In fact, we had a call from someone in the road who had seen you go into the house and who thought, under the circumstances, it was rather odd.'

Good God, you couldn't blow your nose in Breckton without someone seeing. There must be watchers behind every curtain. Time for a tactical lie.

'In fact, officer, the reason I am here is that, as I say, I stayed with the Meckens a few times and on the last occasion Mrs Mecken was good enough to wash out a couple of shirts for me. Now all this terrible business has happened, I thought I'd better pick them up without delay.'

The policeman seemed to accept this. 'And have you found them?'

'Found what? Oh, the shirts – no, I haven't yet. I've been looking around, but I'm not sure where Mrs Mecken would have put them.'

'Ah. Well. Would you like me to accompany you round the house while you find them?' It was phrased as a question, but it wasn't one.

Like Siamese twins they went through the house They looked in the airing cupboard, they looked in the wardrobes. Eventually Charles produced the solution he had been desperately working out for the last few minutes. 'Do you know, I think Mrs Mecken must have mixed them up with her husband's clothes and put them away in his drawer.'

'Well, sir, I dare say you'll want to be off now.'

Charles didn't argue.

'And, sir, I think, if you don't mind, you'd better give me that key. I'll see that it gets put with the rest of Mr. Mecken's belongings. I think, under the circumstances, with the possibility of further police investigations, the less people we have walking around this property, the better. I quite understand why you came in, sir, but if a key like this got into the wrong hands…well, who knows, it might be awkward.'

'Of course.' Charles had no alternative but to hand it over.

'Thank you, sir.' The policeman ushered him out of the front door and closed it behind them. Then he stood in the middle of the doorstep. 'Goodbye, sir.'

Charles walked across the gravel and along the road in the direction of the station, conscious of the policeman's eyes following him. He wasn't going to get another chance to get inside that house without breaking and entering.

Still, the search had not been fruitless, In his pocket there was an envelope.

CHAPTER TEN

'YOU REALIZE IT'S probably illegal,' said Gerald grumpily. 'It's withholding evidence...or stealing evidence or...I'm sure there's something they could get you for.'

Gerald was being unhelpful over the whole thing. He didn't want to hear how Charles had spent the rest of the morning and manifested the minimum of interest in his findings. Also it was clear that he didn't like having his friend round the Grosvenor Street office. Charles Paris was a reminder of the Mecken case and Gerald didn't want to be reminded. He wanted to re-immerse himself in his regular work, wrangling over small clauses in film and television contracts, or even sorting out the odd divorce. Having clients charged with murder upset him; he thought it was irresponsible and didn't want to dwell on it.

'I don't care,' said Charles, 'I think it's important. I had a look at the book on the train, but couldn't make much of it, so I thought two heads might be better than one. You always said you wanted to be included in any of my cases.'

'Charles, there is a difference between what one does professionally and what one does as a hobby.' Gerald could be insufferably stuffy.

'Murder's a funny sort of thing to have as a hobby. Anyway, just give me five minutes of your time to look at this stuff and then I'll leave you alone.' Gerald looked dubious. 'Good God, do I have to pay for your time?'

This at least brought a smile to Gerald's lips. 'You'd never be able to afford my rates, Charles.'

He took advantage of the shift of mood to redirect attention to the envelope on the desk. He shook it and out came a thin, blue-covered book and a beige plastic envelope. 'Let's concentrate on the diary first.'

He flicked through the pages. Gerald,' in spite of himself, craned over to look. 'Not much in it, Charles.'

'No, that's what makes it interesting. Why make such a palaver about hiding a book that contains so little information?'

'Presumably because the little information it does contain is extremely secret.'

'Yes. In other words, it had to be kept secret from Hugo. I mean, there was no one else in the house to hide things from, was there?'

'No.'

'The interesting thing is that there's nothing at all until May. Then we have this entry – Saturday May 23rd, Backstagers' Party. Now I know that

Charlotte hadn't been a member of the society long, so I reckon that could well have been her first contact.'

'Seems reasonable, but it doesn't get us far.'

'No. Then we get these four dates in early June – *Seagull* auditions. That's self-explanatory. And isn't it typical of that Backstagers lot to make a big production out of it and have four whole evenings of auditions.

'As we know, Charlotte was successful in the audition, because then in July we start getting rehearsals marked. Okay, that makes sense. She started the diary when she started getting involved in amateur dramatics.'

'Not really something you'd treat as a big secret, is it, Charles?'

'No, the secret bit comes later. But there's something odd about this diary even from what we've seen so far. I mean, I can understand why she enters all the rehearsals – they're quite complicated and she'd need to make a note of them – but why are there no engagements before the Backstagers' party? I'm not going to believe that was the first time she went out in the year.'

'No.' Gerald sounded as if he was losing interest again.

Charles picked up the pace. 'I think I know what it was. Not the first time she had gone out, but the first time she had arranged to go out herself., So far as I can tell, it was round that time that she and Hugo ceased to communicate. I think starting this diary was an identity thing for her. All right, if Hugo and I are not having a life together, I'll damned well make a life of my own. And this little diary was a symbol of that determination, of her separateness. And if that's why she started the diary, it explains the later entries. The Affair.' He pronounced it portentously to whet Gerald's appetite. 'Look.'

Starting late August, in the midst of all the Seagull rehearsals, there was a new series of notes. Lunchtimes. 1.0 – Waterloo. 1.0 – Charing Cross. 1.0 – Charing Cross again, then back to Waterloo. A whole sequence of them.

The last was different. It was for the Tuesday of that week. 1.0 – Victoria. But that was one railway station rendezvous Charlotte Mecken did not make. Because by then she was dead.

'You reckon it was a lover?'

'It would fit rather cosily, wouldn't it, Gerald?'

'But I thought you were working on the idea that she was having an affair with someone in the Backstagers. Surely that'd be strictly local.'

'Not if they wanted any degree of privacy. To have an affair in a place like Breckton would be like having it off in the middle of Wembley Stadium on Cup Final day.'

'Hmm. So you reckon it was someone who worked in Town.'

'Which would apply to every man in Breckton.'

'Yes. It still seems odd to me that she should write all these things down. Surely it was courting disaster. I mean, if Hugo had found this book...'

'I think that danger was part of the excitement. Anyway, it would have been just as damning if Hugo had found these.' Charles indicated the small beige plastic envelope.

Gerald picked it up and slid out a rectangle of foil round the edge of which was a line of transparent blister, some of which contained small white pills. The solicitor looked up blankly. 'What is it?'

Charles laughed 'Oh Gerald, what touching. naïveté. Have you never seen these before? Of course, they're not really of our generation. We and our wives and girl friends did not have such modern conveniences at our disposal.'

Gerald coloured. 'You mean these are contraceptive pills?'

'Exactly.' Charles couldn't resist a little further tease. 'I think that's a very heart-warming comment on your marriage, Gerald. That you shouldn't even recognize these new-fangled inventions. Fidelity is not dead. If you'd spent as much time as I have hopping in and out of unsuitable young women's bedrooms, you'd know sure enough what – '

Gerald was not amused. 'I think you'd better put them away, Charles. Polly might come in.'

'You're beautifully old-fashioned, Gerald. I rather think Polly would recognize them.'

Gerald took refuge in a look at his watch. 'Look, I've got rather a lot to get on with.'

'Okay. I'll stop sending you up and be quick. These pills are the final proof that Charlotte was having an affair. Not only because of the way in which they were hidden, but because I happen to know that Hugo was in favour of more primitive methods of contraception.'

Gerald's eyes opened wide. 'How on earth do you know that? It's hardly the sort of thing you'd talk about.'

Charles laughed again at his friend's sedateness. 'He did mention it actually. But look, that's not the only thing these pills tell us. There's something else strange about them. Look.'

Gerald cast an embarrassed eye over the foil and shrugged. 'Don't see anything.'

'The last pill was taken on a Wednesday.'

'So?' Gerald was looking distinctly uncomfortable. The conversation was straying beyond the boundaries of what he considered suitable masculine subject matter.

'Charlotte was killed on Monday night and yet the last pill was taken on a Wednesday. It wasn't the end of her cycle because there are still pills left. So it means that she stopped taking the pills at least five days before she died.'

'Maybe she just forgot them.' Gerald's interest was beginning to overcome his embarrassment.

'Unlikely. Though I suppose she was very tied up with the play and it's possible. But you would have thought a married woman in the middle of an affair would be extra careful.'

'Unless the affair had broken up and she no longer had any use for the pills.'

'That's a thought. That is a thought.' The existence of a jilted lover opened new vistas of motivation. But there was a snag. 'On the other hand, if we look back at the diary, there's that Victoria assignation for the Tuesday, not to mention a Charing Cross one for the Monday. Which rather suggests that the affair was still swinging along. So that can't be why she stopped taking the pills.'

The flow of logic had stopped. Charles sighed. He was buzzing round something important, but he hadn't found it yet. He had got the right pieces, but he wasn't putting them in the right order. 'Oh well, I suppose the first thing is to find out who the lover was.'

'I should think, if he exists, the police would know by now.'

'Do you reckon?'

'Of course. They're not stupid. Maybe you can keep that sort of thing secret from the nosey parkers of Breckton, but the police can go around and question everyone who knew Charlotte, they can talk to the railway staff who saw her travelling up on her assignations, all that sort of thing.'

'Yes. Well, if the police happen to tell you who the lover was – or any other useful snippets of information – you will pass them on, won't you?'

'If they are the sort of things I think I should pass on, yes.'

Charles had an urge to punch Gerald right in the middle of his formal solicitor's face, but he decided it wasn't worth losing friends that way. 'Maybe I'd better go.'

'Yes. I am meant to be getting on with my work. I do have clients depending on me, you know.'

'Yes, I'm sure we can depend that one of them is paying for your time at the moment.'

Gerald didn't rise to the running joke.

There was a copy of *Spotlight* in the outer office where Gerald's secretary Polly sat. Charles picked up *Actresses L-Z*.

Sally Radford was under Juvenile and Juvenile Character. The photograph showed a strong face dominated by a largish nose. Straight dark hair parted in the middle and looped back like curtains behind the ears. It was one of those faces which in the flesh would either look very attractive or not quite make it. Depend to some extent on the colouring. Beneath the black and white photograph it said '5ft. 6in' and 'Blue Eyes.' The blue eyes were unexpected and promising.

There was no name and number for an agent. Just 'C/O Spotlight' as a contact. That was revealing to Charles as an actor. Probably meant she had not yet got very far in her career and either couldn't find an agent willing to represent her until she had more experience or had decided that for the moment she was going to do as well finding work for herself. It also probably meant that she was based in London rather than doing a season out at some provincial rep. If she were out of town she'd want an agent as a point of contact for inquiries.

Polly graciously granted him the use of her phone and he got through. The girl on the Spotlight switchboard said that Sally Radford was likely to be ringing in and could he leave a number where he could be contacted? He explained that that was rather difficult as he wasn't sure of his movements.

'Is it important?' asked the girl, meaning 'Is it work?'

'Yes, it is,' Charles replied, glad that she'd phrased it in a way that enabled him to reply without lying.

'Okay then, I can give you a number to contact her.'

'Thank you very much.'

Sally Radford answered straight away. Her voice was husky and well-articulated without being actressy. It confirmed the strength of character implicit in the photograph.

'Hello, my name's Charles Paris. I got your name through Spotlight.'

'Yes.'

He heard the catch of excitement in her voice and realized that that was a rotten way to introduce himself to an out-of-work actress. He had better disillusion her quickly. 'Sorry, it's not about work.'

'Oh.' The disappointment could not be disguised.

'No, I'm sorry, it's a rather awkward thing I'm ringing about. I believe you were a friend of Charlotte Mecken.'

'Yes.' The voice went serious. Charles began to think that she was probably a talented actress; her inflections on small words were telling. She continued, not playing it tragic queen, just sad, 'I thought somebody might be in touch. I suppose I was her closest friend – though with Charlotte that did not necessarily mean very close. Are you police?'

'No, I'm not actually. I'm a…' He resisted the temptation to say 'private investigator', which was a bit grandiose for what he was doing and probably an offence under the Trades Descriptions Act '…friend of Hugo's.'

'Ah.' Again the intonation was informative and reminded him that Hugo and Sally had not got on well.

'As you probably know, Hugo's been arrested for murder…'

'Yes.'

'Well, I'm by no means certain that he's guilty. That's why I'd like to meet you and talk if I may.'

'Sure. Anything I can do to help.'

'Can we meet soon?'

'Soon as you like, I don't have a lot happening at the moment.' The understatement spoke of some weeks of sitting by the telephone.

Charles arranged to go round to her flat in Maida Vale at six and put the phone down with the small satisfaction of having made a date.

CHAPTER ELEVEN

SALLY RADFORD DID look better in colour than in monochrome. The strength of the face and its potential hardness were made less daunting by the piercing blue of her eyes. She was dressed in a collarless man's shirt with a brown stripe, well-cut jeans and cowboy boots. Almost flat-chested, but very feminine. A hint of some musky scent.

Her flat showed the same kind of style. Obviously rented furnished, but with sufficient touches of her own to take the curse off the Identikit furniture. A Japanese paper kite in the shape of a bird dangled over the fireplace. Tall grasses in the old green bottle balanced the slumped display of books on a low shelf. The decor was minimal, but assured.

The girl emanated the same confidence. Not the go-getting brashness that Charles had encountered in so many young actresses, but an inner patience, an impression that everything she did was logical and right.

Charles found her relaxing. Partly because of her directness, but also because she was an actress, a real actress to whom he could talk about the theatre without fearing the stupid or exaggerated responses he had come to expect from the Backstagers. It was only as he talked to her that he realized how long it was since he had been with real actors.

She sat him down and offered him tea or coffee. He chose tea, which came in a blue and grey earthenware mug. China with lemon. Good.

'Okay, what do you want me to tell you?' Down to business as soon as the social formalities had been observed.

'Let me fill you in a bit on what I'm doing first. I was with Hugo when he found Charlotte's body...' He then filled her in on the background of Hugo's confession and his reasons for believing that it was not necessarily conclusive.

Sally was silent for a moment, then made up her mind. 'Okay, let's accept your hypothesis for the time being. What can I do for you?'

'Just a few questions about Charlotte. I'm sorry, I know you didn't like Hugo, but I would like to clear up – '

'I didn't dislike him. I don't think he even disliked me. I think he just resented my friendship with Charlotte. Partly because he was jealous of what he imagined to be our closeness – he was terribly aware of their age difference and was afraid of Charlotte seeing too much of her contemporaries in case they took her away from him – which is ironic, seeing how the marriage turned out. Also I'm an actress and I tended to talk about the theatre. I don't think Hugo really wanted Charlotte's career to develop, in case that took her away from him.'

'That's rather what I thought.'

'So he got very uptight if I started talking about contacts or auditions coming up or prospects for jobs or...Though,' she added on a personal note of bitterness, 'I don't think he need have worried if Charlotte's success had been anything like mine over the last couple of years.'

'Work not coming?'

She shook her head wryly. 'You're a master of understatement. No, I'm not exactly fighting the offers away from my door. I've had a few radios, one or two close calls on West End auditions, but...' She straightened up. 'But you know all that. It's familiar country.'

'Right.' There was a pause of great togetherness, of shared experience. 'I don't know Charlotte well, Sally. I only really met her through Hugo and, you know, you view your friend's wives and girl friends through a kind of refracting glass of the friends themselves. What I've been trying to do since Charlotte was killed is to see her on her own, to know what her own personality was like, apart from Hugo. What I really want you to do is tell me if I'm on the right lines in understanding her, or if I'm hopelessly wrong.'

'How do you see her?'

'It's funny, I keep coming back to the image of her as terribly young. I don't mean just in age. I mean young for her years. Immature even.'

Sally nodded slowly. 'That's quite shrewd. Yes, she was. I knew her right through drama school and she was always very naive, sort of wide-eyed about things. She never looked it. So beautiful, for a start, and she had such superb dress sense that everyone thought she was the ultimate sophisticated woman, but it was only a front – no, not even a front, because she didn't put it up consciously. It was when I realized this that I first started to like her. Suddenly I saw that she wasn't a daunting, challenging woman, but just a rather earnest child. I think we're always drawn to people by knowledge of their weaknesses. It's so comforting, that moment when you realize that you don't have to be afraid and competitive any more.

'I think Charlotte had had a very sheltered upbringing. Northern Ireland. Straight-laced, inward-looking family so far as I can gather. Convent education.'

'It seems odd Sally, considering that, that she was allowed to go to drama school. You'd think there would have been family opposition.'

'Yes, it was strange. But she was strong-minded about certain things. And she knew she could act and that that was what she wanted to do. I don't think anyone could cross her once she'd really made up her mind about something.'

'Hmm. She was a good actress. I only saw her in one thing, tatty amateur production of *The Seagull*, but by God it was all there.'

'Oh yes, she was good. That's what made her marrying Hugo so sad. He didn't want her to be a successful actress. He was miserly about her, wanted to keep her to himself.'

'Do you think he even objected to her joining the amateur society?'

'I don't think he was keen. That was something she decided to do very much on her own. Anyway, he could hardly object – I gather he had been a member to take advantage of the bar for some time. But I doubt if they discussed it. By then they were hardly speaking.'

Charles nodded. It was satisfying to have his diagnosis of the marriage and Charlotte's motivation confirmed. 'So she joined as a deliberate attempt to assert her own individuality?'

'Yes. I think she also saw it as a step of getting herself back on the road to the professional theatre. You know how it is in the business – if you don't work for a bit, you lose confidence. I think she had to do something to prove to herself that she could still act.'

'It's surprising that she started at such a local level, that she didn't just up and leave Hugo and go back to the real theatre world.'

'I don't think she really wanted to leave him. She had been very much in love when they married. It was only when he withdrew completely into himself that the marriage foundered. I think she still hoped that one day he would come out of his sulk and everything would be all right again. Deep down she had a great belief in the sanctity of marriage. The Catholic background again. She wouldn't have left her husband lightly.'

'Hmm. But she would have an affair with another man lightly?'

Sally Radford appraised him coolly. 'You know about that then. In fact, I don't think that was entered into lightly either. Charlotte was a very serious girl – as I said, an earnest child. No, I think the affair was because she just had to do something to get out of her spiral of loneliness. And also because she was very attracted to the man in question.'

'You don't, by any chance...?' Charles hazarded hopefully.

Sally shook her head. ''Fraid not. I have this sneaking feeling that she did once mention a man's name to me, but I'm sorry, I can't for the life of me remember what it was.'

'But she did tell you she was having an affair?'

'Not directly. But she came to me for practical advice, and I put two and two together.'

'Practical advice?'

'Yes. It's back to the naïveté we were talking about. Charlotte had always been a bit backward in sexual matters. I mean, at drama school, where all the rest of us were screwing away like rabbits, she kept herself to herself.'

'You don't mean she managed to come through drama school a virgin? I thought that was a technical impossibility.'

Sally smiled. 'I don't know if she was actually a virgin, but I do know that she was pretty inhibited about such things. Needless to say, all the men were panting round her like puppies, but I don't know if any of them got anywhere.'

'Not even Diccon Hudson?'

'Ah, you know Mr. Golden Voice. Yes, he certainly tried as hard as any of them, but I just don't know. He made a point of trying to have everything in sight, really put it about. What do they reckon that kind of manic screwing's a sign of? Latent homosexuality? Not in his case, I think.'

'But did he make it with Charlotte?'

'I think probably not. And I'm sure if he didn't it made him furious. Great blow to the great pride. No, for Charlotte, Hugo was the first big thing in her life. I think perhaps she found the slower approach of the older man less frightening than the ravenous groping of her contemporaries.'

'Yes, of course, we old men do slow down quite a bit,' Charles agreed with mock-seriousness.

Sally Radford realized what she had said and giggled. She looked at him and a new awareness came into their conversation. 'Anyway, Charles, to come up to date...Some time in July, Charlotte rang and asked if we could meet for lunch. We did and, after some small talk and embarrassment on her part, she asked me how she should set about getting on the Pill. Since she had got that far into her married life without it and because she was so surreptitious about the inquiry, I reckon that that meant she had started sleeping with someone other than her husband.'

'Yes, that would fit.' Charles quickly summarized his discovery of the pills in their hiding place in Charlotte's bathroom.

'Anyway,' Sally continued, 'for some reason she didn't want to go to her local G.P. So I recommended the Brook Clinic in Totty Court Road. I'd been there myself, they're very helpful.'

'So we can assume that they fitted her out and the affair continued.'

'I imagine so. I found it a bit sad that she came to me actually. I mean, not that she was so ignorant, that was just part of her character, but the fact that I was the only person she could talk to. I didn't know her that well, and yet she was in a strange way dependent on me.'

'Hmm. When did you last see her or hear from her?'

'We had lunch again quite soon after the time I mentioned. Since then, just the odd phone call.'

'Did she talk again about the contraception business?'

'Only once. Otherwise it was as if it had never happened.'

'And the once?'

'That was quite recently. I think the last time I heard from her. She must have read some scare article about the Pill in a magazine or something. She asked all kinds of things about the dangers of it. Not straight away, but she manoeuvred the conversation round to it.'

'What sort of things did she ask?'

'Practically everything – about the dangers of embolism, could the Pill cause obesity, was it liable to raise the blood pressure, could it harm the foetus if a pregnant woman took it, could it lead to sterility, did it upset the cycle irrevocably – just about every Pill scare that has ever been put out, and a few old wives' tales thrown in for good measure.'

'Did she sound worried?'

'She didn't actually sound worried, but she was a good actress and the fact that she raised the subject suggested to me that she must be.'

'You didn't get any impression which of the particular dangers she was worried about?'

''Fraid not. If there was one in particular she was asking about, she managed to put up an effective smoke-screen with all the others. I assumed that the Pill had just affected her cycle. It often does at first. If her periods had always been regular before, it would probably worry her if things suddenly got out of phase.'

Charles was silent, his passivity hiding the speed with which his mind was working. There were other things that could cause an upset in a woman's cycle.

Sally Radford suddenly spoke again, with more emotion than hitherto. 'God knows why she asked me. That's what I meant by being sad, that there was no one else she could ask, no family, no friendly doctor. As if I were an international expert on contraception.'

The bitterness in the last sentence made Charles look up and he was surprised to see the glint of a tear in her eye.

She dashed it away. 'I'm sorry. It's just that it seems so inhuman – Charlotte dead and presumably dissected on some police mortuary slab while we meticulously pick through her gynaecological history.'

'Yes, but there's something else worrying you, isn't there?'

She looked up at him, giving the full benefit of those blue eyes. 'You're shrewd, Charles Paris. Yes, it was ironical her coming to me with her contraceptive problems. I learned the hard way.'

'An abortion?'

'Yes. Sixth form at school.'

'I'm sorry.' He offered the useless comfort of someone who knew nothing of the circumstances.

'Oh yes.' She tossed her head back to signify her return to a controlled mood. 'Yes, it's not really the emotional shock in my case. It's just the fear that, you know, something might have gone wrong, that I might not be able to conceive again as a result. I mean, not that there's anyone around at the moment whose baby I want to have, but...I don't know, you just have this fear that if you couldn't have children, it'd warp you in some way. It's all irrational. Forget it.'

Charles changed the subject, but he didn't forget it. 'Sorry to have dragged you through all this, but I'm very grateful to you for giving me your time and for being so frank. Can I take you out for a drink to say thank you?'

'Why not?' She consulted her watch. 'Twenty to eight. Yes, I think we can safely assume that all the major impresarios of London have packed their briefcases for the night and that I can leave the telephone unattended without jeopardizing my chances of becoming a STAR.'

They went to a rather camp Victorian pub in Little Venice and drank large amounts of red wine. Then Charles took Sally to a little Italian restaurant where they drank more red wine. When he saw her back to her flat, there didn't seem to be any question of his leaving.

'Why are we going to sleep together?' asked Charles with the deep philosophy of the drunk as he hopped round the bedroom trying to get his trousers off.

'In my case,' Sally replied, pulling her shirt over her head, 'because I like you and on the whole I do sleep with people I like. Also...' she paused profoundly, 'I'm after experience.'

'Experience that will one day be seen in a stage performance by the public?'

'Maybe.'

'Well, it may surprise you to know that even at my advanced age I'm still after experience.' He mused. 'Do you know, I'm fifty this week. Fifty.'

'There, there.' She took him in her arms. 'Rejuvenate yourself with the body of a young woman. Like Dracula.'

'You're nothing like Dracula. If you were you'd have run screaming from the garlic in the pollo sopreso.'

'There, there. Let's hope your body's not as decrepit as your wit. Otherwise I'm left out in the cold.'

'There, there. And there.' She drew in her breath sharply as he touched her. 'I think you'll find all's in working order.'

'Remember,' she whispered as they rolled together, 'no strings. Experience.'

'No strings,' he echoed as their bodies' heats fused.

'And no babies,' she said, nimbly detaching herself and reaching into her bedside drawer. 'Good God, considering our conversation, it's amazing I forgot it.' She flicked the small white pill into her mouth and swallowed it down jerkily.

'Tell me...' Charles's mind fumbled through the fogs of alcohol. '...if you were having an affair with someone, what would stop you from taking your pill? Apart from just forgetting it?'

'I suppose if the bloke walked out, I might – except that I wouldn't because I always live in the hope that something else is going to come along. Or if I wanted to get pregnant – except then I'd be more likely to do it at the end of the cycle.'

'Or...'

'Or, I suppose, if I thought I was pregnant, I'd stop as soon as I realized...for fear of hurting the baby.'

Charles smiled in a satisfied way as he took Sally back into his arms and crushed her flat but oh so feminine chest to his.

It was unhurried and good. As they snuggled together to sleep, Charles murmured, 'It simplifies everything, doesn't it? Sex therapy. Frees the mind.'

'Yes,' Sally agreed lazily, 'it's freed my memory.'

'What do you mean?'

'I've just remembered the name that Charlotte mentioned, the guy who I think must have been her lover.'

Charles was instantly alert. 'Yes?'

'Does the name Geoff make any sense?'

'Yes,' said Charles. 'Yes, it does.'

CHAPTER TWELVE

CHARLES GOT BACK to Hereford Road at half-past nine the next morning, feeling pretty good. So it wasn't all over; it could still happen. His mind started to generalize, filling with images of other nubile young girls through whose beds he would flit.

An envelope on the doormat quickly dislocated his mood. A birthday card. Right on cue. Friday, November 5th. The card was a well-chosen reproduction of an El Greco grandee and continued the message 'Congratulations on half a century. Love, Frances.' It served as a brutal reminder not only of his age but also of his neglected responsibilities. Images of future girls gave way to wistful recollection.

To stop himself getting maudlin, he brought his concentration to bear on Charlotte's murder. Now he knew the identity of her lover, the case seethed with new possibilities. The first thing he must do was to talk to Geoffrey Winter.

The sound of the phone ringing broke into his train of thought. Expecting it would be a boyfriend of one of the beefy Swedish girls who lived in the other bedsitters, he answered. It was his agent, Maurice Skellern.

That was unusual. Maurice was terribly inefficient and never rang his clients. Since he had never got any work for them, there was no point; they could ring him to find that out.

'Charles, I've had an inquiry from an advertising agency about your availability for a voice-over.'

'What, Mills Brown Mazzini?'

'No, another one.'

'That's good. Hugo said that once somebody uses you in this field, you start getting lots more inquiries. Perhaps I've become Flavour of the Month.'

'Well, they want you to do a voice test.'

'When?'

'This morning. At eleven.'

'Shee. I'd better get straight along. What's the address and who do I ask for?'

Maurice gave the details. 'Incidentally, Charles, about this voice-over business. I don't know much about it.'

'Well, there's an admission.'

'What I was going to say was, I'm glad about all the work, but we don't seem to have had too many checks through yet.'

'No, we'll have just the basic studio session fees so far. A few thirty-five quids. It's when the commercials go out and get repeated that the money really starts to flow. I mean, if this Bland campaign takes off…well…Exclusive contract has even been mentioned. And, you see, it's already leading to other inquiries.

'So you reckon there's a lot of work there?'

'Could be. Some people do dozens of voice-overs a week. Mix it in with film dubbing, reading books for the blind, other voice work. Make vast sums. Mostly people with specialist agents, of course,' he added maliciously.

Maurice was too used to Charles's snide lines about their relationship even to acknowledge this one. 'Well, good, good. Obviously the right step for you career-wise. Haven't I always been telling you you should be extending your range, finding a wider artistic fulfilment?'

'No, you've always been telling me I should make more money. By the way, anything else about?'

'There's a new permanent company being set up in Cardiff. Might be worth trying for that.'

'Hardly me, is it – Cardiff? Anyway, if this voice-over business gets under way, I'm going to have to be based in London for a bit. Till I've made enough to keep the taxman quiet. No nice convenient little tellies coming up, are there?'

'Haven't heard of anything. London Weekend are supposed to be setting up a new series about Queen Victoria's cooks, but I haven't heard when.'

'Then let's live in hope of the voice-overs. I'd better get along to this place for the test. By the way, did they say what the product was?'

'Yes. Something for…depopulation, was it?' 'For depopulation? You mean, like napalm?'

'No, no. For removing unsightly hair.'

'Depilation, Maurice.'

The new depilatory about to be launched on the armpits of the world was called No Fuzz and the selling line was 'There's no fuss with No Fuzz.'

Charles used his heavy cold voice again, because that was what they wanted. (If he had to keep grinding it down like that, he was going to ruin his vocal cords.) He dropped into the routine of giving every possible intonation to the new line, waiting for the fatuous notes from the account executive in charge ('Give it a bit more brio, love' and 'Try it with just a smidgeonette of sex in the voice') and let his mind wander. He couldn't lose the suspicion that a properly programmed computer could sew up the entire voice-over business.

He was kept for an hour, told he was super and that they'd give him a tinkle. And he had earned another thirty-five pounds.

In the reception of the agency he met Diccon Hudson. Charles saw the other man's eyes narrow at the sight of a potential rival. Diccon worked hard to maintain all his agency contacts and wouldn't take kindly to being aced out by a non-specialist. 'You up for the No Fuzz campaign?' he asked directly.

'Yes.'

'Becoming rivals, aren't we. First Mr. Bland, now…'

'I haven't necessarily got this one.'

'No.' Diccon Hudson seemed to gain comfort from the fact. His ferrety face could not conceal what was going through his mind.

Charles recalled suddenly that Diccon was on his list of people to check out in his investigation. 'You heard about Charlotte?'

The name sent a spasm across Diccon's over-expressive face. 'I heard. I was pretty cut up about it.'

Charles nodded. 'Terrible, yes. I suppose you hadn't seen her for a long time.'

'I saw her quite recently actually.'

'Not on Monday night, I suppose,' Charles joked, to draw Diccon out.

'No, not on Monday night. I – ' Diccon suddenly stopped short, as if he'd thought better of what he was going to say.

'What were you doing on Monday night then, buddy?' Charles dropped into a New York cop accent to take the curse off his interrogation.

'Nothing.' Diccon hurried on, 'I last saw Charlotte about a fortnight ago. We used to meet for the odd lunch.'

'Regularly?' Charles was beginning to wonder if, in spite of Sally Radford's recollection of the name 'Geoff,' there was any connection between Diccon and the dates in Charlotte's diary.

But the theory was shattered before it was formed. 'I was away in Crete for all of August, but I saw her a few times before and after. A few times.' The repeat was accompanied by a smug smile, enigmatic, but probably meant to be taken as a form of sexual bragging.

'Did Hugo know?'

Diccon gave a contemptuous shrug; the question wasn't worth answering.

Now for Geoffrey Winter. Charles was glad that Sally had come up with the name, because it confirmed a conclusion towards which his mind had been moving.

He had decided that, if Charlotte had chosen her lover from the ranks of the Backstagers, then Geoffrey was the only candidate. Perhaps it was *The Seagull* which had led him to the conclusion. Trigorin. after all, was the older man who seduced Nina. Or maybe it was just that Geoffrey seemed the only one of the Backstagers sufficiently attractive and interesting to be worthy of Charlotte.

He had first got an inkling of something between the two of them at the cast party. Not that they had been together; they had been apart. They had both danced so ostentatiously, both putting on such a show with other people. There had been something studied about the way they had avoided each other. All of the rest of the cast had been constantly reforming and forming in little knots to remember some near disaster or ill-disguised corpse, but Geoffrey and Charlotte had always ended up in different groups.

So Charles liked to think that he would have looked up Geoffrey's office address in the phone book even if Sally hadn't mentioned the name.

When he did, the address gave him further confirmation. Listed under Geoffrey Winter Associates, Architects. And an office in Villiers Street, adjacent to Charing Cross Station and just over Hungerford Bridge from Waterloo.

The office was on the top floor. A door with a frosted glass window bore the name on a stainless steel plaque. He tapped on the window, but, getting no response, tried the handle.

The door was opened. He found himself in a small outer office. It was very tidy, box files upright in rows along the shelves, cardboard tubes of plans stacked on brackets on the walls. The colour scheme and the choice of the sparse furniture showed the same discrimination as Geoffrey's study.

But the outer office gave no feeling of work. It was like the Meckens' house after it had been tidied by the police – too neat to be functional.

The typewriter on the desk was shrouded in its plastic cover, as if its typist had long gone. There were no coats on the row of aluminium pegs.

But there was someone in the next room. Or presumably more than one person, because Charles could hear a voice. Talking loudly, in a rather stilted way.

He drew close to the connecting door, but couldn't make out the words. He couldn't even be sure that they were in English. He tapped on the door, but there was no break in the speech. He turned the handle and pushed the door open.

There was only one person in the room. The first thing Charles saw was the soles of a new pair of shoes resting on the desk. Behind them, a pair of hands holding an Arden edition of *The Winter's Tale*. And behind that the surprised face of Geoffrey Winter.

'Good God. Charles Paris.'

'Yes.'

'Have you come to commission me to build a second National Theatre?'

'No such luck, I'm afraid. It's not work.'

'It never is.'

'Bad at the moment?'

'Not a good time for the architect on his own. No one's building anything.'

'The economic situation.'

'Yes.'

'Like everything else. Like why theatres are cutting down on resident companies, why managements are putting on less shows...'

This banter was conducted at a pleasant enough level, but they both knew that it was only a formal observance preceding something more important. Charles decided there was little to be gained by further prevarication. 'I've come to talk about Charlotte Mecken.'

'Ah.' Geoffrey Winter tensed fractionally at the name, but he didn't give anything away. Charles got the same message that he had got from the performance as Trigorin, that here was a man of considerable emotional depth, but with great control over his reactions. He did not let anything emerge until he had fully considered how he wanted to present it.

Charles had hoped for more reaction and was thrown when he didn't get it. So he blundered on and, after a brief explanation of his belief in Hugo's innocence, asked point blank if Geoffrey had been Charlotte's lover.

The response was an 'Oh,' delivered absolutely flat; it gave nothing. But Geoffrey Winter was only playing the pause for maximum dramatic effect. Charles recognized the acting technique and let the silence ride. At last Geoffrey spoke.

'Well, congratulations. You've done your homework well. There's no point in my denying it, you're right. Since the police know, no doubt it'll all come out at Hugo's trial, so why should I pretend? Yes, I was Charlotte's lover until she...died.'

He changed pace suddenly on the last word, straightened up in his chair and turned to look out over the irregular roofs of London. As if in the grip of strong emotion. Charles always found it difficult to judge with actors. Since their lives were devoted to simulation, it was often hard to distinguish when their feelings were genuine.

He didn't offer any comment; he let Geoffrey play the scene at his own pace. Sure enough, when the pause had extended far enough to make even a Pinter audience feel uncomfortable, Geoffrey turned back from the window and looked piercingly at him. 'I suppose your next question is going to be – did I kill Charlotte?'

In fact, that was not where Charles's suspicions were leading, but he decided to play along with the scene. 'I was going to be a bit more subtle than that.'

'Well, Charles, the answer is no. I didn't kill her. It would have been perverse for me to...I had no cause to break up what was happening...about the best....thing that...' Again he was overcome by real or simulated emotion (or, most likely, an amalgam of the two). He turned back to the window.

'I'm sorry to put you through this, Geoffrey. I realize it must be painful. But Hugo is a friend and I have to investigate every avenue.'

Geoffrey was once again master of himself (if indeed he had ever relinquished control). 'I quite understand. I've been through all this with the police.'

'How did they find out?'

'Not difficult. They checked Charlotte's comings and goings with the staff at Breckton Station, realized the convenient position of my office for such an affair, then came and asked me, more or less as you have done. It seemed pointless to try and hide the facts. It would only have made things worse.'

'Did they ask you if you'd killed her?'

'They, as you intended to be, were a bit more subtle than that. But they did ask a few pertinent questions about my movements on Monday. I think they were just checking; I didn't get the impression they had much doubt about Hugo's guilt. In fact, they came to see me after he had been arrested, so I suppose they were just building up the background to the case.'

Charles must have been looking at Geoffrey quizzically, because the architect seemed to read his thoughts. He gave a dry laugh. 'Yes. I'll tell you what I told the police. I'll establish my alibi for you – as I believe the saying goes.

'Part of it you know, because you were with me in the Back Room. As you recall, we left there together and walked down to the main road. Now, in case you're thinking that I might have immediately doubled back and taken the insane step of strangling someone I loved, it seems that there is proof that Charlotte was still alive and well at nine o'clock. Shad Scott-Smith, you may remember, in the Back Room buying drinks for *The Seagull* cast. Because Charlotte wasn't there, he rang her from his home at about ten to nine. He rang off at nine. The reason he could be so specific is that he heard the opening of *I, Claudius* on the telly and he wanted to watch it.'

'It seems to have cut a swathe through the lives of an entire generation, that programme.'

'It did. Big success. Pity you weren't in it.'

'Yes, there'd be some pretty useful repeats on something like that. I'm afraid I've never been in what's been hailed as a television success.'

The change of subject relaxed the tension between the two men and Geoffrey continued in almost a bantering tone. 'Right, on with my alibi. I arrived home just before nine to find that Vee, as another member of the generation decimated by *I, Claudius*, was all geared up to watch. I left her to it and went upstairs to do some work on my lines for *The Winter's Tale*.

'For the next bit, I have cause to be thankful that I have a bloody-minded neighbour. Apparently, old Mrs Withers next door, who goes to bed at about nine, could hear me ranting away through the wall – her bedroom's right next door to my study. Apparently she's not a great fan of Shakespeare and later on, when I got a bit carried away with the character, she took it upon herself to ring up the police and complain. A very apologetic constable was round at our place for some time saying that old ladies could be very difficult Apparently, according to the police in the murder case, this means that I'm covered for the time of the death'

He paused, not with satisfaction or triumph, but as if he had reached a natural conclusion. Then he added, 'Fortunate, really. Most evenings spent at home, it would be very difficult to account for one's movements.'

'Thank you very much for going through it all again. And for bearing with my wild accusations.'

'That's quite okay. I sympathize with your motives. I'm as keen as you are to find the person who killed Charlotte. I just thought he had already been found.'

'You may well be right. Certainly the fact that she was having an affair would give Hugo even more of a motive. Do you know if he knew about it?'

'No idea. Charlotte and I didn't discuss him.'

'From my conversations with him, I got the impression that he thought she was having an affair, but didn't know who with.'

Geoffrey smiled painfully. 'Ironic though it may seem, Charlotte and I did try to be discreet about it. I mean, never let on what we felt for each other round Breckton. We didn't want to be gossip-fodder for the Backstagers.'

'Very wise. So she always came up here?'

Geoffrey nodded sadly. 'Yes. It started in the summer. You remember the long, hot summer?'

This new note of wistfulness, like everything else, sounded contrived. Charles didn't respond to it. 'Tell me, why did Charlotte come sometimes to Charing Cross and sometimes to Waterloo?'

Geoffrey raised his eyebrows and nodded in appreciation. 'Ten out of ten for homework. To answer that question, I think you have to understand what Charlotte was like. It was her first affair, she treated it with great excitement, and I think much of the excitement came from the secrecy. Corning to different stations was her idea of discretion, of covering her tracks. She was very young. As you see,' he continued with irony, 'the smoke-screen was not very effective. It. didn't take the police – or you – long to see through it.'

Charles felt a glow of satisfaction for his understanding of Charlotte's character. 'And was it for the same reason that she planned to go to Victoria on the day after she died?'

'Victoria?'

'I'd better explain. I found Charlotte's engagement diary down at the house. She'd listed all your meetings by a time and the name of the terminus she was coming to. The last two entries were one o'clock at Charing Cross on the Monday, the day she died, and then one o'clock on the Tuesday at Victoria.'

'Ah, I didn't know she'd done that.'

'What – put the places down in the book?'

'Yes. Yes, that must have been it.' For the first time in their interview he seemed to be in the grip of some emotion that was more powerful than his control. 'I'm sorry, it's just so typical of her, to think that that kind of subterfuge would fool anyone. Going to Victoria instead...I mean, to go out of her way like that to be inconspicuous and then write all the details down in a diary. I think a lot of the affair was just a game for her, like a schoolgirl having a midnight feast.'

'But it was serious on your side?'

Geoffrey looked pained. 'Serious on both sides – in our different ways. It was very good.'

'And it was still going well when she died? I mean, you hadn't had a row or...?'

Geoffrey looked at Charles with some distaste, pitying his lack of subtlety. 'I know what you mean. No, we hadn't had a lover's tiff which would inspire me with hatred to go and kill her. It was all going very well.' He was becoming wistful again.

'And was it going to change?'

'Change?'

'I mean, were you likely to get divorced and marry?'

Geoffrey shook his head and slowly. 'No, it was an affair. I wanted to go on as long as possible, but I suppose some time it would have ended. I've had other affairs. They all end sooner or later. I wouldn't have left Vee. People can never understand how close Vee and I are. I'm just one of those men who's capable of loving more than one woman at a time. Do you understand?'

'I think I do. Did Vee know about Charlotte?'

'I assume so. I never told her, but she's not stupid.'

'Didn't she get jealous?'

'Vee would only get jealous if she thought someone was likely to take me away from her. She knew that no one would. According to my own rules of morality, I'm very loyal.'

Charles nodded. Geoffrey had a male chauvinist vanity which was quite strong enough to blind him to his wife's real feelings. No woman, however liberated, actually welcomes the knowledge that her husband is sleeping around. And Charles knew from the way that Vee had watched her husband at the cast party, she had a strong possessive instinct.

There wasn't a lot more Charles could find out. 'I must go. I mustn't keep you from your work any longer.'

Geoffrey laughed cynically and flapped his copy of *The Winter's Tale*. 'Ah, my work. Geoffrey Winter Associates haven't had a decent size job now for four months.'

'Where are the Associates?'

'Disassociated – or should it be dissociated? I never know. All gone their separate ways, anyway. Even the secretary's gone.'

'So you just come up here and do nothing all day?'

'Sometimes things come up. Odd little jobs, through friends in various government departments. That's the answer these days – work in the public sector. No room for men on their own. I keep applying for jobs in local government and things, but as yet no luck. So I stay on here and wait. May as well, until the lease is up.'

'When's that?'

'A couple of months.'

'And then what?'

Geoffrey Winter's shrug started expansive as if it encompassed every possibility in the known world, but shrank down to nothing.

'So what do you live on?'

'Credit.' He laughed unconcernedly. 'And the confidence that something will turn up.'

Charles went back to Hereford Road feeling excited. He had been glad to hear Geoffrey's watertight alibi because that removed him from the running. And enabled Charles to follow the suspicions which were hardening in his mind. It wasn't Geoffrey he suspected; it was his wife. He could not forget the tensed-up energy he had felt in Vee's body as they had danced together. She was a woman capable of anything.

The chain of motivation was simple. Vee's jealously of Charlotte had started when she was beaten for the role of Nina which she had regarded as hers by right. It had been compounded by the discovery of her husband's affair with the upstart. That, however, she could have borne; what drove her to murder was the discovery that Charlotte was giving Geoffrey the one thing that their marriage could not – a child.

The opportunity for committing the crime was equally easily explained. Geoffrey had been at such pains to establish his own alibi that he hadn't thought about his wife's. While he was upstairs ranting through Leontes, she was assumed to be downstairs watching I. Claudius. So far as Geoffrey was concerned, that was what she was doing. He could presumably hear the television from upstairs.

But a television set conducts a one-way conversation, regardless of whether or not there is anyone watching. Vee, knowing that Geoffrey would get carried away by his performance, had every opportunity to leave the house after the show had started. There was plenty of time for her to have gone up to the Meckens'. Charlotte would have recognised her and let her in. A brief exchange, then Vee had taken Charlotte by surprise and strangled her. Put the body in the coal shed to delay its discovery and a brisk walk home to be back in time for the end of *I, Claudius*.

It was all conjecture, but it fitted. And, what was more, Charles thought he could prove it.

The proof lay on the table of his bedsitter. For reasons mainly of masochism (to see how much work other actors were getting), Charles always had the Radio Times delivered. Since he had no television and rarely listened to the radio, it was frequently thrown away unread. But on this occasion he felt sure it was going to be useful.

It was the Wednesday that interested him. He thought back to the Wednesday night when he had rung the Winters to get Robert Chubb's number. He remembered the time. Twenty-five to eleven, because he had looked at his watch after speaking to Kate Venables. And when he had spoken to Geoffrey Winter, there had been a break in their conversation while Vee was given advice on how to adjust the television for a good picture on BBC2.

Charles almost shouted out loud when the Radio Times confirmed his suspicions. At ten o'clock until ten-fifty on BBC2 on Wednesday night there had been a repeat of the Monday's episode of *I, Claudius*. Geoffrey Winter would not have been watching it, because he had missed so many of the earlier episodes.

So why should his wife watch the same program for a second time in three days? Unless of course she hadn't been there to see it the first time.

CHAPTER THIRTEEN

CHARLES HAD CAUSE to be grateful to sour Reggie for forcing him into joining the Breckton Backstagers. As a Social Member, it was quite legitimate for him to be propping up the Back Room bar at a quarter past seven that evening.

There were not many faces he recognized. Robert Chubb gave him the sort of glance most people reserve for windows and a few others offered insincere half-smiles. The only person who greeted him with anything like conviviality was Denis Hobbs, who bought him a large Bell's. 'You going to do some show or something down here then, Charles?'

Denis without Mary Hobbs was a refreshing change. He remained hearty, but didn't seem to have the same obligation to be raucously jovial which he had demonstrated on their previous meeting.

Charles denied that he was likely to break into amateur dramatics. 'Just a handy bar,' he explained, hoping that Denis wouldn't ask why it was handy for someone who lived fifteen miles away.

But Denis was a man without suspicion. He leaned forward to Charles and confided, 'Exactly the reason I joined. I mean, you can't turn up the chance of a bar on your doorstep, can you?'

'So you don't act?'

Denis erupted with laughter. 'Me? Bloody hell, I could no sooner act than have a baby. Blimey, me an actor – no, I'm a builder, that's what I am. Although Mary keeps trying to get me to say I work in the construction industry.'

The mimicry which he put into the last two words suggested that he was not as devoid of acting talent as he had implied. 'No, the acting bit's all Mary's. Very keen she is on all this arty-farty stuff. I tell you,' he confided like a schoolboy with a dirty story. 'I've been more bored in that theatre next door than a poof in a brothel. Still, Mary enjoys it. Keeps her out of my hair and keeps her off the streets, eh?' He laughed again robustly. 'I'm only here for the beer – and I like to look at the scenery. The young female scenery, that is.' He winked.

They were silent for a few moments. It wasn't an uncomfortable silence, just a pause of drinking companionship. Then, idly, to make conversation, Charles asked whether there had been any further developments on the burglary.

'No, not a thing. The police seem to think their best hope is to catch the villains when they try to get rid of the stuff. Apart from that, apparently there's not much chance. I mean, they've been all through the house and they haven't got any fingerprints or anything to go on.'

'They left it very tidy?'

'Oh yes, everything put back, all the doors closed – very neat job.'

'Nasty thing to happen, though.'

'Yes. Still, we were insured, so it could have been worse. Mary was a bit cut up about what was taken, sentimental value, all that, but I went out and bought her a load more gear and that seems to have calmed her down a bit.'

At that moment the Winters came in. Perhaps it was what Geoffrey had said in the morning, but they did look very together to Charles. As if they did share the complete relationship which he had described.

Denis Hobbs seemed to be slightly uneasy at their appearance, as if he suddenly had to be on his best behaviour. Mary continually told him what a privilege it was to know such artistic luminaries as the Winters.

Geoffrey did a light take, but greeted Charles cordially. As if by mutual agreement, they did not mention their earlier encounter.

Charles offered them drinks heartily. 'What's it to be? I'm just taking advantage of my new membership.'

Geoffrey wasn't fooled by that, but he made no comment. Charles wondered if the architect knew that he wanted to talk to Vee.

It was possible. Certainly Geoffrey seemed to be keeping his wife at his side to inhibit private conversations. A new thought struck Charles. Maybe Geoffrey had discovered his wife's crime and was set to defend her against investigation. That could make things difficult. Geoffrey's was a formidable mind to have in opposition.

But the architect's protection couldn't last long. *The Winter's Tale* rehearsal started at seven-thirty 'and he gets furious if you're late, so I'd better go. Will you be going straight back home, Vee?'

The question was delivered with studied casualness, but Charles could sense the tension beneath it. Vee, either deliberately or not, didn't take the hint. 'No, not straight away. I'll just buy Charles a drink. See you later. Hope it goes well.'

'Fine.' Geoffrey went through to the rehearsal room with a cheery wave. Or was it his impression of a cheery wave? Charles was getting paranoid about Geoffrey Winter's sincerity or lack of it.

He asked for a Bell's and Vee bought him a large one. Denis and a lot of the others round the bar had left and so, whether Geoffrey wanted it or not, Charles and Vee were alone together.

She commented on her husband's departure. 'You know, he almost sounded as if he was jealous.'

'What, of us?'

Vee shrugged. Charles laughed loudly, as if it was the best joke he had heard for a long time.

Interesting – straight away she put their meeting into a sexual context, just as she had done at the cast party. Once again he wasn't interested. And once again he felt she wasn't really interested either.

He decided that he would have to be a bit more subtle in questioning Vee than he had been with her husband. Better start at an uncontroversial level. 'What are they rehearsing tonight?'

'Blocking the first two acts. So I'm not wanted.'

'Oh, I didn't even realize you. were in the production. What are you playing?'

'Perdita. Since yesterday.' She pronounced it with triumph.

'You mean it was going to be...?'

'Charlotte, yes. Of course, it's a terrible way to get a part, but it's an ill wind...' Her regret was merely formal.

At least she wasn't disguising her satisfaction at Charlotte's removal from the scene. She was now back in her position as undisputed queen of the juve leads in the Breckton Backstagers. Charles would have thought she was a bit long in the tooth to be 'the prettiest low-born lass that ever ran on the greensward' and a symbol of youthful beauty and regeneration, but now she was the best that Breckton had to offer. If she had killed Charlotte, then the returns were immediate.

Charles knew he had to play her gently. She was highly strung and information would have to be wheedled out of her. He hoped Geoffrey had been discreet and not mentioned their meeting earlier in the day. He did not want her to be on her guard.

Starting with flattery seemed the best approach with someone as self-absorbed as she was. He asked her about her acting career at Breckton, regretting that he had never had the pleasure of seeing her in a production.

She needed no second invitation. He had in his time met a good few professional actors and actresses who assumed that everyone shared their own consuming interest in their theatrical doings, but never one as voluble as Vee Winter. Perhaps living with another king-size ego who also liked to talk about his acting, she didn't often get the chance to let rip in this way.

He got it all – the early aptitude for mimicry noted by loving parents, the success in elocution exams, the outstanding ability remarked upon by an English teacher, commendations at local festivals, the agonizing decision of the late teens as to whether to try for drama school and take it up professionally, then parental pressure and the final regrettable resolution to deprive the greater public of her talents.

At this point a pause was left for Charles to murmur some suitable insincerity about tragic waste.

'And then of course I married and decided that it would be wrong for me to do something that would take me away from Geoffrey for long periods of time. He is a complex character and can be a full-time job. I often think it's as well that we don't have children, because he needs so much of my attention that they might not get a look-in.'

In this speech Charles could hear two threads of oft-repeated self justification. First, the very common suburban housewife's explanation of why she never did anything more with her life, how the cares of marriage cut off in its bloom a career of unbelievable promise. In some cases – like, he reflected, that of Charlotte Mecken – it's true, but in most, where only moderate talent is involved, it's no more than a comforting fiction.

There was also the second well-rehearsed self-justification, for her childlessness. It was sad that this was felt necessary, but there was a defensive quality to her remarks about Geoffrey's demands on her time. Ironic to Charles, with his knowledge of the other women among whom Geoffrey spread those needs.

But she gave him a cue to find some purely practical information. 'You talk about Geoffrey being a full-time job. Do you actually have a real one?'

'Job? Yes. I teach Speech and Drama at a local private school.'

'Oh.'

This again seemed to need justification. 'It's very close and convenient. I get home for lunch. And of course I think one can give a lot to young minds. If you've got an enthusiasm for the theatre, it does communicate and stimulate their interest.'

'Oh, certainly.'

'Also the little extra money comes in handy.'

Knowing what he did about Geoffrey's business affairs, Charles felt sure it did. He would imagine they must have been living more or less exclusively on Vee's income for some time. Perhaps Geoffrey even conducted his affair with Charlotte on a grant from his wife.

But this digression on Vee's work did not divert her long from the main subject of her dramatic triumphs. She started to list the shows she had been in through a few more drinks, and Charles's attention was wavering when he suddenly heard himself being asked back to the house to see some of her scrapbooks.'

Instinctively he said yes, not certain whether scrapbooks were the latest form of etchings as a seduction bait. The more time he could spend with Vee, the more relaxed she became, the easier it was going to be to ask the questions he wanted to.

It might also be useful to get inside the Winters' house again. If Vee Winter did kill Charlotte, he was going to need some tangible proof of it to convince the police.

Vee made their exit from the Back Room pointed, with loud goodbyes to everyone and messages that she'd see Geoffrey later. Again Charles felt the overtones of sexual intrigue. Vee wanted to be seen leaving with him, possibly to stimulate gossip among the Backbiters. But that was all; she seemed to want the aura of an illicit liaison rather than any illicit action. Or at least that was the impression he got.

He would presumably find out if he was right when they got back to the house.

As they walked back along the path to the main road, Charles looked covertly at his companion. If she had murdered Charlotte as he suspected, then this was the route she must have taken on the Monday night. But her face betrayed nothing.

The air was full of explosions and the sudden screams of rockets. Of course, fireworks. November the Fifth. His birthday. He recalled the old family joke that his mother had been frightened into delivery by a wayward jumping cracker.

On the common the celebrations were under way round the huge bonfire. Presumably there had been an effigy of Guy Fawkes hoisted on top of the pile, but now all was consumed in the tall rippling flags of flame.

To one side of the bonfire, in a roped-off area, some responsible fathers were donating Roman candles and Catherine wheels. Charles knew that this was the new approved policy; for greater safety, families were encouraged to pool their fireworks into this kind of communal party. To him it seemed to take away the excitement and make the exercise rather pointless. Like drinking non-alcoholic beer in motorway service cafés.

And in this case it didn't even seem to be particularly safe. The leaping flames spat up lumps of burning debris, some of which had landed in a nearby tree and kindled the branches. The conflagration was in danger of getting out of hand.

Still, there were lots of responsible fathers to deal with the problem. Lots of over-insured men in their early forties who no doubt drove Volvos with the side-lights on in the daytime. As Charles and Vee passed, there seemed to be an argument among them as to whether they should call the fire brigade or not.

To his amusement, Charles saw that the organising spirit in the pro-fire brigade lobby was sour Reggie from the Backstagers. Taking his role as professional wet blanket literally this time. He scurried about issuing orders, followed by two small children of one sex or the other whose faces were as sour as their father's. It was strange to see the niggling committee man in another context.

Vee waved at Reggie, but he didn't see her. Once again she seemed to be drawing attention to her being with Charles, to set tongues wagging.

A group of over-excited children rushed towards them, involved in some inexplicable, but evidently very funny, game. Vee moved aside to let them pass. As she did so, the flames suddenly threw a spotlight on her face. The expression was one of infinite pain and bitterness.

They walked in silence down the paved path to the main road. There Vee stopped outside an off-licence. 'No drink in the house, I'm afraid.'

She selected a cheapish bottle of Italian red wine. Charles insisted on paying for it and she didn't argue. His new knowledge of the Winters' financial plight made sense of such details.

As Vee put her key in the front door, they heard the distant siren of a fire engine. Sour Reggie had triumphed. For the firework party-goers the evening's entertainment was ending.

But, as Vee Winter laid her arm on his shoulder and ushered him into the house, Charles Paris felt that perhaps his evening's entertainment was only beginning.

CHAPTER FOURTEEN

CHARLES SIPPED HIS wine and tried not to look too downcast when Vee came in loaded with her theatrical memorabilia. Scrapbooks, programs, a box of photographs and – most daunting of all – the cassette recorder that he had seen Geoffrey using. Oh dear, it looked as if he was going to get an Action Replay of her entire dramatic career.

He settled down to be bored out of his mind. Vee, he knew, was inflicting this on him because he was a professional actor. She wanted his commendation, she wanted him to say how impoverished the British theatre had been by her decision to turn her back on it. Maybe she even wanted to gain his praise so that she would compare favourably with those whom he had condemned at the Critics' Circle.

He found her exhibitionism sad. The fact that she needed this bolstering. It showed that Geoffrey had too simple an interpretation of his wife's character. Her insecurity spoke in every nervous action. To think that she would not be jealous of another woman was totally wrong.

The overtones of sexuality which she gave to the proceedings also revealed her insecurity. She needed attention, she needed Charles to be aware that the two of them together was a potentially sexual scenario, but he felt that was all she needed. If he had made a pass at her, he would have got a considerate rebuff. She wouldn't have minded – in fact, she would rather have welcomed it as a boost to her ego and as something else to feel martyred about. She liked to think of herself as a tragic queen, resisting all blandishments from other men, because of her devotion to one man who was not really worthy of her.

Charles had not realized this vein of contempt which ran through Vee's feelings for her husband until the subject of children came up again. It was prompted by a photograph of Vee with another girl in Elizabethan dress who, apparently, had been a terribly good actress, but had given it all up when she started to have children. 'Four I believe she's got now. Four. I suppose that could have been me, if things had turned out differently.' She responded to Charles's quizzical look. 'I mean, if I had married someone else.'

'Oh.' He sounded slightly embarrassed, as if he ought not to inquire further, knowing that this was the sure way to make her continue.

'Yes, with another man, no doubt I would be surrounded with the little brats, spending all my days at coffee parties and tea parties, talking about nappies and nursery schools.' The edge she put into the words showed how much she was an outsider in the great incubator of Breckton. All the thoughts he'd had about Charlotte being ostracized by her childlessness applied even more strongly to Vee.

He continued his embarrassed act. 'Well...I understood that nowadays there were things that could be done about infertility and...er...clinics and so on.'

Vee smiled a martyred smile. 'Maybe, but I don't think you'd ever get Geoffrey along to one of those. He couldn't admit to himself that...male pride in virility or...I'm sure you know all about that.'

Again the remark was sexually loaded. Not quite a come-on, but a reminder that they were a man and woman alone together.

Charles thought quickly as he worked through the file of meaningless photographs. Vee's conviction that Geoffrey was to blame for their lack of family was obviously one of the supports of their marriage. She believed it, because it gave her superiority over him. She could watch with indulgence his philandering with other women, knowing his secret. And she' was not afraid to divulge it.

Charlotte's pregnancy must have threatened the entire fabric of that illusion and Charlotte had had to be removed so that Vee could remain protected in her cocoon of fiction.

He knew he was right. All he needed was proof. It was time he got down to the details of his investigation.

In broaching the subject he was helped by the photographs. There was a picture of Vee surrounded by adolescent youths in togas with laundry marks.

'Portia in *Julius Caesar* at school,' she supplied.

'Ah, real *I, Claudius* stuff,' he commented, grateful for the cue.

She laughed.

'Have you been watching it, Vee?' he asked casually.

'Oh yes. Seen every one. That was the big advantage of not doing *The Seagull*. Meant I could make it a regular date.'

'Every Wednesday.'

'No, I watch it on Mondays.'

Charles took a risk. What he had to say next was going to sound more like interrogation than casual conversation. He hoped she wouldn't notice. 'That's strange. I rang Geoffrey on Wednesday and I could have sworn he said you were watching it then.'

He played it very light, but still threw her. She looked at him, flustered and bewildered. 'Oh...oh yes, I did watch it on Wednesday this week.'

He didn't volunteer any comment. Just left her to explain.

She did a goad performance as someone sorting through her memory. 'Oh, of course. My mother rang on Monday just after it had started. She always natters on so, the show was practically over by the time I got off the phone.'

Charles joked, as if the information meant nothing to him, 'I think everyone's mother's like that.' But he felt sure she was lying.

'Yes, mine always rings at inconvenient times. Still, I suppose I shouldn't grumble, if the odd phone call keeps her happy. Better than continually traipsing up to Lytham St. Anne's to see her.'

That was very helpful. He knew Vee's maiden name was le Carpentier. There shouldn't be too many old ladies of that name in Lytham St. Anne's with whom to check her alibi.

Eventually (and it seemed to take for ever) they came to the end of the photographs. 'Fascinating,' Charles lied.

Vee looked disappointed, as if she had expected more. What did she want him to do, for God's sake, say that she was the greatest actress to tread the boards on the evidence of a load of amateur snapshots?

But it seemed there was more evidence about to be offered. Vee was now turning her attention to the cassette player and the black plastic-covered box of cassettes. 'Actually,' she said with elaborate casualness, 'I've got recordings here for some of the stuff I've done.'

'Oh, really?' Charles gave the last dreg of his supply of simulated interest. 'What, recorded off stage?'

'Some of them. Some I've just done at home – really just for my own benefit, so that I can get a kind of objective view of what I'm doing.'

'I see.'

'I thought you might like to hear one or two little bits. It'd give you some idea of how I do act.'

Charles quarried a smile from his petrifying features. 'Great.' She fiddled with the machine. 'Geoffrey lets you borrow his recorder then?'

'It's not his, it's mine. He occasionally borrows it when he's learning lines.'

'And to dub off his music.'

'What? Good God, no. He's far too much of a purist for that. Only happy when music is being perfectly reproduced on all that hi-fi stuff he's got upstairs. He always says I'm a bit of a Philistine about it. I mean, I've got some music cassettes – popular stuff – which I play round the house, but he gets very sniffy about them. This recorder's only mono for a start and he says you're missing ninety per cent of the enjoyment if you don't hear music in stereo.'

'So he would never use it for music?'

'Not a chance. Look, there's a bit here that's an extract from a production of The Country Wife that we did. I played Mrs Pinchwife. Got very good press. I think this speech is quite amusing. Would you like to hear it?'

The affirmative smile was another triumph of engineering. Just before she switched it on, they both heard a strange wail from outside. A sound like a child in pain. Vee rose and Charles looked at her with some alarm.

'I must go to the kitchen to let him in,' said Vee.

'Who is he?'

'Vanya.'

'Vanya?'

'The cat.'

As soon as she was out of the door, he leapt to the cassette box. Her recorded voice wound on, but he didn't listen. His mind was too full.

When he had first gone up to the study, Geoffrey Winter had been copying Wagner's Liebestod from his expensive stereo on to this cheap mono cassette machine. Geoffrey had given some specious line about it being handier, which had seemed reasonable at the time, but which now seemed extremely suspicious.

If you don't want a cassette copy of a piece of music, then why copy it? Only one answer sprang to mind – in order to cover something already on the cassette.

He felt a prickle of excitement. Now at last he was on to something. Geoffrey's recording of the Wagner had taken place on the Tuesday, the day after Charlotte's murder. The architect must somehow have found out about his wife's crime and known that there was incriminating evidence on a cassette, which had to be removed. But Charles was due for supper just after he made the discovery, so he had to destroy the evidence while their guest was there without raising his suspicions. What was easier than to record over it?

Charles found the distinctive yellow and green container which held the cassette Geoffrey had used. There was a chance, a very long chance, that some part of its previous recording remained unerased. He slipped the thin rectangle into his pocket.

Meanwhile Vee Winter's interpretation of Wycherley ground on.

Suddenly the door opened and Geoffrey walked in. 'Hello, Vee, I – '

The surprise was so great that even his well-controlled emotions were caught off their guard. In the flash of time before he recovered himself, Geoffrey's face bared his thoughts. He found another man alone in his house with his wife. And he was extremely suspicious.

CHAPTER FIFTEEN

GERALD VENABLES WAS much more friendly when Charles rang him the next morning. Maybe he was less tired and the arrival of the weekend had cheered him. Or maybe the fact that it was the weekend meant he could relax his professional guard. Outside the office he could see Hugo's predicament as a case to be investigated rather than as an inconvenient and time-consuming legal challenge.

Whatever the cause, he agreed that they should meet and invited Charles down to Dulwich for lunch. As he signed off on the phone, he said. 'So long, buster. See you at my joint round twelve. Okay, coochie-coo?' An encouraging sign.

As Charles walked from West Dulwich Station, he found that he was casting a Breckton eye over everything he saw, assessing the suburb from a suburban point of view. He hadn't quite got to the stage of pricing the houses he passed, but he could feel it wasn't far off.

Dulwich had the same air as Breckton of quiet desperation. Paranoid car-cleaning, wives pulled in every direction by children, buggies and shopping, determinedly jovial husbands taking the kids for a walk, track-suited executives sweating off some of the week's lunches in unconvinced jogging, others bearing their loads of wood and ceiling tiles from the brochured neatness of the Do-It-Yourself shop to the bad-tempered messes of a constructive weekend.

Gerald's house was predictably well-appointed. Part of a newish development, with that fraction more room between it and the next house which is the mark of success in the suburbs. The front door had a brass lion knocker and was white, with small square Georgian panels. The up-and-over garage door was panelled in the same way. In fact the whole scheme of the house was Georgian, with thin-framed white windows set in neat red brick. It was exactly the sort of house that anyone in Georgian England who happened to own two cars, a central heating oil tank, a television and a burglar alarm would have had.

Gerald was manifesting the schizophrenia of a Monday to Friday worker. He was dressed in a pale blue towelling shirt and evenly faded jeans (the summery image made possible by the blast of central heating which greeted Charles as he entered). His feet were encased in navy blue sailing shoes and a

Snoopy medallion hung around his neck. This last was worn a bit self-consciously. Perhaps it was a fixture, always round the solicitorial neck beneath the beautifully-laundered cotton shirts and silk ties, but somehow Charles doubted it.

The shock of Gerald without a suit made him realize that it must have been nearly twenty years since he had seen his friend in informal gear. For a moment he wondered if he had come to the right house.

'Kate's taken the kids to some exhibition in Town, so we've got the place to ourselves. She sent love and so on. There's some kind of basic pâté lunch in the fridge for later, Have a beer?'

Predictably Löwenbräu. Charles descended into the depths of a light brown leather sofa and took a long swallow. 'Well, are you beginning to think I might have a point?'

'Hardly, Charles, but I am willing to go through the evidence with you and see if there's anything. What do you reckon might have happened?'

Charles outlined his current view of Charlotte's death, moving swiftly from point to point. As he spoke, his conjectures took a more substantial form and he could feel an inexorable pull of logic.

Gerald was impressed, but sceptical. 'I can see that that makes a kind of sense, but in a case like this you've got to have evidence. If you're ever going to convince the police that their nice neatly-sewn-up little case is not in fact nice and neatly-sewn-up at all, you're going to have to produce something pretty solid. All we've got so far is the slight oddness of a woman watching her favourite television program twice in three days. And that could well be explained if it turns out that her story about her mother's phone call is true.'

'I'd care to bet it isn't. Anyway, that's not all we have. We've also got this.' With an actor's flourish Charles produced the yellow and green cassette box from his pocket.'

'Oh yes.' Gerald was not as overwhelmed by the gesture as he should have been. 'You mentioned that. I'm afraid I don't quite see where you reckon that fits into the scheme of things.'

'What, you don't want me to repeat all that business about my coming in and finding Geoffrey copying the Wagner?'

'No, I've got that. What I don't understand is what you are expecting to find on it. Except for Wagner. I mean, he could just have been copying it for a friend or something.'

Charles wasn't going to shift from his proudly-achieved deduction. 'No, I'm sure he was trying to hide something, to erase something.'

'But what? What could possibly be put on tape that was incriminating? The average murderer doesn't record a confession just to make it easy for amateur detectives.'

'Ha bloody ha. All right, I don't know what it is. I just know it's important. And the only way we're going to find out what's on it is by listening to the thing. Do you have a cassette player?'

'Of course,' Gerald murmured, pained that the question should be thought necessary.

In fact he had a cassette deck incorporated into the small city of mart grey Bang and Olufsen hi-fi equipment that spread over the dark wooden wall unit. The speakers stood on the floor like space age mushrooms.

'Now I reckon,' said Charles as Gerald fiddled with the console, 'our best hope is that there's something right at the beginning, that he started recording too far in and didn't wipe all the...'

The opening of the Prelude from Wagner's *Tristan and Isolde* gave him the lie.

'Well, if that was our best hope...' Gerald observed infuriatingly, as he bent to fiddle with more knobs.

When he was happy with the sound, he sat down with a smug smile on his face, waiting to be proved right. The Prelude wound moodily on. Charles remembered how cheap he had always found the emotionalism of Wagner's outpourings. He began to get very bored.

After about five minutes it became clear that Gerald was going through the same process of mental asphyxiation. 'Charles, can't we switch it off? Kate's taken me to this stuff, but I've never cared for it much.'

'No. Some American once said Wagner's music is better than it sounds.'

'It needs to be. I think it's going to go on like this for some time and we're not going to get any dramatic murder confessions.'

'I agree. Let's spool through. There might be something where he changed sides. That's a C90 cassette, forty-five minutes each way. The LP could only have had about twenty minutes each side, so he must have flipped the disc. Might be something there.'

There wasn't. They could hear the blip of the pick-up being lifted off, then the slight hiss of erased tape until the bump of the stylus back on the other side, the tick of the homing grooves and the return of the music.

'No.' Gerald's smugness was increasing.

'Let's try the end. Yes, if there's only forty minutes on the disc and it's a forty five minute tape...' Charles felt a new surge of excitement at the thought.

He tensed as Gerald spooled through till nearly the end of the tape and uttered a silent prayer as the replay button was pressed.

God was apparently deaf. Tape hiss. Again, nothing but tape hiss. 'I think he just left the Record button down and let the tape run through until it was all erased.'

'Yes, I suppose so,' Charles agreed gloomily. Then, with sudden memory – 'No, but he didn't. I was there. I remember quite distinctly. Perhaps he had intended to do that, but because I was there he switched it off when the music stopped. He must have erased the last bit after that. Which would, suggest to me that he did have something important to hide.' Suddenly he got excited. 'Look, suppose he missed a bit just at the end of the music...'

'Why should he?'

'Well, with some of these cheap cassette players it's difficult to press the

Play button and Record at exactly the same time. He might have put down the Play a moment earlier and left something unerased.'

'But surely he would have heard anything and gone back over it.'

'Not necessarily. Most of these machines have another button with which you switch off the sound to prevent microphone howlround. So he wouldn't have heard it. And, given his great respect for music, even in this situation I don't think he'd want to risk going back and wiping the final reverberation of his Wagner.'

'It sounds pretty unlikely to me.'

'It is. But it's possible. Spool back to the end of the music.'

With the expression of someone humouring the mentally infirm, the solicitor returned the controls. It was the end of the Liebestod. The soprano warbled to death and the orchestra rose to its sullen climax. The regular hiss of the stylus on the centre groove seemed interminable. Then abruptly it was lifted off. This sound was followed by the woolly click of the recorder being switched off. Then another click as it had been restarted and, seconds later, a third as the Record button had been engaged.

Between the last two clicks there was speech.

Charles and Gerald looked at each other as if to confirm that they had both heard it. They were silent; the evidence was so fragile, it could suddenly be blown away.

Charles found his voice first. 'Spool back. Play it again,' he murmured huskily.

Again Wagner mourned in. Again the pick-up worried against the centre of the record. Then the clicks. And, sandwiched between them, Geoffrey Winter's voice. Saying two words – no, not so much – two halves of two words.

' -ed coal- .' Charles repeated reverentially. 'Play it again.'

Gerald did so. 'It's cut in the middle of some word ending in *ed*, and it sounds as though the coal is only the beginning of a word too.'

'What words begin with coal?'

Charles looked straight at Gerald. 'Coal shed, for one.'

'Good God.' For the first time the lines of scepticism left the solicitor's face. 'And what about words ending in ed? There must be thousands.'

'Thousands that are spelled that way, not so many that are pronounced like that.'

'No. I suppose there's coal shed again. If the two parts came the other way around...'

'Or there's dead, Gerald.'

'Yes,' the solicitor replied slowly. 'Yes, there is.'

'May I use your phone, Gerald?'

'What for?'

'I'm going to crack Vee Winter's alibi.'

'Oh.'

'Don't sound so grumpy about it. Cheapest time to phone your friends –

after six and at weekends. I'll pay for the call, if you like.'

'No, it's not that. The firm sees to the phone bill anyway.'

'Of course. I'd forgotten. You never use your own money for anything, do you?'

'Not if I can help it.' Gerald smiled complacently.

Given Lytham St. Anne's and the unusual name of le Carpentier, Directory Inquiries had no difficulty in producing Vee's mother's phone number. Charles put his finger down on the bar of Gerald's Trimphone and prepared to dial.

'Are you just going to ask her direct, Charles? Won't she think it's a bit odd?'

'I'm not going to ask her direct. I have a little plan worked out, which involves using another voice. Don't worry.'

'But that's illegal,' wailed Gerald as Charles dialled. 'You can't make illegal calls on a solicitor's telephone.'

Mrs le Carpentier answered the phone with the promptness of a lonely old lady.

'Hello. Telephone Engineer.' Charles was pleased with the voice. He had first used it in a stillborn experimental play called *Next Boat In* ('Captured all the bleakness and, I'm afraid, all the tedium of dockland' – *Lancashire Evening News*). He thought it was a nice touch to be Liverpudlian for Lytham St. Anne's.

'Oh, what can I do for you? I hope there's nothing wrong with the phone. I'm an old lady living on my own and – '

The Telephone Engineer cut in reassuringly over Mrs le Carpentier's genteel tones. 'No, nothing to worry about. Just checking something. We had a complaint – somebody reported that your phone was continually engaged when they tried to ring, so I just have to check that the apparatus was in fact in a state of usage during the relevant period.'

'Ah, I wonder who it could have been. Do you know who reported the fault?'

'No, Madam.'

'It could have been Winnie actually. She lives in Blundellsands. We play bridge quite often and it's possible she was trying to set up a four for – '

The Telephone Engineer decided he didn't want to hear all of Mrs le Carpentier's social life. 'Yes, Madam. I wonder if we could just check the relevant period. The fault was reported last Monday. Apparently someone tried to call three times between nine and half past in the evening. Was the apparatus being used at this time?'

So confident was he of a negative response that the reply threw him for a moment. 'I beg your pardon, Madam?'

'Yes, it was in use.'

'Oh. Oh.' Still, it wasn't necessarily Vee to whom she was speaking. 'Local calls, were they, Madam?'

'Oh no, it was just one call. Long distance.'

'Where to? We have to check, Madam, when it's been reported.'

'It was a call to Breckton. That's in Surrey. Near London.'

Charles felt the concoction of logis he had compounded trickling away from him. 'Are you absolutely confident that that was the time, Madam?'

'Absolutely. It was the time that that *I, Claudius* was on the television.'

'Oh.'

'Yes, you see, I saw it for the first time last week and I thought it was a shocking program. So much violence and immorality. My daughter had mentioned that she watched it, but after I'd seen what it was all about, I thought it was my duty as a mother to ring her up while it was on, so that she couldn't watch it. Do you see?'

'I see,' Charles replied dully. Yes, he saw. He saw all his ideas suddenly discredited, he saw that he must flush every thought he'd ever had about the case out of his mind and start again with nothing.

Mrs le Carpentier was still in righteous spate. 'I think too many parents nowadays neglect their duties as their children's moral guardians. I mean, Victoria's over thirty, but she still needs looking after. She mixes with all kinds of theatrical people and – '

'Victoria?'

'My daughter.'

'Good God.'

'That's another thing I don't like in young people today – taking the name of the Lord in vain. It's – '

'Mrs le Carpentier, thank you very much. You've been most helpful. I can confirm that there is nothing wrong with your apparatus.'

'Oh good. And do you think maybe I should ring Winnie?'

'"Yes, I would.'

He slumped on to the sofa, not hearing Gerald's remonstrances about the illegality of impersonating people over the telephone and the number of laws under which this action could be charged and how the fact that the owner did not stop the crime might well make him an accessory.

It all flowed past Charles. The void which had been left in his mind by the confirmation of Vee's alibi had only been there for a few seconds before new thoughts started to flood in. He pieced them together into a rough outline and then spoke, shutting Gerald up with a gesture.

'Vee's real name is Victoria.'

'So what? What about her alibi? Was she telling the truth?'

'Oh yes.' Charles dismissed the subject.

'Well then, that seems to put the kybosh on the whole – '

'But don't you see – her real name is Victoria.'

'Yes, but – '

'I should have guessed. The way all these amateur actors fiddle about with their names, it should have been obvious.'

'I don't see that her name is important when – '

'It is important, Gerald, because it means that it was Vee whom Charlotte was going to see at one o'clock the day after she was murdered. During the school lunch hour. Charlotte couldn't stand all those affected stage names, so she would have called her Victoria as a matter of principle. And I bet that the reason she was going to see Vee was to tell her she was pregnant.'

'So Vee didn't already know?'

'No.'

'But surely that throws out all your motivation for her to have done the murder and – '

'She didn't do the murder. Forget Vee. She doesn't have anything to do with it.'

'Then who did kill Charlotte?'

'Geoffrey Winter.'

'But Geoffrey didn't have any motivation to kill her. He had a very good affair going, everything was okay.'

'Except that Charlotte was pregnant.'

'We don't even know that.'

'I'll bet the police post-mortem showed that she was. Go on, you can ask them when you're next speaking.'

'All right, let's put that on one side for the moment and proceed with your wild theorizing.' The lines of scepticism were once again playing around Gerald's mouth.

'Geoffrey and Vee Winter are a very close couple. In spite of his philandering, he is, as he told me, very loyal to her. Now all marriages are built up on certain myths and the myth which sustains Vee is that her childlessness is Geoffrey's fault. His infertility gives her power. She can tolerate his affairs, secure in the knowledge that he will come back to her every time. But if it were suddenly proved that in fact he could father a child, everything on which she had based their years together would be taken away from her. I think, under those circumstances, someone as highly-strung as she is could just crack up completely.

'Geoffrey knew how much it would mean to her, so when Charlotte told him she was pregnant, he had to keep that knowledge from his wife. No doubt his first reaction was to try to get her to have an abortion, but Charlotte, nice little Catholic girl that she was, would never have consented to that. Equally, being a conventional girl, she would want to have the whole thing open, she'd want to talk to his wife, even maybe see if Vee would be prepared to give Geoffrey up.

'So she rang Vee up and fixed to meet her on the Tuesday during her lunch hour. On the Monday she went up to Villiers Street for her assignation with Geoffrey and told him what she intended to do. He could not allow the confrontation of the two women to take place. He decided that Charlotte must never go and see Vee. So he killed her.'

Charles leaned back with some satisfaction. The new theory felt much more solid than the old one. It left less details unaccounted for.

Gerald said exactly what Charles knew he would. 'I'm impressed by the psychological reasoning, Charles, but there is one small snag. Geoffrey Winter had an alibi for the only time he could have murdered Charlotte. He was at home rehearsing his lines so loudly that his next door neighbour complained to the police. How do you get round that one?'

Gerald couldn't have set it up more perfectly for him if he had tried. 'This is how he did it.' Charles picked the cassette box up off the table.

'So easy. He even told me he used the cassette recorder for learning his lines. All he had to do was to record a full forty-five minutes of *The Winter's Tale* on to this cassette, put it on, slip out of the French windows of his study, go and commit the murder, come back, change from recording to his own voice and insure that he started ranting loudly enough to annoy his neighbour with whom his relationship was already dodgy. After previous disagreements about noise, he felt fairly confident that she would call the police, thus putting the final seal on his watertight alibi.'

Gerald was drawn to this solution, but he was not wholly won over. 'Hmm. It seems that one has to take some enormous imaginative leaps to work that out. I'd rather have a bit more evidence.'

'We've got the cassette. And I've suddenly realized what it means. The words – it's Leontes.'

'It's what?'

'Leontes in *The Winter's Tale*. One of the most famous lines in the play. When he speaks of Hermione's eyes, he says; "Stars, stars! And all eyes else dead coals".'That's the bit we've got on the tape.'

Gerald was silent. Then slowly, unwillingly, he admitted, 'Do you know, you could be right.'

'Of course I'm right,' said Charles. 'Now where's that lunch you were talking about?'

CHAPTER SIXTEEN

CHARLES DIDN'T WANT to hurry things. He was now confident that he knew how Charlotte had been killed, and he could afford to take time to check it. There was no point in confronting Geoffrey Winter or going to the police with an incompletely researched solution.

He left Gerald late on the Saturday afternoon. (Gerald wanted to watch Doctor Who and Charles didn't really much.) They agreed that Charles should make various further investigations and then report back. Gerald was now more or less convinced by the new solution, but his legal caution remained.

Since there was nothing useful he could do that day, Charles went for the evening to one of his old haunts, the Montrose, a little drinking club round the back of the Haymarket. As he expected, it was full of out-of-work actors (and even, after the theatres finished, some in-work ones). A great deal of alcohol was consumed.

He woke feeling pretty ropey on the Sunday morning and did the tube and train journey to Breckton on automatic pilot. It was only when he emerged into the stark November sunlight outside the suburban station that consciousness began to return.

Blearily he reminded himself of the plan he had vaguely formed the day before. He had come down to Breckton to check the timing of the crime, to retrace the steps that Geoffrey Winter had taken on the Monday night and see if it was feasible for him to have killed Charlotte in the forty-five minutes the tape allowed.

Charles was early. Since he didn't want to run the risk of meeting any of the principals in the crime, he had decided to conduct his exploration after two-thirty when they would all be emoting over *The Winter's Tale* up at the Backstagers.

He arrived just after twelve, which was a remarkably convenient time for him to go into a pub and kill time and his hangover at one blow.

There was a dingy little Railway Tavern adjacent to the station which was ideal for his purposes. The railway line was at some distance from the posher residential side of Breckton and he was in no danger of meeting any of the Backstagers down there.

When he entered the pub, it was clear that the clientèle came from 'the other side of the railway', an expression of subtle snobbery that he had heard more than once from the theatrical circle. On the 'other side of the railway' there was a council estate, yet another socio-geological stratum in the complex structure of Breckton. At the bottom was the bedrock of 'the other side of the railway line', then the unstable mixture of rising lower middle and impoverished upper middle class 'the other side of the main road' (where Geoffrey and Vee lived), then the rich clay of the newer detached executive houses like the Meckens' and finally the lush topsoil of extreme affluence which manifested itself in mock-Tudor piles like the Hobbses'. Across the strata ran the faults and fissures of class and educational snobbery as well so that a full understanding of the society would be a lifetime's study.

Charles ordered a pint which made his brain blossom out of its desiccation like a Japanese flower dropped in water.

Being a Sunday, there was nothing to eat in the pub except for a few cheese biscuits and cocktail onions on the bar, but Charles was quite happy to resign himself to a liquid lunch.

As he sat and drank, his mind returned to Charlotte's murder. Not in a depressed or panicky way, but with a kind of intellectual calm. He felt as he had sometimes done when writing a play, the comforting assurance that he'd sorted out a satisfactory plot outline and only needed to fill in the details.

And little details were slotting into his scenario of the death of Charlotte Mecken. One was disturbing. He was beginning to think that Geoffrey might be on to his suspicions.

First, the interrogation in his office must have put him on his guard, if Charles's phone call on the evening of Hugo's arrest hadn't already done so. But there was something else. On the Friday night, when Geoffrey had discovered Charles on his sitting room, he had looked extremely suspicious. At the time, Charles had assumed that the suspicion had a sexual basis.

But, as he thought back over the circumstances, he found another interpretation. When Geoffrey arrived, the cassette player was running, reproducing Vee's performance of Wycherley's Mrs Pinchwife. Geoffrey had entered speaking to Vee, as if he expected her to be in the room. Maybe the suspicion arose when he saw that he had been fooled by the sound of the cassette player, that in fact he had been caught by his own deception. If that were the case, then he might have thought that Charles was further advanced in his investigation than he was and that playing the tape of Vee had been a deliberate set-up to see how the supposed murderer would react.

It was quite a thought. Geoffrey was a cold-blooded killer and if he could dispose of his mistress without a qualm, he would have little hesitation in getting rid of anyone else who stood in his way. Charles would have to tread warily.

Because if Geoffrey Winter did try to kill him, he would do the job well. He was a meticulous planner. Charles thought of the set model for The Caucasian Chalk Circle in Geoffrey's study. Every move carefully considered. Little plastic people being manipulated, disposed (and disposed of) according to the director's will.

The thought of danger cast a chill over the conviviality of the pub and the glow of the fourth pint. Well, the solution was to get to the source of the danger as soon as possible, to prove Geoffrey's guilt and have him put away before he could make a hostile move.

The pub was closing. Charles went to the Gents with the uncomfortable feeling that the amount he had consumed and the cold weather were going to make him want to go again before too long.

It was after two-thirty when he reached the Winters' road. He walked along it at an even pace, apparently giving their house no deeper scrutiny than the others. Somehow he felt that the watchers of Breckton were still alert behind their net curtains on Sunday afternoons.

The Winters themselves had resisted the suburban uniform of net curtains, so from a casual glance he could feel pretty confident that they were out. But he did not start his timed walk from then. He felt sure there must be a route from the back of the house.

When he got to the end of the road, his hunch was proved right. The gardens of the row of identical semis (identical to everyone except their proud owners) backed on to the gardens of the parallel row in the next road. Between them ran a narrow passage flanked with back gates into minute gardens.

The alley was concreted over, its surface cracked and brown, marked with moss and weeds. Suburban secrecy insured that the end fencing of all the gardens was too high for anyone walking along the alley to see in (or, incidentally, to be seen).

As Charles walked along, he could hear sounds from the gardens. The scrape of a trowel, a snatch of conversation, the sudden wail of a child, very close the snuffling bark of a dog. But except for the occasional flash of movement through the slats of fencing, he saw no one.

And this was in the middle of Sunday afternoon. After dark one could feel absolutely secure in passing unseen along the alley. And Geoffrey Winter must have known that.

When he reached the Winter's garden gate, he pressed close to the fence and squinted through a chink. He could see the distinctive wall-colouring of Geoffrey's study and, outside it, the little balcony and staircase, so convenient for anyone who wanted to leave the room unnoticed after dark.

As anticipated, the pressure on his bladder was becoming uncomfortable and he stopped to relieve himself where he stood. He was again struck by the secluded nature of the alley, which enabled him to behave impolitely in such a polite setting.

Then he started his timed walk. He reckoned Geoffrey must have allowed a maximum of forty minutes. *I, Claudius* lasted fifty, but he could only get forty-five minutes of *The Winter's Tale* on one side of the tape. Five minutes would be a buffer to allow for the unexpected.

Charles set off at a brisk walk. If Geoffrey had run, the timing would have been different, but Charles thought that was unlikely. A man running after dark attracts attention, while a man walking passes unnoticed.

The alley behind the houses came out on to the main road exactly opposite the footpath up to the common. There was a 'No Cycling' notice at the entrance. The path was paved until it opened out onto the common.

It was the first time Charles had seen this open expanse in daylight. In the centre were a couple of football pitches, which were reasonably well maintained, but the fringes of the common were ill-tended and untidy and had been used as a dumping ground by the nice people of Breckton. Superannuated fridges and rusty buckets looked almost dignified beside the more modern detritus of garish plastic and shredded polythene. It was an eyesore, the sort of mess about which aggrieved ratepayers no doubt wrote righteous letters to the local paper. To Charles it seemed a necessary part of the suburban. scene, the secret vice which made the outward rectitude supportable.

The half-burnt crater of the bonfire doused by the fire brigade at sour Reggie's behest gave the dumping ground an even untidier and more melancholy appearance.

The bonfire had been built where the footpath divided into two. The right-hand fork went up towards the Backstagers' club-rooms and the Hobbses' house. Charles took the other path which led towards the Meckens'.

He was feeling the need for another pee, but resolutely hung on, because any unscheduled stop would ruin his timing. He wished he had got a stopwatch, so that he could suspend time long enough to make himself comfortable. But he hadn't.

Even on a Sunday afternoon there were not many people up on the common. A few bored fathers trying to feign interest in their toddlers, one or two pensioners pretending they had somewhere to go. Breckton boasted other, more attractive parklands, equipped with such delights as swings and duck-ponds, and most of the inhabitants were there for their exercise.

It had rained during the week, but the path had dried out and was firm underfoot as Charles continued his brisk stroll. When he got to the other side of the common, the footpath once again had a proper surface of dark tarmac. His desert boot soles sounded dully as he trod.

To maintain his excitement he made a point of not looking at his watch until the journey was complete. He didn't stop when he got to Hugo's house. His memories of the new curtain snooper made him unwilling to draw attention to himself.

When he had gone one house-length beyond (which he reckoned would allow for going over the gravel drive to the front door), he looked at his watch.

Sixteen minutes. Geoffrey, with his longer stride, might have done it in fifteen. Say the same time each way. That gave eight to ten minutes in the house. Charlotte would have recognized him and let him in immediately, so there would have been no delay.

And eight or ten minutes was plenty of time for a determined man to strangle a woman.

If, of course, the murder weapon was to hand. On that kind of schedule, Geoffrey couldn't afford time to look for a scarf. He must have known where it was or...no, there was something missing there.

Charles tried to focus his mind on the problem. He summoned up the image of Charlotte in the coal shed, surprised untidily by the torch beam. He remembered her face. The red hair that framed it had looked unnatural, as if it were dyed, against the horrible greyness of her flesh. And that thin knotted Indian print scarf which couldn't hide the trickle of dried blood and the purply-brown bruises on her neck. Bruises almost like love-bites. He remembered what he had thought at the time, how she had looked so young, embarrassingly unsophisticated, like a teenager with a scarf inadequately hiding the evidence of a heavy petting session.

Good God – maybe that's what it had been. After all, she had seen Geoffrey at lunch time. By then he must have planned the murder. It would be typical of the man's mind if he had deliberately marked her neck, knowing that, respectable married woman that she was, she would be bound to put on a scarf to cover the bruising.

Then Geoffrey could go round in the evening, confident that the murder weapon would be to hand. Under the circumstances, he did not have to leave long for the strangling.

Charles shivered as he thought of the cold-bloodedness with which the crime had been planned.

He felt like an athlete in training for a major event. Everything was moving towards a confrontation with Geoffrey Winter. It was going to be risky to confront the villain with what he had deduced, but he couldn't see any way round it. The evidence he had was minimal and certainly not enough to persuade the police to change their tack. So his only hope was to elicit some admission of guilt from Geoffrey.

The fear of the man was building inside Charles. He felt increasingly certain that Geoffrey had read his suspicions and he wanted to keep the advantage by going to see his adversary rather than waiting for his adversary to search him out.

Within the next twenty-four hours, Charles knew, something conclusive was going to happen.

He went back to Hereford Road on the Sunday evening and rang Sally Radford. He had the sensation of a condemned man deserving a final treat.

But he didn't get his treat. Sally was glad to hear from him, but, sorry, she'd got a friend coming round that evening. Yes, maybe another time.

It shouldn't have hurt him. They'd agreed no strings, but it did cause a pang. The idea of a completely casual encounter with no obligations had always appealed to him, but now it had happened he was full of the need to establish continuity, to keep it going, to make something of it.

When he'd rung off from Sally, he contemplated ringing Frances, but procrastinated once again. He wrote off the idea of female company for the evening and went back to the Montrose. If he could keep on topping up his alcohol level, he might retain his mood of confidence and face the ordeal ahead without too much introspection.

CHAPTER SEVENTEEN

IN SPITE OF the knowledge of inevitable confrontation, Charles still had a career to pursue. Whatever the outcome of his meeting with Geoffrey Winter, he was still meant to be recording the second batch of Bland radio commercials on the Tuesday morning. The events of the week had pushed that from his mind.

It was only when he thought about it on the Monday morning that he realized he had better check the details. After all, it was Hugo Mecken's campaign and Hugo would not be able to conduct it from the remand wing of Brixton Prison.

He rang through to Mills Brown Mazzini and asked for Ian Compton. It turned out to be the right choice. Ian told him with no little complacency that he had taken over the Bland account. Charles wondered how much more of Hugo's authority the young wheeler-dealer had managed to annex since the Creative Director had been off the scene.

'I was just ringing to check that tomorrow's still on as per arrangement. Eleven o'clock at the same studio for the rest of the radios.'

'Yes, I should think that'll stand, though there's a slight question mark over it. May need some time for reworking of the copy. I'm having a meeting with Farrow this afternoon. Won't really know for sure till after that. Can I ring you in the morning?'

'Not quite sure of my movements.'

'You should be. Got to always be on call in the voice-over business.'

Charles ignored the young man's patronizing tone. 'I'll ring you. Either at the office in the morning or – have you a home number where I can get you this evening?'

'Won't be in. Got a film dubbing session at Spectrum Studios.'

'For the Bland campaign?' Charles pricked up his ears. Was Ian Compton getting some other voice-over work done on Bland behind his back?

'No, no. It's a private film production I'm working on. Doing a session with Diccon, just dubbing the voice.'

'Oh, I see.' It was hard to know whether to believe it or not. Ian Compton wouldn't hesitate to lie if it served his ends. On the other hand, he did work on a lot of other projects apart from Bland. 'How is Diccon?'

'Oh, he's in a pretty lousy mood at the moment.'

'What, not getting work?'

'You must be joking. That cookie is one of the busiest voices in the business. Clears twenty grand a year easy. No, he seems very cut up about Hugo's wife. I think he had quite a thing for her.'

'She was a very nice lady.'

'So I hear. It seems everyone thought so except Hugo.' Ian did not attempt to disguise the note of triumph in his voice. He was giving a reminder that Hugo Mechen was no longer a challenge to the bright young whiz-kid of Mills Brown Mazzini.

Charles decided that the confrontation should take place in Geoffrey's office. It would be quiet, no danger of interruptions. He told Gerald what he was going to do. Gerald disapproved, but Charles wanted someone to know in case he didn't return from the interview.

It was about a quarter to eleven on the Monday morning when he entered the building in Villiers Street. He mounted the stairs with one part of his mind immobilized by fright and the other irreverently providing sound track music and offering Sydney Carton's dramatic lines for use when mounting scaffolds to the sneers of unruly mobs.

All of which build-up was somewhat wasted when he found the door of Geoffrey Winter Associates firmly locked.

There was no light on inside. His mind, still running on romantic rails, summoned up the image of Geoffrey Winter sprawled over his desk, the smoking revolver clutched in his hand, his brains spattered on the wall behind. The villain who knew he had been found out and who had done the decent thing.

Wisely recognizing that this image was a little fanciful, he started knocking on the door to attract attention. A light tap produced nothing from inside, so he tried a more robust blow and then heavy hammering.

The last did raise a reaction, but it came from the floor below. An aggrieved young man with elastic bands holding up his shirt sleeves came and complained. So far as he knew, Mr. Winter wasn't in. He hadn't heard him coming up the stairs that morning. And surely the fact that there had been no reply to 'that bloody awful din you're making' indicated that there was nobody in the office.

Charles apologized and left the building. But he was too keyed up to drop it there. He had steeled himself to a meeting with Geoffrey Winter that day and somehow he had to arrange it.

He went into Charing Cross Station and rang the Winters' number from a call-box.

Vee answered. That in itself was strange. If she was a teacher, she should surely be in class at that time. Also she sounded even tenser and more emotional than usual. She had snatched up the phone on the first ring.

'Could I speak to Geoffrey, please? It's Charles Paris.'

'No, I'm sorry, he's not here.' She sounded near to tears.

'Do you know when he's likely to be back? I've been to his office and I couldn't find him there.'

'No, I've no idea. He's...' She stopped, leaving the word dramatically in the air. Charles was conscious of her acting instincts vying with genuine emotion.

'Is he likely to be in this evening? Do you know?'

'No. I don't. I – ' Again she cut short, uncertain whether to confide more. Charles felt a new panic. Had Geoffrey done a bunk?

But Vee could not keep her secrets to herself. In the same way that she had confided Geoffrey's supposed infertility to Charles, she couldn't resist the dramatic and martyring implications of her latest piece of news. 'Oh, what the hell. I might as well tell you. The whole country will no doubt know soon enough. Geoffrey's been arrested.'

'Arrested?'

'Yes, the police came round this morning before he left for work.'

Charles murmured some suitable words about how sorry he was and how sure he was that it would soon all be cleared up and how it must all be a ghastly mistake, but he had stopped thinking what he was saying. He concluded the conversation and then walked slowly, numbly, down to the Embankment.

He looked into the murky, swirling Thames. He tried to tell himself all kinds of other things, but ultimately he couldn't deny that he felt profoundly disappointed.

So that was it. The police must have been following his investigations in exact parallel. They must have worked out in just the same way how Geoffrey had contrived his alibi and managed to leave his room for the vital forty minutes.

Or no, perhaps he was flattering himself. The police had probably far outstripped his feeble investigations. They must have done. They wouldn't make an arrest without convincing evidence. He felt diminished and unnecessary.

He tried to argue himself out of this selfish mood. After all, what did it matter who had found the truth, so long as it had been revealed? Hugo could now go free, that was the main thing.

It didn't help. Depressingly he thought how little Hugo cared whether he was free or not. The release might well be a licence for him to commit suicide or, more slowly, drink himself to death.

Still, right had triumphed. He tried to feel glad about it.

With an effort he drew himself away from the river and started back to the station. Better ring Gerald and bring him up to date. Though if charges against his client were about to be dropped, he'd probably know already.

He didn't. He reacted strongly when Charles told him. But the reaction was not that of Gerald Venables the amateur sleuth; it was all solicitor. This new development changed circumstances for his client. He would get on to the Breckton police immediately.

'Okay,' said Charles dismally. 'Well. I'm going back to Hereford Road. So if there's any interesting development, just let me know.'

But he didn't really think any new development would concern him. He felt excluded, the one boy in the class without a party invitation.

He bought a new bottle of Bell's on the way back to Hereford Road. He was going to drink himself into a stupor. After the tension of the last week, this sudden anti-climax had let him down like a punctured air-bed.

The phone was ringing when he entered the house. He ran up to the landing and picked it up.

It was Gerald. Very cross. 'Are you trying to make me look like a complete fool? I've just spoken to the Superintendent at Breckton. He must think I'm a bloody lunatic. And you're not the most popular person down at the station either.'

'Geoffrey Winter has been arrested, yes. But it has nothing to do with the Mecken murder at all. He's been arrested for stealing some jewellery from a couple called Hobbs.'

'Oh my God.' Charles saw the bottom card being withdrawn from the great edifice he had built up.

'So you were right, Charles. Geoffrey Winter did have something to hide about what he was doing last Monday night. But it wasn't what your fertile imagination gave him to do.'

'But – '

'And what's more – just for your information – I've heard about the post-mortem. Charlotte Mecken was not pregnant.'

CHAPTER EIGHTEEN

LIKE THE CAT in a Tom and Jerry cartoon, Charles Paris continued running after the ground had crumbled away beneath his feet, before the inevitable realization and the windmill-armed plummeting descent to the depths.

Geoffrey Winter must be guilty of Charlotte's murder. All the motivation fitted; Charles couldn't start again the laborious reconstruction of emotion and opportunity with another subject. He refused to accept it.

But like the cat, he became increasingly aware that he was running on air. Whichever way he worked it, Geoffrey could not have committed both crimes on the Monday evening.

Unwilling to relinquish his theory, Charles went down to Breckton to time it all out again. He felt none of the elation of the previous day; as time passed he saw his logic falling apart.

He tried the trip from the Winters' house to the Meckens' via the Hobbses', he tried it the other way round, going to the Meckens' first, but there was just not enough time for anyone to have committed the two crimes.

Visiting the two houses added another five minutes to the round trip. Which left five or less for murder. Which was cutting it fine by the standards of the most experienced assassin. He tried adding the extra five minutes which he had reckoned Geoffrey would have left as a safety margin, but the sums still seemed pretty unlikely.

They seemed even unlikelier when he remembered that he had not allowed any time for the actual theft from the Hobbses' house. He had only timed the round trip of going past the house. If that were all that had been involved, the murder might have been possible. But even if Geoffrey knew the house well and knew exactly where Mary Hobbs kept her jewellery, it was still going to take him some time to break in, get through the house in the dark armed only with a torch and grab the loot. The absolute minimum was four minutes. In fact, considering the care with which Geoffrey had covered his tracks, it must have been six or eight.

Which left very little time to murder Charlotte Mecken.

Charles sat down on a bench on the common as it started to get dark. He was furious. There was no way it would work.

It wasn't just the timing. If Charlotte hadn't been pregnant, then none of his complex sequence of motivation worked either.

Depression took over. So everything was as obvious as it seemed. Hugo Mecken had killed his wife and Geoffrey Winter, in desperate financial straits because of his failing architect's business, had stolen some jewellery from the richest people he knew. The fact that the two incidents had taken place on the same evening had been mere coincidence.

The new turn of events changed his opinion of Geoffrey. While he had thought of the architect as Charlotte's murderer, he had had a kind of respect for him, for the cold blooded intellect that could plan such a crime. But now he knew that all that planning had been for a petty theft, a mean robbery from some supposed friends.

And Geoffrey's was not a great intellect. He had shown remarkable ineptitude in the execution of his crime, however clever the original conception of the cassette alibi. For a start, there had been his confused exit from the Hobbses' house when he saw Robert Chubb pass. Leaving his torch behind on the window sill was the real mark of the amateur.

The way he had been caught had been equally incompetent. Charles heard it all from Gerald. The thief had gone along the jewellers' stands in the Portobello Road on the Saturday morning trying to sell his loot. One of the dealers had bought some and then, becoming suspicious, alerted the police. From a description and from some remarks Geoffrey had carelessly let slip to the stall-holder, they had had little difficulty in tracking the culprit down.

So Geoffrey was relegated to the status of a shabby sneak-thief and Charles had either to concede that Hugo had killed Charlotte or start investigating somebody else.

The only two people left who seemed to have had any emotional relationship with Charlotte were Clive Steele and Diccon Hudson. Clive was supposed to have been in Melton Mowbray auditing at the time of the murder and no doubt Diccon would have some equally solid alibi. Still, wearily Charles supposed he must try to get interested again and check their movements. But the spark had gone. Any further investigation was going to be just a chore.

Since he was down in Breckton, he might as well start with Clive Steele at the Backstagers. The Back Room opened at six. Just sit a little longer on the common to kill time.

'Evening, sir. A bit dark to be out here, wouldn't you think?'

He looked up to. see the outline of the same policeman who had found him inside the Meckens' house the previous week.

'Yes, I suppose it is dark.' While he had been wrapped up in his thoughts, it had changed from dusk to blackness.

'You intending to sit there all night?'

'No, I wasn't. I was just going.'

The policeman held his ground and watched Charles out of sight along the footpath towards the Backstagers. He obviously thought he was watching a potential rapist or, at the very least, a flasher.

Charles decided that, considering how low his stock stood with the Breckton police, any alternative murder solution he took to them was going to have to be backed up by absolutely incontrovertible evidence.

There was no sign of Clive Steele in the Back Room, nor of anyone else Charles knew until Denis Hobbs came in at about half-past six. He was his usual boisterous self, though there was a slight strain beneath the bonhomie.

He had come in for a quick one on his way home from work. Charles wondered if he needed his regular drink to fortify him to face the redoubtable Mary.

They got talking naturally and Charles bought drinks. Denis had a pint, Charles a large Bell's. After some social chit-chat, Charles said, 'So you've got your man.'

Denis recoiled. 'What do you mean?'

'Your burglar.'

The builder's eyes narrowed. 'What do you know about it?'

'I know who's been arrested.'

Denis Hobbs looked at him steadily for a moment and then downed the remaining half of his beer. 'We can't talk here. Come round to my place for a drink.'

Inside, the Hobbses' house was, decoratively, exactly what the mock-Tudor exterior with its brash stone lions would lead one to expect. The tone was set before you entered. A china plaque by the doorbell showed a little girl in a crinoline and a boy in a tasselled cap leaning forward to kiss over the legend 'Denis and Mary live here'.

It must have been Mary's taste. The same eyes which had chosen her turquoise trouser suit and rainbow-coloured lamé slippers had certainly picked the jungle wallpaper. And the Raspberry Ripple carpet. And the green leather three-piece suite. And the miniature cluster of swords and axes tastefully set behind a red shield on the wall. And the three-foot-high china pony pulling a barrel. And the wrought iron drinks trolley with the frosted glass top and gold wheels. Denis was content to let her make decisions about such things. After all, she was the artistic one.

It was to the drinks trolley Denis went first. He poured a pink gin for his wife, a Scotch for Charles and got out a can of beer for himself. When he had poured it into his glass, he crushed the can in his huge paw. The metal flattened like tinfoil.

Mary's greeting to Charles was distinctly frosty. She had not forgotten his reservations about her Madame Arkadina.

But Denis cut through the atmosphere by saying, 'He knows.'

'What?'

'About the burglary.'

'Oh.' Mary looked downcast, as if rehearsing for a tragedy.

'How did you find out?' asked Denis.

'I spoke to Vee on the phone this morning. She told me.'

'Damn. I hope she's not telling everyone.'

'Why? What does it matter? Presumably everyone'll know when it comes up in court.'

'If it does come up in court. I'm trying to see that it doesn't.'

'I wouldn't have thought you stood much chance. I mean, if the police picked him up, they're going to bring charges.'

'I don't know. I'm going to ask them not to proceed. I'm going to stand bail for him and try to keep it as quiet as possible.'

'But why? I mean, there's no question as to whether he did it or not.'

'No, he's' admitted it.'

'Then why shouldn't he pay the price of his actions?'

'Well, he's...' Denis was having difficulty in framing his thoughts (or his wife's thoughts) into words. 'He's a friend.'

Mary took over. 'It's terribly embarrassing. I mean, he's been in and out of our house so often. This place becomes a sort of Backstagers' annex when the Back Room closes – particularly when we've got a show on. Geoffrey's a very close friend.'

'I can see it's embarrassing, but the fact remains that he has stolen your property.'

'Yes, but people are so materialistic, Mr. Parrish. What's a bit of jewellery?' Mary sat surrounded by the fruits of middle class affluence as she posed this ingenuous query.

'The thing is,' Denis contributed, 'we didn't realize the financial state he was in. We could have helped, lent him some money or something, not driven him to this.'

'Hardly driven. He did it of his own free will, presumably to get himself out of a spot.' Charles was bewildered by their reactions. Instead of being affronted and disgusted by Geoffrey's betrayal of their friendship, they were trying to justify his actions.

Mary gave Charles the patronizing smile of sainthood. 'It may be difficult for you to understand, but we feel an enormous loyalty to Geoffrey. He is a wonderfully talented person and we just didn't understand the terrible time he had been going through. To steal from us was a terrible lapse, which I'm sure he's regretted bitterly, but it's only an expression of the dark side of his impulsive artistic temperament.'

Now Charles had heard it all. That old fallacy about artists being answerable to a different code of morality from the rest of society. It was a view he had never subscribed to in the cases of the extremely talented writers and actors of his acquaintance who had tried it on, but for it to be used in the context of a moderately talented amateur was ridiculous.

Denis Hobbs nodded as his wife continued to expound her views. Charles was saddened by the sight of a man so emasculated by marriage. He wanted to get Denis on his own again and find out what the man really thought, not just hear him echoing Mary's opinions.

'You see, Mr. Parrish,' she continued, 'it's often difficult to explain to people that we don't just believe in materialistic values, that we have an appreciation of art – the theatre, poetry, painting.' She gestured vaguely in the direction of a Hawaiian sunset scene luminously painted on black velvet.

'We've been lucky, we've made a lot of money...'

Charles thought it was magnanimous of her to include Denis in this statement. She spoke of money as if it were an unfortunate skin condition. He was surprised Denis didn't get up and knock her block off. But her husband's brainwashing had been completed too long ago for him even to notice the slight.

'So what we feel is, Mr. Parrish, that it's our duty – being of limited artistic talent ourselves – ' She simpered in expectation of some complimentary remonstrance, but then remembered Charles's expressed view of her acting abilities and moved hurriedly on. ' – to share some of our good fortune with more artistic people. That's why we make this room a second Back Room and provide lots of drinks and things...' (she couldn't resist quantifying their altruistic generosity.) '...so that we can do our bit for the spread of cultural ideas, stimulate lively conversation, discussion of the arts and so forth.'

Charles began to understand her cock-eyed reasoning. Mary Hobbs saw herself as the leader of an artistic salon, the Madame de Staël of Breckton. Geoffrey Winter's crime was just the errant behaviour of one of the young geniuses she was nurturing. In fact, it was a challenge to her values, an opportunity for her to show how far above material considerations she was.

He wondered to what extent Geoffrey had anticipated this reaction. If he had known that the theft, if it ever came out, rather than ruining him socially, might increase his stock among the Backstagers and build up his mildly roué image as a man above conventional morality, then it was not such a risk as it might have appeared.

'Oh dear.' Mary Hobbs gave a tragedienne's sigh. 'I wonder if the police will be persuaded to drop the charges against him.'

This abstraction seemed to be directed at Denis. 'I don't know, dear. I doubt it. But perhaps Willy will be able to get him off lightly. Our solicitor's looking after Geoffrey,' he explained for Charles's benefit.

Good God. The man broke into their house and stole their property and there they were leaning over backwards to defend him. 'What'll happen, Denis? Will he be up before Breckton magistrates in the morning?'

'Yes. My solicitor's going to ask for bail. We'll be going down to give moral support. We've got to get him free as soon as possible.'

Mary agreed. 'Otherwise it's going to interfere dreadfully with *Winter's Tale* rehearsals.'

Charles kept having to remind himself that these people were real when they came up with remarks like that. 'And then straight on as before...Geoffrey rehearsing, no mention of the theft, coming back here for drinks after the Back Room closes.'

'And why not? Geoffrey's a friend.' Mary's constant repetition of this was like a child's assertion that someone is 'my best friend'. In children it is always symptomatic of insecurity and only heard from those who have difficulty in making real friends. And in adults too.

Charles found something infinitely pathetic about the Hobbs trying to buy friendship with a constant supply of free drinks and afraid to lose a friend even when he abused their trust so disgracefully.

Denis seemed to think Mary's view of Geoffrey needed endorsement. 'Oh, he's a very lively bloke, Geoffrey. I don't suppose you've ever seen him in full flood. Life and soul of the party. Always full of ideas for games and what-have-you. What was that thing he started here after the first night of *The Seagull*, love?'

Mary Hobbs giggled with the memory. 'Oh yes, it was a great game. One of you goes out of the room and dresses up and then when they come back in, you all have to ask questions to find out who they're meant to be. You know, you can be politicians or show biz people – or members of the Backstagers, if you like.' She laughed again, a comfortable 'in' laugh. Her Backstagers' identity was a vital support to her life. 'Do you remember, I pretended to be. Reggie, the secretary?'

Denis guffawed at the recollection.

'Actually he wasn't very pleased, was he, Den?'

'No, can't take a joke, our Reggie.'

'Did Geoffrey himself have to go?' asked Charles.

'Oh yes. He was a riot. He did Margaret Thatcher. He found a wig of mine and a smart overcoat and...oh, it was hysterical. He'd got the voice just right, hadn't he, Den?'

Denis agreed on cue. 'He was great. Oh, it was a great party, that. Charlotte – she looked really lovely that evening – wore this long check sort of smock thing.'

'Yes, well, she's dead,' snapped Mary with unnecessary brutality. Denis recoiled as if struck. Mary hastened to paper over the rift. 'Oh, it was a marvellous night. We had so much fun. Of course, Charlotte spent most of the evening with young Clive Steele.'

This seemed to be put in as another rebuff to her husband. His attraction to Charlotte must have been the subject of some marital tiff. She went on. 'Such a clever boy, Clive. And so good-looking. You know, I think he had rather fallen for Charlotte. He certainly seems very cut up about her death.'

'I suppose he's only just heard,' said Charles.

'What do you mean?'

'Well, he was away working all last week in Melton Mowbray, wasn't he?'

'Oh, no, apparently that was called off. No, Clive was here all last week.'

CHAPTER NINETEEN

THIS TIME CLIVE Steele was at the Back Room bar when Charles went in. The young man greeted him patronizingly and graciously accepted the offer of a drink. 'Don't know why I bothered to turn up this evening. I get here to find the rehearsal's off.'

'Oh.'

'Yes, we were meant to be doing all the Florizel/Perdita scenes tonight. But Vee Winter's cried off. Apparently not well.'

Or too upset over her husband's arrest to face anyone, Charles reflected. 'You're playing Florizel?'

'Yes. Terribly drippy part. But I suppose I really am too young for Leontes,' he conceded as if youth were the only possible bar to his being given the lead. 'Still, it's parts like Florizel that need real acting. It takes a bit of talent to make something of that kind of weed, so I suppose it's quite a challenge.'

Charles saw a chance to move the conversation his way.

'So, but for recent events, it would have been another Clive Steele/ Charlotte Mecken partnership. Florizel and Perdita.'

'Yes.' Clive looked shaken, childishly near to tears. 'Oh my God, it was terrible. For her to die – Charlotte who had so much to give – for her just to be strangled by that drunken brute.'

'Hugo?'

'Of course Hugo. You know why it was...?' Clive leaned across to Charles confidingly. 'Hugo was jealous.'

'Oh yes. Of whom?'

'Of me.'

'You?'

'Yes. It's no secret that Charlotte and I got pretty close over *The Seagull*. There was a very strong mutual attraction. I think Hugo must have realized and killed her in a fit of jealousy.'

Charles was almost amused by the young man's arrogant assurance. Are you saying you were having an affair with Charlotte?'

'Ssh,' Clive hissed loudly and waved his hand in a rubbing-out movement. 'Don't say a word about it here.' His dramatic behaviour must have drawn the attention of everyone in the bar. Fortunately, for a moment there was no one there.

'Well, were you?'

'Not exactly. I mean, nothing had actually happened. You know, she had a few scruples and I didn't want to rush things, but it was inevitable the way it would go. Only a matter of time.'

This seemed very much at odds with the state of the relationship which Charles had gathered from the conversation he overheard in the car park. He had surmised from that that Clive had misinterpreted Charlotte's natural niceness as a come-on and that she was disillusioning him in no uncertain terms. But Clive seemed to have forgotten that encounter and retained his belief in his irresistible magnetism for her. Maybe, now she was dead, he found that a reassuring fiction to cling to. It flattered his ego and gave him an opportunity to feel tragic.

He was certainly putting on a performance of feeling tragic. 'And now she's dead – it's awful. She was so young, so ripe for loving. I think love is for the young and beautiful.' This was clearly a category in which he would include himself. 'I mean, it was disgusting, the idea of Charlotte being groped by an old man. Someone like Hugo.'

Charles didn't rise to the implied insult. He was a great believer in letting people ramble on when they were in spate. It was a much easier method than interrogation and often quite as informative.

'Or Denis Hobbs,' Clive continued.

'Denis? Did he grope Charlotte?'

'Well, he was always putting his arm round her, you know, casually, like it didn't mean anything, but I got the feeling he was enjoying handling the goods.'

'There was one night I remember – Wednesday before last it was, first night of *The Seagull* – we all went round to the Hobbses' place. I think Denis must have been a bit pissed, but he certainly seemed to be after Charlotte.'

'Oh.'

'We'd all decided we wanted to play silly games and Denis kept saying we ought to play Postman's Knock (which I should think is about his level), because that meant kissing people – and he made a sort of grab at Charlotte to demonstrate.'

'But you didn't play Postman's Knock?' Charles fed gently.

'No, we played a much better game that Geoff Winter knew. Dressing up sort of thing. But Denis didn't give up. I went upstairs with Geoff to sort out some dressing-up clothes and then I came down while he was changing – actually he got himself up as Margaret Thatcher, he was bloody marvellous – anyway, when I got down, there was Denis with his arm round Charlotte. He was pretending it was all casual again and she was sort of joking, but I don't think she really liked it. And I'm damned sure Mary Hobbs didn't like it. She came out into the hall at that moment and you should have seen the look she gave Denis.'

'When did you last see Charlotte?'

'After the cast party.'

'That was the last time? You didn't talk to her again or anything?'

'Well, actually I did. I rang her on the Monday afternoon.'

'The day she died.'

'Yes.' Clive seemed poised to launch into another self-dramatizing lament, but fortunately didn't. 'I was trying to fix to meet her that evening. The fact is, we hadn't parted on the best of terms after the cast party...'

Ah, now the truth, thought Charles.

'Silly thing, really,' Clive continued. 'She was talking about leaving Hugo for me and I was saying no, it was too soon, we should let things ride for a bit...you know, the sort of disagreement you get between two people in love.'

Charles couldn't believe it. Clive's self-esteem was so great that he actually seemed to have convinced himself that he was talking the truth. Charles was glad that he had heard the real encounter between the two; otherwise he might have found himself taking Clive seriously.

The young man rambled on mournfully. 'So I wanted to meet for a drink, you know, to chat, sort it all out. But she said she couldn't, so I got a bit pissed off and went to the flicks with an old girlfriend.'

'Did Charlotte say why she couldn't meet you?'

'She said someone was coming round.'

'She didn't say who?'

'Some friend from drama school.'

Charles took a taxi from Waterloo to Spectrum Studios in Wardour Street. He told the uninterested commissionaire that he wanted to see Diccon Hudson and was directed to the dubbing theatre.

The red light outside was off to indicate that they weren't recording at that moment, so he went on through the double door. It was a large room, walls covered with newish upholstered sound-proofing. At one end was a screen above a television which displayed a film footage count. On a dais at the other end was the dubbing mixer's control panel. On a low chair in front of this Ian Compton lolled.

He looked quizzically as Charles entered. Some explanation of his presence was called for.

Charles hadn't really thought of one and busked. 'I was in the area and I thought I'd just drop in to find out about tomorrow's session. Save the phone call.'

Ian Compton looked sceptical and Charles realized it did sound pretty daft. But no comment was made. 'No, in fact tomorrow's off, Charles. Farrow's not happy with the radio copy and I'm afraid it's all got to be rewritten. Take a few days. I should think we'd be in touch by the end of the week.'

'Fine.'

'And don't worry, you were booked for the session, so you'll get paid.'

'Oh thanks.' Charles's instinct was to say, 'Don't bother about that,' but he bit it back. He must develop more commercial sense.

Ian Compton looked at him with an expression that signified the conversation was over.

'Actually, I wanted to have a word with Diccon too.'

A raised eyebrow. 'Really?'

'Yes.'

'Well, we're just about to start doing a few more loops. Then we'll break in about half an hour when we've got to set up a new machine.'

'May I wait?'

Ian Compton shrugged permission.

The film that was being dubbed appeared to be about a young bronzed man fishing for octopus on a Greek island. Charles need not have worried about Bland work being done behind his back.

Diccon Hudson was working at a table in a box of screens. He wore headphones. The film was cut down into loops of about thirty or forty-five second durations. On each loop a chinagraph pencil line had been scored diagonally, so that it moved across the screen when the film was run. When it reached the right hand side, it was Diccon's cue to speak, adding his voice to the Music and Effects track.

He worked smoothly and quickly. He needed only one run of each loop and timed the words perfectly each time. A master of all forms of voice work.'

When they had to break, Ian Compton went out to the control room, where the new machine was being set up. Charles went into the box of screens. Diccon Hudson looked up nervously. 'To what do I owe this pleasure? Coming to get some tips on voice technique?'

'No.'

'On dubbing? The great con-trick. Wonderful the things you can perpetrate in dubbing. That bloke on the screen, the diver who does all the talking, is Greek. Talks English like a broken-winded turkey. But by the wonders of dubbing, he can speak with my golden cadences. It's magic. He does his talking at one time, I add my voice at another and in the cinema, so far as the audience is concerned, it all happened at the same time.' He had taken this flight of fancy as far as it would go and paused anxiously. 'But you didn't come here to talk to me about dubbing.'

Charles shook his head slowly. 'No, I've come to talk about Charlotte Mecken.'

Diccon coloured at the name. 'Oh yes, what about her?'

'When we last met, you said you used to see her from time to time. The odd lunch.'

'So?'

'I've come along to ask if you saw her a week ago today. Last Monday.'

It was a shock. Diccon gaped for a moment before replying. 'No, of course I didn't. Why should I? What are you insinuating?'

'I'm not insinuating anything. I'm just asking you what you were doing last Monday.'

'I was out.'

'Out where?'

Diccon hesitated. 'Out with friends.'

'Friends who I could check with?'

'No, I...' He tailed off in confusion.

'Did you speak to Charlotte that day?'

'On the phone, yes. When I got back to my flat after an afternoon session, there was a message on the Ansafone for me to ring her.'

'Someone else she spoke to that afternoon was told that she had a friend from drama school coming down in the evening.'

'She wanted me to go down and see her, but I couldn't.'

'You went out with friends instead.'

'Yes. What are you suggesting – that I strangled her?'

Charles shrugged. 'Well, I don't think Hugo did.'

'I didn't. I swear I didn't go down there. I went out.'

'But you won't tell me where.'

Diccon hesitated and seemed on the verge of saying something. But then, 'No.'

'But you did speak to her?'

'I've told you, yes. She wanted my advice.'

'On what?'

'She wanted to know if I knew the name of an abortionist.' This time it was Charles who was put off his stroke for a moment. 'But she wasn't pregnant. The police post-mortem showed that.'

'Well, she thought she was. And she said she'd decided she couldn't keep the baby.'

'Why not?'

'I don't know. Presumably because Hugo didn't want children.'

'You think it was Hugo's?'

'Why not?'

'Not yours?'

'What?' His surprise seemed genuine. 'Good God, no, I never scored with Charlotte, I'm afraid. Though I tried a few times.'

'Then why did she ask you about the abortionist?'

'I don't know. I suppose I was the only person she knew who might have that sort of information. I have been around with quite a few women, you know,' he added with a touch of self-assertive bravado.

It had the ring of truth. If Charlotte had wanted to get rid of a baby, in her naïveté, she wouldn't have known where to begin. She could only ask a friend. Why not Sally Radford? Perhaps Charlotte knew of the girl's emotional reaction to her own abortion and didn't want to upset her by asking.

As to the pregnancy, that must have been a phantom, some freak of Charlotte's cycle, probably a side-effect of going on the Pill.

But if what Diccon had said was true, why was he being so evasive about the night of the murder? 'I'd like to believe you, Diccon, but I'd feel happier with an alibi I could check. Where were you at the time Charlotte was strangled?'

'I...I won't tell you.'

'You tell him.' A new voice came into the room, harsh and electronic. It was Ian Compton on the talkback from the control room. He must have had Diccon's microphone up and been listening to their conversation for some time.

Diccon turned towards his friend behind the glass screen and shouted, 'No!'

'All right then, I'll tell him.'

'NO!' Diccon Hudson rose and ran out of the screens towards the glass as if he could somehow smother Ian's speech.

But the talkback talked on inexorably. 'Diccon was with me. We went together to a club called *The Cottage*, which you may know is a resort of homosexuals or gays as we prefer to call them. We went there because we are both gay.'

'No,' muttered Diccon, tears pouring down his face.

'For some reason, Charles, as you see, Diccon does not like to admit this fact in public. God knows why. He's only discovered his real nature recently and still tries to put up a straight front. That's why he lunches all these pretty little actresses, like Charlotte Mecken – to maintain the image of the great stud. Which is in fact far from the truth.'

Diccon Hudson found his voice again. 'Shut up,' he said feebly.

Charles decided it was time for him to go. He didn't want to get into a marital squabble and he didn't think much more useful information was likely to be forthcoming. 'I'm sorry to have caused a scene. Thank you for telling me all you have. It's going to help me clear Hugo.'

'Clear Hugo?' Diccon repeated in amazement. 'You can't still think that I – '

'No, not you.'

But something that Diccon had said had released a block in Charles's mind and he was now certain who had killed Charlotte and how.

The next day he was going to confront that person.

CHAPTER TWENTY

CHARLES FELT CERTAIN that the person he wanted to see would be at Breckton Magistrates' Court the next morning.

It was nearly twelve o'clock when the little group came out of the main entrance. Geoffrey was in the middle with Vee, and they were flanked by Denis and Mary Hobbs. A man in a pin-striped suit, presumably the Hobbses' solicitor, followed slightly behind. The atmosphere was more celebration of the return of a conquering hero than the release on bail of a man accused of petty theft from a friend.

Charles went forward to meet them. 'I'm terribly sorry, Geoff. Vee inadvertently told me what had happened.'

'That's all right. Thanks for coming.' Geoffrey wore a mask of relaxed affability. 'I suppose everyone will know soon.'

'Yes, but it'll blow over pretty quickly,' asserted Denis Hobbs. 'Don't you reckon, Willy?'

'We live in hope,' the solicitor replied smugly. Charles wondered whether smugness was something that all solicitors have to take on when they're articled in a sort of primitive ceremony like a circumcision rite.

'Anyway, don't let's talk about it,' said Denis. 'Charles, we're all going out to lunch – how'd you like to join us? We're going to put all this behind us and think of the future. I hadn't realized how badly things were going with poor Geoff. But I think over lunch we might have a bit of a discussion about one or two openings there might be for architects in my business.'

He looked to Mary for approval. She smiled and he glowed visibly. So that was it. Not only was Geoffrey going to be forgiven for his crime; he was also going to get a new job to sort out his financial problems. Mary Hobbs loved being in the Lady Bountiful position, using her husband's money and influence to share a little of the reflection of Geoffrey's talent. And to gain power over him.

Charles declined the lunch invitation with thanks, but said he'd walk along with them a little way.

He fell into step beside his quarry. 'I wonder if we could have a chat at some point. Something I'd like to discuss.'

'Certainly. How about this afternoon? I'll be at home when we get back from this lunch.'

'Okay, fine.'

'About three.'

Charles nodded. It had all been very casual, but they both knew it was a confrontation.

The house was empty but for the two of them.

'Well, Charles, what can I do for you?'

No point in beating around the bush with social pleasantries. It had to be direct. 'I know how you did it.'

'Did what?'

'Killed Charlotte.'

'Ah.' Charles had to admire the other's control. Even total innocence should have given more reaction. 'So that's what it is, is it? All right, intrigue me, tell me how I did it.'

'It was a very carefully worked out plan. A work of genius, one might say.'

'I'm touched by the compliment, but I think it may be misapplied. Incidentally, before you tell me how I committed this crime, would you be so good as to tell me why I did it?'

'You did it, Geoffrey, because Charlotte told you she was pregnant and as a good Catholic she said she wouldn't have an abortion. So you had to get rid of her out of loyalty to Vee. She was coming to see Vee the day after she died. She'd fixed it by phone. You couldn't risk Vee finding out about the pregnancy. It would have destroyed your marriage.'

Geoffrey left a pause before he responded. Maybe it was in reaction to what he had heard, but when he came back, his voice was as firm as ever. 'I see. So that's why I did it. Now perhaps you will continue with telling me how I did it.'

'Right. Last Monday night, after we parted at the main road, you went home. Vee wanted to watch *I, Claudius*, as you knew she would. As soon as it had started, you put on a previously prepared cassette of yourself doing the lines for *The Winter's Tale*, then left this room by the balcony. You walked briskly along the path at the back, over the main road and – '

'Look, I hate to break in on this magnificent piece of deduction, but I would just like to congratulate you and say you're absolutely right. Except in one detail. I did all this, but the crime which I committed in the time thus gained was not Charlotte's murder, but the theft from Denis and Mary for which I appeared in court this morning.'

'If you will wait a moment, Geoffrey, I was coming to that. This is where your plan was so clever, because it involved a double alibi. If anyone worked out the cassette dodge, then you had a second line of defence that during the relevant time you were doing the robbery. On Friday you thought I was on to the cassette – in fact, you flattered me, I hadn't quite got there by then – but that was sufficient to frighten you into implementing your second plan, getting rid of the stolen jewellery in such an amateur manner that you knew it was only a matter of time before the police arrested you.'

'I see.' Geoffrey's voice was heavy with irony. 'So, according to the Charles Paris theory, in the time I had at my disposal, I stole the jewellery and strangled Charlotte in two different houses half a mile apart. Hmm. You obviously have a very high opinion of the speed at which I work.'

'No, I haven't finished the Charles Paris theory. What I am saying is that you didn't do the robbery.'

'Oh, I see. Magic, was it? The jewellery suddenly appeared in my pocket. Or maybe I had a leprechaun as a henchman and he spirited the stuff away. Was that it?'

'No. You did the robbery, but you didn't do it on the Monday evening.'

'But that's when it was done. That's when Bob Chubb saw the light in the Hobbses' house, that's when the police came and found it had been done.'

Charles shook his head slowly. 'All you did on the Monday night was to break the window, open the catch and leave the switched-on torch on the window sill, so that Bob Chubb or whoever else happened to pass couldn't fail to see it. You'd actually taken the valuables on the previous Wednesday evening when you'd been round at the house. You'd put a lot of planning into the thing. You'd suggested the game of charades at the Hobbses' and while you were upstairs dressing up as Margaret Thatcher in Mary Hobbses' clothes, you helped yourself to the jewellery.

'So, on the Monday, you only had to stop at their house for thirty seconds rather than five minutes. That was why everyone was so surprised at the tidiness of the burglary. Everything left as if it hadn't been touched. It hadn't been. No one went inside the house that evening.

'The crime was done like a dubbed film – one part of the action at one time and the other later on. The theft was committed before the break-in. And everyone thought they had been done at the same time.'

Geoffrey's face remained impassive. Impossible to judge what was going on behind that mask.

Charles pressed on. 'Then you went to Meckens's house. It was easy. Hugo played into your hands. Apart from the convenience of his constant outspoken attacks on Charlotte, you knew he wasn't going to leave the Back Room until it closed. And that then he'd be in a state where his reactions and memory could play him false.

'Charlotte was all set up. You'd seen her at lunch time. In the excess of your passion you'd marked her neck with a lovebite, so you knew she'd have a scarf round her neck. Maybe you'd even said you'd drop in, so that she'd open the door quickly and you wouldn't be seen.

'Strangling her must have been quick. She was totally unsuspicious, off her guard. Then you put her body in the coal shed to delay its discovery and you were off home. Back before the end of *I, Claudius*. Just in time to pick up from the cassette and start bellowing your lines with such vigour that your next-door neighbour was bound to complain, thus even getting the police to corroborate your first alibi.'

There was a long pause. Geoffrey kept the usual tight rein on his emotions. 'Well, Charles, you give me credit for a lot of ingenuity.'

'I do.'

'And I can see that, if all your assumptions are correct, it would have been possible for me to kill Charlotte. But you need a ripe imagination to follow the twists of what you've just told me. I think you might have difficulty persuading the police of it all – particularly as at the moment they have two crimes and for each one they have a self-confessed criminal.'

'But Hugo only confessed because he couldn't remember and because he didn't care.'

'If he didn't care, then why should we?'

'I don't know. I just want the truth to come out.'

'Admirable sentiments. Well, I'm sure as soon as you can produce evidence to back up your preposterous allegations, the truth will come out.'

Yes, there was the rub. Charles knew he had nothing except his own convictions to support his theory. It was right, but, as Geoffrey observed, it was going to be almost impossible to persuade the police to take it seriously. Particularly if the persuader was someone who stood as low in the estimation of Breckton Police Station as Charles Paris.

He felt his confidence begin to ebb and, with an effort, tried to regain momentum. Maybe he could shock a confession out of Geoffrey. 'What makes the whole crime so ironic, even tragic, is the fact that Charlotte wasn't even pregnant.'

'What!' This time Geoffrey reacted. This time, for a moment, the mask crumbled. And from that instant Charles knew for certain that he was right. He might have got some of the details of the plan's execution wrong, but Geoffrey Winter definitely killed Charlotte Mecken.

'No,' he continued coolly. 'The police post-mortem revealed that she wasn't pregnant.'

'But – '

'Oh, she thought she was, but it was just some freak effect of her going on the Pill. If she'd had the nerve to go to her doctor about it, he could have quickly disillusioned her. But no, she told you she was pregnant; she said, as a Catholic, she was going to keep the baby and, what was more, if you wouldn't tell your wife about it, then she would. When she made that decision, she signed her death warrant.'

Geoffrey's eyes were closed and he was breathing deeply. Charles turned the knife in the wound. 'And, if you're looking for further ironies, between the time that she saw you on the Monday lunch time and the time that you killed her, Charlotte had decided that she would have an abortion. She rang up a friend for advice on how to end the pregnancy that never was. So her death was doubly unnecessary.'

Geoffrey was badly shaken, but he rallied. There was only slight tension in his voice when at last he spoke. 'This has been very interesting. May I ask what you are going to do now, Charles?'

'Nothing. I'm going to go away. I'm going to leave you with the knowledge that I know exactly what happened and see how you react. Maybe you'll come round to the conclusion that you ought to devise another equally ingenious method of disposing of me. My knowledge makes me just as much of a threat to your way of life as Charlotte was.'

'You sound almost as if you are issuing a challenge.'

'Yes, Geoffrey. I am.'

CHAPTER TWENTY-ONE

THE NEXT FEW days were an agony of vigilance for Charles. He hadn't really meant to challenge Geoffrey to kill him, but without evidence he saw no other way of drawing the man out into the open. All he had to do was to keep on his guard and see Geoffrey before Geoffrey saw him.

In case the worst happened, he wrote down a detailed reconstruction of what had taken place on the night of Charlotte's murder and lodged it with Gerald. Then if Charles Paris were found murdered, it could be delivered to the police, who would know where to start looking for their murderer.

But Charles didn't intend to be murdered; he intended to catch Geoffrey Winter attempting to murder him. That attempt would be tantamount to a confession to Charlotte's murder.

Charles tried to live as normally as possible. He stayed round Hereford Road a lot, so that Geoffrey should have no difficulty finding him. He drank less, so as to remain alert. He rigged up an elaborate alarm over the door of his bedsitter so that he should not be surprised in the night. And he waited.

Meanwhile he tried to continue his career, as funds were getting low. In this he encountered an unexpected setback.

He rang through to Mills Brown Mazzini on that Friday to find out when the next Bland recording session would be. Ian Compton told him with ill-disguised glee that the housewives of the Tyne-Tees area had given the thumbs-down to the Mr. Bland television commercials. They had found the animation too frivolous for something as important as a bedtime drink and they didn't like the name.

As a result, Ian had worked out a completely different approach for the product, and it had been approved by Mr. Farrow. The new campaign for the drink (now renamed Velvet-Sleep) was to feature a young couple who had just finished a hard day's decorating. The voice-over was going to be done by Diccon Hudson.

So that was it. Charles was paid off for the Tuesday's cancelled recording session and suddenly the heady vistas of infinitely repeated commercials bringing in infinite repeat fees shrank down to a few solitary session payments. Needless to say, there had been no long-term contract signed. The dazzling prospects had existed only in conversations between Charles and Hugo. With his sponsor still remanded in custody, Charles was suddenly out of the voice-over world. He never heard the result of the No Fuzz test.

He rang Maurice Skellern and said he would audition for the Cardiff company. He had to live on something.

He also kept thinking he should ring Frances, but didn't get round to it.

On the Saturday morning he received a letter.

Dear Mr. Parrish,

Thank you so much for letting us see your play, How's Your Father?, which we read with some amusement.

We regret that we do not feel it to be suitable for our World Premières Festival, as we feel it is too slight and commercial a piece for production in what has increasingly become one of the main outlets for modem experimental theatre in this country.

We have also been fortunate to receive a new play by George Walsh. It is called Amniotic Amnesia and concerns the thoughts of a group of foetuses awaiting a fertility drug-induced multiple birth. It raises many interesting questions of philosophy and ecology and is much more the sort of work we feel the Backstagers should be doing.

We will hope to see you down here for our next production, The Winter's Tale by William Shakespeare.

Yours sincerely,

Robert Chubb

World Premières Festival Sub-Committee

PS Your script is being returned under separate cover.

It was over a week before the truth sank in. That Geoffrey was not going to be drawn, that so long as he didn't rise to Charles's challenge, he was safe He knew that there was no evidence and he did not intend to supply any.

Charles felt ridiculous when this dawned on him. He had nothing; he should have realized. Geoffrey Winter had killed Charlotte Mecken, but it could never be proved.

Charles was furious. Having got so near, to be thwarted at the end…Hugo would be sentenced to life imprisonment and maybe come out after eight years to drink himself to death. Geoffrey would get a fine or a short sentence or maybe – if Willy, the Hobbses' solicitor, were really good – a suspended sentence for the crime he'd had to commit as a cover-up. Then he'd take up a job with Denis Hobbs in the 'construction industry' and continue to play all the leads at the Breckton Backstagers. And Mary Hobbs would have the satisfaction of feeling that she had done something direct and positive for the artistic life of the community. And memories would heal over and the case would trickle away.

He couldn't stand the thought. He resolved to get back to Breckton for one last try. There must be something he had missed.

* * * * *

It was Monday. Exactly two weeks from the night that Charlotte had died. Monday. November 15th. It had been a bright autumn day, but was dark by the time Charles arrived once again at Breckton Station.

Nearly seven o'clock. Instinctively he walked towards the Winters' house. As he rounded the corner of their road, he stopped.

Geoffrey and Vee were walking ahead of him towards the main road.

Of course. Rehearsal. Up to the Back Room for a quick one, and then ready to give artistically at seven-thirty. Leontes and Perdita, played by Geoffrey Winter and Vee le Carpentier. The stars of the Breckton Backstagers. Oh yes, he knocks around a bit with other women, but they're really very close. No children, no. But they're very close.

He tailed them at about fifty yards distance, but they didn't look round. It was uncannily silent. Geoffrey, like Charles, must be wearing his favourite desert boots and Vee's shoes also must have had soft soles, for there was no sound of footfalls on the pavement of the footpath. Just the occasional chuckle from up ahead. Geoffrey sounded more relaxed alone with his wife than Charles had ever heard him in company. Oh yes, he needed Vee. When Charlotte threatened that relationship, she had to go.

Charles followed them all the way, keeping the same distance behind. It was sickening. He knew what had happened, the criminal was right in front of him and yet he could do nothing about it. Nothing without proof.

By the time Charles got to the Hobbses' house, Geoffrey and Vee had disappeared inside the Backstagers. Everything went on just the same – drink, rehearsal, home, work, drink, rehearsal…Why should he try to break it up? Hugo was long past hope – what did it matter whether he despaired in prison or at large? He had nothing to live for. Geoffrey Winter at least had his love for his wife, his acting, his little affairs. What was the point of trying to break that pattern?

Charles decided he would go back to the station, get the train back up to Town and forget the case had ever happened.

A feeling almost of nostalgia for the time he had spent retracing Geoffrey's movements made him take the long way round past the Meckens' house.

It stood dark and unfriendly. Presumably, after Hugo's trial it would go on the market, someone would buy it. There would be stories of what had happened there. If the buyer were imaginative, Charlotte's ghost might even be seen. If not, it would all be forgotten. Sooner or later, all would be forgotten.

As he stood there, he was seized by an impulse to do it once again. One more retracing and that was it.

This time just as Geoffrey must have done it two weeks before. He slipped across the gravel drive to the side gate. He no longer cared about the net curtain snoopers. Let them report him if they wanted to. He was about to leave Breckton for the last time.

The side gate was not locked. He lifted the latch and let himself into the back garden. He had a small pencil torch in his pocket and he shone it on the ground before his feet as he walked towards the coal shed.

It was a shock not to find Charlotte's body still there. That embarrassingly sprawled figure had so etched itself on his subconscious that he felt cheated when there was only coal in his torch-beam.

He stood there for a moment looking round. Nothing. Not the perfect crime, but a crime that was by now undetectable. Maybe at the time, maybe if Geoffrey had been the first suspect, there might have been something which would have given him away. Maybe the blood from the abrasion on Charlotte's neck had been on his hands as he walked home. But if so, that blood had been long washed away, long dispersed and unidentifiable. Now there was nothing. Not a chance of anything.

Charles's footsteps crunched in the coal-dust as he sighed and left the coal shed. Back across the drive, along the road and down the tarmac footpath to the common.

There was no one, about, of course. No one to see him, just as there had been no one to see Geoffrey Winter a fortnight before.

He walked doggedly along the hard mud path skirting the football fields towards the path to the main road. He passed the untidy bit, the dumping ground, still dominated by the washed-out crater of the Guy Fawkes bonfire.

He reached the paved path and walked a couple of paces. Then he stopped.

He felt a little tremor of excitement. Twisting one foot round on the paving, he heard the crunch of coal-dust.

Good God, it stayed on. He'd have thought it would have been wiped off by the walk across the common, but no. The little grains of coal embedded themselves into the rubber sole of the desert boot and took a lot of shifting.

And if he had noticed the difference in sound when he came on to the paving, so would someone else have done two weeks before. Could Geoffrey have taken the risk of carrying that incriminating dust into his own house?

No, surely he would have tried to remove the evidence. Charles looked at his own sole with the pencil torch. Little chips of coal glinted in the beam. He tried to scrape them off. Some came, some stayed. He could have got them all out, but it would have taken time. And time was the one commodity which Geoffrey hadn't had. His tape gave him a maximum of forty-five minutes.

And on the morning Charles had visited him in his office, Geoffrey had been wearing new shoes.

Charles looked round. There was only one obvious place to dispose of a pair of shoes. You could throw them into the bushes, but there they'd be retrieved by the first nosey dog who came along. But in the bonfire.

After all, so long as suspicions were held off for four days, the evidence would be burnt publicly and no one any the wiser. And as soon as Geoffrey heard about Hugo's arrest, he could relax. He had only to wait till November 5th to be absolutely secure.

But sour Reggie had reckoned the fire was out of control and it had been doused by the fire brigade. There was still that soggy mess of ash. If Geoffrey had shoved the shoes into the middle at the bottom to be inconspicuous, there was a long chance that they might still be there.

Charles scrabbled through the damp debris of ash, half-burnt sticks and charred rubbish by the light of his torch. He spread it all flat on the ground. There was nothing big enough to be a shoe. One half of a heel might have come from a lady's sandal, but otherwise nothing.

He sat down deflated, mindless of the debris. Oh well, it had been a good idea. Too easy though, really. Geoffrey wasn't stupid. He'd have found a way round the shoes, scrapped them or changed them, destroyed them at home. Or just put them high enough in the bonfire to ensure that they would burn quickly.

No, the case was over. Charles put one hand down on the ground to lever himself up.

And felt close round a soft flesh-like lump.

He had the object up in his torch-beam. At first it seemed to be a plastic-covered ball, which had survived by rolling to the bottom of the fire before it was doused. It was shapeless and blackened with ash.

But then he saw that it had once been a pair of plastic gloves, rolled together. Now deformed and fused by the heat, but recognizably a pair of gloves.

But that wasn't what brought a catch of excitement to his throat. It was the fact that the gloves had been wrapped around something. Something soft.

The melted plastic had made a little envelope which gave easily to his fingernail. Inside, preserved like a packet on the supermarket shelf, was a handkerchief.

A blue and white handkerchief he had last seen when Geoffrey Winter lent it to him in the Back Room. On the night of Charlotte's murder.

The brown smudge across it showed why it had been thrown away to be burned in the fire.

It was blood.

Blood that could be identified by a police laboratory.

Blood from' the scratch on Charlotte Mecken's neck.

And was it fanciful for Charles to catch a hint of a familiar expensive scent?

As expected, the police took a lot of convincing. When he first started to expound his reconstruction of events, Charles could feel how unlikely it sounded.

But when he showed them the handkerchief, they got more interested. After about an hour they agreed to go up to the common with him to look at the bonfire. A plain-clothes man and a uniformed constable.

They didn't talk much. They inspected the scene and started assessing times and distances. Charles didn't push his luck by saying anything.

Eventually the plain-clothes man spoke. 'Well, it's just possible. Of course, we won't really know until we get this handkerchief looked at by forensic. But I think we'll go and talk to Mr Winter, get his version of events. Where did you say he lived?'

'He won't be there at the moment. He's rehearsing a show for the Breckton Backstagers.'

The rehearsal was in full swing when they arrived. The cast were doing the awakening of the statue of Hermione.

The queen stood frozen centre stage, with Geoffrey as Leontes on one side of her and Mary Hobbs as Paulina on the other. Vee, as Perdita, knelt behind her husband. By her side stood Clive Steele as Florizel.

As Charles and the policemen entered at the back of the rehearsal room, Geoffrey was declaiming. They stood in silence while he continued.

'O! thus she stood,
Even with such life of majesty, – warm life,
As now it coldly stands, – when first I woo'd her.
I am asham'd: does the stone rebuke me
For being more stone than it? Oh – '

As he acted, Geoffrey took them in. Charles could see the pale grey eyes flicker from him to the uniformed policeman, then to the plain-clothes man and finally come to rest on the soiled handkerchief which the detective was still holding gingerly in front of him.

When Geoffrey saw the handkerchief, his voice wavered. There was a little gasp like the beginning of a giggle.

The supposed statue of Hermione let out the snort of a suppressed laugh. Then Mary Hobbs went off into uncontrollable giggles. Vee and Clive started laughing too.

None of them knew what the joke was, but soon all the Backstagers in the room were roaring their heads off. It was one of those moments that often happen at rehearsal, when suddenly a tense scene breaks down into the ridiculous. A mass 'corpse'.

Gradually, one by one, the actors stopped, slowing down to gasping breaths, and wiping tears from their eyes. Then they turned to look, with growing concern, at Geoffrey Winter.

But he just kept on laughing.

Printed in the United Kingdom
by Lightning Source UK Ltd.
115986UKS00001B/127